THE SHATTERED HORSE

S. P. SOMTOW

THE SHATTERED HORSE

TOR

A TOM DOHERTY ASSOCIATES BOOK

This is a work of fiction. All the characters and events portrayed in this book are fictional, and any resemblance to real people or incidents is purely coincidental.

THE SHATTERED HORSE

Copyright © 1986 by Somtow Sucharitkul

The excerpt from the libretto of the opera *King Priam* by Sir Michael Tippett on page 383 is copyright © 1962 by Schott and Company, Ltd., London. All rights reserved. Used by permission of European American Music Distributor Corp., sole U.S. agent for Schott and Company, Ltd.

First printing: August 1986

A TOR Book

Published by Tom Doherty Associates, Inc.
49 West 24 Street
New York, N.Y. 10010

Cover art by David Mattingly
Cover design by Carol Russo

ISBN: 0-312-93730-X

Library of Congress Catalog Card Number: 85-52260

Printed in the United States

0 9 8 7 6 5 4 3 2 1

To Lady Smansnid Walton,
who (when I was ten years old)
showed me a Greece of the imagination;
and to my father,
who (when I was grown)
led me to Greece itself

Contents

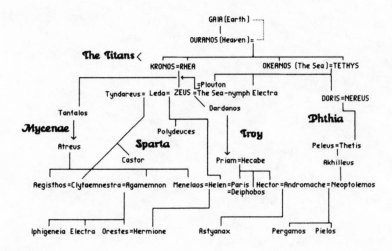

Notes: the above shows the relationships between some of the principal characters in *The Shattered Horse*. However, numerous alternate genealogies have been passed down. Among them:

Iphigeneia was a child of Helen by her previous abduction by Theseus, whom Agamemnon and Clytaemnestra adopted out of pity.

Plouton (a female, not to be confused with Hades) was a daughter of Kronos and Rhea, and Tantalos a result of the adulterous and incestuous union of her and Zeus.

Some generational steps have been omitted between Tantalos and Atreus, and between Dardanos and Priam; nevertheless it can be seen that both the Atreidai and the house of Priam are approximately equally descended from Zeus, both through a union with a daughter of Okeanos (the sea).

Also, note that Aigisthos is actually Atreus's adopted son; his real father was Thyestes, Atreus's brother, who seduced his own daughter Pelopeia and impregnated her. Later, Pelopeia married her uncle Atreus, compounding the situation further.

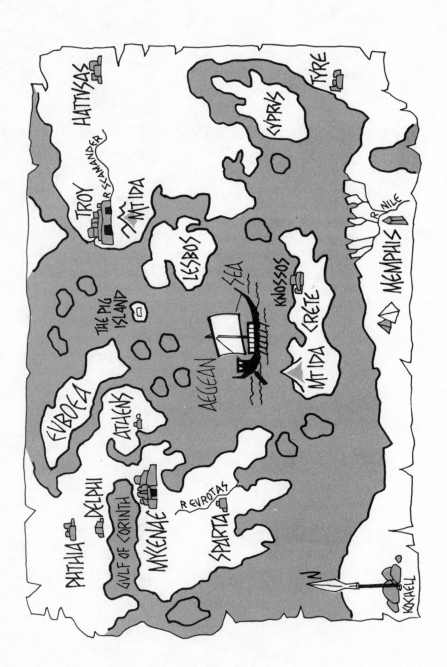

Book One: King of the City

τί καί ποτε
γράψειεν ἂν σῷ μουσοποιὸς ἐν τάφῳ;
τὸν παῖδα τόνδ᾽ ἔκτειναν ᾿Αργεῖοί ποτε
δείσαντες;

> What epitaph will the poet write upon your tomb?
> "Here lies a child whom the Greeks killed
> because they were afraid of him"?
> > —Words of Queen Hecabe over the body of
> > the child Astyanax
> > Euripides, *The Trojan Women*

Chapter I

⟦ⱡⱡⱡⱡⱡⱡⱡⱡⱡⱡⱡⱡⱡⱡⱡⱡⱡⱡⱡⱡ⟧

The Thousand Ships

By the time I was thirteen or fourteen they were already talking about the thousand ships. I knew better, but I held my peace; it would not do to let them know yet what I was. They might have killed me. They did not love the House of Priam, though they spoke of it still in fearful whispers. When they looked at me they might have suspected something, for even then I had my father's eyes, his flinchless gaze; but they said nothing because they knew I was dead.

I had been dead for ten years.

In those days I had become old enough for my stepfather to leave me alone on the mountain to tend the sheep for days on end, as my uncle Paris had once done before they found out what *he* was. On clear days I could see far down into the Phrygian plain, west past it to the beach and the sea; sometimes, even, the shattered horse, its wooden head propped up against my grandfather's broken city walls. I was not forbidden to go there; my stepfather could forbid me nothing, because, in spite of the pretense we kept up for the villagers, he could not bring himself to forget whose son I was. He was an old man, past fifty; when he first took me in I fancied him old enough to be the shepherd to whom my grandfather entrusted my uncle Paris. All shepherds looked the same to me then, and even at five years old I had known that he must respect me. After ten years I still could not love him, though I was thankful that he left me alone, and that he did not often beat me. It was out of this deference, then, that he did not tell me not to enter the accursed city.

But until my fifteenth year I never did. I listened to the talk in the village, always knowing better than they, seeing myth already in the making. Nights, I watched the plain.

3

Often the chill wind roared, drowning out the bleating of the
flock. I would build a fire and warm a little wine in a vessel
of baked earth. One night, a clear night, I saw the dead city
glow. I knew the people were moving back, squatting in old
storerooms of my grandfather's palace, laying down their
sleeping mats on the cracked steps of its great staircases. I
peered hard at the city—I have already said that I have my
father's eyes—and saw the shattered horse touched by the
pinprick light of many torches. Through its empty eyes the
firelight shone, two piercing rays that ran along the sand and
into the wine-dark sea. For a few moments the torchlight
animated the dead artifact; it seemed to glare at me, angry at
the deception I practiced daily.

Why do you tend sheep on the mountain? it seemed to say.
But the voice I heard was my own voice: childish, half
changed, awkward. *You're not a shepherd,* it said, *but a
king.*

I answered myself, "Kings are for dreams. This is real: the
icy wind, the ass-prickly scrub, the stink of sheepshit. You belong to a time that has already become a myth."

*You mummify the past; the past, only ten years old, and
those who lived it not yet dead! You, who saw the fortress of
Priam, the thousand ships!*

"There were no thousand ships," I said wearily. "Do you
think there were even a hundred ships? I do not think I ever
saw more as I stared out, pressed against the stone of the
parapet walls."

A thousand ships, said the shattered horse. But the fire in
his eyes went out as the uninvited guests in my grandfather's
palace moved their torches elsewhere or extinguished them so
they could sleep.

All night long I was angry, remembering the old fires,
other fires. They had long since been put out, but for me they
still burned.

Chapter II

□□□□□□□□□□□□□□□□□□□□□

The Ancient Fire

. . . the fire on my father's shield. The gorgon's eyes, blinding in the sunlight, making my own eyes burn.

"He's frightened of the shield." The hands gripped me tight about the shoulders, they swung me up high high high in the sun over the battlements.

"Hector."

He let go of me; I fell into an embrace of muscle, metal. My mother had come out onto the ramparts. "I must bring him here," he said, responding to her unspoken rebuke. "Throw him up, catch him, throw him up, catch him."

"Hector."

"I'm not afraid," I said solemnly. "Truly." He dropped me; suddenly my chin was down against a depression in the wall, and I looked out over the battlefield: gray tents, a ship that burned on the water. I turned around; if I stretched tall, my eyes were level with his sword hilt. He was worrying at a spot of green on it, scraping at it with a fingernail.

"Will you take me out to the field?"

"Just like his father," my mother said softly, wonderingly.

"When it's over," said Hector. "Before you turn five." He walked away. I saw the sun dance on his helmet.

"Why are you crying, Mother?" Her tears had bleared the kohl that lined her eyes.

She didn't answer me at first, but wiped her cheeks with a fold of her chiton; I saw her breasts for a moment. "Just the sun," she said at last. "A hero's wife doesn't cry." She turned away from me to gaze out over the battlefield. I stood with her. She did not always smell sweet like my aunt Helen. Eventually she told me to go away and play with Leontes, my foster brother, my slave.

5

I did not see my father again. That evening they told me he had died, and all night long the women's ritual shrieks blended with the crickets and the frogs. When they burned him they would not let me see the body. Ten years later, a shepherd boy now, I had still not wept for my father, nor shorn off a lock of my hair for him—that was one reason I was so afraid to visit the dead city. I did not want to meet his shade, to see his eyes reproach me: his eyes, my eyes . . . I did not dare to stand there and hear in the wind the ghost of chariot thunder.

. . . fire of reflected moonlight on the mirror of burnished bronze that took up almost a whole wall of the room where Leontes and I slept, I on the pallet, the slave boy on the floor. He was older, but we were the same height. "What are you staring at, Astyanax?" He sat on a cedar chest where I kept my toys: chariots of terra-cotta, a wooden horse.

"Is there someone else here?" My gaze never left the mirror. Out of the corner of my eye, a shape: gray, cloaked. A death's head?

"No." But as I spoke a cold wind brushed the nape of my neck, though it was summer and the air thick and moist, and all the doors of the palace were wide open to let in the slightest breeze. And the figure again. "You see something in the mirror?" Leontes said. Unlike the other townsmen, he never spoke reverently to me; his mother had been my wet nurse. They had chosen him for my companion; and when I was bad they would sometimes beat him, because I was the prince, not him.

"Behind you," I said, "the moonlight, a ghost."

"Or a god. I can't see them, but *you* can, because you're the six-times-great-grandson of Zeus."

What god, though? For just a second I thought I could see something clearly, bony fingers reaching out of the dark corner of the room, caressing Leontes' hair. "Thanatos," I said. Leontes gave a shrill shriek. "Don't worry. Soon I'll be where Father is." The figure had melded into the gloom, but I could hear his slow breath and feel its chill. "Light the lamps, Leontes. Do you want to play a game? Open the chest.''

We knelt by the cedarwood box and tipped it over, and it yielded its riches: the chariot, the horse doll, and some things my father had given me: a helmet and a little sword, no toy, the bronze honed against his own grinding stone. There were screams coming from far away, outside the palace. I did not know if Thanatos was really there beside us. My grandfather had sometimes entertained gods; I had heard that it had once been almost commonplace in this palace. I had the power to speak to the gods, diluted though it might have been by the six generations since Skyfather had sired my ancestor. It was not strange that Death should show himself to me. I could not feel afraid, though. I had not even seen my father's corpse; I only knew that he had gone to a far gray country, where one day I would go. I had only heard of the great horse they had dragged into the city that day, because Leontes and I had been playing hide-and-seek in an old wing of the palace.

Leontes waited, wondering what game I wanted. I picked up the toy helmet and put it on his head. He laughed. "You be the prince," I said, "and me the slave." I unclasped my chiton and so did he; it was a game we played often. We traded. I liked the unfamiliar roughness of his chiton, and the funny sweaty smell. "What is your will, master?" I said, aping one of my grandfather's lackeys.

"Fetch, carry, or I'll beat you to a pulp!" He waved the sword.

"Of course, master, yes, master," I said, scurrying to obey. He chased me to my pallet, and we tussled in front of the mirror. He had me in an armlock, and I looked in the mirror and saw the skull face even more clearly, brilliant in the moonlight, and I saw how alike we looked, Leontes and I; maybe it was true that Hector was his father as well as mine.

"Don't you want to play anymore?" he said.

I wriggled free and pushed him onto the stone floor. The sword slipped, gashed my arm. I cried out. Then men with torches burst into the room, and I heard for the first time the

thud of metal footfalls in the palace, and the screams of
dying men in the streets outside. I knew that I *had* seen
Death. My mouth opened but no cry came out. They were
Akhaians who had come in. Blood was on their faces, their
arms. A young man swaggered into the room. He stopped,
looking from me to Leontes. "Ah," he said. An adolescent's
voice, a cruel voice. "My prince." I trembled. But he picked
Leontes up in his arms. Of course! The chiton of good wool,
the helmet, the sword—I stared at the soldier and the slave
boy.

"I'm the prince," I said, my voice very small.

They laughed: men's laughter, raucous, derisory. But their
leader, still clasping my slave in his arms and gagging him
with one hand, looked at me with compassion. "You don't
have to," he said. "It's not your duty. It's not your war. We
have to kill the prince; it can't be helped. Run away. They
won't see a kid out there in the smoke, the falling debris." I
must have stood there like a statue. Another soldier shook
me. "Such a lovely child," the young leader said. "You
could almost be of royal blood. Run now, run; maybe you
can make it to the mountains."

Leontes' eyes: struggling not to cry, to play the role of
prince so that I would not be discovered. He did not scream.
Thanatos had not come for me, though I, blessed with
Skyfather's eyes, had been able to glimpse him in the shadows.

"You are too compassionate, Neoptolemos," said one of
the soldiers to their leader. "We really should kill him."

"Go!" Neoptolemos shouted. The soldier had drawn his
sword. Some of our Trojans, half out of their armor, leapt
out of the shadows. I saw Neoptolemos swing Leontes like a
club and smash a Trojan's face with my toy helmet. Blood
streamed from the soldier's eyes. I ran panting into the fire
that raged outside. The street was crisscrossed with rivulets
of blood. They were raping a woman against the flank of a
stone lion. It was Leontes' mother. I tripped over a severed
arm. I ran into an alley, and a cloud of smoke swallowed me
up. I could hear nothing but the hiss of spurting flames and
the shrieks of the dying. I ran like an animal, I, Prince

Astyanax, son of Hector and Andromache, last of my line, while Leontes took my place for the last time.

. . . and fire in the alleyways . . . a flaming woman falling from a rooftop, and the tiles clattering after . . . I found Skyfather's temple at the heart of the city. I crept in, mouselike. A single flame burned: the altar flame. An old man clasped the altar. There was no statue of Skyfather such as the Akhaians sometimes built, with a beard and a stern face; only a smooth black stone that had fallen from heaven. The old man wore a robe of white wool, as though he were to be sacrificed. He did not notice me, his grandson, in the deep shadows. I could not see his face.

Rough shouts of men from a corridor outside, the clanking of bronze on bronze. King Priam looked up. Neoptolemos was there, and some other Akhaians. One had my foster brother's body slung over his shoulder. Now was my moment. I could show myself, insist on my identity. But I was too scared to leave the shadow.

I heard Neoptolemos say, very quietly, "I have come to kill you, King."

My grandfather said, "I know." He did not move.

"Will you not come to me and face death like a man?" Neoptolemos said. He seemed as frightened as I, for a moment. "I don't wish to kill you, a suppliant in Zeus's temple; it is impiety."

"Laomedon was my father," Priam said softly, "who built the walls that you have breached, boy. His father's name was Ilos; Ilos's was Tros, who gave his name to Troy. His grandfather was that Dardanos who crossed the Aegean Sea to found a kingdom in a land of shepherds. Dardanos was a naiad's son, conceived when the breath of Skyfather kissed the wavecrests of the sea. Look, boy, at the stone; it is my father's father's father's father's father's father, and you profane his place."

I have not forgotten these words, because my nurse, Leontes' mother, had made me recite my lineage over and over. When I faltered, she had slapped her son.

They threw Leontes down on the floor. He did not move. Was he already dead? They surrounded the altar in a circle, closing in. I saw a sword fly up and catch the altar glow, and then blood splattering the flames, hissing, bubbling. My grandfather's head rolled down the steps to my feet. The soldiers spun around, following the gray round thing. Neoptolemos saw me. I sprinted from the shadows to where Leontes lay. "Leontes," I whispered. My eyes blurred, stung.

A man seized the boy, who stirred a little. He held him tenderly, like his own son.

"I thought I told you to run away," Neoptolemos said to me. "You're very loyal to your master, little slave. But don't follow us around anymore. Tomorrow we're going to dash your little master's brains out against the walls Laomedon built."

I fixed him with an intense look, a look of hatred. This was my enemy. Even he seemed unnerved. "Quite the warrior, aren't you?" he said. "How old are you?"

"Five."

"Tall for your age. Don't think that I enjoy this, little warrior. This old man's son killed my father." I started to cry. "There now." He hugged me then, he put his blood-stained arms around me. "A man's got to do these things. Avenging the deaths of kinsmen." Even I could feel the insincerity of his words. He needed to be justified somehow. He was only a boy too, after all. He needed to feel loved, to feel compassionate, this butcher. I did not yield, but held myself stiff like a doll. I saw them tossing back and forth the head of my grandfather like a leaky wineskin.

"Let me go!" I whimpered.

He set me down gently, like a delicate carving or a bolt of purple cloth. "Run, run," he said, "and don't let me see you again."

I looked into his implacable eyes. I *will* see you again, I thought, and then I'll kill you! When I'm big.

The soldiers turned smartly around and clanked down the corridor. I ran to the smoldering altar. I embraced the cold black stone. What was it Neoptolemos had said? "A man's got to do these things. Avenging the deaths of kinsmen."

"Skyfather, give me revenge, revenge!" I cried in my tiny voice, knowing the word only from old songs they sang at Grandfather's dinner table. Skyfather did not show himself to me. I have met many of the gods, but never my six-times-great-grandfather, who always hides behind thunder when he is needed.

. . . and pale fire on the battlements, against the brilliant sunlight. I had fallen asleep on the street; I woke up in the shadow of the great wooden horse. The town was empty. Staying in the walls' shadow I slipped down to the Skaian Gate. Only a gutted portal stood, and piles of stone and burnt timber.

I went by a secret path down to the beach where Leontes and I had played. My mother and grandmother and other women were in a pen, chained up, like watchdogs. I did not dare go close, but there were boulders where I could hide.

They brought my mother Leontes on my father's shield. The one with the gorgon's eyes whose flame I had once feared. His head had been crushed open like an egg. His brains were drying on his mouth like old puke. I was not surprised my mother did not know him. It was better that she thought I was dead. But in a way I never forgave her for grieving over the wrong child. I would have run out to her but I saw Neoptolemos and other Akhaians, and I knew he would kill me this time. I slid farther into a nook of the rock. The burning city behind me smelled of charred meat.

Suddenly my aunt Helen was there, behind the Akhaians. It seemed that the sacking of the city had not touched her at all. She had been twelve when my uncle Paris stole her from Sparta, and now she was a grown woman with breasts and golden hair that caught fire from the sun and the city's burning. "Whore! Whore!" the women were screaming at her. I heard them say that my mother was to be given to Neoptolemos, to be his slave. There was more discussion that I could not follow. Aunt Helen looked away, from boredom or guilt, I do not know; she toyed with a strand of her hair. And then she caught sight of me. I had not ducked my head in time.

I saw her eyes: they were the color of the summer sky. Her father's eyes. That was how we were kin, for she was Zeus's daughter, and I his six-times-great-grandson. Her eyes were even bluer than mine. If she had seen Thanatos the night before, she would have seen him much more clearly than I had; I saw at six generations' remove, and she at one. Our eyes met; I knew she recognized me. I had often sat on her lap and played with her hair. She spent a lot of time with the palace children, because the women hated her. She had a special smile for the children she most loved; it lit up her soft features.

I ran from that smile, I ran ran ran to the high mountain. Because Aunt Helen's smile was more terrifying than anything else that had happened in that night and day of fire.

Chapter III

The Shepherd and the Ghost

All night I dreamt of fire. At daybreak came dawn over the black mountains. The light awoke me. I had not meant to sleep, to dream; I hoped the sheep had not strayed too far. Philemon my stepfather was beside the fire; he had figs and goat's milk and fresh bread. I moaned. "Wake up, wake up," he said. "I didn't save your life to have you fall asleep and lose my flock." He laughed gruffly; he was not angry.

I said, "The shattered horse spoke to me, Philemon."

"Fantasies, fantasies!" he said. Fear flecked his gray-green eyes. Whenever we spoke of the past he would always grow afraid. He had lost all his children that day because he had sent them to the city, to market, and not gone himself, though it had been a festival day because they were bringing the wooden horse into the city. "I wish you wouldn't think of those things, Aster." They all called me Aster, the star, and not by my true name, for fear that people would find out.

"I can't help it," I said.

"Yes." He broke bread and wrapped it around a piece of goat's cheese.

"I want to go into the city."

"I have never forbidden it."

"I will go this very afternoon."

"Of course. What do you want to find there? Dreams of glory?"

"I don't know." In one swift motion I got up and hugged my stepfather tight. "I dreamt about Leontes last night."

"Will he come back to life, boy, when you go back to Troy?"

"I'm not a shepherd." I let go of him. He smelled of sweat; a wine stain ran down his gray chiton.

"You're a king." He looked at me steadfastly, ingenuously. "I've tried to make you into a child of mine, but you're not, you can't be."

"I love you, Father." But I do not think I did. I was grateful to him for rescuing me from the burning city, but it grieved me that he could not remember certain things with me: the toy chest smelling of cedar oil, the gorgon-eyed shield, my father shining in the sun, Aunt Helen's special smile, and the chariots plated with silver-chased bronze that streamed from the city gates in the dawn. When I tried to talk of these things he would shush me and say, "It is senseless to remember these things as though they were real; let the memories grow old and turn into myths. The days will be darker from now on, Aster, and we can't go back." For him, the war had meant a change of masters, nothing more. I did not love him because he did not understand my wonder. Was it merely because he did not carry within himself some spark of Skyfather?

I said to him, "This afternoon I won't herd the sheep. Get another lad. I am going to the plain. To speak to the shattered horse."

I had not used that tone with him before. He smiled suddenly, as though relieved that he no longer needed to pretend to be my father, and he said, "Yes, my prince," as all the palace slaves used to once.

Then I started on the warm loaf he had brought. I had kept my cloak wrapped firmly around me, but the morning was still chilly. I folded an old rag around a second loaf and tucked it into my cloak. Then I started walking down the mountain.

Philemon called after me. "Aster!" I turned. I saw his gray face, leathery, worry-lined. I waited. He said softly, "Leave the myths be. Let the hundred ships become a thousand, and the palaces grow into topless towers, and the walls encompass ten cities. Don't shatter the dream, child."

"That's just the trouble," I said. "I don't think I *am* a child. Not anymore."

"Be careful." He smiled uneasily.

I turned my back to him, away from the sun.

I walked downhill to the village, following the dirt path that wound along the contours of the mountain. I kept my eyes fixed on Troy as long as I could. At last, as the trees grew taller and the grass thicker, I lost sight of Troy completely.

I met a shepherd boy going uphill to take over from his father. I recognized him and called his name. He seemed not to hear me. Perhaps he was just ignoring me. Or perhaps he already sensed something different in me this morning. I turned and saw him disappear at a bend in the path bounded by boulders. The new feeling that had come over me . . . it was almost as though I breathed the air of the gods themselves . . . there was exhilaration in it, but also aloneness. But I had to go on.

It was noon when I reached the plain. There was no sun. Only a patch of searing haze, a circle of burning gray over the dull gray of the sky. I walked on. There had been a great road here. It led from a small temple in the foothills all the way down to the city, and was wide enough for chariots to pass each other without being driven into the mud. In ten years there had come first a skin of earth and pulverized rubble, then moss, then grass at last, and the road showed only here and there, bald spots in the tangle of weeds and grass and wildflowers. I could not see the city at all now. But I walked resolutely. I paused only once, to break off a hunk of gritty bread and to drink from a stream.

I smelled the sea before I saw the city. The wavewind, moist and pungent—to me it had always been the smell of home and homecoming. Though I had been walking since morning a new energy possessed me and I began to run. I ran hard and desperately. It was the same angry desperation with which I had once ran away from Troy. The city reared up with startling suddenness. I had not seen it before because, at ground level, it was smothered with dense overgrowth, suffocating under dirt and vines. I almost ran into it.

Then I paused, for this was the city I had not dared enter for ten years. It must be thick with ghosts, this city where I should be king. I stood and waited for my courage to return, nibbling at what remained of the loaf of bread and trying (as a vulture worries at a corpse) to pluck true memories from the confusion that was the consciousness of a five-year-old child. At first all I could remember was Aunt Helen's smile. I walked around the walls. They had not been leveled. How could men topple stones that the gods had set in place? Except . . . yes. There it was. I saw it in the dimming light. A massive rent wide enough to admit an army.

The Akhaians had not done that, I reminded myself; we did it ourselves! To let in the horse.

I stood in front of the Skaian Gate now. They had taken away much of the masonry to build shelters against winter, but the gate still stood. The sun was still out but the sky was even more gray; I do not think there had ever been a sky of brilliant blue since the last time I had stood here, ten years ago. I could hear the sea where lived the naiad my ancestress. I had drawn my cloak tightly around my shoulders. Not really for fear . . . I do not know why; there was nothing anyone would do to a shepherd boy. And it was not yet cold. Looking past the archway, I could see the street. It was much narrower than I remembered it. Beyond it the palace of my grandfather, a tumble of gray stones. There was still paint on the walls, an old mural depicting the story of Herakles and Laomedon. I remembered that each frame of the story was bordered in gold leaf, which also highlighted the heroes' hair; powdered gold was mixed too in the pigments, so that the mural would seem to come to life at twilight, with the light of the sunset falling on it through the gratings of the gate. The gold was gone. There was strident graffiti in the Mycenaean syllabic script, painted in red:

두ᅮ

Ta-na-to-
Thanatos.

There were names too, all written in the script that the Akhaian nations had borrowed from somewhere in the lands of barbarous tongues and awkwardly twisted to the Greek language. I stood in the shadow of the gate and read the names, not daring yet to go in. Someone had attached an exaggerated phallos to Herakles in one frame.

At first I had not noticed them, but people were wandering in and out, bedraggled people, some staring curiously at me. Farther into the city there was a market of sorts; I could hear the noise.

Why had I even come, I thought. Better to cherish the memories. I turned away.

But just then a hand tugged at my cloak. "Get away!" I hissed, wishing I had a dagger. I did have a small pouch with two silver pellets, though, tied to my belted chiton. I had to protect it. I whirled around to grab the thief.

A boy oozed through my fingers . . . a high-pitched laugh in the air, a sudden chill. Bewildered, I looked up. A god? Death was the only god I had ever seen; he had not even come for me then, and only the divine sight in me had let me chance to see him.

"Who are you?" I shouted.

Two boys I knew from the village ran past, paused to look at me, chuckled, ran on.

"Quick," said a small voice. "Behind you." I stepped over the threshold and into the city.

"Who are you?" Still I saw no one.

"Whisper! I don't want to be caught."

"Caught? Caught how? Who are you?" I caught sight of him suddenly, shadow-slim, slipping into the gateway's penumbra. "Leontes . . ."

He was so gray, so gray. "Let me look at you," I said. "I dreamed of you last night, and the shattered horse spoke to me."

I saw him again, a vague shimmering against the disfigured mural of my grandfather's palace. I could almost see through him. His eyes were lifeless. "Leontes . . ." I could not speak. I remembered him lying on my father's shield, where I should have lain, bearing my wounds, my broken head, my spilled brains.

"I can't stay long. Come with me. Come to our old room, Astyanax."

"I should have died," I said. "You should be herding sheep in the mountains, and I should be there, in the dead lands."

"It's much too late." Again the tiny six-year-old voice; his lips did not move in time to it, but were frozen in a grim smile. "Come on, come on!"

"But how can you come here? Aren't you safe on the other side of River Styx?"

"You ask too many questions, master. I flit back and forth, I haunt the places where we once played."

I ached for him. "When I die," I said, "I'll bring a rich gift, and we will both pay the ferryman."

"Why bother? *You* won't need a gift. You're family. Hades is your six-times-great-grandfather's brother, isn't he?"

"They aren't exactly friends," I said. I crossed the stone courtyard fringed with broken columns. Peasants were sleeping in the great hall; they had lit a fire on the cracked stone floor. Leontes passed right through them. I was sure they could not see him. Some of the steps to my old room were broken, and I had to climb on hands and knees. The marble

facings were dirty; in places the stones were veined with
moss. As we reached the room where we had slept together
as children, I could see him more and more clearly. It was
shadowy in the room, and vines blocked the only view. But
the very darkness fed his image, lent color to him; behind the
dead gray of his face there was a trace of pink, and now and
then life flickered in his eyes.

"I come here all the time, when I can get away," said
Leontes. "Why did you come back?"

"Why do *you* come, Leontes?"

"To wait for you," said my foster brother. "I knew you
would come back, one day. Look behind you, in the vines
where your pallet used to be."

I reached behind, my eyes still fixed on the shade of my
dead slave and friend. It was something: a box. It fell apart
when I touched it. I turned; a toy chariot fell onto the stone.
"I kept it for us," said Leontes. "When they came to loot
the room, I haunted them. Bloodcurdling howls, skull-faced
apparitions, images of a child with his brains slowly squish-
ing out of the top of his cracked head."

"Why?"

"I need you. You're my only friend. I went down to the
riverbank where the shades wait for the ferryman. I wore
your clothes, your toy dagger, your glittering helmet, I came
on your father's gorgon shield, but I wasn't you, Astyanax.
They don't accept me. Even in Tartaros there is degree. A
slave doesn't ape a king. I escape when I can."

"What do you want?" I said. "Me to change places with
you?" I did not like living a lie. If I could have died then I
would have; it was nothing to me. I wanted Leontes to take
my place in the land of the living, truly. But Leontes shook
his head. For a moment, just a moment, his eyes had glowed
as brightly as a live boy's. But their light went out again.
Like pouring water on an ember.

"Too late," he said. "It's done now. But I can hover
around you, help you, feed on your soul a little."

"Are you a vampire then? Will you suck the life out of
me?" I had heard stories from the villagers, who were quite

superstitious; they feared such things even more than the gods themselves.

Leontes laughed, a thin little laugh; the temperature fell. He said, "Revenge, Astyanax! I was all yours once. I worshiped the places where you'd been, where your sweet smell lingered. I was your slave not only because King Priam commanded it but because we had suckled at the same breasts, and because I loved you. . . . Is this love to be worthless then? Look, I even took your death upon myself. And because it wasn't really my own death, I couldn't really die either. I can't cross the river, I can't rest, I have to haunt this room, this ghost of a city. Can't you avenge me, Astyanax? For the sake of this half death that I'm living through."

I could not look at him. I was so angry, so frustrated. "Of course," I whispered, "there must be vengeance. I am the king, you know. My kin are all dead, I'm the last of Dardanos's line. My grandfather had fifty sons, nineteen of them from my own grandmother. They're all dead."

"I know. I saw them pass over the river."

"Can't you be more solid? Can't I embrace you, or wrestle with you like when we were children together?"

"I'm the past. You can't hold the past in your hands." I reached out; he was so near, so clear against the gloom. But I only hugged the chill air. "I told you so," he said.

"What do you want me to do? Sail over to Mycenae and kill them all? I'm a boy, I don't even have a sword."

"Listen. There was a great commotion by the riverbank today. All the dead knew we would meet. When the war was being fought, all the universe centered on the Trojan plains: the gods watched, the dead watched. Now the fires have gone out, and you living have become as dismal as the dead. Have you noticed how gray the sky has been since the war's end? Color is fading from the world. Soon the past will become a myth. But it wasn't a myth! Myths don't kill, but for this so-called myth my skull was dashed against the walls of this city! Your grandfather's grizzled head was chopped off as he prayed to Zeus!"

I was burning with rage now. I cried out, "How can the gods let this happen?"

"Do they care? No gods visit *us* as we gibber by the bank of the Styx."

"Come," I said, making to leave the room. I had resolved to make some gesture, impotent though it might be, toward vengeance. If it was the blood of heroes that kept the sky blue and the grass green, I would fight someone. I would call on Skyfather himself. He had to listen! I was his son's son's son's son's son's son's son's son. I had a spark at least of the divine sight. "Come on, Leontes."

"Where?"

"To Zeus's altar," I said. "He's got to show himself to *me*! He's got to!"

"What will you do? Start the Trojan War all over again?"

"I don't know!" I cried out. It had not then occurred to me that the Trojan War might be waged again, although I was anxious enough to start out on my personal vendetta against Neoptolemos.

I walked out, my right hand lightly skimming the balustrade. As a child I had always had to reach over my head to touch the smooth stone. It was cracked now, scarred as the face of King Priam when as a child I reached out to touch it and wondered at its irregular texture. I descended into the hallway. The roof of the great hall had given way; over the chamber in which my grandfather had once held court, night was falling. I was afraid now. Night is the time of the dead, and I was leading a dead child into the street, a dead child that should have been me.

Chapter IV

Skyfather's House

A colonnade: pitiful stumps now. There: the courtyard of the stone lions; two were still standing. The alleyway I had hidden in, masked from the moonlight by the lions' shadows.

Leontes: a patch of grayness on the lion's back. "Where are you taking me?" he said.

"To the temple."

I slipped into the alley, my cheeks brushing the moist rough stone.

"No," said Leontes' voice. "I don't want to relive it again."

"I must see Skyfather. I *will* see him."

There was the temple: it had no roof. A pack of dogs ran past us; their eyes glittered, their mouths slavered. I was not afraid. Dogs shy away from the shades of the dead.

I looked up: on the lintel, some Akhaian had reached up to carve an initial. He must have been a giant of a man. I remembered looking way up to see that lintel. Now I found I could reach it with outstretched arms. I stepped over the threshold; the far wall was jagged as a distant mountain range. In the center was the altar. Rivers of grass had riven the flagstones; they scratched my feet as I walked up to Skyfather's stone. They had not touched it, but it was overgrown with moss; in the moonlight I saw that it had cracked, and that in the crevasse grew a solitary white flower.

I had not remembered it so. I knew I should not have come. I should have remembered it the way it had been when Priam took me there, riding piggyback or in his arms. He would set me down on the altar itself, beside the eternal flame. If Hecabe, his wife, was there, she would say, "Now, now, that's sacrilegious." But Priam would answer, "Hecabe,

21

the kid's his six-times-great-grandson! Let him sit here and listen to my stories. Let him know truly what he is.''

The stories . . .

"Once," he told me, as I played with the sacred utensils, the gold-chased chalices, the little bronze ceremonial axe, "our Skyfather did not rule in this land. A different, ancient ruler lived here. She was of the earth. They called her Snakemother, the Triple Goddess, the Queen of Magic. Our ancestor brought with him a sacred stone from Skyfather's house, above high Olympos. There was a king here; he was young and beautiful, and king only because he was married to the living goddess. Each year they killed him and cut him to pieces and fertilized the soil with his blood; they had learned farming from somewhere in the east, where the custom still prevailed. Dardanos became the shepherd-king, and the farmer-king too, for he loved the living goddess, a woman a thousand years old, for she remembered the Silver Age and she had once visited Prometheus as he lay crucified upon a rock. This woman was ageless. Her face was the face of a girl of twelve, just the age of marrying. It was said that she bathed in virgins' blood, to stay so young. Our ancestor loved her. But when the year was up he would not die. He said, 'Skyfather does not demand such savage sacrifices from his sons!' But the living goddess said, 'You will blight the crops, and a terrible plague will come, because the ground hungers for a king's blood.' But our ancestor was wily. He found a slave whose features resembled his. He dressed the slave up in his garments and invited him to play a game: let the slave be the king, and the king the slave. And the priestesses came to kill the king, and they caused his body to be fed to the earth, and his flayed skin, stuffed with grain, to sit on the throne for three dark days. On the third day the living goddess came to the megaron to dispossess the empty body of the king, for she had found another lover. But the corpse moved and spoke to her; for Dardanos had come in the night, and spirited it away, and had sat in wait all night for her to come to him. She said, 'You *must* die. You have tricked Snakemother.'

"But Dardanos said, 'I will not die. I have fooled the earth, and I will fool her again. I will set up Skyfather's stone on the altar of Snakemother, and I will rule in your place, for the reign of women has come to an end.'

"The goddess said, 'I will be avenged. I will blight your issue and destroy all your works.'

"But nothing happened for a hundred years, little one. We grew strong; Tros built this city. Grain sprang up plentifully in the fields. The flocks multiplied. And then the day came when Tros decided no longer to sacrifice a young slave to be plowed into the earth. And still the crops and flocks were not struck down. So tell me, who rules the universe: Skyfather, or the Queen of Magic?"

I asked my grandfather where the Snakemother had gone; she frightened me. He said, "She has vanished, my grandson, as the night is dissolved by the sunlight. And now the days are brighter than they've ever been. The stones of the palace are adazzle with gold dust."

I said, "But Grandfather, Grandfather, my dreams . . . the gorgon on Father's shield. . . ."

But Priam said only, "She has gone to nightmares, to shadows. She no longer dares to show herself in the light. She has no virgins' blood to bathe in, and so she has become a hag. Her eyes are like coals, and her hair a mess of writhing snakes. Her offspring are as hideous as she. But we can't be afraid of a nightmare, can we, boy? We'll put them on our shields to frighten the enemy, but *we* must not fear them. We are the light, and they the darkness."

"But won't the Snakemother know one day that we have stopped killing the king? Isn't she hungry, Grandfather?"

"No." Priam played with my hair. I trusted him more than anyone. He was the oldest man I had ever seen; I thought he must have been born at the beginning time. "No," he said firmly, "we have withheld the kings' blood so long, we have starved her to death."

"But the gods are immortal!" I said.

The king looked away then. He was grieved; I did not know why. He should have been happy, because the temple was awash in sunlight, and a breeze blew in the portico, fanning the altar flame.

But now, across the ten years' chasm, I understood his grief at last. I had reminded him that the gods do not die, and that they do not have compassion as we know it. They are immortal, but they have never grown up, either.

"Leontes . . . I just remembered . . . how Dardanos overcame the Snakemother by killing a slave when he should have been killed himself. . . ." That was what I had done to Leontes. The war had wiped out the kings' blood, all but mine. Perhaps Leontes had fooled Snakemother; his mangled corpse had fooled *my* mother, after all. The Fates weave endlessly, but there is only one tapestry.

The wind wuthered in the dark streets; perhaps it was Leontes crying. "Don't cry," I said, "be comforted. I'm sorry for stealing the life from you, Leontes. If you were here, we could herd together, you and I, and when one of us fell asleep the other would still be watching. Oh, I know. I always fell asleep before you; it was your duty to see that I slept, and my whim was to stay up playing by myself; you had to watch me, rubbing your eyes to keep awake. Maybe it would still be that way."

"You don't understand," Leontes said. "I am dead, Astyanax. Do what you came here for."

A stillness fell in the ruins of the shrine. I went to clasp the stone of Skyfather; I knelt beside it, burying my face in the moss.

"Forgive me, Skyfather," I said. "I've been a coward, I've waited ten years to come back to you, I tried to run away from the pain. The Akhaians have gone back to Mycenae and Sparta and Ithaka and Phthia and Argos. My mother is a slave in the house of Neoptolemos, whose father, Akhilleus, killed my father. Will you give me vengeance, Great-Grandfather?"

I got up. I gathered wood from the street: fallen branches,

dead twigs. I piled them up on the altar, and I rubbed two
twigs until I kindled the heap and relit the altar flame. "You
see?" I murmured to my ancestor. "You aren't forgotten.
Perhaps you'll shine on us tomorrow, and stain the sky blue
for us again. Please, please, Skyfather, show yourself to me.
There must be a reason why I was saved and Leontes sent to
the dead lands in my place. Surely you didn't decree this for
nothing, Skyfather! I will rekindle all your altars in this land.
I will rebuild what your son built. Skyfather, listen to Priam's
last grandchild."

I heard an explosion, infinitely far. Could it have been
thunder? My heart leapt up with hope. "Skyfather!" I cried.
But there was no answer. I fed the flames until they blazed.

Skyfather did not answer me. And then the fire began to
drip from the altar like liquid. Streams of it over the flagstones. Jets of fire poured skyward. From the altar came
curving lines of light that spun around and around, building a
whirlwind of fire around it, and I stood numbed with fear as
the fire enveloped me and the heat scorched me but did not
scar me. I screamed and screamed. A boy sprang out of the
flames, stamping on them. I saw winged sandals. His hair
was gold and fiery; I could not tell where it ended and the
flames began. The roar grew stiller. The boy cried petulantly,
"Out, out! You can't burn me, so go away!" And he stamped
his foot again and again; each time the fire subsided a little.
Suddenly he saw me, and behind me, the gray shade of
Leontes.

"Hey, you spirit-thing. Dead or alive?" he said. His voice
was inhumanly beautiful.

I whirled round to see Leontes. "Dead, my lord," he said,
his voice quavering; already he was fading, melding with the
gray stones.

"Begone!" said the boy out of the fire. "I've business
with *him*."

"He can stay," I said. "He's my friend."

"This is the business of kings."

"Are you Skyfather?"

He laughed, a silvery, impersonal laughter. "Skyfather!

Skyfather! You're joking, of course. Skyfather does not come when a boy calls, not even a six-times-great-grandson. Do you know how many six-times-great-grandsons he has, my little cousin? Thousands! Only desire can rouse Skyfather now. Io. Europa. Leda. You look a bit like him, boy, but you're no Ganymede. But here I am, little cousin. What do you want?''

"Who are you?"

Another laugh. He sat on the altar, swinging his legs, an impatient boy. "I am your cousin Hermes, little one. You should feel honored that you got even me to come down to this gray, dank world." He touched my face; his fingers were cool, like marble. There was a certain family resemblance between us, but I wore a chiton of coarse wool while he was clothed in sheets of blinding light.

I said, "I want to be king."

"You already are, aren't you? Who has taken that away from you?"

"You know very well. Let me speak to Skyfather." I tried to push him aside, to get to the altar and repeat my prayer.

Hermes caught my arm and twisted it. A sharp pain. "Now, mortal cousin, don't overstep yourself. How foolish of you to think that my father would talk to you in person, that you could just drop into his house and demand to see him! Does a slave demand to see a king? You should know better. Remember Semele, the mother of the god Dionysos. She demanded to see Skyfather. The sight of his glory seared her, burned her up, killed her. You are so young, little cousin."

"If I am to be king, give me the instruments of vengeance."

"Such as? A gorgon-faced shield, perhaps?" He reached behind the altar and plucked it out of the air. The eyes of the gorgon caught the light; for a second I was a five-year-old boy again.

I gasped. "Where did you get it?"

"What are gods for, little cousin?" I reached for it, but he yanked it from my grasp and set it down on the altar. From

behind he drew out a helmet, a sword . . . I recognized the
sword, with the syllabic signs

A⦿Ŧ

E-ko-to etched into the bronze blade. I remembered the
helmet and the armor. "You can't touch it yet. Are you
worthy? Can you prove you are Hector's son?"

"Will you ask me riddles?"

Another boyish laugh. "You've heard too many old men's
tales. Of course there aren't any riddles. Am I a sphinx? I'm
only your cousin, come down from heaven for a nighttime
chat."

"There must be a test!" I said.

"Indeed," Hermes said, sighing. "Skyfather's light is
such that he must clothe himself forever in a thick darkness,
or the world would be blinded. That, at least, is how the
divine rhetoric goes. And me? Fetch and carry, flit hither and
thither, that's me. We're not that different, you and me,
except that I have to go on forever. Forgive me, Astyanax,
for mocking you."

"You are a god. How shall I forgive you?"

"From where I am things don't look as clear as they do to
you mortals. Oh, Astyanax, little cousin, Skyfather has sent
me to tell you this: that in exchange for your father's armor,
which will win you great glory, you must do him a favor
too. . . ." He reached into his tunic of light and pulled out a
golden apple. He threw it up; I caught it. There was an
inscription: *for the fairest.*

"For the fairest! But my uncle Paris already went through
that."

"Mortal wars end, Astyanax, because you all must die.
But war in heaven goes on till the end of time. Look, behind
you."

I turned.

There were three women . . . or were they one? Sometimes they were beautiful; sometimes their faces shimmered
and became harpy faces with serpent hair.

"There they are," said Hermes. "Hera, Queen of Heaven; gray-eyed Athena; and Aphrodite. You shall give the apple to the most beautiful. It isn't hard. It's been done before."

"This isn't how I heard the story!" I said. The women shifted faces; now they were all beautiful. "You aren't the three goddesses at all; you're the Snakemother, the Triple Goddess. How can I choose when every choice is the same?"

"You must choose, little cousin."

"I won't," I said. "I'll go home and tend the sheep, and sleep nights on the mountain watching the stars, and I'll forget I ever was a king."

"No, you won't. We are what we are. It's not hard, Astyanax. Ask them how each will bribe you. That's how your uncle did it."

I spoke to the whirling light that was one woman, three women. I said, "Hera, my Skyfather's wife, what will you give me if I choose you?"

A voice came from the whorl of radiance: a grave, mature voice. "Astyanax: power is mine, and kingship. I will make you king of all the Akhaians. You will rule for a long time; in your reign Skyfather and I will be reconciled. I will not begrudge him his many loves; I will mother the world and give it peace. You want revenge, don't you? I will give you power over all those who killed your father and your grandfather."

I was tempted. I held out the apple to her; but as a ray of light shot out to seize the apple I remembered the story of Dardanos and the Snakemother. I said, "You are Skyfather's enemy. You'll twist my fate against me." I snatched the apple back. "And you, Athena?"

Came a second voice out of the light: mild, haunting. "You are right, little cousin Astyanax. She has always hated our father. There's no reason she would change suddenly. But I will give you both wisdom and strength in battle. In war you will be invincible; in peace, all-wise, compassionate. Of all the gods, I have the most compassion, because I am a piece of Skyfather, born without woman. Of all the gods, I am most kin to you. . . ."

"Oh, Athena," I said. "A man must wreak vengeance on his father's killers. If you give me your compassion, my revenge will give me no joy."

"That you know this," said Athena, "shows that you already have within you the germ of a great compassion. We are so akin."

I was more tempted by her words than by Hera's. But sometimes, as the light flickered, I still saw the withered face of the earth serpent. I doubted. I asked for Aphrodite.

The light resolved into a woman. The woman smiled. Aunt Helen's smile. The smile I had run away from ten years before. Now I knew why I had been so afraid. I had foreseen this moment. She smiled, the fire of Skyfather blazing in her eyes. "No!" I cried. "No! No!" With all my might I threw the apple into the womanflame. It sputtered and was spent.

Later it would be said that I had chosen, as had my uncle Paris, to put beauty and love above all the other virtues. I do not know if that is what happened. But it was the choice I was supposed to have made, and I came to suppose that I had chosen thus. But now I was alone with my cousin Hermes. There was a small fire on the altar, and a moonbeam fell on the green-black stone from Skyfather's house.

"You have chosen," Hermes said.

"Yes." A mockery of a choice.

"They will come again in their thousand ships."

"Yes." Though I knew there were not that many ships left in all the world, and that the heroes all were dead.

"Come, take Hector's armor. You have earned it. Skyfather is pleased with you." I stared long and hard into my immortal cousin's eyes; they were so familiar. Of course they were. My father's eyes, Skyfather's eyes.

"Do you pity me, Hermes?" I said.

"Pity?" The boy stood up on the altar. The wings on his feet fluttered so fast that they could not be seen, like dragonflies'. "Pity? I am a god."

It seemed to me that he thought those words explained everything. I wanted to detain him somehow, to ask him whether he understood what I meant by the word "pity." But he was gone before I could open my mouth, and the fire that had wreathed the altar had collapsed back into the black stone that had fallen from the sky. I rubbed the stone: it was shiny in a way not quite like silver, and it was hard, harder I thought than bronze.

Had this stone always concealed this metallic fire in it? Or was this something new, a sign? I remembered that Snakemother had even now been seen in this temple, had profaned Skyfather's holiest place. I shuddered. I hefted the sword. I could barely lift it. I thought, I must be worthy of Hector.

The three symbols of my father's name, deeply patined, gleamed like malachite. Power was in my father's name. I was his son. The power was mine. But I could not quite feel it yet.

Chapter V

🔳🔳🔳🔳🔳🔳🔳🔳🔳🔳🔳🔳🔳🔳🔳🔳

King of the City

The night did not pass swiftly. I was haunted by the images of the three goddesses, the one goddess, as I lay on the smooth stone softened by moss. In my dreams Aunt Helen came to me with her arms outstretched and her smile brighter than Skyfather's sun and she was naked and faintly fragrant, just as I remembered. But her face was also Snakemother's face. I was fleeing from her, fleeing, fleeing into the sea. I could feel feet sinking into sand. The tide was rising. Water rose up in a wall, the wall of cyclopean megaliths crowned with crenellations, and I knew that if I did not stop running, I would crash against the wall and my head would split open and I would see gray brains dripping down the rock face. I had to turn, I had to.

"Aunt Helen," I said.

I felt her arms around me. I was aroused. I squeezed my eyes tight shut. Her arms wrapped themselves around me, sinuous, snakelike. Were they the snakes that were her hair? Did I dare look?

But I had to. I was the last of the House of Priam, and only I could undo the tangle that the threads of the Fates had knotted themselves into.

Slowly I turned and opened my eyes. I was nauseated from the scent of ocean and of raw sex. I saw her face only for a moment, beautiful and terrifying. Her eyes shone. Deep, deep blue, the forgotten color of the past.

Then she yawned. From her open mouth a black stone fell. I screamed, "That's the Skyfather stone; it's not yours to cast down from the sky." I was full of rage; I beat her with my fists but they crashed down on emptiness. . . .

Then I was a child in my grandfather's arms. What surfaced was not a dream but a memory. Soft light on his soft face. I asked (my voice sounded thin and childish to me now), "Grandfather, what is my name? No one will tell me my name. Sometimes they call me Little Star. But I know it's not my name, I know it."

"It is a good name, Little Star," my grandfather said, looking away sadly. I knew it was the old time because the sky shone brilliant through the wide windows of the palace on the walls faced with white marble and the columns freshly painted, red and gold. And I was a child squatting on my grandfather's knee and wondering at the strange soft weave of his chiton. ("It is called silk," he told me once, "and comes from very far away, on the other side of the world, from the land of tin.")

"But don't I have another name?"

"You have a sacred name. But it is really a title. I gave you that name; it is wrenched from my heart. It was foretold when your uncle Paris was born that Hector could never bear this name if Paris lived. So it is yours now, Astyanax."

When he uttered my name I felt power flow from his lips into me. I was suddenly afraid that he would die right there in the burning sunlight for all to see. I knew magic was at work. "Quick!" said King Priam. "Take the name from me before it is lost!"

I repeated it in its most ancient form: *"Astu-wanakas, King of the City."* I felt the warmth drain from my lips. "Grandfather, don't die!" I cried out in a childish hysteria.

"Oh, child, how did you know?" But his voice held no rancor. "It doesn't matter. There will always be a piece of me in you now, for all time."

"Oh, Grandfather, I love you so much! I don't want you to die!"

"Don't worry. I will live forever." I did not believe him even then. I was three years old, I think.

In the dream I remembered that moment. And I remembered the skystone in the temple of Skyfather. And over and over I whispered, "Forever, forever."

Philemon was shaking me awake. "Nothing is forever!" he was saying. "Once you were a shepherd boy and now you are a king!"

"Was I dreaming?" I moaned. I reached up to rub my eyes; my fingers found metal. The helmet. "Philemon—"

"I knew you'd be here. Look, the sky, Aster."

I stretched, stood up. I was wearing the armor of my father. I took off the helmet and placed it on the altar. I looked skyward: something had splintered the grayness. Something like painted lightning bolts, zagging across the sky, and behind them a soft blue light. Skyfather was beginning to peel back the curtain of grayness.

Philemon said, "Outside there are lads from the village, waiting for your words." He seemed nervous. He wiped at my breastplate with an old torn chiton. He had turned overnight from a father to a slave.

"You don't have to tend me, Father."

"It wouldn't be right for you to call me that, master. Not in front of *them* outside."

"But . . . whose arms will hold me when I falter?" I was panicking now. So much had changed. The cracks in the gray sky showed that what mortals did could affect things in heaven itself. I was more afraid than I had ever been before.

"Whose arms will hold you, master? You are the king. It is

you who will comfort *us* when we suffer, who will feed us, oversee our births and deaths. Troy has been kingless for so long, and people have forgotten a lot. You are our only link with the gods. . . ."

"The gods are not as you suppose, old man," I said, and I remembered Hermes, golden-haired, petulant, pitiless. "I have seen them and you have not." And I told him what had happened: how I had had the chance to choose a new path for Troy, to choose the way of Hera or Athena, but instead had doomed myself to follow that smile of killing beauty. "But before I pass on to the underworld," I said, "I will see the cosmos restored to its full color, and I will see Troy strong again, I promise you."

Philemon was trembling now. "To think I had you in my home, I nurtured you, hugged you to sleep when you were a baby. . . ." He was weeping.

I said, "I have not stopped being your son, Philemon, just because I am Hector's." I wanted him to hold me, even to punish me for coming into the city. "I've done nothing to prepare myself for being a king," I said. "I'm not ready."

"You were ready to come down into ruined Troy, weren't you?"

"But I didn't know!"

"You are the last of the Dardanids, Astyanax, the last of the Trojans to possess your Skyfather's vision. What *you* cannot see, how shall one of *us* see?"

I looked around. I tried to see Leontes' shade. But he too had gone; for he was a thing of the night, easily dispelled by the sunshine. In the unwonted brightness, the jags of moss in the flagstones glittered like slivers of emerald.

"What shall I do now?"

"Show yourself," said Philemon, "to your people. Go to the palace; stand on the balcony that overlooks the market-place."

I thought of something suddenly. "The flock, Philemon! Who is looking after our sheep?"

He just looked at me. His eyes sparkled.

"You—" I said.

"The time of shepherding is over for me."

I walked to the entrance of the temple.

First came the wild dogs, barking at the gleaming armor. Then—our sheep, swarming in the street, and laughing boys at play. They looked up when they saw me; they tittered among themselves. Finally one of them said, "Hey, Aster! Where did you get those clothes, that fancy armor?"

"Sold all your father's sheep in the night?"

"Sell your ass to a Phoenician sailor in the night?" another said derisively. It was the same one I had passed on the mountain on my way from the village to the city. I feinted at them. They made as if to parry, but something made them hold back. As if I was somehow a different person now.

There was no enmity in their voices, though; so I just smiled. Presently they stopped making fun of me, because they saw that Philemon had fallen on his knees before me. Some older men, Philemon's friends, had come down this street, attracted by the commotion. When they saw me they became agitated. One cried out, "Hector, Hector to the life!" And he began to weep; soon the old men were all weeping, and shouting for their wives to come.

The boys stared at us; this talk meant little more to them than the drunken war reminiscences of braggart fathers who had probably cowered behind the lines in the real war. The brave ones had all been killed, including my fifty uncles.

And then the old men took up the cry, "Will you rebuild the walls, and make us strong again? And will you bring Helen back to us?"

I remembered the half-smile of Aphrodite that had caused me to reject all reason and to throw her the golden apple. . . .

I heard their cries now: "You'll bring her back, and you'll fend off the thousand ships again. . . ."

"Glorious Hector's son has come back to redeem his people's honor. . . ."

I did not want war. I wanted it to be like the age of Dardanos, when we had duped the Snakemother and imposed peace on the land. I tried to speak out, but I could not, for the shepherd boys, exhilarated at the talk of bloodshed, surged forward now to touch my armor, to drag me up, high, riding on their shoulders, to the ruined palace.

As we turned the corner that led to the square of the shattered horse, I saw that the news had already stormed the town. Thunder and lightning and portents had been seen as far away as Mount Ida, and stray flames leaping from Zeus's altar had incinerated the thatching of village huts ten stadia from the walls. Or if it were not true there were a dozen willing to swear it so. There were several hundred people squeezing against the walls, squatting between the horse's legs, their children squirming on their shoulders, their dogs and pigs and sheep playing tag among the sea of legs. I raised my father's gorgon shield, and a dozen infants wailed in terror, as I had once. Then came a ragged raucous cheer, punctuated by the bleating of lambs and the yelping of dogs. It was strange to me, who could vaguely remember long lines of soldiers leaving the Skaian Gate like links unreeling from a long gold chain, and the crowd roaring summer thunder and the lightning from sun-drenched shields and helmets of burnished bronze. The young children had no idea, and the old ones did not see the reality, only the past, ten times more glittering in the thousandth telling. . . .

Philemon was by my side now. I turned to him, desperate. I said, "I'll order the walls built; order the youths trained in fighting; order that games be held to celebrate; intercede with Skyfather on the kingdom's behalf. But surely I'll not go and fetch Aunt Helen back from Sparta, and revive all the ancient horrors. How can the old men have forgotten how terrible it was? I'll have peace here, do you hear?"

"It's not me you have to convince," Philemon said.

And in my heart I knew that I had sworn vengeance against Neoptolemos that day ten years before, an oath that my own Skyfather had witnessed in his most sacred shrine; that the world was sick and gray and I wanted the color to return to it, even if it meant pouring out my life's blood in libation, to appease the earth mother my ancestor had wronged a hundred years ago. I knew what the gods wanted.

But perhaps I could buy time. "After all," I said aloud, "we haven't any ships."

But the crowd roar swelled up, deafening me, killing our conversation.

I raced for the palace now, the crowd running after. I reached the threshold: the old frescoes scarred with the Akhaian's graffiti were on either side of me. I hesitated. Was it hubris to pretend that I could be like my father, who slew Patroklos and a hundred other heroes? I drew my father's sword.

The crowd was hushed, awed, waiting. Now and then a child jostled another. I stepped across the threshold into the first roofless courtyard. The pillars, fire-scoured, showed only traces of their once bright red paint. Ahead was the balustrade; on the steps, a man lay in a woman's arms, wrapped in a cloak. They were asleep. I was kicking them awake in a moment. "Up, up," I shouted. "I'm home now, the king is home."

They sat up; the woman held the cloak up to her naked breasts. The man was burly, curly-haired. "A boy in shining armor," he mocked. "Come to oust us from our only sleeping place!"

"I'm the king, I say."

A few of the crowd had crept in behind me. They shouted encouragingly, "That's our boy! That's Hector's kid! I'd know him if I was blind."

The man laughed. "It's not even your armor, boy; it's far too big for you."

I was furious. I raised my sword, hefted it from hand to hand. I did not mean to kill the man, but the sword was too heavy for me; it dragged my arm down, smashed into his neck. Blood gushed up from an artery. He looked at me stupidly, then toppled. The blood ran down the stair, clotting against the moss veins of the stone steps. I was appalled for a moment.

The woman stood up, naked. She was middle-aged, perhaps thirty years old, but still firm-bodied. Her hair was long

and black and fell in ringlets over her breasts. She stared at
me like a snake poised to strike. For a second I thought I saw
vipers writhing in her hair. Then the woman said, "It is good
that the man die. You are king, but you have not paid the
price of blood. Now you have fooled the Snakemother, and
your reign will be prosperous . . . until you forget that she
still lives, boy."

"I am of Skyfather. Your Snakemother has no place *here*,
in the land that Dardanos wrested from her. Who are you?" I
said wonderingly.

"Ha, ha! Priam had many secrets, little one. Didn't you
know that the Snakemother was never really exiled from
Troy, that there was only a truce, not the victory Dardanos
claimed?" She cackled unpleasantly. I saw that her teeth
were rotten. "Come, child, anoint your face with this suppliant's blood, that you may dupe my mistress for a few more
years. . . ."

I bent down. The blood burned my fingers. I smeared it on
my face; it hissed like vitriol. I said, "Get out of this palace,
woman! Practice your witchcraft in the mountains. Here we
will have only light." And even as I spoke the sky's blue
seemed to deepen, and the sun to shine more fiercely; there
were puddles on the flagstones, and they shone like mirrors.

The woman said, "The sky may be your father, little one,
but remember that the earth is your mother. Do not forget her
on whose bones you daily tread." Before my eyes she shriveled; her face wrinkled like an old rag, her teeth turned
black. I saw the snakes clearly now, twisting, twining around
her head.

"Go!" I shouted.

She vanished in a whirl of smoke.

Now the others surrounded me. Some of the children
poked at the dead man; others stared at me, knowing awe at
last. I saw a shepherd boy I knew; we had kept each other
company on cold lonely nights on the mountain. I called out
his name: "Dion, Dion. Won't you come embrace me, your
old friend?"

He looked away.

"She's gone, that ugly old bitch!" I said. "I have sent her away."

I looked from one to another. Suddenly I realized that none of them had seen what I had seen: only that I had killed a man and exerted my right to be king. Perhaps they had seen a young woman running away in tears, wailing for her husband's death. They had seen no Snakemother. They did not believe in the old gods, after all.

Then Philemon came up out of the crowd. "It's all right, King," he said. "All things have a blood price, kingship included. It was a divine madness that seized you; now the gods have had their libation."

"Who was this man?" I said.

Someone turned him over. "Don't know."

Another said, "Stranger. Never seen him in my life."

I said, "Take him. Bury him with kingly honors." Philemon looked at me strangely. "I know what I'm doing, old father," I said.

The old man turned to the crowd; they had all streamed into the courtyard and were crushed together, squeezing against the walls, straddling the broken columns. He kissed me on both bloody cheeks, calling me by the ancient title of *wanax,* king above kings. At the utterance of that sacred word excitement rippled through the crowd: and soon they were all shouting, *"Wanax! Wanax!"* And the sun's rays shot through the slits of the eyes of the shattered horse, whose head reared up from the nearby square over my stunted walls. It was too much. I ran up the stairs, slippery with the blood offering, into my old room, which was still cool and dark because of the overgrowth of vines.

"Leontes!" I cried. "Leontes! I need you now; my kingship has orphaned me and made all my friends afraid of me. . . . I can't bear it, Leontes, I wish I could change places with you. . . ."

Suddenly, like a little boy, I began to cry.

And I heard my mother's voice, from ten years ago, before the walls fell and the city was burnt up: "A hero doesn't cry, Astyanax."

But I could not stop now. Thank the gods that I was alone. I was ashamed. I could not bear to be seen.

Presently my sobs subsided. I knew they would be waiting outside, and that I would have to come down with decisions, plans.

I sat down on my old pallet.

I picked up the terra-cotta chariot and put it down and gave it a shove. At that moment I became aware of another's weeping in the room. Or was it a trick of the wind? A little child weeping helplessly, fearing darkness perhaps. . . . "Leontes?" I said. There was no answer, but I think I felt a little comforted.

I said out loud, "I am a hero. I am a king." And suddenly, for the first time, I felt those words ring true. For I had taken my name from Priam, and I could trace my lineage down from the sky.

It was a day of glory, that first day of my kingship. But I was not, as Priam had been, High King over dozens of lands and tributaries. I knew it was going to be uphill work restoring Troy even to a shadow of what it had been under my grandfather. There was so much to do: emissaries to be sent out to the Hittites and the Egyptians, trading to be resumed after the ten-year interregnum, my subjects to be convinced that I was my father's son, for not all had seen me with the sword and shield and helmet that the gods had returned to me from the underworld.

These duties took up all my time. My vision—of wreaking revenge, even of recapturing Aunt Helen, of rescuing my mother from bondage—began to drain away my thoughts. At the back of my mind there remained the knowledge that the time I had was dearly bought, that I had tricked Snakemother into submission much as my ancestors had done, and that eventually the blood price of my kingship must truly be paid. That was the meaning of my meaningless choice between the three goddesses.

I tried not to think of any of this. I avoided it almost completely for three years, except in my dreams, which I could not control, and which tormented me increasingly as the city prospered. I did not mind. I thought I was getting off lightly, trading the city's rapid expansion for a few bad dreams. I tried to be happy.

But in the third year, almost to a day, there came a ship into the Trojan harbor, a ship with black sails. From the ship there came a king's messenger. Nothing extraordinary in this; in the old days foreign kings thronged my grandfather's halls.

But this messenger came from a king who had been dead for more than a hundred years.

Book Two: The Blue King

Some say . . . that Astyanax survived and became King of Troy after the departure of the Greeks.

—Robert Graves, *The Greek Myths*

Chapter VI

The High Council

I was king but not king. I had the title of King of Troy without being ruler over all that my grandfather King Priam had ruled: the subject cities and the tribute-bearing territories. We had won no wars and therefore had few slaves save those who had inherited their servitude, and these few unruly and untrained. When I had first become king it seemed that I would almost instantly realize the fantasy of crossing the sea and carrying Aunt Helen back to Troy and beginning the Trojan War again. All this had been foretold by my meeting with Hermes and the Triple Goddess. But as time passed the dream receded. For though I was king in name, I was king over an impoverished and dispirited people; I could no more go sailing to the west than could a shepherd abandon his flock to the mercy of the wolves.

First I had to establish at least a semblance of the former order. That, and not the eyes of my Aunt Helen, was what occupied me for the first three years of my reign.

For the sake of form we called it the High Council, but it was not as solemn as it had been during the war, when Priam sat in stern and kingly state on the throne my ancestors had wrested from Snakemother. But I think I gave a reasonable outward appearance of kingliness. When they grew too rowdy I would invoke my father's name.

I was doing so just at that moment, in fact, pulling the gorgon shield up from where it lay at my feet and brandishing it in the sunlight that streamed in through the slits and fissures of the makeshift roof we had put up over those pillars that still stood. "Marriage!" I was saying. "That's all very well, but I'm not going to sit here and have you people manipulate me politically. I mean, I *am* the king, aren't I?"

The shield was heavy and I hastily set it down on the step and sat down. "Philemon," I said, "what do you think?"

The old man, who sat as advisor at my feet, said, "My king, I think you are right to overrule them. But perhaps you should . . . well, it has been rumored . . . forgive me, my king—"

"What?"

"That you are . . . sexually backward." I saw in his face that he feared he had said too much, that he was afraid of what I might do. So I calmed him with a smile and encouraged him to go on. "It's bad for morale, King. But you know I shouldn't really speak at all. I'm only a shepherd, and you are king." I saw that he was embarrassed at being admitted to the High Council and uncomfortable in his position as my advisor.

He sat back down. I looked at the gathering of second-rate nobles who had honored me with their presence. They reclined on woven mats, their arms resting on their helmets or on imported ivory pillows. I had long since ordered the moss scrubbed clean from the cracks in the flagstones, but here and there it lingered like the patina on a bronze shield.

I said, choosing my words carefully, "In the past three years I have been rebuilding the walls around the citadel." The walls were, after a fashion, rebuilt; but how could I imitate the seamless joins of the old cyclopean stones? "I have irrigated; I have bred sheep; I have traded." It was true enough; these things had prospered more than before. For the land needed a king as a man needs a soul; in the interregnum the land had been as a corpse, a mere simulacrum of a kingdom. "But we simply haven't attained the kind of power necessary to make a political marriage alliance possible. And who with? The west or the east? More and more we are becoming the crossroads again, and we have to balance one power against another." This last I spoke was more brave blustering than fact. We were not gold-rich Troy of the old time through which all ships and caravans had to pass, the junction of the silk road west and the tin road east. The roads were collapsing all over; it was not only that Troy had fallen ten years before; it was as though the entire universe were coming to an end. The few foreigners who came to my court would often tell me how dangerous the seas had become since the Akhaians had begun their raiding. But I had told myself that I must accept the world as it is.

I had pushed the remembrance of Aunt Helen's smile into the remotest corner of my mind. It will never touch me again, I thought. (I often thought this, but I knew I could not flee forever.) But at that moment, when my nobles were examining my sex life as casually as one might inspect a slave's genitals in the market, I saw her smile again. Her beauty was my pain. I barely heard the nobles as they went on.

"We're not talking about political alliances," my second cousin Leukippos was telling me self-righteously. "Well, to be honest, a number of jokes have been circulating about . . . about, well, sheep . . . O King." (That title sprang reluctantly to his lips, I was sure.) "It has been said, also, that the reason for the diminished corn harvest—"

"Nonsense!" said Philemon. "You know that it is Snakemother's minions who have been spreading that sort of talk."

Silence fell.

At last I said, "There are some advantages, cousins, in being a shepherd. One isn't so afraid of uttering the unutterable, for instance. Philemon is right. If we ignore them, they will grow strong."

"There are snake-haired women in the hills," Leukippos said.

"Superstition!" said Phoinix, a bastard son of Anchises.

"Maybe not," I said. "We should negotiate with them." I remembered the woman on the steps of the palace on the day of my accession, the blood libation I had been forced to pay. "Perhaps we must make at least some minor concession to the institution of the sacred marriage to forestall any further action from the Snakemother."

Phoinix turned to me, "*You* must deal with them. In your

capacity as"—he edged his words with contempt—"Sky-father's living representative and god-king."

"Don't make fun of the boy!" Leukippos said. "He's doing the best he can. Look at what he inherited. Look at what we have now."

"He's not even a man," Phoinix said angrily. "At least Prince Hector knew how to fuck! Perhaps you're saving yourself for your aunt Helen!" And I vividly remembered Leontes and how they had always said how alike we looked and how we might have been brothers. Where was Leontes now? For three years I had slept in that old room (I could not bear to use the chamber where my parents had slept, let alone the apartments of my grandfather) but Leontes had never visited me again.

"Since you have the effrontery to ask," I said, "I am not as backward as the rumors seem to say. You have but to send to the village where I grew up and ask for the sister of Dion, a young shepherd."

Phoinix said (knowing better, I could not help but laugh), "Shepherd's sisters are little better than sheep themselves. Filthy things. And all that was three years ago. I think it's politically expedient to forget our cousin's little sojourn among the—"

I said, "Be still, Phoinix. You may not like it, but I am the king. And we are not like the Egyptians, whose kings are so high above the peasants that they cannot even address them directly. The father of my fathers was a shepherd. And when Apollo built the great walls of Troy for my great-grandfather, he came to earth in the guise of a shepherd. You would do well not to disdain a shepherd, for it is a shepherd and a grandchild of shepherds who rules over you."

Phoinix pouted and did not speak.

Leukippos said, "But there's still the problem with the corn harvest and Snakemother's faction." My cousin was often pompous and almost always self-righteous. But it was true something should be done to appease the darkness.

"I agree," I said. "I want to eliminate all these problems with one action. I'll go as an emissary to the Snakemother

and I'll consummate my theoretical marriage to the earth.
That way we will dispel both the blight and the allegations
that I am a virgin." I spoke more bravely than I felt. In a city
sacred to Skyfather and the light, as Troy was, the devotees
of Snakemother did not live openly, but concealed themselves among the tholos tombs beyond the city walls. For
when Dardanos wrested this land from the ancient powers,
they fled into darkness, and what is more dark than death?
Moreover, though I knew they would never drag Dion's
sister into the High Court to give testimony on my sexual
prowess, I had not exactly told the truth, or rather I had lied
by concealing. What had I and the girl done? On the mountain, huddling against the freezing wind, we had explored our
bodies, fumbling, in the dark. That was all. But I knew she
would not betray me. More likely, now that I was king, she
would babble of how a god had touched her on the hillside.
No other woman had ever touched me in my secret places,
except, of course, for Leontes' mother, my old nurse, who,
when I was a baby, had often set me to dozing by softly
stroking me down there. But it was not proper to allude to
such a thing, for the relationship between a man and his
nurse is a sublime mystery.

Those were my secret thoughts as I agreed to perform an
act which might conceivably have affected my very kingship.
Not only that, but I knew it would bring me closer to what I
dreaded, what I knew to be inevitable: the consequences of
that night when I met Hermes and faced the Triple Goddess
and chose what could not be chosen. I tried to maintain a
mask of composure; I concentrated so hard on it that I
missed some of the discussion that followed, and when I
drifted back to my senses I could hear Phoinix speaking
again, his dark eyebrows knit together and hands gesticulating.

"The tholos tombs," he was saying. "It's a perfect opportunity to replenish the armory. And fund the war, if we're to
have one as I think we must."

"What?" I said.

Philemon whispered in my ear, "He wants to take advan-

tage of your visit to the Snakemother's lair to break into the
tombs and—''

"It is sacrilege," I said, glaring at my cousin. "Besides,
we can't think of war yet." An image surfaced: Neoptolemos
beheading my grandfather in the temple of Skyfather, and the
blood streaming, steaming from the altar, spattering in the
sacred flame. . . . I thought of that war daily! How could I
blame the nobles when I burned as much as they did with the
shame and the desire for vengeance? But I said, "We should
be patient." It was the kingly thing to say.

But I thought of the tombs outside the city walls. My
ancestors rested there. Their locations were so secret that I
did not think the Akhaians could have touched them. Arms
and gold, I thought. And specters guarding them. Rotting for
centuries in the dank and dark. But I was the child of their
children and my blood was as much their blood as it was the
blood of Skyfather. And I thought of Aunt Helen's eyes.
They were like pieces of a summer sky captured and polished
into smooth gems. Except that there had been no such sky in
thirteen summers. The eyes, the smile were of another age.

Creatures of darkness lived in the dead men's burial places,
I knew that. Some outrage, some unquenchable thirst for
revenge kept them from crossing the river of the dead into
their proper kingdom. But perhaps I could constrain their
rage. If I could somehow prove to them that their gold might
buy their vengeance as well as our victory. If only they could
see our desperation. . . .

"But I am tempted," I said at last, and could not look my
cousin in the eye. But I could tell that they were all relieved,
and that they did not envy what I must do next.

Chapter VII

The Messenger

At the first new moon I sent a runner to the land of the dead. He carried a tablet on which was written this message: *The king of the sky has come to take the land to wife. If she hides, he will come by stealth. If she resists, he will seize her by force. He will seed the land and give her many children. It is I, king of the city, who speaks, and the sky is in me.*

I walked with my messenger as far as the Skaian Gate. Then I watched him begin to run swiftly toward the mountains. The stars were thick, but they could not drive out the gloom that pervaded the city; the light seemed lifeless, desultory. I think the runner was afraid even though I had given him an amulet with a piece of Skyfather's own rock mounted on gold. Once a man who wore such a talisman would have feared nothing: not battle, not death, let alone the mere night. Like so much else, this was a token of how far the shadow had encroached upon our lives.

I turned back toward the palace, walking alone through the unlit streets, finding my way by feel. Some hours later, before dawn, the messenger came and knelt by my bedroom door. I do not know how long he waited. In my sleep I heard one of the dogs growling, and I stirred and leaned over the side of my bed to nudge my body slave. The boy groaned and continued to snore until prodded a few more times; then he sat up abruptly.

"King . . . the dogs . . ." he said sleepily.

"Yes, yes. I'm not sure which one, but take him out. All the way downstairs; I don't want to step in it when I get up, understand? Or you'll be in trouble."

"Yes, King." I could hear him groping for his chiton.

Faint light through the window; dawn was close. "Oh, Astyanax—"

"What?" I was too tired to rebuke him for his insolence.

"There's a man in the hallway." Through crusted eyes I saw the slave pulling on his chiton and behind him a man silhouetted in the flickering torchlight of the corridor.

"It must be my messenger," I said, sitting up. "I had better receive him formally."

"But it's not even morning yet!"

"Take care," I said.

"Yes, King." He ran outside to get a torch; he stuck it in the bracket over my bed. Firelight licked the damp walls and played over the hunting murals, now peeling and faded. One day I would have to have them repainted, one day without crises. If any who still practiced the arts could be found in the city.

As I sat at the edge of the bed, the slave covered me with a robe of purple lambswool. It needed hemming; its gold-thread fringes were in tatters. I said, "Approach, messenger. What word from the queen of darkness?"

He did not answer me, but remained kneeling in the doorway.

"Answer me!"

Something was wrong. I ordered the slave boy to go and lead him in; surely there was nothing to be afraid of. The boy slid over to the doorway, kicking one of the dogs aside. When he came back he was quaking and could barely talk. I waited and he said, "Astyanax, he's—"

I got up. I was not sleepy anymore. I went to the messenger. He was still kneeling, his eyes staring forward, unblinking. He did not speak. I touched his face, his shoulders. Like marble, cold. Even his cloak was stiff, like thinly shaved stone.

Softly I said, "Did you break the tablet over the city of the dead, as I instructed? Is this how Snakemother greets the messenger of Skyfather?" I prodded him and he tumbled over backward and he was lying on the floor, face up, but still in the kneeling position with his legs pointing at me. I recoiled and made the sign of aversion. The slave was crying and one of the dogs was whimpering like a whipped child.

Suddenly a snake darted from his crotch, wound around the stiffened folds of his chiton. It coiled and glared at me with bloodshot eyes. I cast my eyes down, for Snakemother's gaze is an intolerable cold, and found myself staring between the messenger's legs, where his phallos had been ripped out by the roots. And then I heard a soft seductive laughter in the air.

"Quick! The sword from the chest beneath the bed!" I shouted to the boy. He crawled over to me and thrust it at me. The snake had to be killed. I hefted the sword, my father's sword, and brought it swooping downward onto the serpent . . . but there was only crimson smoke and a trickle of congealed blood.

"Turned to stone. Like the old stories," the slave boy said. "Did Snakemother show him her real face?" He cowered by the window. "I thought it was just a story, just a story!"

"The snake!" I staggered up with the sword and began thrusting at the air. There it was, slithering under the bed, twisting itself around the legs of cedarwood. All snakes are supernatural. That was why the boy was so afraid. "Come out, serpent," I whispered. "This is not a house of darkness. You do not belong here. This is Skyfather's place. Come, come," I said, my voice taking on the singsong of a priestly incantation. To the boy I hissed, "Make a run for it! Get help!" He dashed into the corridor, almost tripping over the messenger whom Snakemother's magic had petrified. I stood my ground, waiting, singing softly to the serpent. "Are you so lust-starved, Snakemother, that you thought the king's poor messenger the king himself? Did you show yourself naked to him, stripped of the filth that hides still more profound abominations?"

The snake: coiling, uncoiling, thrashing against the big treasure chest and the cedarwood toy chest. I have to meet its gaze, I thought. I am the king. I did. Its eyes were brilliant crimson. Like Helen's eyes, their color seemed to have been plucked out of time, fragments of the bright past.

"You will die! You must die!" I screamed, and ran blindly forward with my father's sword outstretched. The sword seethed as it met sizzling flesh. A cloud of red dust swirled upward and within that cloud stood Helen. . . .

Not the Helen I had last seen standing among the wailing women in front of the burning city, but a nymph-Helen just past puberty, the age she must have been when my uncle Paris stole her from the land of Sparta: Helen with her golden hair billowing in a wind that was no wind; Helen solemn, star-sapphire-eyed. "Helen, Helen," I whispered. "I don't want to flee anymore. I must run run run toward the light. Helen, Helen."

She beckoned to me across the cloud banks tinged with red fire. "Shall I run to you across the burning lands?" Her mouth parted as if to speak. A wind I could not feel gathered up her skirts. She was attired in the antique fashion, with her breasts bare. What was she saying? I heard the rushing of the wind, her voice was barely audible above the roar.

But it was not her voice! Only the voice of mocking Phoinix: "Perhaps you're saving yourself for your aunt Helen!" and the snake exploding slowly, slowly, as though time had dilated itself to let the gore hang vaporous in the air. Then, in a frenzy of accelerating time, the snake collapsed to a single point and winked out of existence, and only the laughter of my cousin Phoinix remained behind. "Be quiet!" I shouted and whirled around to find him standing in the doorway. "Get out of my room. You're an apparition, you aren't real."

He came toward me warily. I must have looked fierce; he stopped. He said, "Your slave boy came running for help. I have a few of your men outside, what few I could rouse." He was panting; he had been running. "What's happened to the runner?" He stubbed his foot hard against the man of stone and groaned. "Unnatural things, bad things." To someone still outside the room: "Come in, there's a corpse to get rid of."

I said, "Take it away. And in the morning send to Philemon's village. Ask for the shepherd Dion; tell him to send his sister to me."

"You're abandoning your challenge to Snakemother?" said Leukippos from outside. "After only one man's death?"

"No. But I think we should go about this another way."

"Another ruse to trick the queen of darkness?" Leukippos said. "I remember well the story of Dardanos and his corpse stuffed with grain."

"Another old myth to aggrandize the Dardanids," Phoinix said, for his kinship to me was through the maternal line and he could not properly bear the title of a descendant of Dardanos, and it had always rankled him. "I don't believe any of the stories."

"There is truth in all old stories," I said to him, "for those who are able to see it. I will tell you only once: I have a plan and I am king." I rarely used this tone with my kinsmen. It chafed him, but he held his peace. "Now go."

At last they left me. The slave boy curled up at my feet with the largest of the dogs. I was suddenly overwhelmed by torpor as I slumped back onto the bed; I knew that I was in the presence of Hypnos, the brother of Death. Sleep swooped down on me like a bird of prey. Such sleep is magical and comes only as a prelude to prophetic dreams. I had a plan to force Snakemother to submit to me; as I slept and dreamed, its details began to take shape.

In the first dream I was about to be married. My bride was veiled; a robe billowed about her. We stood in front of the palace; I heard the crowd cheering and looked up at the brilliant sunlight and heard the groan of a white heifer slaughtered at the altar and the incantations of priests and acolytes. I lifted my hand to my bride's face to strip away the veil. But it was the eyes of a skull that stared back at me, and the hands were of bone, and the crowd that cheered me on were gibbering shades of the dead, thirsting for mortal blood.

In the second dream I was staring at the disk of the sun until my eyes burned and the tears came spurting. And I was riding a white horse to do battle with a writhing serpent coiled around a mountain. But when I approached the serpent, it reared up and twined itself around me so that I could not kill it without also injuring myself.

In the third dream I watched the skystone in the house of Skyfather. It glowed, became incandescent. I seized it in both hands, marveling that it did not sear them. Then I hurled it high into the sky, so that it raced toward the golden sundisk. The skystone grew a comet tail and burned blinding against the brilliant sky, and I thought: I have killed my father, yet I rejoice.

I screamed as I awoke. The dogs were howling beside my bed, and the slave boy was chattering to hide his unease. When I had calmed him down he told me that they had already dispatched a messenger to the village to summon Dion's sister Dione into my presence.

She was dark-eyed, fearful. She moved as I remembered: in swift, anxious jerks, like a rodent. As she came toward me she fidgeted with a louse she had plucked from her hair. At first I must have shown disappointment; my memory had made of her a more glamorous creature than this.

"My lord, my lord," she said quietly, and prostrated herself at the foot of my throne so that the gloom of the throne's shadow enveloped her.

"Dione. You should not be humble. We are still friends." I touched her head, stroked her tousled, greasy hair. She looked up at me. Her cloak was sweat-stained; she and the messenger must have run all the way from the village. "I need you, Dione. Village women live close to the forces of the earth. They aren't afraid to face dark things. I need to send a message to the queen of the dark city."

To my surprise she seemed relieved. I asked her why; she said, "I had thought you were going to summon me to be . . . your concubine, Astyanax. What else could I believe? You commanded me to bring bridal vestments to the palace. Even now they are following behind me in my father's oxcart. My mother will be here by evening to help make me

more beautiful. I am not a princess, so you cannot make me
queen. There's only one reason you would want me here.
Because of the night we—"

"You still remember."

"My father has promised me with thirty sheep and two
bracelets of bronze to—"

"No matter. You love him?" She had not told me his
name, but I imagined it was one of the local boys I had
played with as a child.

"Oh, my lord . . ." She looked me boldly in the face; she
threw her arms around my waist and kissed my chest, my
neck, at last my lips. "I am sorry, I presume . . . You are
still Astyanax, my friend, who explored my body under a
warm blanket under the chill stars. Oh, I thought you were
going to destroy my life, just because you are king now and I
am still a shepherd girl."

"Are you afraid to go as emissary to Snakemother?"

"I am a woman," she said. "Your god is ruler, but we
still have our goddess."

Ours is a world of men; and woman is by far its greatest
mystery.

I said, "When we have done this thing, I will see that you
are married properly. I'll dower you away myself. He will
know that you have my favor, and that the two of you will
never want, so long as I am king."

She smiled and said, "I always knew there was something
more to you than you let on, do you know that? I always
knew. No one ever told me that you were the prince, but I
just knew. That night, when we were alone together on the
mountain, I *really* knew."

"How could you have? I had almost forgotten myself."

"Because, though I gave you so many opportunities, you
didn't rape me."

I knew that princes were as prone to acts of savagery as
anyone else. But I could not bring myself to disillusion her.
In some fashion, because we had shared one night of adolescent groping, I would always love her a little.

Chapter VIII

The Transformation

I waited fourteen sleeps, until the first night of the full moon. In all this time I did not set eyes on Dione at all; she was sequestered in the women's wing of the palace, in her mother's care; her parents had been let in on the plan.

At sunset it was time for the ritual bath. As a boy I had never entered this most sacred chamber, though it was only a few doorways down the corridor from my own room. Like the other princes I took my baths in the courtyard, splashing myself with rainwater from the tall earthenware amphorae that lined one wall, each one painted with bright geometric patterns. I remember that once I asked Leontes' mother what lay behind that closed door whose always damp and fragrant wood was incised with signs that only half made sense.

She forced me to avert my eyes (they were level with the skirts of her chiton with their heady, familiar smell) and said, "That was a bad place once. That was where they used to kill the king. Walk quickly by and don't read the marks on the door."

I said, "But they don't even mean anything."

"They are in the tongue of Snakemother." Then she said, as she maneuvered me beyond the doorway, "There are old things that a male child should never learn. Or else the world will come to an end." She was rarely this stern, this serious; I had only seen her take this tone with Leontes the slave boy. Was I not a prince, and the son of the greatest hero in the world? I was angry at first. But after that I would slink guiltily past the door and pretend not to see it.

It was only when I returned to Troy as a young man that I was tall enough to see the icons pictured on the upper half of the door. Oddly, though the paint on the corridor walls had been ravaged by the Akhaians, and the neatly concatenated ocean-wave designs around the doorway were now riddled with chars and cracks, the door itself was untouched, almost as though the Akhaians had feared to fire it. How strange, I had thought. They had not been afraid to profane the temple of Skyfather himself, yet they dared not burn this relic of the dark times.

Later I would learn that they feared the darkness even more than we; for they were closer to its source.

I remembered that once, running to my grandfather in terror because of a story Leontes' mother had told me, I had been comforted with these words: "Astyanax, sweet child, it is so no more. In the old times, yes. The sacred bathchamber was where the king was killed each year. He was encased in a fine net and his body was smashed with the two-headed labrys, which the living goddess herself wielded. But such things have ceased. We are not barbarians here. Don't fret, my child."

"But will it happen to me?"

He only smiled. But for many weeks thereafter I dreamed of it. And I would hear the howling of murdered kings, and would awake in pain, calling for my nurse.

I knew now that I would have to use the ritual bath. I had to draw Snakemother out, to challenge her. The crops were bad this year but not disastrous; next year things could be worse. I knew such things were not mere superstition, as my bastard cousin Phoinix would like to believe. Had I not seen a god with my own godlike eyes? But it was with unease that I commanded the seal broken and the bathroom aired out, and the tub filled with hot water scented with sulfur, which is the hardened bile of Snakemother.

The steps were broken and pinched my feet. I had stripped naked while a priest of Skyfather censed me with unpleasant fumes; now at last I lay soaking in the prescribed fashion, letting the fumes and heat permeate my pores and cleanse me. My body slave sat at my feet, strumming on a kithara he had made himself from sheep's gut and the shell of a tortoise. The moon had just risen and completely filled the small high

window. I sat in a swath of radiance and watched the fumes
drifting and listened to the wind as it tore through the tall
trees in the garden. My slave sang a mournful song about
ancient times, about how Theseus wrested love from Ariadne,
priestess of Snakemother, centuries ago. Suddenly he looked
so much like Leontes that I wondered how my companion
could have sprung to life. But Leontes would have been my
age, and I had seen his brains caking and his blood congeal-
ing on my father's shield.

I said, "How is it that you became a slave? You've served
me for almost a year now, and I haven't even asked your name.
But you remind me of—" No. I should not trouble his
childish mind with such thoughts.

He broke off singing and said, "King, my mother was a
slave here, and she died only a year ago. She would have
died giving birth to me, I think. But she wanted to make sure
I was enrolled in your service before she died. The pain was
terrible in the last years of her life; I lived with her in the
slaves' quarters and tended her. I have no name, of course,
other than whatever you care to call me. But . . ." I saw in
his eyes that he was concealing something.

"Speak. I won't do anything to you."

"Oh, King, something about this room . . . Don't be
angry. I am half Akhaian. My mother was raped. During the
sacking of the city. But she crawled away to safety. Before
she died she told me I was never to tell you unless you
demanded it of me. My mother . . ."

"Tell me what?" But I suddenly knew. When I was
running from the burning palace that night, I had seen a
woman being raped against the flank of a stone lion . . .
Leontes' mother. Quietly I said, "You should have told me.
I would have set you free."

"My mother said, 'If he is truly the king, there will be
sunlight in his eyes, eyes that can pierce through falsehood
and divine the truth. At the right time, he will know who you
are without words. Then you'll know that he really is Astyanax
and not some pretender.' "

"She told you that? She gave you such a burden? Poor

boy." I thought of the times I had scolded him and even
beaten him; how he must have been tempted to reveal his link
with my boyhood. I knew then that his loyalty to me ran true,
truer than the pompous lip service of Leukippos or the sneering obedience of Phoinix. I saw the boy was frightened that
he had said too much, and I said, "Do you know what I am
about to do, boy, tonight?"

"I think so, King." I suspected that in the slaves' quarters
they probably had a far more accurate picture of my plan than
did my nobles. Slaves have an astonishing ability both to see
everything and not to have seen anything, an ability that they
depend on, often for their very lives. I saw how useful this
boy could be to me; he could tell me what the people really
thought of what I did.

So I asked him, "Do you think I will survive tonight's
encounter?"

"Oh, my king, you must, you must!" he said. There were
tears in his eyes. He was more than useful to me. I was
moved by what he said, more moved still by his months of
silence.

I said, "Boy, I will raise you up. You will be as one of my
own kinsmen. Your love for me is greater than theirs. I need
people I can trust."

But he said, "No, King, you mustn't! It doesn't look good
to raise a slave up . . . not yet, not while your kingship is
still frail." Such sage advice, from the lips of one so young!
"I won't be any less loyal because I'm still a slave. Besides," he went on, reading my mind precisely, "if you put
me above the other slaves, they'll resent it and they won't
talk to me, and I'll have nothing to report to you."

"But I must honor you. Come here. Come, up the steps,
squat there on the rim of the tub, let me look at you closely."
He clambered up awkwardly. I said, "I'll raise you up in
secret." I kissed him on both cheeks, as is proper with a
kinsman, and said, "You are free." In the moonlight from
the slit-window I could see his eyes, bright with joy. "Rejoice," I said to him, greeting him as I would a friend,
acknowledging him for the first time.

He said nothing for a moment. Then he started to cry. I put my hand up to still him, but he said, "It's nothing, my king, only . . . I don't even have a name!"

"Shush. You shall have one. What do they call you?"

"Usually they call me Stupid, or Pigmy. The ones who like me call me Cat."

I said, "A cat is like a little lion. Because your brother was Leontes, and because you were conceived on the flanks of a stone lion, I will call you Leonidas, lion-child. It will be a secret. But one day I will call you openly by name, and you will be great. Now go and bring in those priests. Rituals, rituals, rituals!"

He scurried away; I heard the patter of his feet in the corridor outside.

I watched the moon.

In a moment I would face Dione; she would come to me dressed as a bride. We would go to the dark city and practice another deception on Snakemother. She would be waiting for me at the gateway of the outer court of the palace.

I remembered the first of the three dreams I had had last night . . . the skull face draped in the veil of virginity . . . the laughter of living corpses. Dione, Dione, I thought, I hope I have not decreed your death.

For though I wanted to bring back Helen and destroy the Akhaians, I also wanted to be a good king, a merciful king. It was not for nothing that I had known both a palace and a shepherd's hut.

I thought of my childhood dreams once more. Alone in this chamber, steeped in water heated to the temperature of living blood, it was easy to relive those dreams, to imagine the screams of a dying king, muffled by water, transmuted by stone and echo into the whine of the empty wind. A sound from ancient times. Would I ever hear such a sound in reality? Did I not long to turn back time and bring back glittering heroes to the Trojan plain? What if I overstepped my ambitions, and so contorted the fabric of the universe that the dark times of Snakemother were brought back? I told myself that it was useless to think of such things. I had already gone too far when I chose between three goddesses, knowing that they were all the same goddess. I had already gone too far by being born under a king-making star.

And so, as the priests came to robe me for the forthcoming ordeal, I stilled the war within by telling myself that the choices had already been made, and not by me. As they robed me in Phoenician purple and hung me with stones and talismans, I became more and more transformed. I stared into the mirror of bronze that two slaves held up for me; I saw my face, yellowed by the gleam of the metal and wavery from its contoured surface. I barely knew myself. Then they placed a gold mask over my features, as though I were a dead man. And braided my hair and tied into it pieces of lapis lazuli and Egyptian faience and a nugget of tin from the world's western edge.

I was a man no longer; I was what destiny had made me, both more and less than human.

Chapter IX

The Undead Goddess

Moonlight on stone in the outer courtyard of my palace. The wind seemed to change as I descended the great staircase weighed down with the emblems of my kingship and the coming ordeal. Below, matched pairs of naked children danced, their rhythms thrown by the cracks in the flagstones; there was a small band with a double flute, finger cymbals, a kithara, a hearthrobbing tympanon. At the gate was the woman I had disguised as my bride.

A small crowd had gathered; as I instructed, they had come in festive clothes, but all the colors were grayed by the moonlight. As they saw me come down, the dancers stopped, stumbling in mid-step. I went up to Dione, whose face I could not see, for she was veiled like the skeleton-woman of the first of my three precognitive dreams. I reached out to grasp her hand, fearful that my hand would encounter bone. But her hand was fleshy, human, palpitating.

"Don't be afraid," I said, "the ordeal will soon be over, one way or another." I signaled to the girls who had accompanied Dione from the women's quarters to begin strewing our path with flower petals. The wind was hot in our faces.

"Leonidas." I called the boy who had once been my slave; he had been peering from behind the ranks of my nobles. I saw him dart out from behind the wall of shields, all of black oxhide stretched over frames of wood and painted with the faces of demons and exotic beasts.

"My king," he said, kneeling before me.

"Go in front of me and cry out my name."

"Astyanax!" His tiny voice wavered in the wind. I wanted to stifle the wind, but I knew that to live near the gods, at the summit of the citadel, as befitted a king, I must endure the ceaseless battering of their breath.

Hearing the boy's cry, the crowd parted and fell in behind me. The gate was opened. The street wound steeply downhill, gradually broadening as the slope became more gentle, until three or four could easily walk abreast. Behind us the girls were chanting a wedding song, their voices listlessly rising and falling. They were all afraid they might lose their king that night.

The marketplace: pieces of the shattered horse had been dragged here and set up. The torchlight danced over the trunkless legs. The torso had become a wineshop. The head was half buried, but someone had tied a rope to one of its ears and used it to stretch an awning over.

I looked into the horse's eyes; the horse did not speak to me as it had once done when I watched from the mountain. I could not help feeling a strange sense of betrayal. There was something wrong in what I was about to do. Once more I seemed to hear Phoinix's mocking words: "Perhaps you're saving yourself for your aunt Helen!" It sounded so real that I looked around to see if he was walking right behind me; but no, he was off with the other nobles, behind the chanting children, in the slow processional that wound ever downward, downward.

We walked on, with painstaking deliberation, as was appropriate for so solemn a ceremony. The inner city walls were mostly only waist-high and covered with scrawls. We passed on. Granaries now, and a courtyard where my warriors loved to spar. The full moon lent all our faces a ghastly sheen. But that was as it should have been, for we were going toward the city of the dead.

At the Skaian Gate we picked our way gingerly in the half dark over the rubble. I insisted on crossing through the gateway itself, though the wall had cracked in a dozen places, and already the other celebrants, impatient, driven a little mad by the moonlight, were abandoning their ranks and clambering over fallen rocks and charred timbers. I looked behind me and saw my city. Silvered by Snakemother's light, it was as tomblike as the tholoi toward which we progressed.

I clutched Dione's hand again; she pressed it firmly. She was less afraid than I, I sensed.

"You are a king," she whispered from behind her veils, "but you are also a man. Men burn but women smolder; always we are the stronger, and your subjugation of us is an illusion."

I was afraid at this; they seemed not to be the words of a shepherd girl. I wondered whether Snakemother had somehow possessed her, had already divined my plan.

We walked on until we reached the river; a raft ferried us across. The pathway ended and our procession moved through a sparsely wooded terrain. At last we began our descent into a chasm, partly natural and partly built by my ancestors and partly built in ancient times, when the worship of Snakemother was ascendant. We climbed down into the pit, holding onto ledges in the rock; presently the rough stone gave way to steps carved into the chasm walls. Centuries of use had made the steps concave, and in each hollow was a pool of stagnant water. Now, at the bottom of the little valley, we faced the entry into the necropolis. Moonlight fell directly into the pit.

My people were huddled on the steps and crowded against the rim of the chasm.

I looked around. The pit was perfectly circular; it was said that a fist from the sky had smashed it out of the solid rock. Ahead was the passageway that led to a network of tholoi. Farther into the rock were more primitive tombs; farther still, and deeper, were tombs of those who had lived in other ages of creation, before Snakemother yielded up the gifts of farming and of bronze, and before Prometheus snatched fire from the sky. Though in the citadel the wind never ceased to blow, here the air was thick, close, motionless. The gods' breath is mighty, but the dead do not breathe at all. It was unsettling, but I had to begin the ceremony.

"Music!" I cried, waving frantically at the orchestra, gathered at the crater's edge. They began to play halfheartedly. "No," I shouted. "More, more! I want rejoicing . . . rejoicing that will wake the very dead! We're here to celebrate a wedding, not a funeral!"

They began to play in earnest now. Flutes sobbed, their high tones jabbing at the still air. I felt Dione's hand in mine, encouraging me. Drums pounded, a slow tat-tat, tat-tat that accelerated into a frenzy.

I spoke to the passageway that led into the rock. "I sent you my messenger, Snakemother, to tell you of my purpose: I, the son of the son of the many-times son of Skyfather, am come to possess you as a man possesses a woman. But you spurned him and turned him to stone. I will heed you no more, Snakemother! I will profane the dark places with music of life. I will take a mortal woman to wife amid song and light . . . I will take her here, in the secret places where you dwell . . . for you have lost all your power. The days of the sacred marriage are no more. I will strip from you even this shadowland to which you have fled." I turned to the musicians. "Louder! Louder! Make a noise that will drive out the darkness!" And then, firmly grasping the arm of my veiled bride-elect, I marched forward to the entryway.

"Look, dark one!" I screamed. "I kiss this woman. You are dead, Snakemother, and can do nothing." The chanting

swelled up; I heard the crash of great cymbals and the tinkle
of little ones, the twanging of kitharas, the banging of timbrels, and always the keening of the flutes, like lightning
over the thunder of the drums.

I seized Dione and unveiled her. She was not beautiful, but
the chalk powder and the kohl and henna had been applied so
artfully that she resembled an antique statue. "Kiss me," I
whispered. I felt her lips on my lips, her darting tongue. I
was aroused; I pressed her hard to me, remembering the night
on the mountain three years ago.

The ground began to shake.

I stood my ground. "You are nothing," I said. "You are
powerless. You are a jealous old woman. But I am young
and my bride is young. We will make love on your graves.
We will trample your bones. You are no more."

The rumbling went on. Suddenly I felt Dione go limp in
my arms. "No," I shouted, "don't succumb, be strong!" I
called out to some of my men to come and support her. Her
eyes . . . dead, stone, cold. And laughter from within the
tholoi, cavernous, witchlike.

Dione stirred. She was not dead. But my ruse was working. Snakemother was feeling threatened; jealousy was stirring in her. I felt it in the quaking of the earth. Rocks
tumbled. One hit me in the temple. Blood gushed out, but I
tore off a fold of my frayed ceremonial robe and bandaged it,
unmindful of the pain.

There came a voice from deep within the darkness: "You
are bold, little king. But can you plumb my depths? Can you
fuck darkness itself? Come, come, enter me . . ." It continued in tones that parodied seductiveness without seduction. I
held onto Dione's hand. I cried out—the hand had changed
from flesh to bone, digging into my palms, sharp and dry.
The voice said, "Foolish woman! Did she think she could
defy me, who am all women, mother of mothers? Enter me,
little king. Come. I will receive you. I will not turn you into
stone. Oh, there was a time when we did not need you, when
the wind itself planted life in a woman's womb. That time is
gone, gone, gone with the coming of your Skyfather."

Blue light from the stone doorway. The air was chill though it was still late summer. "Louder," I said to the musicians, and I could see them flailing away at their instruments, but their sounds were receding further and further. A terrible cold came, and the skeletal hand clutched me and would not let me go.

"Return her to me!" I said. "She is innocent."

"You dared, little king, to tempt me forth from my houses of darkness. Do you come even here? Shall I not have a fissure in the earth to dwell in? Shall I have no one to exercise power over? No! You will win her from me yourself. Dare, dare, dare to ravish me, the darkness itself. If you are truly king, you will pass through my searing cold unscathed. Do you dare, dare dare?"

"But the woman is innocent," I said. I could not do anything as Dione's face began to peel away, the flesh melting, her mouth torn open in an unformed scream. "Give her back to me."

"Do not make bargains," said the voice of Snakemother. "I have spirited away her soul; it has already begun on its journey into the shadowland. Perhaps you may wrest her free. But first we shall make love, you and I, earth and sky, king of light and mistress of shadow, the lion and the snake!"

The bony hand clutched mine, rigid. I pried it loose. I saw Dione fall backward, heard the crack as bone met stone. I could not bear it. "Illusion!" I shouted. I could not hear the crowds, though I saw their faces, corpse-faces all. It was the first dream! And only I could avert it! By making love to the foul heart of darkness.

It did not comfort me to know that this was what I had set out to achieve—to draw Snakemother out, to force her once more into Skyfather's chains . . . to make the crops grow taller next year, to show my people I was a man.

But I could not let them see I was afraid. I straightened my robes and made sure my talismans and amulets were securely fastened, so that magic shielded me on every side.

Then I walked boldly into the blue light, where darkness waited for me in the shape of a woman.

*   *   *

At the entrance I paused. A young boy was tugging at my hand. "Leontes—" I said involuntarily, thinking for a second that it was the slave brother of my childhood. But it was Leonidas. "How did you get down here," I said, "through the press of people?"

"I am only a boy," he whispered, "and only a slave. People don't see slaves, let alone child slaves. King, it's a labyrinth in there. I think she's trying to trick you into getting lost forever."

"Perhaps."

"King, do you know the story of Theseus and the labyrinth?"

"Yes. But that was centuries ago, in the days when Snakemother ruled all the known world."

"But her power was already beginning to fade. Remember the song I sang to you as you bathed, King? Of Ariadne, priestess of Snakemother, who betrayed her own goddess by giving Theseus the thread that allowed him to find his way back out of the labyrinth?" I understood what he was saying then. I had to have a way out, but . . . "King, I have no silken thread from the easternmost edge of the world. But you see, my chiton is frayed at the hems." He picked at it until a thread pulled loose. I watched, dazed, as he tied it around one of the talismans I wore, a miniature golden lion. "King, I'll be your anchor to our world. I won't fail you." He watched me with clear catlike eyes. I embraced him.

"No, King. Remember, my freedom is a secret. Don't show me too much favor."

I entered the blue light, feeling a slight tug as the hem of Leonidas's garment unwound behind me.

The cold, the cold . . .

The walls of the cavern narrowed. Earth and rubble blocked my path. It was illusion. I pushed my way through it; it was like sinking into quicksand. I checked to make sure the thread was still attached to me; it pulled taut as I straightened myself. It was dark, so dark. I thought I would never get used to such darkness. The air was stale and putrid. I did not know whether I was in a huge cavern or just another tunnel. Boldly I went on. The air was so thick that walking was almost like swimming.

Almost imperceptibly the dark began to shift. I was stepping on soft, pungent earth; now and then bones snagged at my robes. Here and there a yellow gleaming: gold. Gemstones. Hidden forever from the light, swallowed by Snakemother's shadow.

Then came the voice, murmurous, so quiet that it seemed to come from inside my head: "Little king, you have come. We will complete the mysterious circle. Come, come."

I felt soft hands now, touching me. Moist lips moved over my face, though I saw nothing. If only it were not so dark. I saw eyes now, burning red. Their radiance played over rotting kings. Here a crown caught the light and glowed for a moment. Here a white skull rubied by the red shining, its cracked eye sockets seething with hungry worms. The walls: brick piled upon brick, bending inward to form a ceiling-vault. Armor stacked against the wall: priceless armor with cunningly articulated joints such as had not been seen in a hundred years. The eyes, being the only light, transfixed me: though they burned, they contained no emotion.

The voice: "How wrong you are, little king, you and your priests of Skyfather, to turn your back on me. Don't you know that earth and sky are one?"

"That is not true!" For it went against all I had been taught as a child. "The light does not spring from the darkness. Forever they will be at war, until the end of time." I was angry, thinking of my messenger turned to stone, of Dione stripped of her mortal flesh.

"Light! Light is an illusion. Darkness is eternal."

Again the hands caressed me. The body I could not see exuded a heady fragrance. I crushed myself against the darkness, feeling in it the curve of a girl's breasts, my hands roving over a nymph's hairless pubis that ran slick as I touched it. I had never felt such arousal. The breasts swelled in my hands and hardened, and sometimes the skin seemed taut and sometimes slack and fleshy. "Does it surprise you?"

the voice whispered. "I am all women. You cannot live without us, Astyanax, though you have banished us to the gateway of the kingdoms of death."

And we settled onto the floor of the tomb; we lay down on the bed of crushed corpses and glittering treasure. I closed my eyes against the cold glare of the crimson eyes, squeezed them shut and let myself be swallowed up in the rhythm of her sexual movements, I felt . . .

A scream rent the air! Suddenly there was a blinding radiance in the chamber, and I saw for a split second Snakemother's image, monstrous and snake-haired and also beautiful as Helen, and in a rasp, like the groaning of rocks against each other in an earthquake, she spoke to me, her voice screeching along the walls incandescent with white fire: "Why have you come? Why you, of all men? Why have you invaded my final sanctuary?" And she began to wail, her ululations like the mourning of women who have lost their husbands on the field of battle, as the light bombarded her and she shriveled and faded, faded into the all-consuming brilliance. . . .

What had happened? I whirled around, lunging for what I thought was the entrance. The cave walls had been torn away and I could see clear through to the pit outside—it was brighter than broad daylight. I saw Dione restored to life. I saw Leonidas, his tunic now in tatters, weeping for joy. I could not understand what had happened. Around me lay the skeletons of kings, crowned, swords at their sides, of horses caparisoned in gold, of slaves. Against the wall leaned wicker chariots painted in blue and red; wheels were stacked in another corner; piles of goblets and neckpieces and age-greened weaponry. I ran for the entrance, where I was greeted by cheers and laughter.

"You've done it!" Leukippos said, admiring for once. "You have mated with the earth, as is required by one of your high blood. Now we can get on with our lives. And the treasure of the outer tomb—it's a gift from Hades!"

I looked down at the earth. I dared not tell him the truth—that I had not yet consummated my union with

Snakemother. Some outside force had burst in upon us and sent the Snakemother fleeing whence she had come. Was it the grace of Skyfather, visiting me at last after three years of desultory kingship? I could not know. I looked at my nobles; none seemed to know that I had not fulfilled my duties; my reputation, at least, was secure. Then I looked at Dione and Leonidas, who had served me so faithfully. They did not look me in the eye. I wondered how much they had divined: the one from having temporarily visited the periphery of the shadowland, the other from being linked to me by a frayed woollen thread through my ordeal.

Philemon (I saw him thrust himself out of the crowd) cried out to me, "You have brought out the sun in the middle of the night, my king."

More shouts from above. I was anxious to be as far away as possible from Snakemother's domain, and I began to elbow my way up the damp steps. The crowd parted, broke up in confusion, as I reached the top of the pit. The sun—or something like the sun—was indeed out; the whole sky was alight. It was not blue but white and white-hot, as though particles of fire were scattered throughout the air.

In the distance a horse whinnied. It was a messenger from the city. The horse reached us, reared up; the messenger dismounted and knelt before me. He was trembling. "King . . ."

"Speak," I said.

A hush fell over the throng. In the distance I could hear birds of dawn, wakened by the artificial brightness. A hot wind, tasting of salt and moisture, was blowing in from the sea, just beyond the western horizon.

When I looked at the messenger's face I saw that it was the very one who had been turned to stone. "Speak," I said. "How has the spell been broken?"

"I—I—don't know, O King. Suddenly I regained consciousness. I thought I was still in the lair of Snakemother! Oh, I was afraid, King. But then I looked out over the battlements, at the sea. And I saw light bursting out over the water. There was a kind of sun, King, but it rose in the west, out of the dead lands! And it seemed to come from a ship with black sails. In the harbor now. A ship . . . brilliant! We're all afraid. Someone is coming from the ship. Here, now, coming.''

I looked up ahead. There, hidden by a line of olive trees, was the river; upon it something flashed gold. "Have they rowed it upstream?" I said.

"No, King. It's a huge ship, with at least fifty rowers. They sent an emissary upstream in a boat, to find you.''

I heard Phoinix cry out, "The Akhaians! They're back! They must have heard that Troy is rebuilding itself.''

"No, Phoinix." I turned to him. "Sheathe your sword. They may be Akhaians, but that doesn't explain why the sky is on fire and why Snakemother flees in terror. Whatever has come to Troy, it concerns the gods." I did not add, "It cannot therefore concern you, Phoinix, because the blood of Skyfather does not run true in you." I did not have the heart to say it, but he knew anyway.

Sullenly he turned to address his warriors. "Be ready for a sudden attack on our king," he said.

"The procession will go to meet this man now," I said.

For the second time that night I acted far more bravely than I felt, and I led the entire ceremony of Trojans toward the bank of the Skamander. I commanded the musicians to play something joyful, and presently their piping and singing filled the air; I was glad of the sound as it pounded at my thoughts, for I was afraid to imagine what kind of ambassador could magically transform day into night, and shatter even the spells of Snakemother.

Chapter X

The Mage

When I could bring myself to bear the bright light, I saw him in a palanquin borne on the shoulders of eight slaves, who were bald and wore white linen kilts, each fastened with a string of gold. It was the slaves I noticed first. At first I thought the blue slickness on their bodies was oil or sweat, transformed by a trick of the light; but moisture always moves, and this substance that covered them was hard, like the deep blue faience glaze that the Egyptians use. Egyptians—that was who they must be.

I looked at the figure in the palanquin. I had never seen such a man before. His nostrils flared like those of a horse, and his lips were wide. His skin was completely black. Though he seemed immeasurably old, his face was unlined, and his body was sleek and well muscled. He wore a tunic of white linen; earrings of gold and malachite depended from beneath his clustered hair.

I said, "You must be an emissary of Skyfather, because when you came you brought the sunlight with you and routed the forces of darkness . . . yet—"

"You are surprised," he said, "because I do not appear fair and blue-eyed, like you."

"I admit it. I've heard stories about people like you; you come from Upper Egypt, or perhaps from even farther, at the southern edge of the world, where the Anthropophagoi live." I shuddered at the thought that he might be one of these . . . that he might thrive on human flesh. If so, I would find it difficult to offer him the guest-friendship proper for a visiting dignitary.

"Why, why, Astyanax!" he said. His voice was rich and

72

oily. "You don't remember me? I fought beside your father in the war. But you were only a child then."

"What is your name?" I said dubiously.

"I am Memnon."

I knew that there was an Egyptian hero by that name who had fought on the side of Troy. But if he had been a hero fourteen years ago he must be frail and withered now, and he was not. "Can you prove it?"

"I am not . . . entirely mortal, young king. But for proof you will have to visit the king I serve. And he is not free to leave the ship. He is not entirely mortal either, you see."

"Riddles!" I said. "It seems I should be grateful to you; perhaps I even owe you my life. Yet you give me conundrums and presume on an old friendship with my father which may well prove a lie."

He laughed. I had the uncomfortable feeling that I was the butt of some joke. I tried to cast my mind back to the war, to what little I knew of the name "Memnon." An image, a tale my nurse had told me maybe: "Memnon . . . of the singing statues?" Yes. That was what Leontes' mother had told me about the warrior Memnon: that he was a mage, and that he had placed a spell upon certain statues, that at the rising of the sun an eerie singing escaped their stone throats. I disbelieved it even as a five-year-old; now that I saw the results of his magic in the night sky, I was more ready to believe.

Memnon smiled again. His teeth were white, so white; I could not imagine what made them so. Reading my mind, he said, "I polish them with a dentifrice of powdered marble mixed with oil." I must have shown startlement, but he went on regardless. "The king I serve cannot come ashore. But he has a knack of knowing when he is needed. I came in the nick of time, you say. That's what your father said too, though it turned out badly in the end. There's destiny in our meeting, though you may think it an accident."

I knew better. There are no accidents in this universe; I had discovered that when the gods forced me to choose between three goddesses and made them all the same. There was a wrongness about this man. I knew he was concealing something.

A little miffed, I said, "I offer you friendship and hospitality—whether or not you are Memnon the warrior-mage who knew my father."

"Thank you," he said. His eyes sparkled.

"You will join our procession? And come back to the palace with us? Tonight, though it's late, we will feast to celebrate our small victory over Snakemother."

"No, O King," said Memnon. "One of the unfortunate features of my present situation is that I can no longer use . . . conventional modes of transport. It is forbidden for my feet to touch the ground, you see."

"An inconsistency! How did you then fight at Hector's side?" I had him there, I thought.

"Ah, but I had not then reached my current . . . ah . . . stage of development. Well, my boy, you spoke of a feast? I will be waiting for you at the palace!"

Confused, I said, "I will have my slave prepare a chamber for you. We don't have all the amenities we used to, but . . ."

Suddenly I noticed that he was gone. "Where is he?"

Leonidas, who had been standing at my side, said, "He simply vanished, my king." The boat, the litterbearers, the mage, all had disappeared, and no one could tell me when it had happened.

I said, "I think the man mixes lies with truth, the better to impress his listeners. But he's obviously a very powerful mage, and worth having as an ally."

I summoned my nobles to me. I called Dione to my side, and said, "Tonight we'll celebrate your wedding to the man you truly love." And I kissed her on the cheek, like a kinswoman.

But she only said, "I have seen the other side, Astyanax, and now nothing will ever be the same."

"But how did you manage to reach the city before we did?" I was a bit drunk before I dared broach the question to my guest. "And how is it that you came here at all, and apparently just in time?" I waved at Leonidas, who brought in more wine.

Memnon, reclining beside me, said, "Let us say simply that I have managed to obtain the fastest litterbearers in the world."

"You must know a good slave market." I glanced at the bearers, who were standing behind the mage, still as statues, and still startlingly blue; I watched one of them for several minutes, wondering. It suddenly occurred to me that I had not seen him even breathe.

"Indeed not," Memnon said, reading my mind.

Surprised, I turned. "Don't do that. You unnerve me."

He laughed a little. "I am an old friend of the family," he said, "and it would be terrible if my presence were to unsettle the son of one I fought beside as brother." In all this time his feet had not touched the ground at all, for the couch he sat in was actually part of his palanquin, detachable from the canopy. The king he served must be wealthy. But I did not think there were blue men even in Egypt. "So," he said, "no magical displays . . . not tonight. We've probably had enough spectacle for a single evening anyway, no?"

I looked around me. The long table was laden with the leavings of our feast; torches competed vainly with the false daylight. Rich smells in the air: the roasting carcass of a sheep, the bread piled high, the dark wine on the beards of my nobles, many of whom lay on the floor or leaned against the walls or were slumped on the table itself. Only a few still stirred. It was as if a magical slumber had fallen over them. "No magic!" I said, waving at them as their snoring started to fill my grandfather's dining hall. "But you have not yet bewitched Leonidas."

"I sensed that you have an extra pair of eyes and ears, and that they are in the keeping of that slave who is not a slave."

"So you admit it!"

He nodded at Dione and her new husband (I had performed the rite myself, after we got back from shadowland), who was, as it turned out, the loutish Philippos, a nephew of Philemon's and thus my adoptive cousin. They were dozing in each other's arms, a wreath of summer flowers halfway down the young man's face, and the bride smiling. "I admit

that you and I need to talk, and that it's just as well that these
others have fallen asleep,'' Memnon said. ''Do you know
why I am here, young king?''

''No.''

''Can you guess the name of the king I serve?''

I could not. Yet he would not tell me.

''It is not a name that can be uttered. It is a name whose
characters have been painstakingly erased from every monument in the world. It cannot even be written, for it does not
exist.''

''Then write it in *my* language,'' I said. ''I know that
names contain the greatest concentration of magic. But perhaps, in another tongue—''

''Ah, misdirection! A magician's greatest gift. You know
much for your years, young king.'' And he dipped his finger
in wine, leaned over, and began to write on the table:

$$\text{T} \oplus \text{F} \text{L}$$

''That's easy,'' I said. ''The four symbols are *A, KA, NA,
TA*—''

''Try putting it together,'' said the mage, suddenly assum-
ing an expression of smugness I did not much care for.

I started to say the name, and . . . I was tongue-tied.
''Wine!'' I said, and Leonidas quickly refilled my goblet. I
drank, I tried again and once more the name stuck in my
throat like a fishbone.

''You see?'' The mage shrugged.

But though I could not say the name, I knew at once who
it was. It chilled me. I remembered the story only vaguely.
There was a king, once, a hundred years or more ago, in
Egypt. He had built a great city to Skyfather, whom he
worshiped in the shape of the circle of Helios. So much did
the city bask in the sunlight that all the other gods were
banished. So brightly did the sun shine that the city had no
night, and Snakemother had no place to hide. And she became angry, and stirred up the hearts of the priests and
priestesses of the banished gods; they toppled the king from

his throne. But the city of the sun has been left to the ravages of sand and time, and no one knows now where it stands. The king's name was on the tip of my tongue.

"Don't try," said Memnon, "or you'll hurt yourself!"

"I don't trust you," I said slowly.

He said, casting his eyes furtively about as though not certain that his spell had worked, "Whether you trust me or not is really immaterial, my son. The threads of fate are spun already, are they not? So let me tell you. My master, the king whose name may not be spoken, waits aboard his ship. One day, he hopes, there will come a man who will speak for him at the gates of the dead, and utter the unutterable, and he will be permitted, at last, to sail across the bourne of life and death. But now . . . You see? Without a name, he must float forever down the river. Always the gap narrows, but the goal is never reached. The river widens to encompass the ocean that surrounds the world. You see? And still, though he has died, he cannot be numbered among the dead. His own souls, his ka and ba, do not recognize him without his name. Yet he is a good man, and he does what he can." Memnon looked sharply at me.

"Thank you," I said uncertainly.

"Well, we have reached a turning point in the history of the universe. Once, Astyanax, there was a Golden Age; then a Silver Age; we now live in an Age of Bronze. I think there will be a new age soon, though what it will be like I cannot tell. Darker still than the present, I imagine. The upheavals in our world presage it."

"You mean the fall of Troy?" I said, draining my goblet again and beckoning for more.

"Oh, child, you are so provincial. You think your petty walled village the center of the universe, don't you?" I could not bear to be patronized so, and downed more wine, disliking my visitor more and more. "The Akhaians are sweeping over all the world, and you think history ends with Troy's destruction—"

"Troy will rise again!" I said. "And soon."

"Not without my help."

I stared at him. "Is that why you were sent?" I stammered.

He smiled sadly. "When you have been adrift as long as I, you acquire different perspectives. Let me tell you about myself, young king." I could see that he was about to embark on the traditional telling of tall tales; it is something strangers always do at feasts. I have always thought that it is because, far from their homes, travelers know that no one will bother to contradict them.

"I was born," he said, "far, far beyond Upper Egypt, beyond the fourth cataract of the Nile, in a land whose people do not know the art of writing. They speak a language called Dinka and practice ritual anthropophagy. It was just after puberty, when I lay recuperating from my circumcision, that I came to be interested in magic. It was an exciting time for me, a twelve-year-old boy: a war, a tremendous victory (though we fought with weapons far more primitive than are known to you), and captives to be eaten. It was my duty to feed the captives, whom we kept tied up in a cage that hung from a tree in the central clearing of our village. Oh, I forgot . . . Our country is one of impenetrable forest, and moisture hangs in the air like the breath of a dragon. Oh, it is oppressive. But feeding the captives—we had to keep them fat, you see, for the feast. Do I disgust you?"

"Continue," I said, not particularly believing him, though I saw that Leonidas had left his station and was sitting, wide-eyed, at our feet, stroking a puppy who worried at a bone.

"One of the captives was not like the others. He spoke with an atrocious accent. He said to me, 'Free me, boy, and I will teach you . . . oh, astounding things. I will teach you to raise the dead and use them as slaves!' I said, 'That is absurd, old man. You'll say anything to escape the fire.' But he said, 'Do you see that woman?' and he pointed to one who huddled in a corner. 'She is sick; she will poison anyone who eats her. Kill her; take her body into the forest; and I will teach you the spell. You need only free me if the magic works.' I saw that he was in earnest, so I called the woman to me and broke her neck with my bare hands. I buried her deep in the forest, and that night I whispered over the shallow grave the words that the old man taught me. That very night she returned and stood outside my hut, her eyes glazed, her skin ash-gray in the moonlight. I was very frightened. I led her back to the cage, not wanting even to look at her, and tied the door shut. In the morning, the prisoners were all in a panic. They screamed; one even beat his own brains out with a wooden paddle, he was so terrified. Over and over they whispered the word 'zumbi.' My father came to see what all the noise was about; he saw the woman sitting in one corner, and the others squirming in the other, and he decided that, in order to quiet them down, the woman should be removed and eaten immediately, before the feast. This was done. I never had a chance to use her as my slave, nor did I dare tell my elders that she had died once already and had been resurrected. But everyone knew that something was wrong, for her meat tasted bitter, as though it were not human flesh at all. This was my first taste of the dark powers."

"And how did you come to Egypt?" Leonidas said with an eagerness I did not share.

"That came soon enough. I kept my end of the bargain; in the dead of night I released the old man and allowed him to flee into the forest. When this was discovered I kept silent, but our chief called the entire village together. His magician performed a ceremony with bones and rattles that proved me the perpetrator, and my father beat me savagely. So I too fled. I followed the trail of the strange magician until I reached the Nile. When I found him he adopted me as an apprentice. We journeyed downriver. I begged for him, I shilled for him. He used to beat me regularly. I ran away from him in Upper Egypt and found work divining harvests for a local magistrate . . . and then, at last, I came to the sea, and met with the king I now serve."

"And what happened to your former master?" Leonidas asked.

"To this day I have not seen him."

"And your feet?" said the boy. "Why can't they ever touch the ground?"

"My child, in the service of the king without a name I set behind me all the dark arts. I have learned to practice only that magic that comes from the sky. Through the years of my service to the mysterious king I have distilled so much sun essence into myself that I am a reservoir of sky magic. And Snakemother watches me constantly that she might wrest my power from me. On the sea I am safe; here I must ever be wary."

His stories were incredible. I thought: He thinks of me as a little king, an ignorant king; perhaps he doesn't even believe that I too am born of Skyfather. There is doubtless some truth in his boastings, but . . . "If you have the power to bring the dead back to life," I said, "why aren't you surrounded by walking corpses that do your every whim?"

"I have told you, young king, I have turned my back on the darkness forever."

It all sounded too convenient. I knew he was hiding something, and these bizarre tales made me ever more suspicious of him. Once again I asked him why, if we were so insignificant a kingdom, he had sought me out.

"Ah, but you are a pivotal figure in the coming battle," he said.

"What battle?" I thought of my three dreams; I thought of the great dream—that of recapturing Helen and leading my people back to our days of greatness. But what could the magician understand of these things?

"The battle," he said, "that will herald the coming of the new age, the one that will replace our Age of Bronze. But, young king, to learn more you should come aboard my ship, and speak with my master as king to king. I am but an emissary."

"Nonsense," I said. "What nonsense." I did not like the theatrical casualness with which he had broached the invitation. A thought flashed into my mind: perhaps he is really from the Akhaians; they've guessed that I want to go to Sparta to win back Aunt Helen, and they've sent this messenger to tempt me, perhaps to kidnap me, to kill me? It was an outlandish theory, but no stranger than all else that had happened that day. But his talk of war in heaven and of a new age dawning was impressive. I was angered by it; it made me feel small, and this was improper. I was even more angered to admit these shortcomings to myself. Was I not king? Had I not planned the ruse that defeated Snakemother, even though Memnon's coming had aided that defeat? I badly needed to convince him—and more than that, myself—of my importance, of Troy's importance. I drank more deeply now. The light from the torches seemed to stream like comet tails, and the hunting scenes on the wall wavered, seemed almost to come to life. . . .

"A hunt!" That was what we needed to impress the visitor. A formal hunt, with all the pomp and panoply of Priam's days! On the far wall, faded and stained and cracked: the chariots thundering through the plains. A lion's roar. A wild boar leaping. Javelins dripping blood. Wild, wild. "You come here, magician, mouthing your arcane mysteries and boasting that you can raise the dead. I will show you that a provincial king can be grand! Tomorrow at dawn we will hunt lion in the hills. We'll have chariots! We'll have archers and spear-thrusters! You'll not despise us, Memnon!"

I looked around me and saw that the nobles were beginning to rouse themselves and rub their eyes. Whatever it was that Memnon had meant to tell me must all have been said. It's all trickery, I told myself, sleight of hand.

"A hunt?" I heard Phoinix's voice. "That's the spirit, King! No use brooding now that we can look forward to a decent harvest again."

"A hunt?" It was Leukippos this time. "A h-h-hunt? When?"

"At dawn!" I shouted, jumping up and throwing the goblet down onto the table. A wild joy had seized me. I could do anything. I *had* vanquished Snakemother. There *was* something to rejoice about. I leaped onto the table and danced wildly, heedless of the flying sheep bones and spilt wine. They were all catching my excitement, all telling one another, "A hunt! Dawn!" I staggered the few steps to where the black mage was sitting and shouted in his ear, "Do you hear? We'll go hunting. At dawn. You talk of great events, but even here in this backwater we can show you an event or two, can't we? Dawn!''

The mage closed his eyes. He was disquietingly serene. The blue men swayed forward as one, ready to lift up his couch.

He said, smiling, ''It is dawn already, young king.''

''Yes!'' I called to my nobles, kicking some of them awake. We ran out into the courtyard. The air was bracing. The false sun-disk was no longer there, for the real sun had dragged rosy-fingered dawn out from the world's edge.

I was standing at the top of the citadel. My city was stirring. I was king. I had bested Snakemother at her own ritual. I was king! We were going to hunt down the great golden beast. I yelled out my joy.

It all seemed immeasurably distant, all this talk of cannibals in dark forests . . . of dead kings in sailing ships . . . of the walking dead . . . of the end of the world as humans knew it. Absurd! We would go hunting, and my guest, eccentric as he was, would receive a king's entertainment.

Chapter XI

The Lion of Death

''But, King,'' said Phoinix disdainfully, ''we have no chariots.''

I said, ''Ransack old storerooms. Surely not everything was destroyed by the Akhaians. . . .'' I was still drunk. ''Leonidas! Tell them to prepare the bath. We're going hunting!''

''Yes, King.''

''And Memnon—''

''I will meet you at the Skaian Gate,'' he said.

There was an ominous note in that simple declarative

statement. What was he really saying? Dimly I saw him through the miasma of my drunkenness. The blue slaves bent down in unison to lift his couch while others bolted the canopy in place above him.

"Good," I said, and then under my breath: "Madman. Raising the dead indeed! And that king-king-king-A-A-A-A-Ka-Na—" Still I could not say the name. The magic that had removed his name from the earth was strong still, after more than a century.

The effort of trying to recall the ancient king's name was so great that I collapsed onto the banquet table in a stupor.

I must have slept for several hours, for when I woke I could hear the hunting drums banging in the courtyard outside. I was lying in my bedchamber, and Leonidas was methodically oiling my body and scraping the dirt off with a strigil. Now came the sound of wind instruments on the breeze; the dogs pricked up their ears and set up an eerie howling. "The hunting music! They must not have heard it in years," I said, wincing from the aches that besieged my whole body.

"Don't talk, Astyanax," said Leonidas. "Turn over so I can do your back."

"Listen! Listen!"

The clatter of chariot wheels on the broken flagstones . . . the whinnying of horses.

"Chariots!" I said, delightfully. "Hurry up so I can go to the window."

But Leonidas's face darkened, and he went on rubbing my back resolutely, forcefully, making me groan.

"Well, what's wrong, boy?" I said. "Aren't you pleased about the chariots?" He did not answer. "Speak to me, boy, or I'll—" I raised my hand.

"You freed me, remember? Now stay there while I get your hunting clothes."

"I don't have any hunting clothes."

"The women found them in a chest in their quarters. They belonged to your father."

"My head—"

"Quickly now, my king. The nobles are waiting for you."

* * *

Fully attired, I ran down to the courtyard with the dogs at my heels and with Leonidas beside me. I saw Phoinix and Leukippos, both brandishing swords more splendid than I had known them to possess. Horses pawed the flagstones and neighed as their grooms soothed them . . . and there were chariots, fine chariots! One in particular I noticed, its frame covered with fine leather tooled with gold and blazoned with ancient lettering.

As I approached, the horse reared up. I tried to read the gold letters but could not. I felt a sudden foreboding: the script was the old tongue, the language of the snake.

"What storeroom did these chariots come from?" I asked, turning to my kinsmen.

Phoinix said, strutting to show off his cloak of purple and gold thread, "Storeroom? King, don't you remember? You opened for us the treasure houses of the earth!"

"Then these chariots came from the shadowland, from the city of the dead?" I was dismayed at this, though I should have guessed that Phoinix might do something like this. And I knew, too, that no storeroom in Troy contained such finery, for the Akhaians had looted what they could not burn. Already, still drunk as I was with wine and my apparent victory, I had the feeling I had inadvertently set some grim new sequence of events in motion. I started to rebuke Phoinix, but he would not hear of it.

"Nonsense!" he said. "The appearance of the sun-disk by night showed clearly that Skyfather has given us permission to raid the kingdom of Snakemother. What is there to worry about, cousin?" I flinched when he called me "cousin," for that was not strictly speaking his right. He looked at me darkly for a moment, then said, "I follow you for now, Astyanax. But not forever."

I did not answer him, but called to Leonidas, and stepped up into the car of the chariot. I recognized it now; when last I saw it it had lain among the putrefying bodies of dead kings. It was too late to turn back, for I had given the command that

there would be a hunt, and I could not countermand my own
word lest I seem weak.

"The dogs!" I shouted. At once they were loosed from
within the palace, their trainers running briskly behind them.
I could barely hear what Phoinix was saying above their
yelping. But I did not want to listen to him. Leonidas crouched
at my feet, my bow and quiver crushed against his chest; the
charioteer, really no more than a groom, tugged at the reins.
At once I felt the wind of flying against the breath of the
gods, and the warm sun edging from the clouds, and I heard
a cacophony of neighing and barking and shouting and clanging such as I had not heard since childhood. We were lurching forward now, hurtling past the courtyard gates and into
the steep streets, toward the Skaian Gate, where Memnon
would be waiting for me.

"Halt!" I cried as the broken gate reared up ahead.

The great wind of the citadel was hushed here; there was
only a faint sea breeze, stifling in its pungency. I looked
around at my companions: my two kinsmen and others in the
chariots they had stolen from the dead; the ill-trained charioteers gangly and coltish and tentative in their control of the
twinned horses; the oxcart that was to follow behind, guided
by Philemon and tended by two old slave women, laden with
wine and refreshments for the evening, for I did not know
when we might return.

"Splendid!" I said, though I did not quite think so. For I
saw that my cousins were as mismatched to their chariots as I
had been, as a boy, with the armor and shield of my father
Hector. Yet the chariots and weapons themselves were magnificent; treasure had indeed been forced from the bowels of
Snakemother. "But where's the Egyptian?"

A slow pounding in the distance. The sun high now: the air
hazed, blurry. There he was, a smear of burning gold against
the moss-streaked rubble of my city, his chariot completely
plated with gold and inlaid with lapis lazuli and rubies that
pointed to a sunburst reliefed in the shining metal. His horses
were golden too, I saw, as he approached me, and the
hollow, rhythmic thudding was from a drum, the circumfer-

ence of a man's height, borne on poles and beaten with a
padded human thighbone. I called out his name, "Memnon,
Memnon. You've come."

He came nearer. Behind him were a dozen of the blue
slaves; a blue youth drove his chariot; a blue maiden stood
behind, fanning him with the feathers of a giant bird. We met
just beyond the shattered walls. He was so much more resplendent than I that I felt shamed. It must have shown in my
face, for he said to me, "Young king, you must not be
grieved at my wealth; I have paid a terrible price for it."

"But I wanted to show you something of the old Troy," I
said, as my driver brought my chariot abreast of his and our
company started across the plain toward the foothills. "I did
not want you to feel that I was some provincial kingling." I
did not add, "And I was angered at your boastful tales." But
he sensed it, I think. And so we rode on in silence until we
reached the river and, our procession hugging the bank,
continued away from the sea. It was hot. Even the wind
burned; its moisture was stifling. The dogs whined continu-
ously, not knowing where we were going, for they had not
been trained to hunt. I had a feeling the outing would be a
disaster. And Memnon knew it too. "Don't mock me," I
said testily, though he had said nothing.

"I did not say—"

"But your expression!" I wanted to charge on ahead.

"Young king . . . it is in your mind. But that is the worst
kind of ailment, I think. Come, let us enjoy ourselves."

We passed the place in the river where I had crossed over
into the kingdom of Snakemother. As it disappeared from
sight, and there were no earthquakes or other signs of the
underworld's wrath, I began to relax a little. The air became
somewhat cooler as the land began to slope gently uphill.
There were crags bursting from the blanket of dull green, and
in the distance I saw a flock of sheep on a mist-covered
hillside. My heart ached, for I knew that I would never be a
child again, that I would never sit all night on the mountain
beneath the starlight and know the special loneliness of shepherds. It is a loneliness that sears you from within. It had

changed me; I was not like the kings who had gone before
me. I was an end and a beginning. These confusing thoughts
whirled in my mind as we drove toward the mountain's edge.

"Good," I heard Phoinix's voice from behind, over the
babble of barks and shouts. "Sheep there. Where there are
sheep, there may be a lion."

"Lion!" I said. I felt Leonidas shiver against my leg.

"I'll go on ahead," Phoinix said, anxious to prove himself. He cuffed his charioteer, who flailed at the horses.
Suddenly he was ahead, and vanishing.

"Quick," Memnon said, "he may get into trouble."

"Quick!" I shouted. I knew that Phoinix seldom thought
before he acted.

Our chariots sped up now. I saw the chariot of Memnon
accelerate. It was uncanny to watch his gold-skinned horses,
their feet moving in unison, unnatural almost. I urged my
own horses on and the others followed. We pursued Memnon,
but it was like trying to catch a star; a comet tail of dust
trailed from the smudge of gold flame that was his chariot.
"Faster, faster!" I shouted. Hooves thundered, stones flew, I
could barely see through the dust haze. Where was Phoinix?
There he was! And Memnon gaining on him. We hastened.
Leonidas squealed as we zigzagged through a clump of trees.
We flew against the stony terrain, almost choking on the
smell of the sweating horses. Sweat drenched my eyes and I
could barely see. The supply cart was left far behind. We
raced on. A dog was trampled and crushed by Leukippos's
chariot wheels; I saw its spinning carcass shoot up and
splatter on a mound of stones. The bloodsmell maddened the
other dogs, the horses, the men . . . like dark wine. My
throat was parched; I barely croaked out my commands to the
charioteer; and still we rushed onward, chasing the distant
gold that gashed the gray-green hillside. . . .

Clattering, whinnying now, as we struggled uphill, and the
rocks cascading beneath . . . "There, King!" Leonidas
shrieked, pointing. We turned hard. The car bucked. "We
can't go on!" he said.

We stopped . . . in time to see the others leaping from

their chariots, javelins held high. I could see Phoinix now, sprinting through the trees. Above us, in the shadow of overhanging rocks, a tawny flash spearing the dark. "Lion!" I whispered. My heart stopped still for a tiny moment. Then I heard the tumult from somewhere uphill. I turned to Memnon. "You are not coming?"

"No. I may not touch the earth. When my litterbearers catch up with me . . ." From far below, there came the heartbeat thudding of his ceremonial drum.

"I'll go without you then. Leonidas! The quiver. The bow." I seized two javelins from the chariot and started uphill. The noises were faint, then loud again, then deathly quiet.

"Leonidas! Stay with me, this isn't a childish game."

We rounded a haunch of bare gray rock. "Leonidas!" Where had he gone? I was alone. But there was no time to lose. Where had the last sounds come from? I looked skyward . . . an eagle crossed the blue-gray cloudbanks. They must be uphill somewhere. Resolutely I began climbing. From somewhere overhead there came a low growl. I followed the sound, clambering over the sharp stones. Where could the others be? From where I had heard the growl came more sounds: scuffling, a child's whimper, the patter of dogs' paws on gravel. I climbed feverishly, hugging my javelins against my chest, skinning my hands and knees.

I stood upright. My back was to a wall of rock. I heard neighing from below. There was no one in sight. I looked out over an unmoving expanse of the Skamander Valley. Mist, shot with sunlight, tendriled through rock mounds. And then, condensing from the fog, the dark shape. A lioness. We stared at each other for a long moment. She dared me to defy her stony gaze. There was no hatred in her eyes; there was nothing at all. Her flesh rippled. This was not like the time I had stared at Neoptolemos, I a mere child and he a soldier crazed with bloodlust. I did not know her for my enemy. She tensed, her head moving from side to side. Then, as though urging me to follow, she began to bound away. I eased myself away from the rock wall, selected a single javelin, and tiptoed behind her, keeping myself upwind.

She sprang to another ledge. I barely clambered across. Again and again she leaped. I did not want to lose sight of her. I saw her disappear into a crevice between two crags. A steep pathway seemed to be a shortcut; I half stumbled, half slid down it, only to find myself staring the lioness full in the face—she was so close I could have touched her. She made no move to attack. I kept the javelin poised to strike.

We were in a clearing. There was a cave behind the lioness. Rocks had been piled up into a makeshift altar. I knew suddenly that this was no natural lion, and that men had built this place. For some reason the gods had led me to this place. "Who are you?" I said to the lioness, who still stared into my eyes. Trying to appear calm, I inched my way toward the crude monument. . . .

Now I heard human sounds. My companions could not be far. They must have been following the lioness too. Softly I called out their names: "Phoinix! Memnon! Leukippos!" There was no answer; some property of the rock walls trapped the sound of my voice and prevented its escape from the clearing.

The lioness pounced onto the altar and continued to glare at me.

I moved closer. There were names scratched on the rock, already half worn away:

Ͳϒ   ＢＴ☖

A-ki—
Pa-to-ro—
A sudden rage seized me. This was where the Akhaians had left the remains of Akhilleus and Patroklos—their greatest general and his lover! Akhilleus, who had dragged my father round the walls of the city by a meat hook fastened to his chariot; Akhilleus whom my uncle Paris had killed. I knew who else must be buried here. For though I fled the

burning city into the hills that day, I had heard the story many times in the years that followed. They had sacrificed my sister Polyxena at Akhilleus's tomb, to be his consort in the world of the dead.

I no longer feared this lioness. I rushed into the cavern. And there she was, a skeleton fettered to the walls. I could not bear to look at her empty eye sockets. Pieces of a bridal gown still clung to her breastbone and her cracked pelvis; a silver token was clamped between her teeth to pay her way to the world of the dead. The ancient anger came upon me with redoubled force. With the point of my javelin I sawed at my hair, unmindful of the pain. I hacked like a madman, threw down hanks of golden hair on the cavern floor as signs of my grief. Blood ran down my forehead, mingled with my tears, my sweat. I beat my fists against the jagged walls. I did not notice the commotion outside for a time. When I turned around it was too late. . . .

The others were all standing at the cave mouth. Between them and me stood the lioness, pacing, preparing to spring at me. The others were cowering and thrusting up their shields. I saw Leonidas, eyes wide with terror, trying to push through the wall that the grown men had put up.

I had no more fear.

"Who are you?" I shouted at the lioness. "Why have you brought me here?"

She leaped up, claws out, jaws wide, teeth glistening. I was choking on the fetor of her breath. There was a moment outside time, a long still moment in which the lioness seemed to hang in the air. In that moment I heard a still voice in my heart, the voice of a child: "Astyanax! Have you forgotten your true purpose? Have you forgotten me?"

And the eyes of the lioness turned to blood, and I knew her for Snakemother's servant, sent to punish me for violating her domain. I knew I could delude her no longer, that she had come to collect the king's death that had been due her for so long. At last she roared. I did not close my eyes. I will not flinch from death! I thought—

Abruptly Leonidas broke through the barrier of shields and

thrust himself in the path of the lioness's pounce. I fell back, shattering the skeleton of my sister. I heard the snap of the boy's neck. Blood spurted in my face. He had not even had time to scream before the lioness had ripped his throat open. His head thudded onto the ground and rolled away. I remembered the soldiers tossing my grandfather's head back and forth over the altar of Skyfather. I screamed and rushed at the lioness and slammed the javelin's point hard into her throat. I felt it sink in as though into mud, I felt myself collapsing onto shuddering flesh.

It was only then that the others came stomping into the cave, spearing the dying animal again and again until it was a mass of fur and blood and swaying javelin shafts. . . .

"You cowards," I said to my two cousins, who had been at the forefront of the attack on the felled lioness. They looked away.

Light filled the cavern mouth.

My companions parted, retreating from my anger. And now I saw that they had brought in the mage on a litter, and set it down on the backs of crouching slaves, who trembled as they looked from the lioness to me.

The mage said, "Is this the young king of the city, who has restored gold-rich Troy to its days of glory, who will cross the ocean and bring back Zeus's daughter, and make the plains run red again with heroes' blood?"

I hung my head in shame.

"Is this the king?" he said. "A king indeed, who lets children be slain in his place, who will not face the gods as their equal!" He beckoned to the slaves to bring his litter forward. They did, still crouching. A dog ran into the cave and began to worry at my sister's bones. I was so gripped by despair that I did not even shoo the dog away.

Then Memnon's tone softened. "It is time, young king, to listen to the voice of your destiny. . . ." I went to him and fell weeping at his feet. He lifted my head. His hands were gentle. I knew I did not merit his compassion. I wept bitterly. "A king does not weep," he said. "But here in this cave, with your companions waiting outside, fearful of your wrath, you need not be king, but only a man."

I summoned up the strength to cuff the dog; it ran, yelping, out into the open. "It's not for shame that I weep," I lied, "but for anger, anger, anger!" I tried to work myself up into a passion, but I was too spent. "Two children have died for me. Why? I am not like the god of the Phoenicians, who demands infant sacrifice." There was the torso of Leonidas wrapped around the lioness; in death the headless boy seemed like a suckling seeking protection from its mother. There was his head. One eye dangled from its socket; but the lips were curved in a smile, and strangely beautiful. "He died for me and didn't even think twice. He was glad to die. He lived only for me." But the thought did not comfort me. I cried, "You come here, with your impressive stories about waking the dead and anthropophagoi and dead pharaohs sailing the sea. . . . I only wanted to make some dent in the splendor of your tales, I envied you. If you're so wonderful, bring him back to life! Oh, I hate you and your fantasies. Bring him to life, do you hear? Stitch his head back onto his body and bid him speak! I demand it as a favor, as a gift appropriate for my hospitality!" I should not have said that. For such a demand, in the name of guest-friendship, is binding in the sight of Skyfather. And I was a king who spoke, and that made it doubly binding. . . .

"My poor poor little king," Memnon said. "You do not know what you ask. And I am bound to grant that favor. Even though it cost me—"

"What do I care how much it costs you?" I screamed, beside myself. "I demand, demand, demand."

"Then gather up his remains. There is little time. For this cave, like all caves, is a mouth of the underworld, and I fear his soul may have strayed too far already."

Numbly I rose and scooped up the pieces of the dead boy and laid them at the mage's feet. I still did not believe him, could not believe him. I covered the corpse with the tatters of his chiton.

The mage said: "There are mysteries here that you must

not gaze upon. I must wrestle with darkness. It may be that I must soil my feet upon Snakemother's earth; it may be that I will lose my own soul. So go outside."

I did so. But first I pulled off my cloak and wrapped up the remains of my sister Polyxena, so that she might take up her proper place in the necropolis of Dardanos's descendants. I had barely known my sister. But I hoped that, from the world beneath, her shade would see my shorn hair and rejoice that her blood yet lived upon the earth.

I gave the bones to Philemon, who had even now arrived with the wine and food. I watched him stow them in the back of the oxcart—the bones of a princess of Troy!—but I wept no more. For the kinsmen of the king were watching, and I dared not show sorrow lest the whole land suffer.

For a long time we waited at the mouth of the cave.

It was late evening when the blue slaves bore Memnon out of the funeral cave. My shame had gradually been giving way to anger. I had drunk several goblets of wine. I cried, "I knew it! There is no boy with you. You are a fraud."

The slaves moved smoothly; his litter seemed to sail across the clearing. In the twilight his body gleamed, reddish and metallic, like copper. "Hush, young king," he said softly. He gestured to the cavern.

"I won't look! I won't fall victim to your fanciful claims." But all my companions had fallen suddenly silent and were staring, openmouthed, at the dark entrance.

He came forth from the black mouth of the underworld: whole, his face pallid, his lips bloodred. There was a new beauty in him, unearthly, like that of flowers that bloom only in moonlight.

"Leonidas . . ." I said.

"It is a good name for the slave," Leukippos said. "His second birth was from the womb of a dead lioness."

The boy smiled at me, a wan, joyless smile. "He isn't the same," I said, "not the same at all."

The mage said, "Of course not! He is twice-born. I reached out across the barrier, calling his name. His body I washed with Stygian water and sewed together with threaded moon-beams.''

I called his name. He looked about, seemingly bewildered. The mage said, ''He does not know yet where he is, does not understand that he has come back.''

''Leonidas . . .''

The boy stepped forward. He was naked. I touched his shoulder. No, it was not the same. He felt abrasive, like the skin of a shark. I snatched back my hand. ''Gradually,'' the mage said, ''he will seem more lifelike. But you are right in this: all that I practice is illusion. But is not life itself only a wind that passes through dead flesh and animates it for a moment? And is not wind illusion?''

''Wind is the breath of the gods!'' I protested. It was what I had been taught.

''Yes. All truths are true,'' the mage said. ''Perhaps *now* you will hear my message.''

I said, ''I am sorry. I should not have doubted you.''

The mage called me to his side and spoke so that I alone could hear him. ''Didn't the lioness speak to you?'' he said.

''No. But there was a child's voice; it sounded like Leontes. It reminded me . . . of my destiny, of the vengeance I once swore.''

He said, ''The time has come, young king, for you to embark on the next stage of your journey. I am sent to prepare the way. Did you not vow to sail to Akhaia and recapture Helen? Have you thought, in the past three years, of your mother Andromache, still a slave in the house of Neoptolemos? Do you not remember him who killed your father, who demanded the blood of your sister, whose ashes rest beneath your very feet? Do you not remember the man who butchered your grandfather?''

''Yes. He spared my life.''

''Why? Because destiny, once set in motion, moves forward by its own inertia. One man does not have the strength to stop it. Not even an entire people! Young king, your efforts to flee the Fates have failed. You've thrown yourself into rebuilding your city. But all the while you have been haunted by your vision of Helen. Confess it, Astyanax.''

I felt the destiny in me like a mighty wind. But still I fought against it. "Who will govern my city? Incompetent Leukippos? Cruel Phoinix? I must have a regent while I am gone.''

"That is why I have come.''

"You want me to set you up as king in my absence! They would not accept you.'' In truth, I feared that he would win my people by sorcery, and that I would lose my throne forever. I still did not trust him, even though he had breathed into Leonidas an eerie imitation of life.

"No, no, young king. There is another way. But to find that out you must come into my master's presence.''

"The undead king from Egypt? But I cannot even say his name!'' But I was only putting up a token resistance. I knew that Memnon was the ineluctable agent of my future.

"When you cross into his little kingdom, my friend, you will know his name.''

Night fell at his words. I looked away. The Leonidas-creature came to stand at my side. He waited for a command, unnervingly still. Not looking back at Memnon, I said, "Very well. Tomorrow at dawn I will wait by the shore. You will send a boat to me. And I will speak with the king who has no name.''

Chapter XII

The Ship of the Sun

A blue-skinned oarsman rowed Leonidas and me over to the pharaoh's ship. I saw it in the pink-fringed gray of dawn, its sails great sheets of darkness, floating in a pool of fire. The fire was in the beaten gold that smothered the wood of the ship; reflected fire burned on the sea. The prow was carved into the shape of a dog-faced god; beneath its visage was a huge eye made of inlaid lapis and bordered with ivory and onyx. Overhead, atop the high mast, was a golden sun-disk about the height of Leonidas; I tried to look at it, but it hurt my eyes, and hot tears spurted down my cheeks. Shielding my forehead with my hand, I tried once more to gaze on it. When I did not look directly I could see that shards of light were raining down continually from the sun-disk, each fragment shaped like an ankh, their sign for life. It was strange to see such an image on a ship of death. . . .

At length the oarsman brought me astern, and I and the boy climbed aboard on a golden cord they tossed to me.

Memnon smiled at me. His skin gleamed in the light. "You're standing! But your feet—" I said.

"May not touch the ground. But this is not the Snake-mother's earth. This is a different kingdom completely. This tiny island is a domain outside the war of earth and sky, young king. But now you will tell me the name of the nameless king."

"Akhenaten." It fell easily from my lips. I had always known the name, had I not? Yet . . . some power had stopped my tongue. Until now. "Akhenaten . . . the heretic king . . . who toppled the gods from their thrones and made Skyfather the one god in the form of the sun! Akhenaten, Akhenaten . . . Here I can say it, here the spell is broken."

"Yes. This ship is like a crossing between worlds. It sails two oceans: life and death. You may come by one ocean and leave by another. The spell of unnaming does not reach this kingdom, for it is not part of the human universe."

I saw the terror in Leonidas's face. I put my arm around his shoulder. He hid his face. "It's too bright, my king," he whispered. "I think I'll go blind."

"You did well to bring the boy," said Memnon. "Eyes other than your own must see what you will see; or who will ever believe you? But it is time to see the pharaoh."

He turned to face the prow. I saw that on his back there hung the skin of a lioness, her head dangling, her eyes gouged out and replaced with rubies. Leonidas screamed.

Could this be the very lioness that . . . ? Surely not. Yet I did not know what they had done with the beast whose embrace had killed Leonidas. I felt the boy's slim form as he clutched my side. It was as though death's cold still clung to him. Since our return from the hills, he had seemed normal at times, but at others he regarded me with a kind of distant contempt, as though from another plane of existence. Now he seemed afraid, as any young boy would be on a magical ship, confronted by a black mage who served a dead king.

"It *is* the lioness," Leonidas whispered. "Oh, Mother, death, embrace, darkness, life."

"What are you saying?" But he looked lost and far away. I said, "We must follow the mage, Leonidas."

"Yes, King," he said almost inaudibly.

As we walked the length of the ship, the rowers stood one after another, raising their oars high in salute. The oars seemed golden too. Their light lanced the air, the water. The ankhs fell constantly from above. I tried to catch one with an outstretched hand—it glanced off my skin and left a tingling, like a snowflake. The ankhs whirled in the breeze. Out to sea they seemed like birds of fire; farther out, like dust motes in a shaft of sunlight.

"Below is where my master lies," Memnon said. A trapdoor in the deck, painted with icons of sun-disk and mystic eye. It opened to receive us. We trod down worn wooden steps, squeaky and pliable, into a vestibule.

Four walls surrounded us; there were no passageways, no entrances. But on each wall was painted a door, and upon each was a long inscription in the Egyptian picture-writing; I could make no sense of it.

Memnon told us to face one of the doors. We linked hands; his burned like a fresh-forged sword; I howled in pain. He shushed me. I gritted my teeth and held on. Leonidas showed no emotion. But I knew he had passed through death before.

We slid through the image of the door and found ourselves in a funerary chamber.

* * *

After the brilliance outside, I could barely cope with the darkness within. I held Leonidas's hand tightly while my eyes became accustomed to the dim light that seemed to emanate from the walls themselves. My eyes followed the murals, which seemed to tell a story: there was the pharaoh depicted on his throne of gold, an ugly man, pot-bellied and long-chinned, presiding over the building of the city of the sun; there was a hunting scene—was that not a lioness that the king pursued in his gilded chariot?—there was the pharaoh's wife Nefertiti, standing solemnly beside him, painted at only one third of his height and with snow-pale skin. Was it illusion, or did the figures in the murals move? Magic was in those walls. I followed the images, reading from right to left, until my eye rested on the far wall. Then I saw the king himself.

A stone sarcophagus leaned in a niche in the wall. It was open. A mummy stood within it. Linen bandages, age-yellow, swathed it. A neckpiece of gold and faience covered the shoulders and upper chest; a golden pointed beard was affixed to the chin; a wig of solid gold topped the skull features; the arms and legs were hung with every kind of precious stone. As I watched, horrified and fascinated, the dead king moved, painfully, jerkily, as though constrained by the bindings and the weight of gold and jewels. An acrid smell filled the air; later I would learn that this was the perfume of embalming.

Feigning courage, I said, "I have come to you, king to king, brother to brother. I greet you in the name of Skyfather."

The voice: not human at all, but more like the chirping of crickets; a brittle, high-pitched sound. "Astyanax." And then: "Come closer, little king. You are the same age as my brother-son, the one I named Tutankhaten . . . whose name they changed to Tutankhamen so that none would ever know how I honored the sun. He died a hundred years ago, but he was your age, little king. Oh, what can you know of those bright times? Bright, bright. This ship is all that remains of the ancient brightness. . . ."

"Then it's true," I said. "Color is leaving the world. . . ."

"The brightness! The brightness! Do you think I was mad?" So dry, his voice, like a desert that has never known water. "Do you think I enjoy this magical captivity? Oh, free me . . . free me!"

"From what must I free you, Pharaoh?"

"From death! From life! From knowledge! From ignorance! Oh, child, you cannot know this cold eternity, this shadow beyond all shadows, this undeadness. Oh, you must free me, free me. Break the spell."

Even I knew that there was only one way to shatter the enchantment that prevented Akhenaten's ship from reaching its destination in the realm of the dead. His name had been deleted from every monument in the world, scratched from every papyrus, chiseled out from memorial steles and inscriptions. The spell of unnaming had been spoken. The magic that makes a name a *name* and not a jumble of sounds had been dissolved. Akhenaten's name existed only in this fragment of reality, unmoored from the stream of time. To free the king, the life would have to be breathed once more into his name; his name would have to be uttered in the land of the living. But I had tried to speak it before, and my lips would not make the sounds.

I said, "I am no mage, Pharaoh. How shall I set you free?"

The mummy laughed then, a harsh, bitter laugh; it was a sound like an amphora being shattered against a wall. Or a human skull, I thought, remembering Leontes in my mother's arms, his head smashed.

Akhenaten said, "You will, little king. You will free not only me, but yourself . . . and everyone else! The Bronze Age ends, little king, and your fate is tied up in its ending!"

"I don't understand."

"It is not good that you should understand. Your innocence is what makes the whole thing possible, you see. You are an empty vessel, the tool of the gods."

"No! I am king!"

He laughed again.

"There's nothing you or Memnon can do," I said angrily.

"I will go to the Akhaians without your help. I will wreak revenge—alone, if I have to! It's no concern of the gods."

And Memnon too laughed: a rich, musical laugh that did not blend at all with the pharaoh's raucous rasping.

"You yourself told me the problem," Memnon said. "That you need someone to govern Troy in your absence."

"I'll get Phoinix or . . . No, Philemon! He's only a shepherd, but he's old and wise." But I knew that no one would obey him, for he was not a descendant of the sky; even Phoinix had some meager claim to that.

"Yet there is a better answer," Memnon said. "If you dare. . . ."

"Maybe it's not a question of daring," I said, "but of destiny." For I felt the wind of Skyfather in my very soul, though the air of the chamber was musty and death-still.

"The answer," said the undead king of Egypt, "is to fashion a blue king out of clay, and to give your name to him, and animate him with a part of your life's breath."

"What do you mean?" I said. "That is no kind of answer at all."

But I thought of the blue men who rowed the boat, and the blue servants who had carried the palanquin of the mage, and even the blue-skinned woman who had fanned him. The answer, then, was magical.

The king said, "Follow the mage."

I obeyed. The skywind roared through my bones. No one else felt it. "You are here, Skyfather," I whispered, "within me. I'm in your hands. I'm your six-times-great-grandson." I knew now I would never escape the consequences of that choice that was no choice.

We left the king's chamber through another of those illusory doors. I was beginning to suspect that there were far more rooms here than one could expect to find beneath the deck of a ship; perhaps we had departed the ship altogether and flown by magic to some secret place. I asked the mage how this could be.

The three of us (Leonidas still followed timorously behind)

stood in a chamber covered with dust. My head hit a mummified cat, suspended by its neck; I brushed it out of my way. It swung back and forth. Magical utensils were heaped upon a worktable. The only light came from an earthenware lamp; it illumined little more than the dancing dust.

At last Memnon deigned to answer my question: "Reality resides in the names of things, young king. When one writes down the true names of places in the prescribed fashion, and says the right words over the papyrus, and folds that papyrus and stuffs it in his tunic, he wraps away also the reality of the object. Here, in the hold of this small ship, there are whole worlds enfolded. Their names are written on scrolls throughout the ship. Some names will never be uttered, for men have lost the art of reading them, just as men may no longer read words written in the tongue of Snakemother."

"I don't understand," I said.

"Good," he said, and motioned Leonidas to sit on a low stool against the door mural. "Wait there, boy. As for you, Astyanax . . . Do you know what an ushabti is?"

"No."

He swept a space clear on his worktable. Metal jingled as it hit the floor. There was no motion here such as one normally feels in ships; it confirmed my suspicion that we had entered another realm entirely. He rooted through the piles of apparatus and scrolls and finally retrieved a wooden box, from which he plucked a small clay figure glazed with faience. It was a brilliant blue, the only bright object in the room.

"The blue slaves—"

"Ha! Our young king is slow, but not unintelligent. Yes. When a man is dead, there are many tasks he must perform in the underworld that he may find unpleasant. The ushabti answers for him while the dead man continues to enjoy the good life—hunts, banquets, women—that was painted into his tomb. Why not an ushabti to rule a kingdom? It's only for a little while, no? Until you avenge your father and grandfather, and bring your aunt Helen back to Troy."

It seemed too good to be true. Until I saw the catch in it. "In order for an ushabti to take my place, I first have to—"

"Die!" It was Leonidas's voice, small and terror-stricken. I did not want to look at him, to see into the eyes of one who had already crossed the boundary.

"Is it so bad, then, death?" I said.

"It will not be a final death. But you will want me to explain how the magic works." Memnon was searching frantically through the box, flinging aside broken ushabtis that clinked on the debris-strewn floor. "We, the Nile peoples, have studied the human soul for millennia. We know that at least two souls exist: the ka, the shadow-double, which we draw in the form of a homunculus, and whose symbol is arms outstretched in prayer; and the ba, the spiritual essence, whose symbol is a bird. I will draw your ka from you, young king, and breathe it into a clay figure." He found what he was looking for: a crude statuette of reddish clay. "I will inscribe your name upon the biscuit," he said, "and glaze it with faience; then I shall bake the figurine in the fire of life." He was already applying to the clay a reed dipped in black paste, murmuring to himself in a language I could not understand, and I could see the hieroglyphs take shape. "Now for the glaze itself," he said, taking the ushabti and dipping it in a powder. "These are mysteries. Do not look." I averted my eyes. I felt a blast of heat from somewhere. "Now, we may begin. If you don't mind, we must now go to another chamber."

We passed through the door drawn on the wall. It was the same door as before, but we did not go into the chamber from which we had entered his laboratory. This was a bare chamber; a stone sarcophagus, its lid propped up against its side, filled most of it.

"Climb in!" he said.

Leonidas whimpered and was afraid. "Don't cry, child," I whispered. "It's only a trick." Hoisting myself up by my arms, I got into the coffin and lay face up, my hands crossed over my chest; for I had seen the mummified pharaoh make that gesture, and there was no room to rest my arms on either side of me. Leonidas, standing on tiptoe, could barely peer over the granite wall. I saw his eyes, big with fear. "Don't cry!" I commanded. I touched his hair with my hand; presently his feet became tired and the top of his head slid out of sight.

Memnon lay a gold neckpiece on my chest. In my hands he stuck a crook and flail. To my chin he attached one of those pointed beards, a circlet of cold metal on my skin. To my brow he affixed a miniature sun-disk of beaten gold.

"Close your eyes," he said. "There, there. You are drifting, drifting. You feel the cold of death upon you . . . drifting, drifting . . . you are dying, King, dying."

I felt as though I were sinking, sinking into a bank of snow. More and more snow seemed to pile up over me, smothering me, crushing me with intense cold. I squeezed my eyes shut against the pressure. As the snow seemed to bury me, I lost all feeling in my limbs, and I saw nothing . . .

Except, for a tiny moment, the smile of my aunt Helen, as vivid and as frightening as that time in my childhood in the smoke of the burning city . . .

Then, again, nothingness.

Then the voice of Memnon, over and over, intoning.

After an immeasurable time I felt the crushing cold ease. Metal touched my heart; I could hear it pumping, the only sound in the stillness. Then it touched my lips. I moaned. At last I felt it touch my eyelids, gently, left and then right; I opened my eyes and saw that Memnon was putting away a wooden rod tipped with silver.

"You are dead now," he said, "and yet not dead, for I have performed over your immobile body the ceremonies of death. The earth will be fooled for a while."

"Misdirection!" I said, remembering our drunken conversation at the banquet. Had it only been two nights ago?

I looked about me. I sat up. I was no longer in the sarcophagus, but on a couch on the deck. The sun had risen. Leonidas was kneeling beside me and diligently cleaning my hair with his fingers. Ankhs were still falling from the sun-disk on the mast.

"Do not be afraid, young king," Memnon said. "I have pulled your ka from you with my rod; soon I will send it into the ushabti."

He placed the figurine on the deck between us.

It began to grow.

"Don't panic!" Memnon said. "It's all part of the magic, you see!"

It was the height of a man now.

"In the name of my master, Nefer-kheperu-Ra Ua-en-Ra Aakhu-en-Aten," the mage cried out, "I constrain thee, grow no more!"

The blue man stood motionless. His face mirrored mine exactly. "King, he's just like you!" Leonidas said. "Not just his face . . . his whole body, even his private parts!" For the man of clay and faience was naked.

"Do you feel curiously light?" Memnon said to me. "It is because your ka rests in my rod. Soon you will be free."

"I don't think—"

He silenced me with a gesture. Then he pulled out a scroll from his robe. "This is your name." I saw:

"A king's name!" Memnon said. "Pera-en-Nu Astu-wanak, King of the City!" He wrapped the scroll around the loins of the blue statue. Then he lifted the rod and touched the lips, eyes and heart of the blue king, saying over and over, "Oh thou ushabti of Pera-en-Nu the king, may thine eyes and lips be opened; may the breath of the king animate thee; go thou forth." The figure quivered. Growing angry, Memnon smashed the rod against the figure's features, and I felt a sharp pain in my face.

And the figure spoke in my voice: "I am here. Tell me thy bidding."

Memnon said, "Thou must take this name unto thyself for a time. And in this name must thou rule over Troy, until he that possesses the ba return to reclaim the ka, and thou become as dust once more."

"I will need . . . the trappings of kingship," said the blue king.

"Give him your crown, your crook and your flail, your jewels," Memnon said to me, and gestured to Leonidas to help him strip me of my finery and bedeck my surrogate. At last I was naked and he was garbed in the splendid vestments of a king. Memnon said to him, "Say thy name."

He said, "I am Pera-en-Nu Astu-wanak, King of Troy."

"Now," Memnon said, turning quickly to me, "say *your* name!"

"That's ridiculous," I said. "I am called—" I stopped. I could not remember my own name! Surely it had something to do with the blue king who stood before me, but . . . my name, my name . . . I looked wildly about me. "My name is—my name is—"

"Do not be afraid," Memnon said. "Your name still exists; you are not lost to the afterlife! You are twice-born now, and you will need a new name for your second life."

"My second life . . ." I was thinking, he has miscounted, because twice already a surrogate has died for me: Leontes and Leonidas. "I see what you mean now. You mean that I have now gone through the motions of death and practiced a deception on Snakemother." I was still confusedly trying to recall my name. It must be some silly magic trick, I thought. Misdirection! Wasn't that the word he always used? Misdirection . . . deception—was that not the nature of magic?

"You're wrong," Memnon said. I was startled that he had read my mind. "Magic is truth!" He stared into my eyes. I dared not flinch, for in my heart I still knew I was a king, though I could not force the words from my throat. "You will have no name, nameless king, until a stranger names you. And that new name will be your name until your twin souls are reunited."

Leonidas spoke up now. He said, sobbing, "I wasn't

deceived! I know who my lord is! I won't stay in Troy. . . . I will go with you to the land of the Akhaians. . . . I will serve you forever!''

"Leonidas," said the blue king in a cold, compassionless voice.

He turned at once, as a dog who hears his master call. I saw that he was drawn toward the blue king, that some power was pulling him away from me. "No!" I cried out. "I may have no name, but I can't lose you to that walking statue—"

"Master—master—" he was calling to me, I knew, but he kept walking toward that other one. The magic was too strong for him.

"Be comforted," Memnon said to me. "He cannot go with you. You must face the next stage alone. But it is good that he has seen the ceremony. We must have a witness. For . . . Ah, I should not have forgotten to tell you. What we have done today is . . . irregular, you see. And most dangerous. That creature possesses your ka. For all intents and purposes, he *is* you. The longer you stay away, the harder it will be for you to reclaim your soul."

"You tricked me!"

"No, young nameless king, never. There is no deception here, but a deeper reality."

"Words."

"Truths." He smiled and flicked back a paw of his lionskin cloak.

I said, "They'll know him for what he is, that blue king; for one thing, he's blue. For another, his movements, his gestures, his pronouncements—"

"The blue will fade as your ka takes hold. By tomorrow no one will know the difference. Except, perhaps, your boy here."

"What do you mean, 'perhaps'? Leonidas will always know me."

"It will be a test of his love, his loyalty. Remember that he is staying behind in Troy. Perhaps he will forget what he saw here; for it is hard to reconcile such an experience with what passes for reality. Perhaps he will think it is a dream. . . ."

"My lord," Leonidas said, and I could tell that he formed the words with difficulty, "I will always know you." But he faced the blue king. And he wept.

"Very well," Memnon said. With his bare hands he tore the two front paws from the skin of his lioness. He drew two bronze chains from his robe. He pierced the paws with a dagger and threaded them on the chains to form two amulets. When he tried to put one around the boy's neck, Leonidas recoiled.

"How can you do that?" I cried. "He knows it for the lioness that took his life!"

Memnon said, "There is no other way." The boy no longer resisted him. And I too took the talisman and put it on; it was the only thing I wore, for the blue king had taken my clothes along with my name. "The lion of life and death—that has linked the two of you from the beginning," the mage said. "Let it be so still."

"Then the lioness was not from Snakemother?" I said.

He did not answer. I persisted, and finally he said only, "All things come from all other things."

And so it was that I was readied for my great journey of love and vengeance . . . born anew, like a baby, without even a name. The sun was setting now; I saw the hills' shadow on the plain, and the dark outlines of my city. In the gathering dark the three of us were rowed ashore. The blue king led the way; his servant followed; I, the nameless king, came last.

Nor could I remember the name of that other nameless king, the one who inhabited the floating kingdom of the sun; for I was once more in the grip of the spell of unnaming.

Chapter XIII

The Blue King

I did not awaken in the royal bedchamber but on a straw pallet in the slaves' quarters of the palace. A guard was shaking me roughly. "Begone," I said. "Can't you see I'm—"

"The king has summoned you! Get up at once!"

I knew that the blue king was king and that I was a man without a name; I knew that to proceed on the next step of my journey I must leave Troy. I was beginning to perceive that my departure would not be entirely voluntary. But I did not truly grasp these facts—not until I saw the blue king sitting on my throne. I wanted to shout out, "Impostor!" and rush up angrily and grind him back to gravel with my fists. But I quelled my rage. I looked at the faces of my erstwhile companions: Phoinix was disdainful as always; Leukippos haughty. Philemon stared curiously at me. He did not know me.

"Philemon," I said, "Phoinix—"

They looked away.

The blue king said, "Because of your physical resemblance to me, it will not do to have you in the city. It is not expedient to have here one such as you, for your appearance may stir dissension and cast doubt on the legitimacy of this kingship. And it is a terrible omen. Thus I will banish you."

The court—my court!—applauded.

"But I am compassionate. I will provide for you a boat with twenty rowers. Leave immediately! My boy will attend you."

He summoned Leonidas with a crooked finger. The boy stepped forward. There was no glimmer of recognition in his eyes.

108

"Leonidas . . ." I whispered.

"Do you know my name?" he said.

I was lost. "My kinsmen," I said, "surely you can see the difference between us. . . . He doesn't talk like me." I laughed uneasily. "He utters those pronouncements in a sepulchral monotone. I planned this departure, but I did not plan to leave so ignominiously . . ." Yet inside I knew it was the only way. Misdirection, as Memnon had told me, was the key. "You must recognize me!"

Phoinix shook his head sadly. It was clear that he thought me a madman. "He is far more kingly than *you*," he said. I saw that he was sorry for me. I was still naked except for the lion's paw talisman and a makeshift loincloth I had fashioned from a rag.

"Of course he isn't like you!" Leukippos said derisively.

"If you're the king," the blue king said, "surely you would know your own name!"

"I am—" I could not say it. My mouth was hemmed shut by the magic. Could they not see that the king was blue? Evidently not. Only I, blessed and cursed with the eyes of Skyfather, could see the clay and the glaze beneath the skin of the false *wanax*. For it was faience, the color of the ancient sky. I stood, stung by their rebuff, gaping at what I myself had wrought.

But still I could not speak my name, and still I was the impostor in their eyes.

On the beach, Leonidas wept and embraced me; but he did not call me by name.

It was a small ship, the kind that can be brought all the way up onto the sandbanks. The rowers, I noticed, were old men and adolescents; I could not imagine we would get far. How I wished for a ship like the ones in the stories! But I knew even as a child that the stories had become more and more grandiose in the telling. The Akhaians had come in ships like this one, crammed almost to bursting. I boarded.

*   *   *

At sea, I stood with my face turned away from Troy. I must never look upon Troy again, I thought, until I have fulfilled the oaths of my childhood. Neoptolemos will die, and the war will begin anew.

As I stood there, trying to erase the past from my mind and to think only of the future, I remembered the three dreams I had had the night the messenger had come to me and turned to stone. . . .

The first dream was accomplished, for I had seen my mock wedding with Dione, had seen Snakemother steal away her flesh, had seen the mage bring her back from the shadowland.

It was the second dream that must now be fulfilled. The mountain, the serpent, the sun . . . I fighting myself—was it the conflict between ka and ba to which Memnon had referred? Where was Memnon now? His ship had vanished without a trace, and along with it the mummy-king whose name I could no longer utter. Doubtless he could have divined the dream's meaning. The sun-disk I had seen, but the serpent? The dream told of perils to come: dangers both from without and from within my divided soul, I was sure of it . . . and of the battle between Skyfather and Snakemother. But had that not been won centuries ago? Or was that victory an illusion?

And the third dream! That had been the strangest of all. For why would I cast the skystone back into the sky, and give up the most sacred object in the universe? And what was it that glittered in the stone? Some hidden treasure? There was no reason in it. We would never lose Skyfather . . . not unless the entire universe came to an end.

And the universe was not ending. No, it was beginning! For I was twice-born, and Troy could be twice-born too. And though I had no name, I was riding the waves and racing the wind in the direction of the sun . . . in the direction of Helen! Helen, my kinswoman, Helen of the bright eyes and killing smile! Phoinix's mocking words had been true after all. I was saving myself for Helen: Helen the swan-born, Helen the daughter of the limitless sky.

Book Three: The Mad Queen

ⲦⲮⲮⲨⱲⲰ⊕

The point of the story is that Paris gave the prize to Aphrodite, not because she bribed him, but because she was beautiful. After all, it was a contest in beauty, though Athena and Hera started a discussion about wisdom and power. It was they who tried to bribe him. They had their merits and they had arguments, but Aphrodite was the thing itself.

—John Erskine, *The Private Life of Helen of Troy*

Chapter XIV

The Beginning of the Journey

We journeyed for a long time. I, who had seen time only as a shepherd sees time, sitting still on the hillside while the stars wheel, could not tune myself at first to the new rhythms. I was no longer king save by an inner knowledge others did not share; but I tried to behave as a king, sitting unruffled on a plank astride the stern, hiding my nervousness at the ship's ceaseless motion. At night the stars were the same as they had always been, but they swayed. The wind was quite different, though. I should have been used to the gods' breath, living as I did at the summit of the city; but here there were no walls and no means of hiding. It smelled different: it lacked the fragrances of flower and cedar, of young women scurrying down corridors, of the rushes laid down to catch the excrement of the palace animals. It overpowered me at first, this new smell, as a sudden darkness might after one has gazed on a many-colored mural. But at length, after some days at sea, I found myself able to distinguish the myriad scents: the raw fish odor, the tang of fresh kelp, the sweat of the rowers, the pungent saltiness of the air. Breathing it I felt keenly the possibility of newness in everything. I felt lighter—or was that simply because I now possessed only one soul, and that soul the spiritual, birdlike part of me? And because I had no name?

Inwardly I knew this namelessness to be another illusion, another example of Memnon's reckless misdirection. But I was only then beginning to comprehend that truth and falsehood were not two separate ideas, and that a thing could be both true and untrue. I suppose that this lesson, though it was but a casual comment of the mage's, was the beginning of wisdom for me.

Some days, to avoid the tedium, and because I pitied the untrained rowers and their arrhythmic plying, I joined them. We moved slowly, hugging the coastline, trying to synchronize ourselves with the thump of the drummer; but he himself was old and blind and did not keep time. After a day or so the wind became more consistent and we were able to rest our oars and unfurl the sail, which was painted with an eye so that the ship might see its way clearly. Eventually the drummer's uneven pace became so annoying that I took the beater myself and sat for hours pounding. The sun turned the wind to fire; it shone with such unwonted steadiness that I felt I must be traveling under the sigil of the undead pharaoh himself. For some days the sailing was so smooth that I was afraid. Excessive good luck can be a bad omen.

There was only one person on board who had had much experience of the sea. He was a Phoenician. He was somewhat more able-bodied than my own crewmen, but had only one eye, and was so tall that I heard the other seamen calling him a cyclops. His face and arms were scarred, perhaps from brawling, perhaps from battling; his back was crisscrossed with weals of scar tissue, from a flogging perhaps. I remembered him, a criminal whom I had planned to expel from the city, a day or two before that conference in which I had decided to challenge Snakemother's power. I do not remember exactly what he had done; I think he had tried to cheat an old woman out of a side of lamb. Whatever it was, it had not really merited banishment, but the Phoenicians, whom the Egyptians only barely kept under control, were fond of piracy and were, besides, worshipers of Snakemother. That was what really made me want him gone. Indeed, I had considered using him as a ritual scapegoat if we could find no other way of improving the harvest.

I had not been pleased to see him on my ship, though it was only logical that the blue king would think like me . . . would use the departure of my embarrassing self to get rid of other undesirables. At first I thought he should be thrown in the ocean in case he was a vehicle for Snakemother's intervention; but the days passed and we journeyed smoothly, and I reflected that he rowed well, and might prove useful.

One day, when the wind was stilled, I squatted beside him as he plied his oar. The deck was barely wide enough to sit comfortably; I complained of this. He grunted and said something in his own language. I knew he did not have Skyfather's tongue, which is known only to Akhaians and Trojans; but I could speak the Luvian language of the Phrygian shepherds, which had been known in our land long before my ancestors crossed the sea to found my kingdom. I asked him in that language what he meant.

"I barely understand you," he responded in yet another tongue, whose words sounded vaguely familiar and quite different from the raspings of Phoenician. It was the language of the Hittites, I realized, which bears a few resemblances to our own. We conversed after a fashion, then, in a mixture of Luvian, Hittite, Skyfather's tongue, and the universal language of gesture. I laughed at the complexity of our situation.

"Our ships much better than yours," said the Phoenician. "Our ships have . . . fifty, even more oarsmen."

"That seems unlikely," I said, always the doubter. For even Akhenaten's ship of the sun, which had had rooms beneath its decks, had not boasted more than fifty rowers. Surely a contraption like that would sink beneath the weight of human flesh.

"No. True!"

"Not sink?"

"No. For the Lady's wind blows through them."

"Blasphemy!" I said, flinching from his use of the honorific *potnia* for the mother of darkness. "The wind of the sea is the breath of Skyfather." In truth it disturbed me to hear such ethereal things attributed to the shadow powers. I said, "Is it true that in your cities you have statues of Snakemother filled with milk, that you fashion the nipples of the statues of wax . . . and when you throw babies in the sacrificial fire, the burning of their flesh melts the wax so that her breasts seem brimming with the milk of compassion? Oh, you are a monstrous people.'' I had heard the story once from King Priam.

"A silly story," he said. "Where the Lady rules they tell such things of you people too. But I have been in your land and know they are false."

I was uncomfortable with the subject and thought it best to let it drop.

I said, "Have you ever been to the lands of the Akhaians?"

"I do know something of them." He continued to row sullenly.

"Do you know where we are headed now?"

"No. Only that our way lies west. The coast we hug is Thrace. We have passed Lesbos"—he spat into the sea—"your former ally."

"*My* former ally! You know who I am, then?"

"You are some leftover prince of the royal house. Astyanax has cast you out for fear you take over the throne."

"My name—" I could not say it. Oh, I would have given up the whole enterprise if I could have uttered my name only once, to show this barbarian what king I was. But the magic chained my tongue. Roughly I said, "We're going to Phthia . . . Phthia, the kingdom once ruled by Akhilleus . . . Phthia where my mother serves Neoptolemos as his slave!" I could not conceal my bitterness.

"Who is your mother?"

"Andromache," I said, "the wife of Hector, who would have been Queen of Troy."

"I did not know she had any bastards," said the Phoenician.

"I'm not—" I was confused. My name was on the tip of my tongue but . . . it was useless. I sat beside the foreigner in silence, knowing that I could not argue my way out of Memnon's ensorcellment.

One day we put in at an island somewhere off the Thracian coast. It was a dismal day, and Phalas (that was, I found out, the Phoenician's name) was the first to leap ashore.

There came to greet us a priestess, bare-breasted, who held a snake in her bosom. We had no tongues in common, but

Phalas understood her after a fashion. She did not answer him directly, and he addressed only the ground at her feet. She was attended by women, all naked to the waist, who wore the flounced skirts I had seen in ancient murals and on the walls of the sacred bathroom in the palace. After they had exchanged words in this curious fashion, the priestess clapped her hands, and about a dozen pigs came trotting out of the village behind her; they stopped in a row in front of her, almost as though they understood her commands.

She gave another order, at which a swineherd came forward and began to slit the throats of the pigs. What was strange to me was that the animals made no complaint, but waited for death as though bewitched. The swineherd was the only man I had seen; for all I knew he was the only one in the village.

They held a feast afterward, and the girls who served the priestess each chose one of my oarsmen for herself. They vanished into their huts with the men. A sobbing, frenzied flute music issued from some hidden place. I resisted the one who tried to pull me away, for the village was sacred to Snakemother, and I was afraid of being bewitched away from my mission.

So I went to the ship to sleep alone. Once in the middle of the night I awoke to the strains of an obscene chanting from the village; the words, over and over, were "piggy-fucker, piggy-fucker." I sat up, listening carefully, until I was absolutely certain those were the words. I was glad then that I had not joined the orgy. The smell of roasted pig's flesh blended with the brine-laden breeze; the mix was almost suffocating. I did not sleep well after that, but dreamed again the three precognitive dreams. But they were not as vivid as they had been the first time. Perhaps it was because I, having lost my ka, dreamed with only half a soul.

Toward dawn I sensed, from the ship's rocking, that the others must be staggering back, some drunk, some worn out from sex. I felt a twinge of jealousy at that. I rubbed the crusts from my eyes. I saw my men through the haze of my half-dreaming. Were they men or pigs? I almost choked on the smell of roasting meat, yet . . . they *were* pigs! I sat straight up, stared wildly in the half-light as the animals overran my vessel.

"No!" I shouted. Then I felt a hand on my shoulder. It was the Phoenician Phalas, and he was laughing. "They've all turned into pigs!" I blurted out, panicking.

"Strange you should say that. The priestess of the Lady told me that very thing. I don't know why you turned down the honor of making love to the goddess yourself. Because you declined, it fell to me, you see, who knew her tongue."

"You mated with Snakemother and . . . my men are cursed; they're all pigs!" I could barely control myself.

He laughed again. "The sun is rising. You will see for yourself."

I looked again, my eyes getting used to the half-dark. To the east, in the direction of Troy, sunlight glimmered, bronzing the face of the sea. I saw my men dozing against the sides of the ship, some resting against the oars, some with their hands trailing in the water, some picking at the sheets of hide that kept us waterproof. A pig ran grunting down the deck. "You remember now! We negotiated for those pigs. And, because I performed . . . adequately last night, we are rewarded with more meat. You should thank me."

I saw the humor in it now, and laughed aloud. The voyage must have been more of a strain than I had allowed myself to think. Pigs indeed!

"But," Phalas said, "she did tell me that she has that power. Indeed, she says, the pigs we feasted on are all Akhaians whom she transformed by magic; they were shipwrecked here years ago, on their way back from the war."

"What a sense of humor that priestess must have."

"Yes, women like to tell one such odd stories as they lie sated with love."

I sat in silence for a time, watching the dawn light dappling the water, waiting for wind.

Presently, when a few of the men seemed more awake, I gave the order to depart. I dived down to help the dozen or so sober ones. We pushed the ship out, swimming after it; the water was chill, exhilarating. I pulled myself up hand over hand over the sleek slippery skin-clad wood, and vaulted aboard at the stern. "There's a wind," the boy who worked the rudder said, looking up. "West."

With the lifting of the sail my oppression seemed to melt away. I called Phalas to me and bade him gauge our direction by the rising sun and the morning star. I felt the ship give into the wind and I thought, Skyfather's breath is blowing me away from that dark place . . . toward Akhaia, the world's center. The time of the second dream is approaching: I must battle the dragon that coils around the mountain of truth. I had glimpsed her on the isle of pigs, in the shape of a priestess.

First to Phthia. I would rescue my mother if she lived, and kill Neoptolemos. Then south, past Mycenae, where the High King of Akhaia held court, to Sparta where *she* was waiting. I would conquer the two sides of womanhood: the dragon darkness and Helen of the starry sky. I thought myself fate's master, not its victim, such was my vanity.

In the few days' sailing that remained, I found my sailors strangely taciturn. Their eyes seemed glazed. I think I must have looked that way when Memnon laid the deathlike spell on me. I wondered what had happened on the island of the pigs.

We were traveling southeast now, with the coastline of Magnesia on our right; I glimpsed Mount Pelion, named for my enemy's grandfather: blue, mist-girt, foreboding. We turned westward into the straits that separate the mainland from the island of Euboia; to the right was the kingdom of Protesilaos. All this the Phoenician told me; for though I had heard the names rehearsed again and again in my childhood, I could not match names to shorelines or kings to countries. More than once I felt inadequate. In the night I seldom slept, but prayed for a sign from Skyfather. But the gods like to tantalize us by opening doors or setting us down at the beginning of the path to some epiphany; they rarely show themselves again, and we must fend for ourselves.

At last we landed on a white beach surrounded by low cliffs.

"Where are we?" I asked Phalas.

"I think that this is Alos," he said. "I remember once we came raiding this far; we even fought a battle on the sea itself. Alos is an outpost of Akhilleus's old kingdom; while the war was going on, it was fair game for us Phoenicians!" I was at a loss for words. "What shall we do now?" he said.

He was deferring to me, but we both knew he had me at his mercy. He had no tie of fealty to me, and he was the only one of us who knew his way on the sea. But I could not think of what he might do. "Go south," I told him, "hugging the coastline but avoiding detection; find Sparta. Once I have reached it overland, I'll find some way of contacting you." I was improvising; but perhaps the gods would find some solution. I took from the ship fresh clothing—I had to look respectable, if not like a king—and a pouch of gold and other small precious items, and a dagger. The blue king had not, of course, permitted me to bring my father's armor and his phasganon.

I watched my companions leave. I wondered whether I would see them again, or whether the gods had provided them merely as a way for me to get from one shore to another. Perhaps Phalas would take control and try to go to Sidon or some other city of his people.

The sea swallowed the ship in a smear of light, and I walked inland.

Chapter XV

Phthia

I knew, from things I had overheard in my childhood, that Akhilleus's kingdom was a desolate one. My grandfather had once told me that Akhilleus was a son of Snakemother herself. Perhaps that was why Neoptolemos had had the effrontery to burst with bloodied sword into Skyfather's temple the day he killed King Priam. I remembered this part well; I was squatting in my grandfather's lap, sucking on a sheep's eye that was supposed to give me luck and strength, and finding it gelatinous and sweet and cooling. I had been saying, "Tell me about the Akhaians!" For like every child I loved monsters.

This is the story my grandfather told me that day. . . .

"In the days when Snakemother had not yet become a monster, deformed and serpent-haired, she ruled over many lands; she lived in many bodies. She rose from the wavecrests of the sea in the shape of a beautiful woman, for dominion over the waters was still under dispute then, and had not yet passed entirely into the hands of Skyfather's brother Poseidon, to whose chariot are harnessed the horses of land and sea and wind and fire, who is one of our city's principal protectors. In such a form she came to Phthia; she called herself Thetis then. She ruled there for a thousand years, unchanging, beautiful, and the people followed the custom of killing the king. In Troy, our ancestor outwitted Snakemother; in Phthia it was Snakemother who outwitted herself, for she fell in love with a mortal, Peleus, and refused to kill him. And so the kingdom existed uneasily for some years, until Thetis's mortal vessel, the priestess who represented her, gave birth to one who should have been her daughter and should have

121

become the vessel of Snakemother in her place. But instead
she bore a son, and for love of Peleus she did not kill him,
but clothed him in women's clothes. When the war came this
proved convenient, for Thetis knew by her own gift for
divination that if Akhilleus went to Troy he would be killed.
But Odysseus found him out by trickery. All the world
knows how he went to the women's quarters of the palace
disguised as a pedlar of rich jewels; how he had a dagger
concealed among them; how Akhilleus could not resist toying
with the weapon and was found out. And when his mother
learned what had happened, she had a premonition that
Snakemother's reign would be over in the land of Phthia, and
she fled screaming into the sea. And that was how Akhilleus
came to Troy.''

I remember asking my grandfather whether I should be
afraid of Akhilleus; he only smiled sadly. That was long
before Akhilleus killed my father. Did my grandfather already know? There were times in my childhood when I had
the impression that everyone was acting out what they already knew must happen, but without much enthusiasm; they
seemed like terra-cotta dolls whom the Fates had animated.
Leontes and I had often made up stories around the figures I
kept in my toy box: warriors, chariots, heroes. It occurred to
me vaguely that the gods were doing the same thing with us.

Alos was not much of a city; the citadel's fortifications
were in ruins, with a few huts clustered outside them. I
found an old shepherd who led me to the king, an ancient
man who kept court in the open, under a tree, beside a well,
while his wives spun endlessly behind him. A single horse,
an old nag, was tethered to the well. I said, ''King, I come as
guest.'' He looked up and closed his eyes again. Hospitality
is a sacred thing, and one of his wives set down her spinning
and ran to fetch me bread, cheese and water. ''This is
welcome,'' I said, drinking deeply. I sat down on the ground
at the feet of the king. The day would soon end, and I was
anxious to continue on my journey, but I had no quarrel with
the king and dared not risk discourtesy.

"Rejoice, stranger," said the younger of the wives. "I see from your dress and bearing that you are descended from the gods." I had been saved by the fact that I have my father's eyes.

"King," I said, "tell me how to get to Phthia. I have traveled far to reach your city, at the ocean bourne of Phthiotis, where Neoptolemos grandson of Peleus is overking. I want to see this great king for myself."

The old king moaned. Another of his wives went to succor him, and the first, who had given me food and drink, said, "He is very sick, and troubled by dreams. Do not take offense at the breach of hospitality, sir."

"Of what does he dream?" I said.

"He dreams . . . dark, terrible things. He cries that there are snake-haired women, inland, wandering the countryside and tearing men limb from limb. Have you seen such people, stranger? If not, can you give him comfort?" I remembered, though, that even in Troy I had heard such rumors; that was why I had needed to trick Snakemother in her necropolis. The woman continued, "I have heard no news at all from Phthia. We don't even know whether Neoptolemos is still king, exactly. When he came back, many years ago, he killed those who had usurped Akhilleus's throne. But since then there's been little word from inland. We subsist here, more or less, on what we harvest ourselves, and on our single herd of goats. We were raided, you know. By Phoenicians, I think, because I could not understand their tongue. They raped us and sacrificed all our male children to . . . to the Lady." Phalas had not lied to me then. But I was even more disturbed at the deferential title that the woman used for the Snakemother. Was not this country ruled by the sky, not the earth? She continued: "We have been barren ever since, and the king has had nightmares, and we have had no help from Phthia, though Phthia is but five days' journey hence, and we sent runners."

I looked from woman to woman; still the king said nothing. One of the women, older than the others, stood up and scrutinized me thoroughly while I ate. I tried to cover my embarrassment, but as she stared at me I found it harder and harder to eat. At last she said, "I think it's him! I think it's the one!"

She pulled out a dagger and prepared to stab the king, who did not resist, but sat still as marble; only his eyes showed he was still human. I was about to protest when the first wife, the one who had greeted me, knocked the knife angrily out of the old woman's hand. "These are not the old times!" she said. "He is a traveler, yes . . . but he's on his way to Phthia. Perhaps he intends to accept the throne from Andromache—"

"Andromache!" At the mention of my mother I lost my cool completely. Was my mother embroiled in some arcane intrigue . . . or worse, somehow snared into the cult of Snakemother?

"Andromache is her earthly name," the old woman explained. "I apologize humbly for trying to kill the king, stranger; but the opportunity seemed too good to pass up. You fulfilled all the criteria for being the local consort; moreover, we all found you comely." The king seemed unperturbed that his own wife had even now attempted to murder him, but the rules of hospitality prevented me from remarking on this.

Instead, trying to keep calm, I said, "What do you mean, Andromache's her 'earthly' name? What other name could she have?"

"Oh . . . you are a stranger, I forgot. From far away, you say? The sea, perhaps? But you do seem to have a slight Luvian accent." The young wife was hedgy now; I knew she was concealing something important. I also somewhat resented the imputation of a Luvian accent to me, for my ancestors came as much from the sky as any Akhaian's.

"I want to know about Andromache!" I said angrily.

She did not answer me.

It was the old one who spoke. "You fools," she said, berating the other wives, "you are still victims of the inglorious past. I will tell you, stranger, that Andromache has become the Lady Incarnate, the earthly vessel of Thetis, whose position was held by Deidameia before her.''

I covered my ears with my hands. I did not want to hear this. I did not want my quest to end with the discovery that the world had slid back into primordial darkness. My own mother . . . It had to be untrue. Then I suddenly remembered her wailing and beating her breast over the smashed body of Leontes . . . and I knew that I still felt that betrayal as keenly as I had done thirteen years before. What could I do, though? At that moment I felt that my whole journey had been made useless. What god was in me? Skyfather had not spoken to me, only my cousin Hermes, a messenger. I was a boy and could barely heft my father's shield.

"Let him go on," said the young queen, who seemed to see a little of my grief.

I turned to go.

"You will see the road to Phthia past the third of those thickets; walk directly away from the setting sun," the young queen said. "And, sir, I will give you ten loaves of bread and some dried goat's meat. But you have not told us your name."

"I do not know it," I said.

"I knew it!" the old queen shrieked triumphantly. "He who shall conquer the queen of night shall be the hero who has no name!"

"I don't know what you mean, Queen," I said. "But I will try to heed what you've told me."

Thus I walked away from Alos, which, they told me, had once been a bustling town. I followed the directions and walked onward. The road was often steep and always stony and had obviously not been repaired since the war. My sandals were soon hopelessly torn and my feet bloody.

I had wanted to ask the king for a chariot, but I had seen he possessed no such thing. It would have been unseemly to ask for a gift he could not give even though I carried suffi- ciently rich return gifts on my person; flaunting one's wealth is not proper for a nameless king. I had seen a lone horse in the king's courtyard. Had its companion died, perhaps? I should have asked for it, seeing that it was useless for a chariot now; I had heard that to the north, in Thessaly, which was also in part under the suzerainty of Akhilleus, there were acrobats who could actually ride on the creatures' backs.

For an hour as I walked inland I entertained myself with visions of flinging myself onto a horse as though it were a ship, and having it carry me, bucking and whinnying, with the wind streaming. A wild, poetic, impossible vision. It was quaint and faintly lascivious to me.

In the forest I surprised a fawn, killed it; I skinned it, scraped it, pissed on the hide and stretched it on a frame of twigs. I made a fire to speed its drying, and in the morning fashioned makeshift coverings for my feet.

On the third day I saw signs of cultivation. There were fields of grain and foothills up ahead; I knew that I would soon reach the citadel of my enemy. I slowed my pace, for I wanted to approach in the right way. And also because, when the women of Alos had mentioned Andromache, I had known, in a way for the first time, that my quest was not some fantasy. But I was afraid of what they had said, and I wondered how profound Snakemother's grip on this kingdom might be. I knew that she could not have established her dominion overtly, for the women of Alos had been reticent, and had bridled their tongues; only the old woman was outspoken about the Lady. Well, I told myself, I had defeated Snakemother before, though I had had help from an unexpected source.

This time I would be alone.

Often, in my childhood, I had dreamed of dying to bring back the glory of Troy; I knew now that I might truly die, and that Troy might not necessarily be the richer for it . . . or even know that I had died, for it was even now ruled by a king who owned half my soul and all my name.

I thought of death.

The death in Neoptolemos's eyes when he struck off my

grandfather's head. I tried to conjure up hate for him. Revenge! I thought. I have sworn revenge!

At last, with the citadel clearly visible, perched on a hilltop, I remembered Neoptolemos even more clearly.

I remembered that when he looked at me his eyes had contained compassion as well as death; that at the same moment that he had decided to kill my slave boy, he had already spared my life.

To kill him—would that compromise the balance of the universe? It might be as impious an act as was the slaying of King Priam before the stone of Skyfather. . . .

I was there at last, in front of the gate. I pounded at the gatekeeper's window and demanded entry.

Chapter XVI

Prince Pergamos

The wooden shutter was drawn aside. A boy's face greeted me: gray-eyed, his dark hair crudely hacked off in places . . . a look of bewilderment and then, abruptly, a warm smile. "You're a visitor!" he exclaimed. "We so rarely have visitors. Forgive me for being so excited, but you're the first good thing that's happened all week." He was about twelve years old, I guessed. "Oh, Zeus, I can't work the latch myself. I'll have to call someone. Hey, gatekeeper! Oh, the house slaves are so decrepit and useless these days."

The small doorway within the great gate was opened; it creaked. Ceremoniously I stepped over the threshold. The boy saw me and said, "Have you come from far away? Have you stories to tell us, wonderful stories? You don't know what it's like here, so far from the big cities like Mycenae and Thebes, and—" He stopped abruptly as an ancient man, the one who had helped him unbolt the door, approached.

"Master—" he said, deferential yet stern.

"Oh. Of course. I'm sorry, I was just so excited." Remembering his manners, he said to me, "Rejoice, stranger. I will have food and drink fetched at once."

"Rejoice," I said in greeting.

"Master, we are in mourning," the slave said, "and your father—"

"No matter," the boy said, "hospitality supersedes all things, you know that! And we need to take a break from our grieving! They've been at it for days, wailing, wailing." Now that the gate was closed behind me I began to hear it, a faint keening from the women's quarters of the palace. "Come in, come in. Oh, stop fussing, gatekeeper; you know Father will whip us both if we don't treat guests properly, mourning or no mourning."

The old man shambled off.

I looked about me. It was a mean, miserable palace. Although it had not been ravaged by fire like my grandfather's, it had not been kept up well: all the flagstones of the courtyard were broken and many were missing; the paint on the columns was peeling; scaffolding showed in the awning over the entrance to the inner court. The boy took me by the hand and led me within, chattering constantly. "I suppose it's not seemly for me to be the first to greet you, but I heard the pounding and I couldn't stop myself. Are you a bard? But you're not carrying any kind of instrument. Maybe you're a prince . . . fleeing from some blood feud . . . chased by the Furies perhaps!"

"Something like that," I said.

"May I ask your name?"

"I am forbidden to speak it."

At this the boy's eyes widened. He let go my hand as if he'd been stung, bolted up the steps at the far end of the court, shouting, "Mother, Mother, it's him, I know it, I know it!"

I realized then who the child must be: Neoptolemos's bastard, my brother. How could I kill the father of my mother's child? I had come for revenge, that was my sacred duty, yet . . . now he had gone to fetch his mother. My mother. For thirteen years I had rehearsed the recognition scene. I imagined it with all sorts of different landscapes in the background: palaces, graveyards, groves. I imagined her coy reluctance to believe, as I presented evidence upon evidence of my true identity. I imagined the smile that would burst out on her face, like the accelerated blooming of a flower in the sun, her eyes shining as on the day we stood, we three, my father and she and I, on the ramparts, Hector's helmet like the sun, the gorgon-faced shield, the gleaming sword. . . . I wanted that day back so badly.

And now a woman was coming down the steps.

She could not be my mother. She was haggard and her dark hair straggly and lusterless. She came slowly toward me. No, it was not Andromache. I knew my mother would look older, but nothing could transform her into a different woman. . . .

"You are welcome, stranger," she said to me when our eyes were level. "I bid you rejoice."

The boy followed her down the steps.

"This is my son Pergamos. I understand you have no name."

A terrible bitterness seized me. "Don't you recognize me?" I shouted. I shook her by the shoulders; she cried out. "Don't you know me? Even though I've lost my name, I still am the one you lost—"

She stopped, looked deep into my eyes. "Oh, are you, are you? The one I dream of. No. Oh, no, no. He is dead."

"It was not I who died—it was a slave who took my place. You didn't recognize him because his brains were spewing out all over his face, but it was Leontes, Leontes!" Pergamos was staring at us in bewilderment. This was not the meeting the boy had planned for us, it seemed.

The old woman said, "A boy . . . brains spewing . . . no, his name was not Leontes, it was . . . Pielos! Pielos!"

"Mother, you're making a scene," Pergamos said. Again he took my hand, unnerving me by his friendliness, and led

me a little out of earshot. Then he said to me, "She's mad,
I'm afraid." He looked sadly at me. "You've got to protect
me from her if you can, now that Father's gone off on some
crazed mission. . . . They're both mad, I tell you!"

I looked at the boy, feeling an uncomfortable mixture of
love and loathing. I wanted to tell him that I was his brother,
but how would he react? I was his father's enemy. And
perhaps he would not even believe me, because I could not
speak my name. "Who is Pielos?" I said at last.

"Pielos was my little brother. He was killed a few days
ago. No one knows how." I saw that he had not quite come
to terms with this loss; he was acting almost flippant about it.
He was hoping it would all go away. He said, "He was
found outside the citadel walls. His brains had been dashed
out. The women know who did it, but they won't say.
Something is brewing. I don't know what. Father went to
Delphi with some loyal Myrmidons, to see if the Pythoness
could tell us something."

"Are you scared?" I said.

"No, of course not!" he said. Then, "Yes. I'm terrified. I
think I know who did it." He looked at his mother. She was
still standing in the same place, her eyes closed, rocking
slowly from side to side; now and then a word escaped her
lips. I did not know the language. "She's been learning to
talk the Lady's talk," he whispered. When I heard him use
the honorific for Snakemother, I became worried. It was
impossible for me to think of the woman as my mother.

At that moment, she cried out, whether in pain or ecstasy I
could not tell; and she flung herself upon me, embraced me.
At first I thought she recognized me at last, but then she
kissed me as lovers kiss, trying to thrust her tongue into my
mouth. I was mortified at such impiety. I knew the story of
Oedipus as well as any man. "You forget yourself!" I
shouted at the woman who was and was not my mother.

She turned and ran up the steps, her sobs echoing. Pergamos
said, "Don't worry, friend. It's part of her madness. She
thinks you're someone else. For weeks now she's been saying

that a nameless hero is going to come and wed her and become the new king. I don't even think it's really her speaking; I think it's the Lady speaking through her."

"Yes. She's possessed." Only by telling myself that could I accept that this shell of a woman was my mother. But deep inside I knew that this was the second time she had failed to recognize me. And I remembered Memnon's prophecy—that my name would be the first name given me in the new land. I had assumed that I would get my real name back as soon as my mother saw me. That was not to be.

"Come," Pergamos said, "I'll take you to your quarters. You're not to see the funeral arrangements; we're not to impose our grief on guests, you know that. It'll be evening soon, and we should eat."

"Pergamos—" I almost revealed myself to him. But how could I?

He led me up the staircase. The structure of the upper level was similar to that of Priam's palace, but there was much that was wood where Priam's had been stone. We turned into a cell of a room, with a window overlooking an olive grove; the walls were brightened by a painting of young boys diving into the sea. I was delighted by the colors: the azure of the sky and the deep green sea and the clay-red skin of the boys. The artist had sketched smiles into their faces with a wavy line of black paint, and dolphins cavorted among the waves. "It is a lovely room," I said.

"Yes, isn't it? We shared it once, my brother and I." He pulled a pallet from a heap of broken furniture and toys. "For you. I know the slaves should be doing all this, but . . . well, they're mostly out farming now; we haven't kept many domestics. Our treasury was depleted by the war . . . You know, *the* war?"

"I know of it," I said.

"Tonight you're going to tell me all about your adventures, aren't you? It's been lonely without Pielos these past days. I miss him, I'm afraid," he added apologetically, as if the admission robbed him of appropriate manliness.

I was in a quandary. I would have preferred to sleep alone.

I had to rethink my strategy. Would I remain here at Phthia until Neoptolemos returned from the oracle? But the longer I remained, the longer I would have to face the specter that my mother had become. And the boy, so lonely, innocently demanding my affection, my mother's son and my own half brother and the son of my greatest foe . . . I could easily resist a bombardment of hate, but could I fend off an assault of love? But there was one advantage in having another person in my room. If my mother, in her madness, should try to come to me in the shape of Snakemother and try to make me her consort. . . .

It was unthinkable! But I might have to defend myself against my own mother.

From far away there came the hollow pounding of a drum. It put me in mind of funerals.

"Oh, don't look so panic-stricken," Pergamos said, laughing. "That's the dinner signal. Come down with me and I'll introduce you to the others."

As we descended the main staircase, I heard once again from the women's quarters the rhythmic ululation that one hears only in times of death. I wanted to get away from the palace that very moment, but I knew that I could not. It was beginning to rain, and clouds covered the sunset. As we stepped into the main hall, it began to rain in full force, and the hall was dark and soggy. A slave came in and lit a few torches.

Outside, the rain pelted down, and rivulets of water were seeping in through the door seams. There was only one chair. It was of ebony crusted with gold; inlaid into the gold was a hunting scene in silver. I recognized the chair; they had stolen it from my grandfather's palace. I was ashamed to see it there. But Pergamos was innocently and earnestly motioning to me to sit there, and I could not refuse. He squatted on the matting next to me, using my footstool as a pillow. I watched the moisture beading on the stone walls. We did not speak to each other.

Chapter XVII

The Consort of the Night

"Well," Pergamos said awkwardly, "I'm sorry our banqueting hall is so—"

"Don't worry about it," I said. I knew that even in Troy things were not as they used to be.

"Shall we wait for Mother?" said the young prince. "Or shall we begin?" In the distance, the choral ululation of the women. "Oh, they are still mourning. I've ordered them to wait until you're asleep, but . . ." He smiled a smile of forced cheerfulness.

Presently a few flabby old men joined us. "They are Myrmidons," Pergamos told me. He referred, of course, to the fabled fighters whom Akhilleus had brought with him to our gates. I could not believe they could be the same men whom I had glimpsed through the chinks in the crenellations of Troy's ramparts, ablaze with bronze armor, screaming their terrifying war paean, sweeping behind Akhilleus's chariot like fire ants overrunning a corpse. I smiled politely. "But you don't want to talk about the war," Pergamos continued. "I understand. You *are* from Troy, aren't you? I could tell by the Luvian words in your dialect. That's why you won't give your name."

"Am I so transparent?" I said as they began to place food before us: a rack of roast lamb, loaves of bread into which figs had been baked, and a stew of hare meat and onions.

"You needn't be so worried we'll have you killed, or something," the boy said. As the senior member of the royal family present, he was mixing the wine and water for me in a golden krater. He was doing it sloppily, and spilled some on the rushes. I only noticed because I remembered my grandfather once scolding Uncle Troilos for the same offense. "The war's over, I mean for good, and none of us can afford another one, right? For all I know, you and I are related; my mother is Trojan, after all."

"Cilician," I corrected him testily. "Andromache is the daughter of Eëtion, King of Cilicia, whom your grandfather Akhilleus killed as he raged up and down the Phrygian coastline, destroying Troy's allies."

Pergamos stared at me. "So it *is* a blood feud of some kind that brings you here," he said at last.

Constrained by the rules of guest-friendship, I could not exactly lie, though I could of course evade the question. I said, "Yes, in a way."

"Are you planning to kill me?" the boy said, holding a gold-chased wine cup up to my lips. "If so, you are offending grievously against our hospitality." The two old Myrmidons moved slightly, getting ready to protect their prince. They were old and unarmed; it would have been a pathetic battle.

I took the drink; accepting it seemed to me to be a commitment. I said to myself, I will end the blood feud with the death of Neoptolemos. Somehow. My brother will not kill me and I will not kill my brother. I said, "Of course I don't mean you any harm, Pergamos."

"You don't have to mean it to cause it," Pergamos said with surprising wisdom. "Look at my parents! They are both mad."

At that moment Andromache entered the chamber.

Again I looked into my mother's face. I could no longer deny that it was Andromache, for she wore the raiment of a queen, and her pinched, withered face was caked with a chalky paste that lent it unnatural whiteness; kohl darkened her eyes, and her lips were stained with the juice of crushed pomegranates. The light was dim in the dining hall, and for a few seconds she projected the illusion of young Andromache. Then I saw the cracks in the chalk, like the fissures in the murals on the walls of my bedroom in Troy. She smiled at me. She was not a monster; it would have been easier to reject her if she had become one. But she still did not recognize me, and though there was no reason for her to, a part of me believed—and will always believe—that her rejection of me was willful.

"Rejoice, stranger," she said. One of the Myrmidons brought in another chair for her. It did not match mine; its legs were the paws of lions, inlaid with silver. "I am sorry I was so . . . forward, earlier. I have no shame anymore. How can I? It's a consequence of being a war concubine. I had great riches once; did you know I was to be Queen of Troy? Tell me, stranger, have you heard of Troy?"

She sat down and nibbled delicately on a piece of bread smothered with the stew. I said, "I have, Princess."

"She's much more lucid than usual," Pergamos whispered in my ear.

She said, "From queen to slave is far to fall, no? But I bear with it. I lost my palace and my gold and my virile, beautiful husband and my fine clothes. All I have left is this withered, wrinkled cunt. Gateway to a barren womb. It wasn't always barren! Look at the sons I bore the man who raped me."

"I'm all you have now, Mother," Pergamos said, sounding suddenly like a little boy. "Remember? You've been grieving all day."

"Where is Pielos? Where is . . . Oh, I remember, I remember, the brains bursting . . . Have you seen a man crush an egg in his fist? That was my son's head! Oh, Pielos, Pielos! How I loved you! Ah, me, pheu, pheu!" Shrieking out the traditional cries of lament, she seized a dagger from the dining table and cut off another plait of her hair and flung it on the floor. A skinny dog, thinking it was food, ran under the table to worry at it.

I wanted to say, "Mother, I am here, your lost son . . . I can end your grieving." But something stopped me from speaking. She had to know me by her own intuition, or the magic would not release me.

Instead it was the boy who calmed her with a single half-pleading, half-reproving "Mother." Andromache returned

to her seat and my brother p(ured me more wine. My mother
sat in silence.

Trying to change the subject, Pergamos chattered on: "Our
friend is traveling on a mission of blood feud, Mother. But it
doesn't concern us. Shall we have our Myrmidons help him?
Or should I wait for Father to come back before committing
our men?"

I could not help wincing at the irony, but dared not speak
yet.

"But then," Pergamos went on, "Father may be full of
the latest prophecies. Stranger, you've found out about the
man with no name who will come and free my mother. Then
there's the one my father is very much taken with. It says he
should only find happiness if he settle in a city with a roof of
lambswool, walls of wood, and foundations of iron!"

"Iron?" I said.

"Iron! You don't know of iron?"

"Of course I've heard of it," I said. "It's a fabulous
metal."

"More than fabulous! Let me show you something." He
pulled a small dagger from his chiton and handed it to me.

I toyed with it for a moment. It must be magical, I
realized, because it was harder even than Hector's two-edged
phasganon. It was a plain weapon with not the slightest
ornamentation; clearly the substance it was made from was
simply too hard to admit elaborate intaglio.

"It's remarkable," I said. "But—"

"Well. Iron, as I said. We've been getting a lot of it
lately, since the end of the war; it seems not to be as fabulous
as it once was. There was a time when it only fell from the
sky."

A thought flashed through my head: the stone that fell
from the sky, the black stone of Skyfather! In the third of my
precognitive dreams it had transformed itself into something
gleaming, hard, deadly. Was that what it meant, then?

I barely paid attention to what Pergamos was saying: something to do with a shipment of iron speartips that the Myrmi-

dons had started to use, that the metal came, some said, from the north, others from the east. Everywhere they said it came from somewhere else.

At that moment Andromache laughed: a shrill piercing witch's cackle. She rose from her chair and swept out of the chamber, murmuring, "It is time for more tears now, more and more tears"; but she did not weep, she only screeched with laughter.

I saw that my brother, seated at my feet, was trembling. He was in the grip of some terrible emotion, rage or grief or terror. "Don't be afraid, little brother," I said softly.

"Why do you call me that?" he said, staring at me with huge gray eyes that were starting to stream with tears.

"I don't know." I wanted to cry too, but I clenched my tears back for his sake, for he needed someone strong.

Dinner did not last long after that; a bard sang some dreary scenes from an epic (it was the story of Penthesileia, queen of the Amazons, who had fought in the war on our side, and her love for Akhilleus her sworn enemy) during which the Myrmidons nodded off. Since Pergamos was my host, I had to wait for him. He wanted to talk, but I had nothing to say. It was as if he were trying to put off the night for as long as he could. At last, when he had exhausted his repertory of small talk, he conducted me upstairs. He placed his sleeping pallet beside mine. Outside, it was raining still. A lamp burned.

He sat by the window and stared outside.

"Aren't you sleepy?" I said. I wanted him to go to sleep so that I could lie awake planning my next move.

He seemed to be waiting for some signal from outside, for he kept craning his neck to look farther out. Presently he seemed satisfied, and blew out the lamp. But he still sat there.

It was I, who needed the time to make my plans, who fell asleep. I was weary from my five days' walk, and this was the first time since I arrived in the land of the Akhaians that I had been given a proper bed.

As I slid into sleep, I thought, At least I will dream of vengeance; perhaps the gods will send me some solution to these new dilemmas.

Instead I dreamt the happiest dreams I had had since childhood. I dreamt of cool glades and clear skies, of nuzzling between my mother's warm breasts, of running after Hector across the palace roof, skipping so that my bare feet would stay in his shadow, off the hot stones.

When I awoke it was still night. "Pergamos," I said, "why are you waking me now?" I clasped the hand that shook my shoulder. It was coarse, callused, a slave's hand. Had Neoptolemos returned in the night? Was I being dragged away to be killed?

I wrestled with the figure, a thin, pathetic figure who clawed at me. It had to be a boy! "Pergamos!" I shouted. I dragged my assailant to the window, where starlight shone brightly, for the rain had quieted to a drizzle. There was cloth over the face, I ripped it off, and—

"Andromache!"

She gripped me hard. She was my mother. I could not just break her arm. Harshly she whispered, "Oh, my husband, oh, my Hector. Fill me with your seed, seed me with your passion." I could not bear it. I threw her down.

She crawled to me, clasped my knees in supplication. "Pergamos, where are you?" I shouted. The boy was nowhere to be seen. My mother began to caress my thighs, to dribble against my phallos. To my horror I began to experience a slight arousal. Shame flooded me. I cried out, "Why, why? Don't you know me? Why did you never know me? Not today, not thirteen years ago. . . ." I slapped down my erection; the white paint of her face was caking on my pubic hair.

"I do know you. I knew you the moment you stepped into this house. . . . Oh, you, young and burnished by sweat and sun, you're my husband come back to me from the dead. Oh, Hector, you've come to set me free. . . . Are you angry with me because I lay with the man who killed your father? Will you beat me? Oh, beat me, but free me. Time has not changed you at all, my dearest husband. . . . Oh, make love to me, I want to have a child. Our child was killed, his head dashed against the . . . Do you know, they're saying *I* did it?''

"Oh, Mother, slavery has driven you mad." I tried to embrace her chastely, remembering how often I had acted out this scene in my fantasies. I kissed her cheek, the paint flaking on my lips, but she tried to turn the kiss into an erotic one.

"I didn't kill Pielos. Was there another one? I forget. But you are so handsome. Have you just come from the battle-field? You will be wanting a bath; I'll have the servants . . . Bath! The golden axe!" Her eyes became like fire. "I will cleave you asunder, man who dares to violate my image!''

"Snakemother has possessed you, Mother. I have come to take you home, not to make love to you. . . .''

"Liar!" She spat in my face. "I will kill the king.''

"Mother—''

"You call me Mother, title of the Lady. You will impregnate me and die in the spring! So it has always been. I am your mother, wife, and sister.''

I flung her from me then. "No! In the name of Skyfather—''

She wailed then, like a pig about to have its throat slit. "That cursed name," she cried out, and then ran into the corridor.

I heard her lurching footsteps and her dying laughter. I had to do something! "Mother!" I screamed as I ran behind her into the lightless hallway.

I collided with a wall. I cursed. It was pitch black here, but I could hear Andromache's padding footsteps somewhere. I had to stop her, to remonstrate with her, to smash through the barrier of her insanity. Clumsily I felt my way along the wall. I was still naked, and the stones had scoured my side. There was a staircase . . . yes. Somewhere below, light. I half ran, half slid toward the source of illumination, a faint

rectangle of yellowish light. A shadow flitted across it. I
reached the bottom of the stairs. I was in the megaron of the
palace; servants and dogs were sleeping on mats on the floor.
Light from the courtyard shone dimly through the great door,
half open, and through gaps in the ceiling.

I stepped cautiously over the sleepers; I did not want them
to think I was an interloper. I listened. Snoring; and outside,
the stridulating of insects after rain. Above the noises . . .

Wailing. Women's voices. And the muffled knell of death
drums. I turned in its direction. It was from the women's
quarters, I was sure of it. It was not quite seemly for me to
go invading, but I could not help myself. Standing naked,
shivering in a room of sleepers, I was haunted by the distant
music, with its plangent yowlings interspersed with meander-
ing chants. I crossed the hall to the outside court, stealing a
cloak that lay on the floor to cover myself, and followed the
music. It was all mixed up in the wind: the singing, the grief
shrieks, the drumbeats, the insects, the frogs, the birds of
darkness.

A gateway to an inner court; I saw fire. An altar. And
gathered around it, women beating their breasts and singing.
Grave goods were piled up in a miniature, boy-sized chariot,
beside an unlit pyre of cedar logs.

I saw Pergamos now. He wore a robe of mourning. And
then I saw, resting on a shield—not a bronze shield like my
father's, but a common shield of cowhide on a wooden
frame—a small boy's corpse. The finery he was clothed in
emphasized his broken, bloody features. Even as I watched
him he was rotting.

Pergamos saw me and came up to me.

He said, "You needn't come, stranger. I hoped to spare
you the sight of our suffering; it is dishonorable to inflict our
private pain on guests."

I said, "Why are you burning him? We only burn our dead
in times of war."

He said, "Since the Akhaians returned from Troy we have
always burned our dead. My Myrmidons explained it to me:

they said, in the old days people were comforted to know that their ancestors were always with them, in the ground or immured in their houses. Now they're afraid of the dead. The dead keep demanding things: you've heard, maybe, how my grandfather Akhilleus wanted Polyxena sacrificed to him?''

"My father was burned when he died.''

"Was he a great hero? Are you here to avenge his death?''

"I don't know!" I said bitterly.

We watched as the body of my youngest brother was placed at the top of the pyre. The wailing crescendoed. One by one attendants placed the funerary gifts on the pyre. My brother went down too. The little chariot was now empty. An old man brought two colts into the courtyard and tethered them to stone posts near the pyre. Solemnly he yoked them to the chariot. Another servant brought in four spoked wheels of figwood, and hammered on tires of copper; then he attached them to the chariot. A wooden image of a charioteer was set within it, and a small quiver with arrows tipped in gold and a bow and a tiny two-edged phasganon of silver—all useless weapons but exquisitely crafted.

I went to stand beside Pergamos. He whispered to me, through his tears, again, "You were not to know of this; we set the funeral for nighttime so that you would never know. . . .''

The colts stood still. They showed no fear; I think they had been drugged. A priest gave Pergamos a torch; then, with a sickle, he slit the throats of the horses. Blood spattered our clothes; my hair and face were drenched in it. Pergamos did not seem to notice, but kicked at the colts until they stumbled into the pyre itself, buckling ungracefully onto the woodpile as they died. Then, looking away, he tossed the torch into the pyre. "You must look!" the priest said, for the torch had rolled onto the stone. Pergamos turned, dived after it, hefted it, and ran halfway up the pyre, trampling on the corpses of the colts, to plant it firmly. Then he ran to me, never once looking back, as the flames soared, fragrant with cedar and rare oils, toward the embrace of Skyfather.

I saw him, frail, skull-eyed, his body racked with sobs.
"Pergamos," I said.
Slowly he came to me.
"Give me the iron dagger for a moment," I said.
He handed it to me dully. I used it to saw off a plait of my
hair. It cut right through with no effort; I marveled at the
metal and wondered what it would have been like to fight the
war with weapons of iron instead of bronze. "What are you
doing?" Pergamos said. "He was no kin to you." I could
see he was moved by my expression of grief. "Not even my
mother would come to the funeral, in the end, but you did."
I returned the dagger to him. "Your mother . . ." What
had happened was so unthinkable that I had been trying to
exorcise it from my consciousness. "What your mother just
did—"
"I think I know. Well, would it have been so bad?" he
said.
"Bad. Yes, bad."
But at that moment about a dozen women came from
within the women's quarters. One of them was my mother. I
cried out her name; she saw me and shouted, "Hector,
Hector." The women swayed. There was something menacing about the way they moved, all in unison, like soldiers.
Shrieking, my mother sprinted toward the mourners. I do not
know whether she was trying to immolate herself or to wreak
havoc. The other women rushed forward too. They all had
daggers. Or were they snakes? Sometimes I saw metal glint-
ing, sometimes I saw serpentine writhing.
Pergamos lifted his dagger. "We need help," I said.
"Pollution of the sacred rites," the priest was murmuring,
wringing his hands in horror. "If Pielos's shade is not properly appeased—"
More women were emerging from the palace now, all of
them clutching daggers or snakes, live ones, and clay ones. I
said to Pergamos, "We'd better get back to the megaron and
wake up some Myrmidons."
Pergamos and I ran back across the outer courtyard, through

the doorway of the main hall. It was darker here, and smelled of death. "Wake up," Pergamos was squealing desperately, kicking and shoving the men who slept.

They did not move.

I knelt down by the nearest one. "He's dead." For my hands had slid into a puddle of warm blood.

"What are we going to do? Are they all dead, all, all, all?"

Quickly I felt a few other bodies. They rolled over, crashed into one another. "Listen," I said. "Listen carefully."

"There's no sound in here. Nothing."

The silence chilled me. "No one is snoring," I said.

"That means—"

"Yes. They're all dead."

Footsteps now from outside. "Help me with the door!" Pergamos said. Together we strained against it, pushing it tight, latching it. "This is the only entrance to this part of the building," he said. "Unless they climb up to the roof and lower themselves through the windows."

A babble of voices by the door, and then . . . the clang of metal on metal. "Is it a battle?" I whispered.

"I don't know. But I can't let them in . . . because I can't fight her. If I injure her, if I become a matricide . . ."

He did not have to continue. I knew that the Erinyes come to hound those whose hands are polluted with a mother's blood. He would go mad. I could not fight her either, and for the same reason; nor could I permit the abomination of incest. We sat together by the door, waiting for something to happen.

As time passed, the air became dank; the bodies were festering. I could hear flies buzzing in the dark. Some settled on my face; I shook my head. "I'm not dead yet!" I muttered.

Beside me, Pergamos sobbed to himself. "This shouldn't happen to you," I said softly, taking him in my arms. "You're just a child. You shouldn't have to face these things, not yet. There's not even a war going on."

"I'm not a child," he said, still sobbing. "I'm a prince, maybe a king. If my father doesn't come back . . . a king!"

I had heard those words before. I had spoken them myself, to ward off my fear of the dark. I knew his torment well. "Cry if you want," I said. "I understand, I really do."

"How can you?"

"I understand." I could tell that weariness was overcoming him. The sounds still raged outside, but for the moment we were safe. His body went limp in my arms. "I understand, little brother," I said very softly, and kissed him on the cheek.

Half asleep, he murmured, "I wish it were true, I wish we really were brothers." Not moving, we both slept, huddled in a corner of this chamber of the dead.

Chapter XVIII

The Road to Delphi

There came a pounding at the doorway. Pergamos jerked awake and stepped away from me; I stirred and saw the room, sunlit now. There were bodies everywhere; already the fetor of decomposition was intolerable. The pounding went on.

A man's voice: "My prince, let us in, let us in!"

"It's Xanthos," said Pergamos, "the priest." He moved to unlatch the door. "Help me."

I was suspicious. "It might be a trick."

They were forcing the door now, twisting a spear shaft into the side, battering it with some device. "It will be too late soon anyway," said Pergamos.

The door gave way. Men came charging in, old men in ill-fitting armor with their green-crusted swords upraised.

The priest, bearded, his robe still bloody from last night's sacrifice, stood behind the soldiers. "My prince," he said at last. "This catastrophe is . . . so appalling . . . I don't know. . . ."

"Where is Andromache?" I asked.

He regarded me coldly. I was a stranger; I should not have been the one to ask. Perhaps he even considered me the cause of the incident, for Andromache had hurled herself at me in full view of the mourners. "Answer him, Xanthos," Pergamos said. I had to admire him; he had not buckled under the strain. "I too want to hear."

"But so many men here . . . murdered in their sleep. . . ."

"They did not fight back," I said. "Doubtless they thought their assailants, being *only* women, were harmless. Perhaps even wives and mothers were involved."

"Andromache and a few other women left the women's quarters in ruins last night. They burned part of the granaries. Now they've bolted, all of them. And we've hardly any men here; the best of them are with the king, on the road to Delphi. It was ill-omened to cremate the young prince; I warned Andromache of it. It has driven her mad."

"She was mad long before that," I said.

"You seem to know a lot, for a stranger," the priest said.

I remained silent, not wanting to reveal more about myself than I could help. "Any idea where the women might have gone to?" Pergamos said.

"Delphi," the priest said, shaking his head.

"Delphi? They've gone to consult the oracle? But my father is already on his way back, or should be by now." He was fully composed now, a prince through and through; last night's hysterical weeping seemed forgotten. I was proud of him.

Xanthos said, "My prince, as Andromache and her frenzied helpers ran through the palace, they were heard to scream out, 'I go to kill the king now! I go to rend him limb from limb!' They were drunk, my prince, wildly drunk; twenty amphorai of wine are missing from the warehouse."

"I will go after them," I said at last.

They looked at me oddly. "Why?" Pergamos said at last.

I could not tell them the truth: that I still wanted to save my mother if I could, and I still needed to find Neoptolemos. I hated him more than ever now. It was he who had brought my mother to this. It was a hatred that my love for my newfound half brother could not mitigate. Instead, I said, "I have an obligation to you and yours, in the name of guest-friendship; you have received me, and I must give you a gift in return." I had to phrase this carefully, because if I overestimated the value of my return gift, it could be seen as a slur on their hospitality. I said, "There is little I can give which you do not already have; but my help I can give freely, intangible though the gift be."

The priest and the Myrmidons understood this. Satisfied, Xanthos nodded. "You are young and can perhaps overtake them before they do something to the king."

"Perhaps."

"But perhaps," the priest said, "you don't quite know how dangerous the road to Delphi is."

"It is a shrine sacred to Apollo; surely no one will attack me on the road!"

"You don't understand. Long before Skyfather and his sons ruled this land, Delphi was sacred to the Lady, who is now become Snakemother. It is the Omphalos, the navel of the universe. At Delphi the Lady was called Pytho; it is the central source of her power. There are bands of women roving the mountains; they are all bound for Delphi. There is a battle being waged for possession of Mount Parnassos, you see, a battle between the Dragon and the son of Skyfather. . . ."

My second dream! The serpent coiled around the mountain! I trembled, knowing now how inexorable fate had led me to this palace, to this meeting, to the aftermath of this hideous massacre.

"The omens indicate that all this may be coming to a head," said Xanthos.

"I will go," I said. "Supply me those of your men who are not grown too old and fat, Pergamos, and I will try to get word to Neoptolemos, and to save Andromache." I did not tell him that this would be a perfect opportunity to see Neoptolemos, and that after I gave him the message I would contrive to kill him. Would the death of her brutish slavemaster break the spell that gripped her? It was my only hope.

"I'll go with you," Pergamos said.

The others gasped. I panicked for a moment. I could not have him present if I was going to kill Neoptolemos! I tried to stall. "You're too impetuous, too young . . . you're needed here besides. You said only yesterday you might have to be king. You must be safe."

"Why?" Pergamos said. "You're a prince, aren't you? Maybe even a king. I saw it in your eyes, last night, when you told me you understood me. I knew you weren't just making sympathetic noises. If you can risk danger, I can too."

"It's too impractical."

"No. It's a twenty-day walk to Delphi, and Neoptolemos has chariots. But Delphi's an important place, not like Phthia. The roads are well kept up; by chariot, you could overtake the women easily. Have one brought in from the warehouse, Doron," he commanded one of the Myrmidons. Impressed by his imperiousness, they all stood to attention, and Doron scurried off. "You'll need a charioteer," Pergamos said to me. "It's as simple as that."

"Why you? Don't you have some slave, some groom, who—"

"I know our horses best. Besides, if you don't do as I say, I'll make you tell me your name."

Since there was no question of that, and he put it in the form of a violation of hospitality, I was forced to accede.

In an hour all was ready. The sun was high as we drove down from the citadel. The road was mud at first; after we rounded the first hill, the paved road began, and we picked up speed. It soon became evident to me that Pergamos had not overstated his talent as a charioteer; the horses moved swiftly, in perfect rhythm, never deviating from the road. We drove on till nightfall, pausing only to piss by the roadside or to drink from a stream.

As the sun set, we stopped at a little wayside shrine to offer up prayers to Skyfather. Pergamos tethered the horses and we entered the grove together. "Look," he said.

Such shrines usually have a stylized stone pillar or phallos; the Akhaians call them herms. But here there was no such thing above the altar. I found the herm lying on the grass, smashed. "How could anyone be so impious?" I said.

And on the altar itself, a crude terra-cotta figure of an obscenely fat woman, her breasts grossly exaggerated. There were words scrawled on the altar in dried blood; the words, I realized, were "Thetis" and "Semele"; I knew them for titles of Snakemother. In front of it were votive objects I was unfamiliar with—men woven from dried cornstalks, a small bloody fleshy object, which I assumed was some kind of meat offering . . .

"It's a human phallos," Pergamos said tonelessly.

I remembered the messenger I had sent down to the dark country—how his phallos had been torn out by the roots, and he himself turned to stone. If Akhenaten's ship had not sailed into the harbor, that man would still be a statue. I said, "Snakemother's worshipers have been here."

He said, "Let's drive on. I'm afraid to sleep. If we don't stop, we'll leave the madwomen far behind, and we'll have plenty of time to warn Father."

"Travel in the dark?"

"The road is fairly straight; the horses know it well. And it's a full moon."

We went on. The constant pounding of hooves on the paving stones kept me from nodding off. Pergamos drove as though possessed. In the moonlight he resembled a statue.

Dawn broke. A mountain towered from the morning mist, blood-colored in the rising sun. It was so tall, I felt I had reached a wall at the end of the world. As we approached, it seemed to rise higher and higher, its gray-white peak impaling the lowering sky. Far away I heard thunder.

"Parnassos," Pergamos said. "The most sacred place in the universe."

As the chariot slowed, he pointed halfway up the mountain. "Can you see the shrine?"

"No."

"It's perfectly blended with the mountain. It's not a great big temple that you build to boast about how your god is bigger and better than your neighboring city's. The shrine goes into the earth itself, into a vaporous cavern."

It was the mountain of my dream, but infinitely more huge. "I saw this mountain in a vision," I said, "but a snake was coiled around it."

"Yes. You will see."

I did. I could not tell if it was real or just a trick of the light, or whether it was a swath of trees that ringed the mountain, their leaves catching the dawn like bronze scales of a monster serpent. I said, "So it's true. The Trojan War is over, but the war between the gods goes on."

"Till the end of time."

"Does it? Is there no way to end it at all?"

He had no answer. We drove in silence toward Parnassos. At length Pergamos said, "I see Neoptolemos's tents ahead!"

"Where?" For I saw nothing.

He kept pointing, and I kept squinting. As I looked at the mountain that filled the sky, I still could not tell if the coiling serpent was a phantom. No tents, but . . . there was something: a streak of gray across the serpent's belly, the gray-green grass. Tents? How could he tell?

"Gray for tents," he said. "Woollen canopies. My father never dyes his tents; he says it's ostentatious. I can't wait for you to meet him; I hope you'll tell him how brave I was, not how I cried last night."

"Of course," I said, stalling uneasily. He quirted the flanks of the horses and urged them to go faster. "Delphi!" he cried. "Delphi, Delphi!"

Chapter XIX

The City of Wood, Wool, and Iron

Of course, we had to leave the chariot at a sanctuary near the bottom of the mountain before continuing our ascent of Parnassos on foot. Neoptolemos's tents were about halfway to the oracle itself. The coiling dragon had disappeared as we began actually to climb the winding pathway. Here and there were steps, carved into the rock. After a couple of hours' climb I was giddy. It was close to noon. The face of the mountain burned my eyes, and the wind too was like fire . . . the breath of the dragon. I felt a subtle wrongness in the air.

Pergamos was scrambling on ahead; he was anxious to see his father. I followed. The sheer scale of Parnassos oppressed me, as did my secret fear of encountering the fate I had chosen out for myself.

After a time we reached a level area where several parties had encamped; I saw the gray tents of Neoptolemos, which Pergamos had seen from so far off, and tents of other colors too, from other delegations doubtless. One tent had Egyptian hieroglyphs painted on its sides, and its flaps were painted with two eyes. I wondered whether Memnon had followed me somehow; I half expected him to come forth and greet me on his litter borne by blue men. But I saw no one come forth from the tents, and Pergamos was urging me on toward his father's. The wind blew incessantly, disturbingly.

I had no weapon except the small bronze dagger I carried strapped to my chiton. I would have to be careful how I killed Neoptolemos; if I challenged him in an honorable and heroic manner, perhaps we would be able to fight, one to one, to the death.

Pergamos lifted the flap of the main tent; we entered. The

150

wind was immediately blocked out, though we could hear its
roaring; inside, the heat was stifling. Through the translucent
woollen canopy there came a ruddy half-light. On the other
side of the tent, flanked by more of the old Myrmidons, these
ones in little better physical condition than the ones he had
left behind in Phthia, was Neoptolemos.

I recognized him at once, though he was older now. He sat
on a magnificent throne; it too had been stolen from Troy. Its
arms were winged, in the Hittite fashion, and coated with
gold; each feather was shadowed in lapis lazuli. His eyes . . .
I had not forgotten his eyes in all this time. But the throne
seemed to dwarf him. He seemed haunted; he was only a
shadow of Akhilleus's reputation. When he spoke it was
haltingly, like a much older man. He said to Pergamos (I had
to strain to catch his words), "My son." Pergamos ran
forward to kiss his father.

"Father," he said, "I've brought a friend."

"Oh? Who is he?"

I glowered at him, focused hard with my mind, tried to
force the memory of our earlier meeting into his consciousness. But he did not react; or if he knew, he gave no hint of
it. Pergamos said, "I don't know his name, but he has been
very good to me. He is a traveler; I think he comes from
Phrygia. He calls me his little brother."

"You had a brother once," Neoptolemos said. "I do not
like to remember what happened to him." He motioned me
to approach. I did, never taking my eyes off his face. This
was my enemy. I had to feel the old hatred, I had to! Or my
life till now would have been lived in vain. "He would have
been about your age. Are you, perhaps . . ." He closed his
eyes, searching out the remembrance. "There was a slave
boy . . . who kept insisting he was the prince. You are not,
by some strange twist of fate . . . ? But that's impossible."

"You do remember me," I said. That was all I could say,
for I could not say my name.

"It was all a long time ago," Neoptolemos said, "and
most of it does not bear remembering." I was surprised, for I

remembered him exultant in his victory. He had killed King Priam as a boy might torture a toad. I steeled myself. I had to harden my heart, for I knew that the vengeance I was about to take was proper and sanctified by the gods. He went on, "But why are you here?"

"Mother's gone mad," Pergamos said. "She and a group of wild women killed a lot of the men in the palace and fled. They're coming to Delphi, maybe to kill you."

"Or perhaps to witness the great battle?"

"Battle?" I said, thinking, hubristically, I know now, that he perhaps referred to the duel that he and I were fated to fight.

"Yes. It's a fine show: every night the cosmic battle between Apollo and the dragon Pytho over who shall possess the truth. I don't really understand it myself. I came here only to consult the oracle; I didn't know there was a struggle going on." Then, remembering his duties as a host, he said to an attendant, "Run along, you! See to it that this fellow gets food and wine."

"I'm not hungry, King," I said.

Silence fell: complete, stunned. Pergamos's jaw dropped open. He jabbed me sharply in the side, hoping, I think, that it was only my ignorance that had resulted in this appalling solecism. But he knew better; he had suspected me all along.

Neoptolemos turned in a rage to the nearest Myrmidon and seized one of the thrusting spears from his hand. He pointed it at me. The guards whirled round and drew their swords. The heat was unbearable. Sweat poured into my eyes.

"You disdain my hospitality," said the king. "However"—I felt him carefully measuring each word—"perhaps you don't understand how we do things here. Pergamos, have food and drink brought for our guest. At once."

"My lord, I am not hungry," I said again, belligerently. I was rather hungry, in fact, because we had not had time to bring supplies from Phthia; but if I had partaken of his food it would have been the grossest possible impiety for me to kill him. Of course, it would only have served him right for the

impiety he committed in Skyfather's temple thirteen years
before; but I did not want to descend to his level.

He considered for a time. Then he screamed, "Kill him!"
and the guards moved forward, raising their swords.

"No!" said Pergamos. "Father, don't! This is Parnassos.
This is holy ground. We can't go around killing people." I
stared at my brother in amazement.

"Pergamos," Neoptolemos said, quietly, menacingly, "this
is none of your business. When we get back to the city I am
going to beat you senseless. I promise it, by Zeus!" Then he
turned to me and said, with painfully exaggerated sweetness,
"My son is, of course, correct. It would be absolutely uncon-
scionable to pollute this most sacred spot with blood—especially
yours."

"But, Father . . . he has come to question the oracle! He's
been ordered to fast. Can't you see? He felt awkward, that's
all."

"Your powers of diplomacy," Neoptolemos said, "are
dangerously promising. Still, I can't help but think there's
something faintly unmanly about diplomacy. Very well, I
shall only beat you half senseless. But you know from experience that that's bad enough."

"Yes, Father."

"As for you, nameless stranger—"

At that moment we heard an immense din from outside the
tent. It sounded chillingly familiar—the high-pitched shrieks,
the rasping, animal chanting.

"They're here!" Pergamos shouted. "How did they get
here so fast? Unless some divine agency—"

Neoptolemos was shaking with rage. Still holding onto the
thrusting spear, he charged toward the tent opening, shouting
to me in passing, "I'll deal with you later—when we're off
sacred soil!" A ripping sound from all around us, the glint of
metal blades—they were shredding the tents and breaking in
from all directions!

Sunlight streamed in from a hundred rents in the wool,
crisscrossing the faces of Neoptolemos and the others, and

the wind came tearing in, whipping the floor rushes in our faces. Women stood all about us, dozens upon dozens. We were outnumbered. We all stood, unnerved, not believing we would have to fight armed and angry women. Then the daggers started to fly—daggers that shifted shape in midair and seemed to become writhing serpents. Pergamos grabbed my hand. "Quick, the throne!" he cried, and pushed me behind it. A dagger flew past me and imbedded itself in the earth beside me. I saw its snakeform waver and become metal, hard. I touched it and felt it pulsating beneath its inanimate surface and knew it for a magical object.

"Skyfather!" I whispered. "Father of my fathers—"

Now I recognized some of the women. There was the old queen of Alos, who had tried to stab her husband in full view of the court; there was the young queen who had helped me, but her eyes were slits of yellow now, and she hissed and I saw her tongue darting out and it was forked. And then I saw Andromache.

She was coming straight toward me. I put one arm around Pergamos and brandished my dagger with the other.

"Hector," she crooned. Her voice was like an owl's, melancholy, death-haunted. "Oh, I have found you. Oh, come possess my throne; oh, become the consort of the night." Her breath was rancid, like sour wine. I am sure she had drunk too much wine, and that she had not mixed it with water at all.

Her arms were outstretched to me; her bosom was bare, and I could see that a serpent twined itself about one of her breasts. I watched transfixed. I could do nothing. She was my mother. I could not defend myself. I said, "You're possessed. I have to get through to you and draw you out. This is a terrible madness that has gripped the whole world. I must heal you. . . ." But my mother came inexorably toward me and I could not flee.

"Andromache!" It was Neoptolemos. Horrified, he had seized her by the shoulders and spun her around.

"My son!" she cried. "My lover, my father. Why have I not killed you yet?" And she howled like a hungry wolf.

Others gathered and surrounded Neoptolemos. They were all moving toward him now, their eyes glazed over. I was reminded of the walking dead, the zumbi, of which Memnon had once told me. They swayed as they clustered around him; they paid no attention to me or Pergamos or the Myrmidons, some of whom lay dead with snakes crawling all over their corpses. The mob closed in; it seemed that they absorbed Neoptolemos into themselves. Then they moved in a herd, bursting through the tattered tent walls onto the mountain ledge.

"Should we follow them?" Pergamos said. "I'm afraid of—"

"Matricide." I hardly dared utter the obscene word.

"I have to save Father," he said.

"So do I," I said. For I still clung, somewhat desperately, to my original plan. I did not want a mob of madwomen to cheat me of my revenge.

"Where are they going?"

I looked outside. I could see them moving uphill; other groups were joining them. I could make out Neoptolemos. He was not dead, but was struggling violently. They were running up the mountainside with such alacrity that I knew that Snakemother had possessed their feet with unnatural speed. Some of the other tents had been torn up too, and one was burning. The only one that seemed untouched was the Egyptian one; it seemed that a powerful magic held it safe against all attack. Men were rushing out of the other tents, waving their weapons.

"Let's go after them now," my brother said.

"First . . ." I bent down among the dead bodies, trying to pry a weapon from a fist that was already beginning to harden.

Pergamos pulled a chest from behind the throne and opened it; he handed me a bow, took one for himself, and filled two quivers with arrows. I managed to loosen the dead Myrmidon's phasganon and used it to cut off another man's hand so as to free a second sword for Pergamos. I shook the hand off.

"Thank you," he said. Then, "I knew that man; he was at the sack of Troy."

"So was I."

"You must have been a baby."

"Yes."

"Let's go after them now."

"Pergamos, why did you try to save me when your father was going to have me killed just now? It was perfectly within his right."

"I don't know." Then he said, "I owed it to you. You rescued me at Phthia. It was a debt repaid, nothing more." But we both knew that it was not that simple. I think that Pergamos could feel our blood tie even though my name had been stripped from me; for the blood of gods ran strong and true in both of us.

We set off, slowed down by the altitude and by the weight of our weaponry. Soon others had joined us: the surviving soldiers of Neoptolemos, and people from the other tents. It seemed only a few moments before our ranks had swelled to several dozen, the size of a respectable raiding party. We climbed, the rocks scraping and stinging our hands and knees, the wind roaring and burning still. The madwomen were farther up. I could not count them; they were jammed together and moved in an undulating line across the scrubby terrain. They wound and twisted their way up the mountain, coiling and uncoiling like a monstrous snake.

I exulted. I knew I was helping to save my enemy only so that I would be able to kill him myself. But it was also true that if I could succeed in saving his life, this would wipe out the life I owed him, the day he killed my slave boy thinking he killed the son of Hector.

For I knew, as by divine inspiration, the meaning of the prophecy of which Pergamos had told me: that Neoptolemos would find his supreme joy in a city of wood, wool, and iron. For the tents he had put up had canopies of wool, and they were supported on spears planted in the ground; and Pergamos had told me they were using iron to tip their spears.

And every child knows the adage, "Call no man happy until he is dead."

Chapter XX

The Maenads

As we struggled up the face of the mountain I became aware of a man clambering up beside me. "They are called maenads," he said. "There are more and more of them all the time. They are wild."

I glanced at the man. He was a dour, dark-haired person. He wore a black himation, and a black chiton beneath that; it must have been stifling in this heat. I looked behind and saw Pergamos deep in conversation with another youth, lanky and coltish. I waved to them; they hastened up to join us.

"Ah, Pylades," said the dark young man morosely. "You've found someone to talk to?"

"This is Pergamos, Orestes. He is Neoptolemos's son, and his mother seems to have joined the madwomen; she might even be one of their ringleaders."

I realized that the man beside me must be Orestes, son of King Agamemnon, who had been High King of Mycenae and leader of the Akhaians during the war . . . and therefore someone to be hated. But I could feel no antagonism toward him; I could feel nothing for him at all, in fact. For, though he was climbing the pathway beside me, and his black cloak occasionally brushed my arm, he seemed surrounded by an impenetrable shield, cold and invisible. Already I knew that he was as obsessed as I, though I did not yet know why.

I said, "Why have you come to Delphi, Orestes?"

"I have to choose between two unthinkable alternatives, each more impious than the other," the young man said. "Perhaps the god will guide me."

"I tried that once," I said, thinking of the three goddesses and the golden apple.

"What came of it?"

157

"I don't know. I think I learned that choice is an illusion."

Orestes studied me oddly, wondering, perhaps, whether I was being flippant or really meant what I had said.

By this time many of the pursuers had dropped out, either from exhaustion or because they needed to go back and see to their wounded, and the madwomen were nowhere in sight. They had disappeared, almost by magic. Snakemother's power was strong here. I dreaded the coming confrontation, but did not turn back.

We reached a more level area, and the scrub had given way to forest. Even here in the shade there was no respite from the heat; the very ground burned. "They must be here," I gasped as I leaned against a tree. "Snakemother's children always dwell in thick darkness."

"I know one," Orestes said, "who dwells in the brightest of all places, and shows herself in broad daylight. . . ."

"Who could that be?" Pergamos said, coming up to us.

"My mother."

We stood in darkness for a while. I too was thinking of my mother; doubtless so was Pergamos. Silence fell in the forest; I could not even hear birds or animals. Perhaps the forest was bewitched.

Then, from somewhere deeper into the darkness, low mocking laughter. Pergamos started. "They're there, somewhere."

Orestes said, "I'll go with you. We seem to have been deserted by your friends the antique Myrmidons."

"You should not be disrespectful; they're responsible for us winning the war, you know," Pergamos said.

"I don't care about the war," Orestes said. "I don't care about anything."

I said, "Then why are you helping us?"

"Because I want to die," said the dark-eyed Prince of Mycenae. "Do you know how it is with me, Pergamos? I'm in hiding; I've been running from palace to palace ever since I can remember, holing up with this relative or that . . . and always knowing I must come here and be told what I already know and do what I already know I must do. Only this stranger friend of yours seems to have any inkling of what it's like.''

I understood him so well. Yet he too was my enemy. I had to beware.

We followed the laughter. At first we did not speak to one another; each walked alone, thinking his private, desolate thoughts. The laughter echoed in the treetops. I broke the silence: "We'd better keep looking overhead, too. They may be lurking in the trees.''

After that we talked more to one another, just to have something to listen to other than the laughter. Was it just the wind whining as it whipped through the branches? Was that what sounded like the mourning of women over a hero's pyre? But there was no wind. The leaves did not stir. The laughter: sourceless, metallic, inhuman. And I was among enemies.

"We might be lost," Pergamos said at last. For the forest had grown so thick that we could barely see. It had not seemed that way when we had entered it.

"Is this truly a forest?" said Pylades, Orestes' friend, who had said little.

"Why do you ask?" I said.

Then I saw what he meant. In the pale light that filtered in through the seams between the leaves, I saw . . . the leaves edged with bronze, slime-laden. Like serpent scales. My imagination, I told myself. Still, the place was uncannily devoid of life. A real forest would have buzzings, chirpings, rustlings. But this one . . .

"I know where we are," Orestes said. In the half-light his eyes seemed dead already. "Yes! I know, I know, I know.'' His voice took on a plaintive singsong. "The belly of the dark beast! Snakemother has swallowed us!''

The laughter swelled. Were those words that mingled with the cacklings? "Sssssssnakemother . . . sssssswallowed . . .''

Pylades said, "Orestes. None of your fantasies. You'll worry our friends.'' To me he said, "You must forgive him. His insoluble dilemma has made him quite mad, you know.''

But before I could reply Pergamos pointed to a circle of light; I could not tell how far away it was. "It's a way out, though, maybe. We should . . ." I fingered the lion's paw that I still kept hanging around my neck. We started in the direction of the light. The boughs overhead were woven together, encircling us in a tunnel of darkness. I felt that we had long departed the real forest and were gliding down the gullet of some monstrous creature. Were we perhaps inside the belly of the serpent I had thought I'd seen as the mountain rose out of the misty dawn? The serpent coiled around the mountain of my second dream?

"It's not a way out at all," Pergamos said at last. We were whispering now. Only Orestes seemed untouched; I was convinced that nothing could touch him. Of the four of us, he was the only one who wanted to die.

We had stumbled onto the edge of a clearing. The light that fell on it was cold, silver-edged. In the clearing sat the women. They were gathered in a circle; we could not see their faces. All were disheveled and naked, their backs and buttocks streaked with mud. Snakes crawled in and out of their hair and the crevices in their bodies.

"Where is Neoptolemos?" I said softly. I reached out to touch Pergamos's arm, for he was standing just in front of me. It was ice-cold. For a moment I thought he had turned to stone, like the messenger I had sent to the land of death. "Pergamos," I said, soothing him. He shivered. He raised his arm slowly, pointing. My gaze followed the crook of his arm, to a pile of raw and steaming meat that lay on the grass near the circle of women, to the severed head of Neoptolemos.

I should feel triumph! I told myself. My enemy is slain.

Instead I felt only a yawning desolation within myself. How could I exult, that my vengeance had been exacted, not by me, but by a madwoman . . . perhaps my own mother? I stared stupidly at the head.

The women moaned, swayed, ceased their chanting and turned around, their eyes, smoldering, blood-red. One woman shook her head, dislodging a piece of meat from her mouth;

it was a human intestine, I realized. I was too numbed to feel the horror.

But Pergamos screamed and ran forward with his little iron dagger and charged into the circle of women. "No!" I shrieked after him. Orestes and Pylades drew their swords. Pylades outstripped the boy and threw himself between him and the women, who had begun a quiet, menacing chanting and who rose now, standing in a line before us, swaying, licking their lips. Pergamos and our two companions stood uneasily, reticent about attacking women with swords. I pulled out my dagger and I was about to sprint into the middle of the clearing when . . .

The line of women parted! And behind them, wearing a crown of leaves and with a necklace of bleeding human hands adorning her bare chest, two serpents twining about her outstretched arms, was Andromache.

She saw all four of us. Called to us in the voice of the wolf, the owl, the hiss of the snake. I could not move, though my dagger was raised to strike. Her stare transfixed me. In that moment of indecision I saw . . .

Pergamos shouting at her, "You killed Father you bitch you Trojan whore."

The women closing in around him. Pylades slicing through them with his sword, Pergamos being thrust to the ground, lunging forward, slashing at a woman's knees with his dagger. Snakes flying like darts through the air. Orestes, stung, screaming, fighting them off as they swarmed over his face.

I could not stand there helplessly anymore. Even a twelve-year-old boy was fighting back. I strode forward. The grass was slick with blood. I slipped, put out my arm to steady myself . . . poked the head of Neoptolemos in the dangling eye, which burst like a pimple. At last the horror dawned on me. Uncontrollable anger now. I rushed forward, striking down a snakewoman who leered before me, sticking another in the neck with my dagger. Blood dripped down my arms, seeped down my chiton. Pergamos was struggling to his feet. I seized him, flung him into the thicket behind. He was protesting. "Stay put!" I shouted. "If you die I'll—"

They had Pylades. Orestes was trying to reach him, slicing his way through a rain of snakes. I surfaced next to Pylades, tried to pry him out of the arms that held him. As I pulled the woman off, other hands reached out, knives hacked into Pylades' flesh. A woman dived in with both hands and yanked out his heart and held it high, a paean screeching from her lips. They were on me now; I felt their bloody hands slipping over my body, and . . .

The lion's paw! The chain I wore it on came loose; it dangled in the air.

The women suddenly let go of me. The snakes that writhed all over Orestes vaporized. What was it about the paw of the lioness? I held it up. A woman whimpered when she saw it and fell silent. Stillness returned, heavy, claustrophobic.

"You are the one," my mother said, as the women parted once more to let her come to me. "I am she who sits astride twin lionesses, and you hold the Lady's paw."

I was becoming more and more perplexed. Memnon had given me this paw; the other he had given to Leonidas. And Memnon was a creature of Skyfather . . . yet these women reacted to the talisman as though it were an emblem of their own dark goddess. I could make no sense of it.

Very quietly, so that only Andromache could hear, I said, "Do you now know me? Can you not name me? Please, give me my name, free me. The revenge I came for has been rendered meaningless. Name me, set me free."

My mother said, "I know your name as well as I know my own."

"Andromache, Mother . . ." Pergamos said from the shadows.

"I am not Andromache!" she said. "I am Thetis of the sea. I am Semele; I am Demeter of the corn; I am Isis. And you are my eternal husband, my consort, my son, my lover, my father."

"Don't you know me at all?" I said, despairing.

"I have spoken! I know you as I know myself."

"You do not know yourself at all, if you say that you are Snakemother."

She laughed. The women began to look guiltily about
them; perhaps the effects of the wine were wearing off. I
clutched my lion's paw aloft, for it seemed to quell their
lunacy. They no longer moved like a single being, a many-
headed hydra; their individuality was returning to them. Presently they began to disperse. I watched my mother go off,
deeper into the forest. I did not follow her. There was no
point. I dared not travel down the same dark road. I only had
half a soul. I was afraid to lose it. I did not call after her
when she vanished into the shadows. I knew she would never
recognize me. It had all been a fantasy, this notion of having
my name instantly restored to me by the mother-phantom I
had idealized for thirteen years.

Orestes said to me, with no emotion in his voice, "You
saved my life."

Then he knelt over the gutted corpse of Pylades. He did
not weep; his face was set in some inconstruable emotion.

But Pergamos did not hide his feelings. He wept bitterly.
He was only a little boy after all. He could not look at his
father's head. I stood there, watching their two modes of
grief. My mother too was dead; though she still walked the
earth, I knew she had lost both her souls. I felt no sadness.
Only an uncanny vacuum within me. I realized that I had
stopped loving her.

I had not loved her for thirteen years. Not since the day I
saw her wailing over the corpse of Leontes. All those years I
had felt ashamed not to feel that love; now even that guilt had
deserted me.

Oh, Skyfather, I envied the grief that Pergamos and Orestes
felt! They were still human, while I was a ghost, a magician's fabrication. I could feel the blue king growing strong
in Troy, feeding on the shattering of my youthful illusions.

"What shall I do now?" I said at last.

It was Orestes who answered me. "I suppose we should
consult the oracle," he said. "Isn't that what we came for?"

Chapter XXI

The Naming

We walked down tunnels moist and misted, into the mountain's heart, Pergamos and I and Orestes. I realized that this trembling boy, his hair hacked off in mourning for his brother and his father, was now a king.

He said, "I'm afraid of what the oracle may tell me."

"What will you ask?" I said.

"I will ask about you," he said softly. We walked on in silence.

We reached an interior cavern; white-robed priests stood guard. The cave mouth was stained with layer upon layer of ancient blood. Fumes tendriled from the opening, a nauseating meld of strange spices and brimstone. The officiating priest said, "Only one at a time."

Orestes and I looked at each other. "I'll go," Pergamos said at last, and entered the swirling mist.

"Why not together?" I said.

The priest said, "Truth is something best encountered alone."

We waited, our eyes adjusting to the light. We were in a natural vestibule; at its center was a stone much like the stone of Skyfather in Troy, the one that had fallen from heaven. It was soaked in blood. As we stood there, a weeping woman entered, clutching a white pigeon in both hands. "They sell them outside," Orestes said. "Do you want one? It is good to set one free; the gods see it as a deed of virtue. But they blind them, or they break their wings, so they can easily be recaptured and resold."

I said, "Orestes, your grief for your dead friend—"

"Why?" he shouted in a sudden outburst of passion. "Why didn't you save him and let me die? I told you I

164

wanted to die! I told you I wanted to be released from my intolerable dilemma!''

"What dilemma?" I said. For I saw the blackness of his garb, the coldness of his manner, as superficial affectations designed to hide his true anguish.

He said, "Do you not know the story of Agamemnon's return from Troy?"

I said, "I was only a child." That was all the magic would allow me to reveal.

"To speed the Akhaian ships toward Troy, my father sacrificed my sister Iphigeneia to the Lady, for she visited him in the form of the moon, the huntress, the shadow." He spoke tonelessly, as though the story had been repeated so often it had been purged of its emotion. But I knew better; I could feel that hidden torment as my own. He continued, "Before the war was even begun, my friend, he had bought the outcome with a blood offering to Snakemother! Later, I remember, Agamemnon put out the story that the Lady had snatched my sister into the air and replaced her with a doe. I was told she lives on some distant island, serving the Lady with human sacrifices. But there are those who saw her die. And so they went to Troy. I was still an infant, my sisters Electra and Chrysothemis were still tiny too. Because Agamemnon had fed the Lady's appetite, she grew strong. For ten years the kings of Akhaia were gone, and their queens remained behind . . . and the women had not forgotten that they once ruled the world, and could do so again, if they revived the worship of the Lady. When my father came home, my mother Clytaemnestra was waiting. She killed him with due ceremony, in the royal bathroom, with the net and the two-edged axe, and made my uncle Aigisthos king. Then she sent me away; although she feared my revenge, she did not want to kill me. For her it was a sacred thing to kill the king; to kill me would have been murder. . . .''

I understood then why he was so tormented. For years he must have known that it was his duty to avenge his father, yet this duty must lead to an even more unthinkable act:

matricide. He would be driven mad if he fulfilled his destiny. "I feel for you," I said. "I don't know what I would do."

"The oracle will tell me, won't it?"

The priest, who had been eavesdropping on our conversation, said, "The answer you hear will depend on which god comes to speak to you."

"What do you mean?" I said. "Isn't this the shrine of Apollo?"

"Sometimes it is," the priest said, "and sometimes it isn't."

"What does he mean?" I said to Orestes.

"The war," Orestes said. "We've all been told that it's over, that Skyfather controls this place completely . . . but it isn't true, is it? The priestess that utters the riddling replies still bears the name of Pytho; she is still the voice of Snakemother."

"But the priest who interprets the response," said the priest, "is the voice of Apollo, Skyfather's son."

"An uneasy compromise at best. And which is to be the truth?" said Orestes.

I said, "I knew a mage who told me that many contradictory things can be true at once."

"That's a dangerous doctrine," said the priest, "and I'm glad we don't follow it here. It would mean the end of civilization."

The boy emerged from the mist-fringed shadows now. He declared, "I asked the oracle whether I should return to Phthia and become king . . . or whether I could be permitted to go with you, stranger who calls himself my brother. The oracle said: 'You will do as the stranger bids you.' "

"That's unfair," I said, "that's not an answer. The oracle shifts the onus onto me." What could I say? Could Pergamos abandon his kingdom and follow me on my quest? At last I said, "I have to tell you to go home. I have to tell you to be king." Even, I thought silently, if it doomed us to become mortal enemies. For I had come to love my newfound brother, and I did not want to see him lose his soul, as I had done.

"I knew you'd say that," Pergamos said. "But I hoped—"

He paused, almost choking. "I mean, I've lost it all, haven't I? My father is torn in pieces, my mother driven mad, my little brother burned and returned to the sky. Why should I be king?" He seemed crushed. How could I console him? I could only tell him the truth that I had learned not long before.

"You *are* king," I said. "It is not a matter of choice."

Pergamos wept bitterly, saying, "I'm just a child. . . . I've been brave long enough. . . . I can't be king."

I said, "You have the courage to weep. You will be a fine king." But the boy would not be consoled. What could I tell him? I had left behind my kingship in pursuit of a dream that was fast proving vapid and senseless.

The priest gave me the sign to enter the inner cave. I composed myself and stepped over the stone threshold.

Mist . . . clouds of thick darkness. An old man stood beside a throne whose arms were the backs of living lionesses. A woman sat on the throne, and the woman was sometimes like my mother and sometimes like the snake-haired goddess . . . and sometimes she smiled, with the starlight streaming from eyes blue as the bright sky, and before I knew it I had said her name: "Helen."

Her face—the features seemed to shift, to mold themselves into more and more different faces, women from my past: Leontes' mother at whose breasts I had once suckled; my grandmother Hecabe, being dragged off toward the Akhaian ships; Dione, the girl whose breasts I had crudely caressed on the slopes of the mountain . . . I whispered their names, and even as I named them they changed form, again and again. There was something in the perfumed mist, some herb that gave me visions. I spoke in a delirium, mixing poetry with obscenity, until I felt the old man's arm on mine and I subsided, quaking, and faced the priestess.

"We meet again," she said.

"Again?" I said.

"Again. Did you not once give me this gift?"

She pulled an apple from her bosom. I saw the gold glint through wisps of vapor. "You?" I whispered. "You are—"

"All things are true at the same time," she said. "That's what the big black sorcerer told you, isn't it? It is also true that nothing is true." She laughed; the laughter was hideous and familiar.

"Mother!" I said involuntarily.

"Your question," the priestess said. "I grow impatient."

"I beg for a sign from Skyfather," I said. "How can I trust you, mother of deceit, mistress of snakes?"

"I will tell you something, little king. Remember that I see into your heart, and I know your question before you even ask it. Come, look into my eyes."

"No!" I remembered the story of Perseus, who lived at the dawn of history, who founded the city of Mycenae: when he battled the serpent, he looked steadfastly at his shield, for he knew that if he gazed at Snakemother directly he would be turned to stone.

"I know what you are thinking. You foolish boy!" She laughed softly, seductively. "That is only a story, a myth; this is reality. Things like that don't happen anymore. And you know why? Because the Age of Bronze is ending. The heroes are all dead or dying. This time you think you inhabit is not a time at all. The Egyptians, you know, have an ancient calendar in which there are days of the year that do not exist. Do you know that? The passage from one year to another is marked by time that is not time . . . for time is not seamless. It is like those cyclopean walls that surround the great cities you men have built. There are cracks between the stones, try as you might to make the walls one homogenous artifact. And you are a creature dwelling in one of the cracks of time."

"I didn't come here to listen to arcane conundrums," I said. "I just want to know how I am to finish my quest. Neoptolemos is dead without having fallen to my vengeance; Andromache is beyond my rescuing. Two of the goals of my journey have already proved useless . . . and I still have no name. Should I go now to Aunt Helen? Or should I just give up? I don't want your answer but Skyfather's."

"Foolish little king," she said. But there was no malice in her voice; instead there was that very gentleness I had dreamed of finding in Andromache. At last I looked her in the eye; if I was to turn to stone now, what did I have to lose? Better to be a statue, not to feel anything at all, than to feel this shame. The priestess who was also the ancient goddess said, "Do you know, nameless king, whom you really serve?"

"I serve the sky," I said, "my ancestor."

Again she laughed, even more gently. "Why then did the lioness's paw serve to quell the maenads' madness?"

"I don't know!" I said. "I go from moment to moment, not knowing why or how."

"What if I tell you that the war between me and Skyfather was over long before it was begun . . . that it is only in the minds of you mortals, that you manufactured it in the name of conquest, centuries ago? What if I tell you that it is man who makes us from the clay of his imagination, and not the reverse?"

"I would say," I said carefully, for I knew that she was trying to trick me into uttering some impious sentiment, "that the universe had become unmoored from the truths it was built on."

"That is true," said the priestess.

I felt a cold desperation inside me, waiting to burst. "What shall I do, then? If nothing is true, if there's nothing for me to believe in anymore, why must I continue on this quest?"

She said, "I did not say you must."

"But you—"

"You have sent yourself on the quest, little king. You have already lost your city, your name, your revenge, and your mother. I have never told you to go on."

"But you tell me that I am your servant . . . that I'm doing your will, not Skyfather's! Is it your will to crush me, to crush everything Skyfather stands for, to drag the world back into darkness?"

"Oh, little king," she said. I saw the softness in her eyes,

Helen's eyes. I could not tell whose voice she was, the voice of
my ancestor or the voice of ultimate evil. "Light and dark,
good and evil, man and woman—these are things you must
unlearn, child. The void stands at the beginning and the end.
I am not your enemy, little king, any more than that
Neoptolemos was. Do not despair. All things are conjoined
in an endless web. The Fates spin a million threads, but
Penelope weaves only one tapestry. Before ever Skyfather
was, I am."

"I don't trust you," I said.

"Have I asked for your trust?"

She stepped down from her throne then, her shape flickering wildly from maiden to mother to crone. She came toward
me. For a few seconds she seemed to be a serpent, her head
darting sinuously to and fro, her forked tongue flicking in
and out. I blinked. When I opened my eyes again she was
Helen as I remembered her. I said, "Aunt Helen. Is it you
who will give back my name to me?"

And she smiled the smile that had caused me to flee into
the mountains; and then she embraced me, laughing. For a
moment I felt her in my arms, wriggling, smooth-skinned,
unnaturally hot to the touch . . . then she dissolved into the
mist that wound itself around the throne, the ancient priest,
the lionesses, me. "Helen!" I said again. My voice echoed.

I turned to the priest. "Interpret!" I said. He did not respond;
I shook him by the shoulders, unmindful of the sacrilege. At
last he gave me to understand, by frantic gestures, that he
was mute. I was angry when I left the chamber.

I saw the anger on Orestes' face, too, when he finally
came out. I said to him, "No answers. Am I right? And the
priest dumb, tongueless."

He would not speak to me.

Down at the encampment, Pergamos commanded the remains of Neoptolemos to be loaded onto a cart. We stayed at
the tent of Orestes, the three of us, drinking. All night we did
not sleep. In the morning Pergamos left. He showed no anger

at me for abandoning him to his lonely kingship. But I could see the reproach in his eyes. I embraced him in farewell. He stiffened and wriggled out of my arms as soon as was decently possible.

Orestes said, "Do we journey together now?"

"I don't know," I said, rubbing my aching head.

"I will go to Mycenae, and do what the oracle says I must do. Then I'll go to Sparta. At birth, you see, I was betrothed to Aunt Helen's daughter Hermione."

Our meeting had been no accident! It was clear to me now. Orestes was my road to Helen. "I'll go with you," I said.

"But you must have a name."

"I have no name."

He puzzled over this for a while. Then he said, "He was my closest friend. He died for me, do you know that? But I was so caged by the conflict within me that I hardly spoke a kind word to him." He spoke, as always, without a trace of emotion. "But the gods have given me the chance to try again. That's why I'm going to call you Pylades."

I gaped. Pylades had been dead less than a day. His shade had doubtless not yet reached the ferryman. A chill seized me. I said, "It's only the drink that makes you speak that way." But it was too late.

For this is what Memnon had said to me: "You will have no name, nameless king, until a stranger names you."

I felt the name fasten itself to me as an owl grips a mouse. I tried to fight it off with my will; but I had only half a soul, half a will. I needed a name. A man without a name is nothing. The name seeped into me like a salve. "No!" I said. "That's not my name, my name is . . ." My lips formed the first syllable "A-" but the sound that came out was "Pylades, Pylades . . ." The dead man's shade was invading me, forcing the sounds from my mouth, twisting my tongue into the foreign name.

"Good," Orestes said. "You saved my life, Pylades. I know we will be friends. I'm sorry I abused you before." Did he really understand what he had done . . . that I was not the friend he had lost, but a man possessed by another's name?

I did not think he would ever understand. Perhaps he was already mad, although the Furies had not yet come for him. Later, when they drove him completely over the edge of sanity, I was to remember that even before we reached Mycenae he had seemed haunted. Sometimes I believe that we can remember the future; that is the meaning of prophecy.

All I knew then was that the trap was closing in on me. I was like Theseus in the labyrinth, only I had lost my thread. I had been named my enemy's best friend. Perhaps I would have to play this role forever. When I left Troy I had thought my mission the most important thing in the universe. What could be more significant than to restore my city, to bring back the heroes, to stop the color from draining from the world?

I knew now that there was a struggle more cosmic and more ancient . . . that the battle between Skyfather and Snakemother, which had been taught to me as a thing of the distant past, was far from over. The answer to every enigma was a further enigma.

Perhaps Helen would solve the riddle for me. For she was Zeus's daughter, a bridge between earth and heaven. All my other plans had ended in disillusion; my meeting with Helen was the only thing that mattered now. I had to see her, even though I came to her with another's name. Perhaps our meeting would mean the end of the age of heroes. Perhaps it would mean the beginning of wisdom.

```
▣▣▣▣▣▣▣▣▣▣▣▣▣▣▣▣▣▣▣
```

Book Four: Kings Without Thrones

```
ΤΦᎡΤ⊕
ᗡΨ�C
```

Eifersüchtig sind
die Toten; denn er schickte mir den Haß,
den hohlaügigen Haß, als Bräutigam.

Jealous are the dead!
For Agamemnon sent me hate, hollow-eyed hate,
to be my bridegroom.

> —Words of Princess Electra to Orestes
> on recognizing him
> Hugo von Hoffmannsthal, *Elektra*

Chapter XXII

[decorative border]

Orestes

At first, the road to Mycenae was smooth, uneventful. We were entering the domain of the High Kings of Akhaia now, and though the war had destroyed much, here they still kept up appearances. The road was evenly paved and wide enough for two chariots to rush past each other in opposite directions. We drove all day, taking turns at being charioteer, all the while hardly exchanging a word. Orestes lashed the horses savagely, as though we rode out to do battle. He was obsessed; he seemed to look through me, his eyes fixed on something infinitely far away. I did not understand him; I resented him for giving me a name I did not want, and although the way we took was the way I had vowed to travel, I still resented him for forcing me to take it. It was no pleasure to sit with my head crammed against the prickly wicker of his chariot car and stare upward at his implacable face.

I did not speak to him at all the first day. Deep into the night, we were both too exhausted to continue. Orestes had been driving; we careened to a sudden halt by the side of the road. Corn grew on either side. One of the wayside shrines stood there; there came a reddish glow from a brazier within.

I did not want to go in. I remembered what Pergamos and I had seen on the road to Delphi. But I followed him; and I saw what I expected. Hundreds of votive Snakemother images in clay and terra-cotta and wood were scattered over the altar, and fresh garlands. "Why are we here?" I whispered. It was so dark. I was afraid of angry shades.

"Hush, Pylades," Orestes said. "We must stand here, tall, facing the shadow. That's what the oracle told me. Otherwise how will we be able to defeat it in Mycenae itself?

175

Quiet, quiet, Pylades; perhaps, if I stand here long enough,
I'll know why the shadow has come back." He turned abruptly
from me and faced the altar. Two lionesses of stone reared up
on either side of it. The paint was fresh on them, and their
flanks were edged in gilt. Someone had sacrificed here recently; that was why there were still embers in the brazier,
and why a smell of cooked meat lingered in the air. "I must
understand, you see," said Orestes. "Or how can I plunge
the sword into my mother's breast?"

"Did the oracle tell you to kill your mother?"

"I don't know!" he said hoarsely, still looking away.

"What were its words? The priestess answered *me* in
riddles," I said. "Did the god come to you at all?"

"Yes. But he said to me, 'I come by stealth, and you
must accomplish your quest by stealth. They have usurped
my kingdom, and I am struck dumb.' "

"What can that mean?" I said.

"My family suffers from an ancient curse," Orestes said.
He spoke without anger, without bitterness. But what desolation there was in his toneless words! "All my ancestors
struck the wrong bargains with the wrong gods. Atreus,
Thyestes, Pelops . . . We sacrifice our children to the gods
and hope to appease them, but instead we seal a pact of
death. Did you know that my ancestor carved up his son and
served him to the gods in a stew? In those days Snakemother
had not become . . . completely dark. It was she, in the
shape of the Corn Mother, who restored Pelops's life. My
father Agamemnon should have known better than to sacrifice his own child Iphigeneia to the Moon Huntress! Didn't
he learn anything? And I . . . what have I learned? I am
going to Mycenae to kill my uncle and my mother."

I was shivering. I threw some dry twigs on the brazier. We
sat together on a stone bench under the thatched awning of
the shrine. "Why? Can't you raise an army, sweep down to
Mycenae and dispossess them? If your mother indeed took it
upon herself to practice the ancient rite of killing the king,
surely you can find enough angry people to—"

"You don't understand, Pylades." I flinched a little, as I

always did, when he addressed me by that name; for each
time it was applied to me I felt the name grow stronger,
tightening around my forsaken ba like a noose. He went on,
oblivious to my discomfiture, "The people aren't angry."

That I could not understand.

"The worship of the Lady is a very old thing, Pylades"
—again I recoiled slightly, and again he did not, or pretended not to, notice—"and it clings to the old stones of
Akhaia."

Yes. I remembered what the snake-haired woman had said
to me when I paid the first blood price for my throne: "Do
not forget her on whose bones you daily tread." I could feel
the presence of Snakemother here, more strongly than ever
before. I shuddered.

"Our ancestors brought Skyfather down—some say from
the north, others the west—and established his name in every
city of Akhaia and many cities of the east, like vanquished
Troy. But the city is not the land—it is something raised up
high over the land, it looks out over the land, it holds the
land in awe and fear of it, but it cannot destroy the land.
Snakemother has never died, and now she is more powerful
than ever before, as you know from the bands of wild women
who roam the countryside and who worship her and her
obscene son, who is called Dionysos, whose flesh they tear
apart and eat again and again in their sacred, bloody mysteries. I don't believe it was always like this, my friend. The
worshipers of Snakemother were great once. They built Knossos
and Mycenae itself, for Perseus, the first High King, was in
truth only the husband of the living goddess Andromeda the
Serpent Queen. How can they have come to this? It is partly
our fault, I think—for centuries we've tried to stamp them
out. My father told me that in his grandfather's day they
would rape the priestesses to death and then proclaim that
Skyfather had seduced them, that furthermore Skyfather's
glory was so dazzling that it made them expire on the spot. Is
it *we* who made madwomen of the Lady's followers?"

"What you say," I said warily, "is dangerous." There
was corruption in what he said, but the memory of my

grandfather's stories seemed very far away. And yet . . . had not King Priam's vision proved false? I cursed myself for doubting the memory of my grandfather, but that doubt was a canker that continued to fester. I said, with a twinge of desperation, "Orestes, we must believe in the supremacy of Skyfather; we must seek to crush the dark! We are enlightened people, modern people, who do not speak as the barbarians do, but in the tongue of the father of heaven himself. We can't give up!"

"Perhaps it's hubris to believe we're the light and they're the dark, Pylades. Perhaps it's the other way round."

"That's a terrible thing to say." Yet . . . I hated to admit it to myself, but it was something that even I had begun to suspect. I had to cast out these thoughts. I had to remain a pure vessel of Troy's vengeance, or I was nothing.

Orestes looked at me. I studied his face in the emberglow. His eyes were like the eyeholes of a deathmask. He said, "That's what everyone says when I mouth these subversive ideas. But they don't have to go through what I go through! Whatever I choose, I'm damned. I fail in my duty to Skyfather if I don't take revenge; I fail to honor Snakemother if I kill her highest priestess. There's no solution. Do you know something? When I sleep I see my father's shade before me, arms outstretched, the blood gushing from his neck. He's struggling to get out of the net, but the axe descends relentlessly again and again. I call out to him, 'Father, Father.' He can't answer me because his throat and lungs are already full of blood."

I could not answer him. I could have told him of my own grief: of my grandfather decapitated, of Troy burning, of my father's broken body hooked to Akhilleus's chariot and dragged around the walls of the city. We could have sat all night exchanging horror stories, each one bloodier than the last, until we were numbed. I only said, "I see now why you rarely sleep. You haven't slept since we left Delphi; that night, after we saw the oracle, I don't think you slept then, either, though I was too drunk to know."

"And still I saw him! His eyes are the most terrible thing."

I closed my eyes, remembering. Had I seen Agamemnon? So many Akhaians, each one glittering in his war panoply like a star against the backdrop of the tents, the sea. Which one had been the father of this man, tormented, unable to sleep for fear of dreaming? I was sure Agamemnon had been splendid. They had all seemed indiscriminately splendid to me then; even the corpses in the field had seemed beautiful, because I saw them from on high, like bronze-plated dolls, and the blood bright as paint.

But so far I had seen no splendor in Akhaia. I had seen a drab, decaying palace; I had seen fat, tired warriors; I had seen women driven insane and turned to cannibals. And this was the son of Agamemnon; he seemed himself a shade, for his face was bloodless and his cheeks hollow and his eyes deep-set and dark as night. What glory would there be in fighting another Trojan War if this was the kind of creature who would lead the Akhaians against me? And it would be even worse if it fell to Pergamos to fight me. I did not think I could bring myself to do battle against my own brother.

Orestes sat very still for a long time. If his eyes were not open, I would have thought he was asleep. I was uncomfortable; I thought I should make conversation. I said, "How much longer till Mycenae?"

He did not answer. I realized that he had fallen into a kind of waking sleep, the same state to which Memnon had sent me when I had gone through my mock death. He had been trying to fight sleep all this while, and now he could do no more.

He started to speak. I made to answer, but he was not speaking to me. It was a gibbering monotone. I could only make out a few words: "Dark, dark, dark . . . you slip in blood, the throne is blood, the paws of the lionesses are soaked in it . . ." In a panic I clutched the lion's paw talisman that still hung around my neck. It had saved my life, but I no longer trusted its magic. I tried to tear it off, but the chain must have been magical; it would not break. "Iron!"

Orestes screamed. "Iron from the mouth of the lioness!" It was nonsense.

Suddenly he got up and strode from the shrine. I followed him. I knew he was still asleep. We were on the path now; but we walked away from the paved road into the fields thick with corn.

I pricked up my ears. Chanting.

"Get away from there!" I hissed. "We've got to stick to the road."

He did not speak but continued on, thrusting into the man-tall stalks. The moon was high, tingeing his pallid face with pale blue. Where was the singing coming from? I knew what it must be. Had the maenads followed us all the way from Delphi? It was impossible.

"Come back!" I dashed after him. The corn closed in around him, like . . . like . . . My eyes must be playing tricks! Were they stalks of grain or were they naked women with crimson eyes? I caught Orestes' arm. I pulled, he turned, I saw arms reach for him, arms woven from thatch. "Orestes!" I shouted. I pulled hard. We stumbled back onto the road. He fell; not crumpling, as a man falls, but stiffly, as though he were made of marble.

I shook him. Slowly he came awake. He murmured, "Help me, help me, Pylades." I was too tired to deny the name.

"To the chariot," I said.

"Mustn't sleep . . . mustn't sleep . . . they're following us."

"Who are they?" I said. I did not know if the women I had seen were real—whether they were the same maenads we had seen on the mountain—or whether I had somehow been sucked into the edge of his dream.

"Please, Pylades," Orestes said, "you must keep me from dreaming. Do you think I'm already mad? But the madness is leaking out of me. I can see you're touched by it, you see a little of it."

"Yes." It was because I had only half a soul and another man's name; I had become so unmoored from myself that, like Memnon's ship, I was able to exist simultaneously within many realities.

"Don't let me sleep," Orestes said. "I may sleep forever, and if I do, the dream will be real forever, and the world will contain only horror." He clutched helplessly at me. "Promise me you'll keep me from dreaming. Promise me, my friend."

"What can I say? I can try, but I cannot promise." For a brief moment he seemed no longer distant, no longer ghostlike. I saw the man within the shell, vulnerable and heartbroken.

He said, "You are the only one who has seen what I am, what I could have been, Pylades."

"I'm not—" I stopped. It suddenly occurred to me that I did not even *want* to know what my true name was anymore. I was sliding inexorably into this man's dark fantasy, and I could not exorcise the name of Pylades from me. I said, "I will be Pylades for a while. If it makes you happy. I'll see you through to Mycenae. But then . . ."

Would it be too late by then?

"Help me, help me." His voice was weak; I shook him awake. I took a cloak from the chariot and covered us both, for it was getting chill. We sat on the ground with our backs against the wheel. "Don't let me sleep," he said again.

But I was so tired I could not keep vigil over him.

As I drifted into slumber I was thinking, We too are kin in our own way; we are both kings, both dispossessed, both tricked by the Fates into embarking on impossible quests. As I am the last in the long line of Dardanids, so he is the last of the Atreidai, and he must bring their family's curse to its final fruition.

And I thought, Do I too seem this way to others, a madman, possessed, obsessed, untouchable? Have I come all this way to look into the face of my enemy, only to see my own reflection, my dark secret self?

These thoughts nagged at me as we rose before dawn, as I gazed at my companion's face, haunted and haggard; as we raced along the lonely road lined with the shrines of Snakemother; as we reached the outskirts of Mycenae itself and saw the city on the hill ahead, its stone walls growing from the living rock like natural formations.

"What do we do now?" I cried. "Will you march into the palace, announce your kingship, kill the usurpers?"

"No."

"What then?"

"It will be done by trickery and stealth," he said.

"Misdirection," I said softly, remembering Memnon and the king who ruled Troy in my name.

Chapter XXIII

The Graves of the Perseids

Stealth. That was what Orestes demanded above all. And so we came to Mycenae in secret. Orestes left the chariot and the horses in a village half an hour's walk from the city gates, using a gold band to bribe a farmer into hiding them.

We proceeded uphill. To see Mycenae filled me with emotion; it was so like Troy before Troy tumbled. The smell of the air was subtly different because the sea was far. But like Troy there were the stone walls built by giants when the Age of Bronze was young. There were the distant mountains. And the road was full of people: tradesmen, beggars, curious children, prostitutes. It had been so long since I had heard a real crowd, chattering, arguing, bustling; not since my childhood, perhaps. A line of noisy children began to follow us, attracted perhaps by Orestes' black clothing. They were playing follow the leader, aping his melodramatic posture, his compulsive stride.

"Where are we going now?" I said. For I had noticed that we were not going straight to the city gates, but had turned down an alley that wound away from the city and the crowds.

"Something suspicious," Orestes said. He stopped to shoo

away the children. One of them, laughing, thrust something in my hand.

It was a clay snake. Recoiling, I thrust it into the dirt beside the road. The child, dismayed, scurried after me, saying, "What's wrong with you, foreigner, why are you scorning the Lady's gift?" I walked faster, but I was barely keeping up with Orestes.

"There! Look!" He pulled me into a passageway between low buildings, warehouses. A low wall overlooked a shallow ravine crammed with people. They were all shouting at once, and there was music playing, but there was something forced about their enthusiasm . . . or was there? At the center of the commotion there were about a dozen men, shoveling up earth.

"I saw the men with spades earlier," Orestes said, "turning in this direction. Don't they know what those places are?"

"What?" But I, who had violated the necropolis of Snakemother, had already guessed what they must be doing.

"Keep low!" Orestes said. We knelt. "This is a dark and secret place. Only my family knows what is here. The graves of the Perseids, who ruled Mycenae in the days of the Lady."

"Only your family? Then why the crowds? And grave robbers wouldn't be digging in broad daylight. . . ."

"Watch!"

Somewhere, the rasp of chariot wheels and the whinnying of horses. I saw someone approaching along the line of cypresses that lined the ravine. A man and a woman.

The woman, pushing her way through the throng . . .

"I'd know the man anywhere," Orestes said. I saw him: a boyish man who bore a slight resemblance to Orestes. He wore a purple cloak; a ceremonial phasganon dangled from his waist, looking curiously obscene. "He is Aigisthos, my uncle," Orestes said. "He has fallen prey to my mother; he has agreed to become king in the old way. But my mother is infatuated with him, and every year, come spring, she finds an excuse not to kill him."

"He's a very pretty man," I said. "But there's a sickness in his face. He's . . . he's much like you, in a way; he doesn't seem quite to inhabit the same universe as other people."

"Perhaps. Why are they digging, though?"

"Who's the woman?"

His face darkened. "My mother."

"Clytaemnestra."

I watched her. The crowd parted for her. She was regal, erect; from this distance I could not tell whether time had lined her face. There was so much gold on her, and so many stones: stones on a neckpiece that hung down to her navel, polished crystals on a headband, gemstones tied to twists in her black hair. Although she was Aunt Helen's sister (for her mother Leda had hatched four children from one egg—two of them mortal, the other two children of Skyfather), she did not resemble Aunt Helen at all. Her eyes were thickly lined with kohl. They were all deferring to her, falling on their knees and raising their palms outward, as though she were the king, and not Aigisthos.

"Why?" I whispered.

"The old things have been restored," Orestes said. "Let's try to get down lower."

The wall we were peering over ended at the warehouse. Through the window I could see clerks counting amphorai and stacking wet clay tablets against the wall. From the wall we climbed onto the roof and crawled to the other side of the building, where a steep stair, carved into the rock, led into the ravine.

We were behind the crowd now. I squeezed between two toothless women. "What are they doing?" I asked them.

One of them said, "The queen has ordered the graves opened, so that artifacts from the past, no longer suppressed, can be put back to use." She seemed not to understand the impiety of such an act. The emotion in her eyes was hope, not horror. Above the mounds of dirt I could see the diggers' heads now, seeming to dance disembodied over the pit. The queen moved to the edge. She was panting. The stones of her neckpiece clanked with the cadence of her breasts.

"Faster, faster," she was saying. "Is there nothing at all here?"

I shuddered. There is only one force that will yield riches from the ground, and that is Snakemother. Truly I was in her realm. Presently there were bones flying from the pit, then skulls, then gold: rhytons, drinking cups, a gold mask with empty eyes.

I whispered to Orestes, "But this is sacrilege! Don't they realize what they're doing?"

He said, very softly, "Oh, my friend, my friend . . . don't you know that the world is coming to an end? These things don't matter anymore."

"I can't believe that! I have to believe that there's still a purpose behind this madness."

He laughed. His laugh did not sound human, but like skeletons smashing into other skeletons.

The mask—that was important, obviously. Queen Clytaemnestra clutched it to her breast. Through the eyeholes I saw the glint of the jewels the queen wore; they made the mask seem alive for a moment. "The treasure of the Perseids," Orestes said. "At least they were no kin of ours. But they would have sealed the grave objects with the usual curses, I'm sure."

"What is the mask for?" I said. Orestes shrugged.

"Why, you must be foreigners," said the old woman who had answered me before. "The deathmask is used for a king-killing. Nothing is to be done in a slapdash way anymore, but with due and appropriate ceremony, according to the Lady's ancient precepts."

I said, "Will they kill Aigisthos?"

The woman hooted with laughter. "What boorish ignorance!" she screeched. But she did not volunteer any more information.

Clytaemnestra held the golden mask up in the air. Dirt clung to it in places; she wiped it with a fold of her antique flounced skirt. The crowd gasped as the queen and her consort walked away and palace guards fell in behind them.

"What now?" I said to Orestes.

"I need to get into the palace. I need a plan."

"You know they won't turn away guests; no one would descend *that* low, surely," I said.

He seemed to be prevaricating. All his life he had been planning his revenge; the fantasy of it had become more real than the reality. I understood this because I too had dreamed great dreams of glory and was now beginning to see them for the sham they were . . . and I longed for those dreams more than ever. The crowd was scattering now; only a few loitered. One, in particular, a woman, crouched in the shadow of a mound of earth. She seemed not to have changed her chiton in years, although the fabric was rich enough. She kept staring at us like a vulture.

"Let's walk a little farther," Orestes whispered. "She's making me nervous." I too was nervous, if only because it is dangerous to stand near an open grave. Especially now that evening was approaching.

A low wall, broken in places, began at the other side of the ravine. We climbed up; there were many footholds, both natural and man-made. "This wall was still unbroken when I was sent from Mycenae," Orestes said. "We used to play here, you and I."

"I, Orestes?" Then I remembered the role the Mycenaean prince had thrust upon me. I rebelled against it, but only briefly, for Memnon's magic was too strong. "Yes. Remind me," I said. "What was this wall?"

"You don't remember, Pylades? Your father sent you here to be my companion, and we had the same wet nurse. We used to play here, with a toy chariot; first I would yoke you to it and you would be the horse, then I would be tied to the chariot and drag you around, neighing furiously. Why are you weeping, Pylades?"

"It's nothing." How could I tell him that I had seen Leontes in my mind, my boy-sized armor on, being wielded as a club by Neoptolemos? It was so clear to me; my old

identity, my old memories, were still all there, all vivid, if I
could but cast off the name that clung to me like Orestes'
black cloak. I turned away, blowing my nose into my fingers. "I have to piss, that's all." I started to urinate against
the wall.

"Oh! You remember!" Orestes said.

"Remember what?" In the sunset, the piss stain on the
wall glowed eerily, like a little red sun itself.

"The pissing contest we had here once!" Suddenly the
shield of isolation dropped. His eyes lit up; he began to
urinate himself. "For weeks I dreamed of pissing farther than
you! I was so furious at you!" he cried out. There was so
much joy in his voice, so out of proportion to the homeliness
of what we were doing. "Oh, Pylades, thank you, thank you
for making me feel, for a few seconds—"

"Feel what?" I looked at him oddly. He covered himself
and embraced me.

"Human! Human again!" he said. I felt his emotion surge
through me, like a thunderbolt; I was shaking. Then, as
suddenly as it had evaporated, his emotionless demeanor
returned.

"Strangers!" A woman's voice. Where was it coming
from? "You come all the way to Mycenae to piss on our
walls! Who are you?"

"Up there!" Orestes said. "In the tree!"

There she was! It was the same woman who had glared at
us from the graveside. She was crawling on a branch, her
thin buttocks haunching like a dog's, her hair wild.

"Why did you follow us?" I said.

"Always I follow the stranger, stranger." She laughed, a
silvery, girlish laugh that belied her haglike appearance.
"Especially strangers who piss on our walls, strangers who
talk in whispers and don't understand our kingdom's weird
ceremonies."

"Who are you?" Orestes said.

"Does it matter?" She sprang down now and half loped,
half crawled toward us. "Ai, ai, I am become an animal."
She turned toward the setting sun. "When the moon comes,

you will see me howl." She looked from me to Orestes, her head jerking back and forth on the stalk of a neck. "And who . . . who are you? Which one of you is Orestes?"

Orestes gasped. He pulled me toward him, whispered in my ear, "Zeus, don't betray me! Maybe she's a spy."

"Neither of us is Orestes," I said.

"And you?" Orestes said. "You're filthy, but your clothes are fine. Unless you're a thief, they must be hand-me-downs; you must be one of the maids who work in the palace."

"Ha! Ha! You might say that I'm a servant there all right." She twisted and turned, and through the rips in her chiton I saw the scars of the lash.

"I see you're a pretty recalcitrant slave," Orestes said. "Well, we do have news for your mistress, Clytaemnestra—"

"She doesn't go by that name anymore. No!" There was bitterness in her voice. "She is the Mother. The Lady. The Great Goddess, who is free to fuck whomever she wants."

"I take it you don't approve?" I said.

"Approve! Disapprove! I am no one."

Orestes pulled himself together. He seemed to have come to some decision. "I wish to see your mistress . . . to inform her that Orestes is dead . . . trampled by his own horses in a far country." So that was the ruse he planned to use to get into the presence of the queen.

The woman wailed, heartrendingly, passionately. The sun had set and the moon was rising. She howled. "Let's get out of here," I said. "This is making me nervous, very nervous. . . ."

Orestes would not leave, but seized the slave woman, gripping her arms, shouting, "Why are you so touched by his death? What's he to you? You're only a slave, aren't you?"

The woman continued to howl; she fell to the ground on all fours and began to scratch at the earth. "The moon!" I said. "Is she a lykanthropos?"

After a long while the woman's cries subsided. She rose. In the moonlight, the paleness of her face matched that of Orestes; they seemed almost to be the same person.

Softly she said, "I will lead you to the palace, and I will

see that you are fed; and tomorrow I will tell them to bring you before the court." There were no more tears in her eyes. Instead I saw something else: emptiness, desolation, obsession.

They were the very things I had seen in Orestes' eyes.

Chapter XXIV

The Chained Princess

The street wound uphill. The woman summoned a boy with a torch to lead the way. "There it is," she said, as the boy held the torch high, standing on tiptoe. "The great gate . . . the inner city . . . the heart of dark Akhaia."

I looked up. Saw an archway topped by a vast triangular slab of rock on which two lions, rampant, pawed the air. I said, "It is said that Snakemother holds court on a throne flanked by such lions."

They seemed to move in the flickering torchlight. I was afraid. But the woman was already beating against the shutter of the guardroom and calling for admittance. When they saw who it was, the gate opened just enough to admit one man at a time. "I may not go in," the boy whispered, awed.

"We'll go on in darkness," the woman said.

I watched the two lions for a few more moments. I fingered the lion's paw around my neck. The boy and his torch were fast descending the slope, but the lions did not lose their glow instantly; a cold light hovered above their inlaid eyes.

"Don't gawk like a tourist!" Orestes hissed at me. "Remember you've been here before, Pylades." He tugged at my arm. "Quick, follow the servant."

I was reluctant to go on. Something about the stone lions . . . in my mind's eye, the image of the mother of Leontes and Leonidas, being raped against the lion's flanks, against the fire and falling stones. I thought of Leonidas waiting for me in Troy, of Leontes stranded between life and death,

waiting by the Stygian banks. It was their remembrance that
made me continue, and not the great vision that had first
inspired me to leave Troy. I was afraid to become like
Orestes.

The woman led us through side alleys to a courtyard
overlooked by two levels of apartments. The court was dark
from the shadow of the upper palace. A whipping post stood
at the center; against one wall, a row of jars to catch rain
water for bathing. A dog sniffed at a pool of blood at the
base of the post. A faint smell of olive oil and cooked fish in
the air; I realized I had not eaten all day. "This is where I
live," she said. "Doubtless, when they hear the good news
tomorrow, they'll move you to princely accommodations.
But I'm sure they don't want to be disturbed now."

"The good news?" In the dancing lamplight from the
apartment windows I saw him wince. "Is Orestes' death
something to rejoice in, then? I would have thought that
mourning rites, at least, would be declared."

"They live in mortal fear of Orestes' return," the woman
said. She led us to the door of one of the dwellings and
knocked. "Open up, we have visitors."

A paunchy man came with a torch and opened the door
and admitted us. His hands were filthy with fuller's earth; he
must work for the palace laundry. He looked nervously at us
before uttering the proper greeting: "Strangers, rejoice."

"Rejoice," we said.

The man shifted his weight from one foot to the other,
making the torchlight wobble. The walls: the whitewash
gray, cracked. A moth fluttered. The man gaped at it, drool-
ing a little.

"Look," the woman cried, "this is what they've married
me to, to try to silence me! Nightly they rut like beasts in the
royal bed, while they insult me by having me submit to the
lusts of this peasant!"

The man turned to us in remonstration. "I see you are men
of high standing, perhaps of royal blood. I beg you, try not to
see the harm in it. The queen forced me, and I have not laid a
hand on her, of course; that would hardly befit someone of

my station." Imploringly he turned to me. "Master, I should not say it of her, but she does tend to . . . worsen her own situation by these innuendoes. Believe me, she is a virgin, and if the political situation should improve, why then—"

"What are you talking about?" Orestes said.

The woman and the man looked at each other and shrugged. They did not seem in the mood to belabor us with the labyrinthine complexities of Mycenaean palace politics, and instead led us to an inner room, where the woman made up some pallets for us; the man brought in an amphora of sour wine, a loaf of bread, some goat's cheese. He seemed hospitable enough, once one got used to his shambling. I wondered why the woman had seemed to despise him so; I surmised that this must have been one of the inner palace servingwomen, who had perhaps fallen from status with the change in regime.

When we were left alone, Orestes spoke. "The dreams—they are worse than before. Just now I closed my eyes for only a minute—I needed sleep so desperately—and I saw him again. The blood, the blood . . . his arms and legs hacked, hacked. Please don't let me sleep tonight, or the dream won't let me go, I won't be free to face my mother. Shall I kill her? Is that really what it comes down to, Pylades?"

There was nothing I knew that could lessen his torment. So I just sat there, chewing slowly on a chunk of slightly stale bread, methodically counting and recounting the stacks of clay tablets piled against the far wall. This was clearly some kind of record-keeping room, not a place for guests to rest.

Before I could think of how to answer Orestes, he had already drifted into sleep. He turned and twisted and breathed uneasily and once or twice moaned words I could not understand.

"Poor Orestes," I said softly, "you always tell me you can't bear to sleep, you can't bear to face your dreams, yet you're always the first to go to sleep. Is it that you *want* the horror of the dream, that you're punishing yourself somehow?" More and more I saw the parallels between him and me; more and more I wanted not to become like him.

Later, in the dead of night, I was awakened by a whimpering sound. At first I thought it must be Orestes. But it was coming from outside, and it was accompanied by metallic clanking.

I threw on my chiton and slipped out. I wanted to find the source of the sounds; but more than that, I wanted to escape, however briefly, from the oppression of Orestes' feverish sleep.

I went through the outer room and into the courtyard. Somewhere, a dog snarled. I saw now the source of the moaning. Someone had been manacled to the whipping post. I could barely make it out; a woman, I thought, lying face down on the stones, her wrists raw from the cuffs. The chains, in the moonlight, glittered like silver. No, they must be iron, I realized. So fabulous a metal put to so mundane a use!

The slave stirred. I stepped into the shadow of the doorway; I did not want to be thought an intruder.

A rustle of cloth against stone . . . a boy bearing a torch . . . behind him a young girl dressed in a flounced skirt, her hair immaculately plaited and combed into delicate bangs over her dark eyes, clasping a clay serpent to her naked breast. She came to the post and stood over the woman. Perhaps her mistress, come to gloat over some punishment. What an unpleasant scene. I had witnessed one or two such as a child, when one of my aunts quarreled with her maid. I myself had never ordered Leontes beaten, though it was my right. My mother had never taught me to be cruel to servants, though a certain implacableness is necessary for a king. Perhaps it was because all through those last years in Troy she secretly knew she would one day be a slave herself? Could she have doubted Hector? I would never know now. Fascinated by the contrast between the two women, I could not leave; I knew too that if I returned to the sleeping room, I might be required to listen to another outpouring of Orestes' grief.

At last the girl said, "I've come here in secret. They don't know. They've terrible plans for you, terrible plans. Oh, no one thinks of us, no one, no one. They just stand in court, striking majestic poses, talking about destiny, destiny. Oh, I'm afraid. If only you would cooperate instead of giving these tasteless displays of self-inflicted pain!''

That was not what I had expected to hear. So I moved closer. They stood in a little wavery puddle of light made by the torch boy, and could not see me; I was practically breathing on them.

The woman on the ground pulled against her chains. More skin scraped on the hard iron. She said, ''He's dead, he's dead. I've just been told. I hugged the information to my bosom and didn't tell them yet. I wanted to put if off as long as I could—''

''Who's dead?''

''Who else? Who else? The liberator, the one I've waited for these long, long years while the stinking laundryman—''

''You know he's never touched you,'' said the girl.

The woman screeched with laughter, reared up. I saw her face clearly. With a shock, I realized it was the woman who had found us by the graves of the Perseids, who had led us into the citadel. So it was Orestes' death she meant. That much was clear. Who was this woman, and why had she taken Orestes' death so much to heart? She said, spitting the words out, ''We have to do it ourselves now, that's all there is to it.''

''What? Do what?''

''What do you mean, do what? There is only one thing to be done.''

''There you go again, sister, talking about what can't be. You can't bring back the old ways. You can't drag Father back from his grave.''

''I can, can, can! He's with us now. Ha! Standing in the fireglow, and the blood sluicing from his hundred wounds. Only he has no face.'' She was staring straight at me! I had no time to hide. She was pointing at me now. But the one who had called her sister would not look. Instead she stared at the ground.

And slowly said, ''I can't stand it anymore. Every day you

make them chain you here. You eat your food from the bowls
we set out for the dogs. When our mother and uncle come
you taunt them. If it were only just you, it would be all right
for you to enjoy torturing yourself in this perverse way, but
there's me to think of. It's about time I thought of myself,
even though I'm the youngest, and barely out of puberty. But
you've never given me a chance. You've poured out all this
terrible, terrible hate more and more and more and more, and
it's like I'm swimming in shit, and I just want to drown, to
die.''

"You weak, feebleminded—"

"Oh, I should be strong like you. Then I could let them
chain me and whip me and I'd still spit in their faces . . . but
I'm not strong, Electra.''

Electra . . . I knew that name. Electra was Agamemnon's
daughter and the sister of Orestes: a princess. Why had they
married her to a peasant? Why was she covered with filth and
sores and weals from the lash? And this other girl, she must
be Chrysothemis, the youngest daughter of Agamemnon.
Perhaps she had never known her father.

Electra moaned again, and turned her face away. I took
advantage of this to slip back into the apartment. Quickly I
found Orestes in the dark and shook him. "You must wake!"
I cried. He groaned and gripped my arm as though in mortal
terror. "You must wake up, that woman's not just some
servant, she's your sister!"

He muttered something. Then he sat up.

"They've done that to her?" he said very softly. "I'm too
late to save her?"

I thought of my mother. "I hope not."

"Let's go."

We went out into the courtyard. Chrysothemis was leaving; we were in darkness. Orestes knelt down by the body of
his sister.

"Electra," he said quietly.

She jumped up, howled, prowled around the post on all
fours, tugging on the chains and drawing more blood. "Oh,
Electra, Electra, how could they have done this to you?"

Her howling had awoken some of the dogs inside the
building. I could hear them yelping. A few ran out and began
to bark. No one else came out to look; it seemed people were
used to Electra's nightly bondage.

Electra said fiercely, "What right do you have to call me
by my name? You've come to strip me of the last thing I
have to call my own. After you tell the queen I will have no
name."

"Oh, Electra, I can't believe they've done this to you—"

"Ha! Does the sight of a woman in chains excite you, little
boy? Are you going to rape me now? Come on, come on . . .
but this cunt has snapping teeth. Ha, ha!"

"Electra . . ." Orestes was sobbing helplessly, hysterically. "I'm sorry, I didn't mean to tell you Orestes was dead,
I didn't know, I didn't mean to hurt you."

But she only laughed and shrieked and howled at the moon
and slavered. Two mangy dogs came running out now,
whining.

"Oh, what am I supposed to do?" said Orestes. "I can't
prove it, I can't prove anything." He touched her face, her
neck. She recoiled and growled.

"Keep your hands off me, do you hear?" she screeched.
"You can fuck me if you like, I'm not human, I eat with the
dogs, I'm just a dog myself, a bitch in heat, in heat."

"No, you're not a dog."

Orestes got up. The dogs were at his feet now, licking his
shins. He said, "You're not a dog. At least the dogs recognize me." He started to walk away.

I watched as she slowly craned her neck to look at him. At
last she said, almost inaudibly, "Orestes."

Orestes wept. He did not look back. I said to him, "My
own mother didn't know who I was. We've been misled by
our myths into thinking that everything depends on these
grand, apocalyptic recognition scenes. But . . . usually we
don't know who we are. For days now you've thought I was
someone else. I don't think"—it was only as I spoke that I
became aware of these thoughts for the first time—"I don't

think we *ever* know who anyone else is, really. I think we're always alone.''

I do not know why I spoke. None of this was my business; I was intruding painfully, embarrassingly, on their most private moment. I spoke only to hide my nervousness. I was really speaking for myself; the truth hurt less when it came out in the guise of words to another.

Orestes said, ''I don't want to be alone.''

I wanted Electra to believe. I wanted Orestes to have someone, someone other than me. I was so tired. The weight of Orestes' guilt and sorrow was crushing me. I knelt down by her side and said, ''Please, please believe him. He is Orestes. He is your brother. He has come to set you free.'' Angrily I shook her, forced her to sit up and look at him. ''Can't you see? Even I can tell . . . the look in your eyes . . . unmistakably the same—hunted, haunted, deathlike. Oh, I'm weary of the way you carry on, the two of you. Just get it over with, just believe him.''

I could see that she had waited for him so long, she had wallowed in her degradation for so many years, that it was hard for her to accept its ending. I went over to Orestes and said, ''It may take some days.''

''Perhaps,'' he said dully. We walked back into the building, leaving the princess still chained to the whipping post.

I slept uneasily the rest of the night, constantly waking to hear Orestes crying out. Whether he was dreaming, or whether he was conversing with some apparition, I could not tell. The dawn came too soon, chill and lifeless.

Electra's husband woke us with bread and milk. When Orestes sat up he prostrated himself and cried, ''Forgive me, my king, my king.''

Orestes said nothing.

The man went on, ''You don't remember me, of course, but once—in the old happy times—I used to wash your swaddling clothes.'' He was weeping copiously; I had to snatch the milk bowl from him. At last, drying his tears, he said, ''Electra has already gone to the megaron. She gave me this to give you.''

He laid a package at Orestes' feet. It was wrapped in many layers of cloth. Orestes untied it. Something heavy, metal-shiny.

A double-edged axe, brown with old blood.

"She has saved it for you, King, these past ten years," said the man.

"The labrys with which my father . . ." Orestes whispered, letting it drop from his hand. It thudded against the floor.

The man nodded. "She intends for you to use it."

"How strange," I said, examining its smooth, unornamented texture. "It's made of iron. It can't be that old, then."

"Iron, copper, bronze—what does it matter?" Orestes shouted.

But it did matter. It was the most important fact of all, in the end.

Chapter XXV

🔲🔲🔲🔲🔲🔲🔲🔲🔲🔲🔲🔲🔲🔲🔲🔲🔲🔲

The Throne of the Twin Lions

We were led through colonnades with scarlet pillars and murals depicting hunts and battles on land and sea. As we ascended the levels of the citadel the hot wind of the height began to blow. First, a courtyard where suppliants waited in an anxious line, waiting to be summoned before the Lady. A pompous basileus, wearing full armor and a helmet of boar's tusks, waved us through. Then a courtyard where priests wailed before a bloodstained wooden image of a bull. Murals of young women at their toilette, holding up mirrors and plaiting each other's hair. A smaller courtyard overlooked by a gallery, where two young boys scuffled; in the dust cloud of their kicking they seemed like little ghosts. When they saw us they stopped fighting and scurried within; I heard their voices echoing inside. When we reached the portal of the megaron they were standing on either side, quite still; they

had somehow scraped the scruffiness from their faces, and
their kilts had become perfectly creased.

Bright-eyed, they cried out in unison, "Rejoice, visitors.
The Lady Queen is pleased to see you."

We stepped into the megaron of the palace.

As the portals closed, the wind subsided. I saw a throne at
the far end of the chamber: the throne of the double lions.
The throne of Snakemother. But there was no darkness here.
Light streamed down from slits in the walls and ceilings.
Orestes had spoken truly when he said that here was an
image of Snakemother that dwelt in the midst of light. For
Clytaemnestra was seated on the throne, clasping a serpent of
gold over her breasts, her hair falling in ringlets over the gold
flanks of the twin beasts, paws upraised.

At her feet was seated a man. He wore a mask: it was the
very mask that had been robbed from the Perseids' grave. It
must be Aigisthos, I thought. Standing beside the throne
were the two daughters of Agamemnon. Chrysothemis did
not seem as attractive in the daylight; she pouted and fiddled
constantly with her hair, and flinched whenever she felt
Electra's gaze on her. As for Electra, though her clothes were
torn and filthy and her hair disheveled, she stood erect and
insolent, and no one in the court dared look her in the eye.

"Here come the messengers," she said, so loudly that the
court came to attention all at once.

"Rejoice," Clytaemnestra said. "I hear you bring sorrow-
ful tidings." Her lip quivered; she was barely suppressing her
glee at the prospect of Orestes' death.

Orestes and I approached the throne. I kept my eyes
downcast. I was supposed to be Pylades, and Pylades had
been Orestes' companion since infancy; but now I was supposed to be Pylades disguised as someone else. I was afraid
of giving the game away. I did not think that Orestes would
exact his revenge here in the open, with the guards in attend-
ance; but he was, after all, mad, and the mad are rarely
predictable.

I heard the queen's voice: old, tired. There was something
in it of my mother's. But of course there was. The same evil

had come to possess them both. "Tell me the manner of it, messenger."

"Lady, we were in Thessaly, where wild men actually ride on the backs of horses," Orestes said. "It pleased the prince to go and catch some wild horses, to break them to the chariot yoke. An accident . . . he was trampled to death. My companion and I saw, but could do nothing."

"I grieve," she said. But I saw no grief in her. "He was my son." But I knew also that he had been sent away because she feared his vengeance, and that she had sent assassins to kill him and promised them gold. The hypocrisy of her words made me look up from the floor. I saw her eyes: dark, rimmed with red. The precious stones of her many necklaces tinkled and glittered, making my eyes water. "But have you proof?"

Orestes pulled, from his chiton, a bloodstained rag he had obtained from the laundryman our host. "This was his." For Electra had kept many of his boyhood clothes hidden in a box.

He presented it, palms up, to the queen. Clytaemnestra did not take it immediately. When she did, she lifted it by the edge, as though it were still alive. The women of the court sighed, all at once; it was as though the wind outside had leaked into the megaron for a moment.

She let it drop. It fluttered to the floor, a great big crimson butterfly.

An attendant spirited it away; for when I looked for it again I saw it nowhere.

Then Clytaemnestra cried out, in a chesty, strident voice, "Ah, ah, pheu, pheu!" and shrilled out the traditional ululation of mourning, stretching her arms out over the crowd. Taking their cue from her, the women began to wail enthusiastically. Chrysothemis screamed and beat her breasts, digging into them with her fingernails and drawing thin lines of blood. Only Electra, Orestes, and I of the false name did not indulge in the display of grief. But in the general frenzy no one saw us. They were competing to see who could mourn most ostentatiously, striving doubtless for the queen's approval.

I heard the queen's voice close to my ear. "Actually," she was saying, "the death, though unfortunate, is not necessarily a calamity for me politically. Do you know, you two young men are rather attractive? I shall have you quartered near the royal bedchamber. You see, Aigisthos has gone into hiding; I mustn't see him for three days. It's the tiresome king-killing ceremony. See the man in the mask? A slave, expendable. I don't care to fornicate with slaves, much. Though as the living goddess I do as I please. And will, my sons and lovers, with you."

I understood. It was said that Clytaemnestra was so besotted with Aigisthos that, though she ruled as the representative of Snakemother in the High City, she could not bring herself to kill him as was the custom. She had done exactly what my ancestor Dardanos had done, though in her case it was out of a sexual obsession; after reinstituting the ritual in order to kill King Agamemnon, she had reinstituted the custom of the ritual scapegoat in order not to kill King Aigisthos. The poor man in the mask was intended to fool the powers of the earth. In three days she would kill him, in the sacred bathroom, using the sacred labrys. Even here, at the bright heart of the dark kingdom, misdirection was rife. It was all so contradictory, so confusing.

Clytaemnestra raised her hand. Abruptly, the chorus of lamentation was cut off. "But I am negligent in my duties," she said, smiling sweetly to the two of us. "You are guests. Electra, fetch the guests food and drink." There was triumph in her voice; evidently she felt she had scored a great victory over her unruly daughter. Electra shot her a baleful glance, then, as she walked out to order us food, collapsed into a fit of giggling.

"Ah, the poor girl!" Clytaemnestra said, "the grief will drive her mad. She loved her little brother, alas, alas. But I will not inflict our family problems on you, honored guests." She clapped her hands. "Music! Festive dancing! Choral odes!" she screeched.

Orestes whispered in my ear, "The bitch! They're for her benefit, not ours. She wants to celebrate my death, and the only excuse she can find is that we are guests and they mustn't burden us with their torments.''

I could not hear what he said next. For a dozen musicians had begun pounding on timbrels and twanging their kitharas and tinkling their finger cymbals. Flutes keened and conchs brayed. A dozen girls, naked save for a string of jewels about their waists, came running into the megaron. A white bull snorted and paced the flagstones; slender brown boys somersaulted over its back and stood on their heads and sang a high-pitched, haunting lyric in a language I did not know, a language rich in gutturals and strangely colored vowels, a tongue not unlike the one in which the Phoenician Phalas had spoken to the priestess of the pigs. I trembled. Snakemother's tongue! It was being spoken again, spoken openly, in the very citadels sacred to Skyfather!

I could see that Orestes was profoundly shaken by it. "My resolve . . ." he said. "I don't know. Am I on the wrong side? Are those who worship Skyfather fated to fall?''

"Skyfather loved Troy," I said, "and yet Troy fell." It was only at that moment that the full implication of that statement dawned on me. Could it be that Skyfather was not omnipotent after all? And then I had another thought, yet darker, which sprang unbidden to my lips: are we all on the wrong side? Is the answer a third possibility, one that no one has even considered yet?

I was about to say something to Orestes when Clytaemnestra clapped her hands. The Queen of Mycenae turned to depart; the slave dressed as a king fell in step behind her, and the whole circus of dancers, animals, and courtiers began to scatter. The megaron emptied in minutes. Clearly this was a highly disciplined court, always tense, always ready at a moment's notice to note and instantly accommodate the caprices of their sovereign. After the long walk from the dismal apartment of the laundryman, through the many corridors and courts, we had had a fleeting vision of glittering spectacle, of the fabled court of Mycenae; like a dream it had dissolved. I, Orestes, and Electra stood alone, dwarfed by the vastness of the chamber, in front of the lion throne.

"Well," Electra said (she still refused to call Orestes by
name, I saw), "I suppose I must obey the queen's instructions and see that you are properly housed and fed. Come
with me."

Orestes looked in dismay at me. "I shouldn't compound
the impiety by accepting food and drink, if I'm to exact
vengeance. . . ."

Electra turned, laughed, clawed at the air, again reminding
me of a lykanthropos. "Worrying about niceties, little boy,
when there's so much else to worry about?"

"Where is Aigisthos?" I said.

"Who knows?" said Electra. "A fine time you've chosen
to come, if your true purpose is what you say it is. They'll
want your presence at the king-killing ceremony, doubtless.
You'll not be able to wriggle out of that one."

"They've spirited Aigisthos away." I saw the dark rage in
Orestes' face. "I thought at the very least I could kill Aigisthos.
As for my mother, I—"

"The real Orestes would never weaken," Electra said
scathingly. "The real Orestes would be Vengeance personified.
The real Orestes would be the arm of Skyfather, wielding the
very thunderbolt of heaven."

"How do you know?" I said, for I understood Orestes'
inner turmoil and I did not think Electra did. "You don't
bear his burdens. You don't have to drive the actual sword
into your mother's breast. You've tortured yourself these
thirteen years . . . but no one forced you to suffer. Revenge
is the son's duty. You're a woman; Clytaemnestra has restored the old way, the rule of women. If they chain you and
whip you, *you're* to blame."

Orestes put out his hand to stop me. But I had said my
piece and it could not be retracted. Electra stared at me,
fierce, defiant. She whispered, "You've always been cruel to
me, Pylades."

It was the first time she had called me by name. I felt the
name grow ever stronger, the knot tightening; I was almost
physically choked by it. While I was venting my feelings, I
had felt the ba of my old self stir, move its wings, poise

itself; her words pushed my birdlike half soul further, deeper into the abyss of my consciousness. I grasped for some memory of Troy. Instead, my thoughts were invaded by remembrances of another's childhood, more vivid than my own: of pissing contests at the walls, of running after my best friend's sister and taunting her and pulling her hair. And I knew that poor dead Pylades' shade was feeding on my life force as a vampire feeds, and that until his name be taken away from me he would never be truly dead. We were two half souls in the same body, each unwilling to acknowledge the other for fear of suicide.

While I stood there, trying to tear myself free of Pylades' name, I heard Electra speak, in a quite different voice, trembling, soft: "He is right, though, Orestes."

"At last you can say my name," he said.

"I've lived under a terrible spell for so long," she said. "Do you know why I've tortured myself? While Father was away in Troy I always dreamed of him. . . . No, not chaste dreams of daughterly loyalty, but dreams in which . . . I felt him touch me, you know, touch me, *there*. Once, Orestes . . . Oh, I see it so clearly, though I've tried for so long to have them flog the remembrance from my flesh. Oh, it was the night you were born! That night—dark, the slaves scurrying back and forth outside my father's chamber, and the screams of my mother in labor—Agamemnon came to me. Did you know that? And he said, 'Daughter, daughter, I wish you were my wife. In a few years you will start to bleed and you will be married off to some prince. My wife is like a stone! Have you ever hugged a stone? Stone, stone, stone . . . Oh, Electra, I love you.' Oh, he kissed me, Orestes. He burst my hymen. He told me to tell the servants I had hurt it while riding piggyback on the shoulders of his barbarian body servant—they killed that servant. I rejoiced when my mother killed Agamemnon, I really did. I hated him. And yet I thought, she's like a stone, a stone, but I'm like a real woman. If I become like a stone too, like a stone, no one will touch me again. Oh, I loved my father! Now I am the stone and Clytaemnestra is the rutting woman. But if you kill her, make her the stone again, I will become—''

"What are you saying?" Orestes said, uncomprehending.

Electra kissed me and said, "He has freed me to say these terrible things. I will always be grateful to him, Orestes."

Her smell lingered in my nostrils: the heady womansmell blended with the stench of the filth with which she had chosen to surround herself. Was this the sordid truth of Electra's years of suffering, of yearning for revenge—not the filial piety which is blessed by Skyfather, but an insane self-punishment brought about by incestuous desires?

"Nothing is what it seems," I said, sounding hopeless, inadequate.

But abruptly Electra assumed her mask of cold fury, and told us to come and be fed, or we would go hungry. She did not call Orestes by name, or acknowledge him her brother again, for three more days.

Chapter XXVI

The Secret Kings

The first two nights passed without event, for we were not summoned into the presence of Queen Clytaemnestra, nor did Orestes seek to appear before her; he was not yet ready to act. Nights he lay unsleeping, or if he slept, he sleepwalked and I would find him gone, and have to lead him gently back to his pallet. Although the queen had made suggestive comments to us during our meeting, we had come to understand, from conversing with slaves and couriers, that she acted this way toward every male stranger who showed up at the palace, and if that man proved forward, would revile him and even, on occasion, have him executed by delivering him into the hands of the maenads who roamed the hills beyond the city walls. We had passed a kind of test, it seemed, and as a result, we were given freedom to roam the palace and the city. But we would not see the queen until the ceremony of the king-killing; they told us she was in seclusion, being ritually purified so that she could perform the sacred, dreadful act.

The evening before the rite, Orestes and I left the dining hall early to retire to the chamber.

On our way, we walked past the sacred bathroom, whose door was covered with mysterious inscriptions like the ones in Troy; I made an involuntary sign of aversion as we walked past it.

This time, as we turned the corner to go to our quarters, we saw a golden cage in the corridor. A man in a purple himation was seated inside, wearing the mask of the Perseids. "It's the surrogate," I said. "Why is he here?"

The man in the cage stirred wearily. "Let me out, let me out," he moaned.

I stood beside him. The latch was easy enough to open; the slave could not reach it through the bars because he had been securely tied to the other side of the cage. "But you're supposed to be the king," I said, "at least for these few days. Why are you in a cage?"

"King for three days!" Hollow laughter, muffled by the mask. "I've been trying to escape. There is a potion to numb my senses"—I saw a lekythos, half full, lying at his feet—"but it is wearing off. King for three days—that's what they told me. A drugged king, powerless. You'll get to fuck the queen, they told me. What a high honor! The drugs make me impotent, and when I complained the queen threatened to castrate me before she killed me."

Orestes and I looked at each other in bewilderment.

"We should free him," I said.

He hesitated. "What can we do?" he said at last. "It would only give us away. I think they put him here, so close to our chamber, to tempt us. It's another test. Free him and we'll be in that cage ourselves."

"I wonder what he looks like under the mask," I said.

"I'm tied down. I can't remove it." The slave struggled

uselessly against his bonds. Moonlight streamed in from the right, for the passageway had window openings that overlooked an inner garden and let in the wind. I heard the wind roar beyond the garden walls; but here it was just a breeze, suffused with the scents of night-blooming flowers. The mask glinted. Through the window, over the top of the far wall, I could see the hills; forests blanketed them, and the treetops were silvered by the moon. From infinitely far came the howl of a wolf . . . but perhaps it was Electra who howled, for I knew now that suffering had turned her into half an animal.

"I want to escape!" I cried. "I want all of us to escape— you, me, the slave here too. The curse of the Atreidai is not my curse, not the slave's curse . . . and it needn't be your curse, Orestes, unless you insist on this revenge that must bring about your own destruction."

Orestes said, "All of them are mad, my friend. The whole world's gone mad. My mother is feverishly working to turn back time. My sister's hour of incestuous passion has turned her into an animal. And my father's dead. And my sister Iphigeneia, sacrificed to seal a bargain between my father and Snakemother—a daughter's blood in exchange for a futile victory, a brief triumphal return, then . . . cuckoldry and death. They're all mad, I tell you! So why shouldn't I be? Don't I have the right to take the same escape route everyone else in my family has taken? I *want* to be mad; by the gods, I need to be mad!" He turned to me, shook me frenziedly. "Oh, Pylades, you almost make me sane when you tell me these sensible things, when you say we should escape. But surely you must see it's impossible. To surrender to the endlessly replicating cycle—that's the easy way out. Not running away. Oh, Pylades, don't say such things anymore. Let me be mad."

I said, "Of all the Atreidai, you're the only one who *knows* he's mad. So you must have some inkling of sanity."

"No! I don't want that! Leave me alone! If you want to free the slave and flee the city, do so. I'll stay and face the consequences! It's *my* fate, *my* curse, and not yours; do what you want."

And he stormed away in the direction of the sleeping chamber.

The slave groaned. "Free me." I saw his eyes through slits in the gold: dull eyes, fearful eyes, not the icy, resolute eyes of the one who would be king.

My hand was on the latch for a long time. But I did nothing. Was it out of love for Orestes? Orestes was my enemy. But he had drawn me into his secret inner world, and in that world I played the role of comforter, of advisor, of friend. I tried to tell myself that it was only because the name of Pylades had been thrust upon me that I felt any concern for Orestes. But perhaps that was not so. Perhaps I did feel a kinship with him that went beyond the magic of naming and not naming, in the depths of my true soul. But I did not want to have it so.

I hesitated for a few moments longer.

In the end I simply did not have the courage. Orestes was right; it was easier to remain passive, not to fight fate. I had my own destiny to think of, though at the moment that destiny seemed impossibly far away.

Slowly I walked away from the caged slave, toward the chamber Electra had prepared for us.

Later that night, however . . .

I had been sleeping for some hours when a creaking sound woke me. It was Orestes again. He was pacing back and forth, muttering to himself; now and then he went to the window and peered out. "Orestes, Orestes," I said, "you must sleep."

He did not speak to me, but continued to mumble. I rubbed my eyes. I saw that the iron axe, which he kept by his bed wrapped in a piece of wool, was gone. He was sleepwalking again; he had not bothered to clothe himself. He started to leave the room.

I followed him, seizing his cloak from the floor and throwing it over his shoulder. He wrapped it lazily about himself and went on, walking quickly down the hall—not in the direction of the caged slave, but the other way, a way we had never gone before. The moon had set; I could barely see him moving against the starlight from the windows. When we reached a back stairway I held onto him, trying to make sure he did not stumble and desperately trying to lead him to retrace our steps; but he went on, his feet resolutely finding the steps, not faltering at all . . . and I felt a chill sweat running down my spine, for I knew that some god was leading us. If I were still King of Troy I might have seen what god it was. But now I was only Pylades, a mortal, lacking Skyfather's vision. All was dark to me. I simply followed.

More corridors, more turnings. Would this palace never end? Deserted courtyards; here and there a guard slumbering at his post, a linkboy sprawled on the flagstones with his torch smoldering at his feet.

Gardens within gardens, and columns crusted with cool gold, a goat tethered to a well, more passageways . . . "Orestes," I said again and again, "turn back, turn back," knowing it was useless because a god possessed him.

Past the courtyard where Electra was once more chained to the whipping post . . .

Somewhere else now, another corridor; when I looked I saw that we were on the other side of the garden our room overlooked, and I did not know how we had managed to circle back to the same wing of the palace. Light from a crack in a door. Orestes pushed it open a little more; we stepped inside. Torchlight.

Shadows striping the face of a stone god, bearded, battered; the jewels had been pried from its eyes. An altar; the smell of incense, fragrant, suffocating. And a man clasping the knees of the statue. I saw the disfigured face of the statue and knew it was Skyfather, for the Akhaians worship him not as a stone but as a vigorous, terrifying old man. Looking around I saw more statues of him: broken effigies stripped of their gold. Arms and legs littered the floor.

The suppliant was babbling: "I'm sorry I let it happen let it stop now let it stop let the queen and her snakes be sent back into the forests and the graves—"

Orestes snapped awake and cried "Aigisthos!"

And I saw that he wielded the iron labrys.

In terror the man whirled to face us, one hand still clasping the knees of the god. "You can't kill me," he said. "I'm a suppliant . . . in the temple of Zeus . . ."

And I saw in my mind my grandfather embracing the stone of Skyfather and Neoptolemos's sword descending, and blind rage seized me and I ran forward, seized the weak and weeping man and dragged him and thrust him on the floor at the feet of Orestes, thinking, I'm involved now, I've become an accomplice to his mission, I'll never escape now. . . .

And Orestes raised the axe, shouting, "Do you know who I am? Do you know, do you know?" and I was smashing my fists into his face and feeling slippery blood spurt over my arms, and Orestes was screaming, weeping, screaming, weeping . . .

Aigisthos threw himself down in prostration. "I know you. You are the agent of Skyfather. Always I feared his retribution, always I knew he'd come back, that Clytaemnestra would go too far. . . ."

"Look into my face, Uncle Aigisthos! Did you imagine me standing over you with my axe poised over your neck when you fucked my mother? Did you, did you?"

"Orestes . . ."

Nephew and uncle looked for a long moment into each other's eyes. "Oh, I have been weak," Aigisthos said. "And your mother—she burns, she is like fire. I was always weak, but when I made love to her I felt manly, all-powerful—"

"And with Agamemnon she was a stone!" Orestes cried out, his voice a bitter rasping. "Oh, oh, how can I kill you?"

"You must, Orestes," Aigisthos said softly. "This moment was fashioned by fate before we were born, before even the world began. It was ordained that you would find me here . . . in the three days before the king-killing, when I am compelled to hide my face from Snakemother lest she know that the dead slave is not the king. I am not Aigisthos at this moment, I am vulnerable. Every year I hid here, and every year I believed you would come."

"Don't weep," Orestes said. "It's much harder to kill you that way."

"No. I won't weep. I am sure that fate has decreed that I should now plead for my life, but we'll take that as read. Just get on with it."

Orestes did nothing. . . .

I said, "Isn't this what you came for, Orestes?" Yet I did not want to see this man die. The circumstances were too much like those of my grandfather. Aigisthos remained prostrate, not trying to ward off the blow he was expecting. But Orestes dropped his axe. It clattered on a shattered marble torso. "But you don't understand," Aigisthos said. "I don't want mercy. I deserve to die. It's the right thing to do, you see? I made no bargain with Snakemother. . . . not like your father. But he was the head of the family. What he did affected all of us. And he was head of the entire Akhaian forces; so his actions affected them, and with them all Akhaia. I prayed to Skyfather in secret, but . . . your mother was so passionate! So beautiful, so warm, so, so, so lonely! We didn't know that they'd ever come back, you see. As for your father's death, *she* said that the ancient laws gave her the right to kill him, even though those laws hadn't been invoked since the Perseids, since the Minoan hegemony, centuries ago! She planned it all! And I stood by and watched, and every night we made love and her kisses sealed my complicity. I know that I must die, Orestes."

I could see that Orestes was searching for some way out. He was a man who hated bloodshed and yet was continually haunted by bloodshed past and future. What could I do? It was not my affair . . . yet that little part of me that had begun to feel for Orestes spoke. "You must kill him without killing him," I said.

"That makes no sense," said Orestes.

"Isn't it true that he is supposed to die tomorrow, that the slave takes his place wearing the deathmask of the king? Well, who's to know that—"

Aigisthos rose to his feet and stared at me. "I accept the fate you have decreed, stranger."

He did not call me Pylades. Orestes had not told him who
I was, of course. I was glad. It meant that it was the I
beneath the I who had proclaimed his death sentence. I felt
my old self stirring a little. I exulted.

Orestes looked at me. "It's not like you," he said at last,
"to be able to dream up so duplicitous a scheme." So he too
acknowledged, somewhere in his crazed mind, that I was not
Pylades! He went on, "But I must say that the punishment
you suggest does fit the crime. Perhaps, too"—there was
longing in his voice—"it will be punishment enough for
Clytaemnestra."

"I don't think so," Aigisthos said. "Zeus, I don't envy
you."

"You don't mind being placed in that cage?" I said.

"Not really. Is there any of the drug left?"

Orestes and I nodded.

"Then I'll scarcely know what's happening to me. The
slave is undoubtedly miserable; one gets inured to the potion
after a day or two. But since I'm to die tomorrow . . ."

I said, "You seem remarkably calm, King, about your
own death."

He said, "We Atreidai are a very fatalistic family, my
friend. We have to be, you know. We live under an ancient
curse." He turned to Orestes. "Kiss me goodbye, nephew. I
do love you, you know."

The two of them embraced, proudly, as kings embrace. I
stood a little way off, in the shadow. I felt awkward, an
intruder in the most private moments of this doomed family.
I felt pity for them. How could I not? But there was another
emotion too; with a shock, I recognized it as envy.

For a few hours, they still would have each other. But I
had no uncles. They had all been killed in the war. So long
ago. Deiphobos, Troilos, Paris, Polydoros . . . I could not
even remember the names of all fifty anymore, or even the
nineteen sons that his queen, my grandmother Hecabe, had
borne King Priam. I just knew that they were dead, and that I
would never know their love.

The palace was utterly still as we led Aigisthos to the

corridor where the slave was caged. It took only a few moments for them to change places. The slave escaped into the night. Aigisthos drank what was left of the potion; when I placed the mask over his head I felt his skin and it was already cold and numb. He was as good as dead, though tomorrow we would have to see him carved up in Clytaemnestra's dark ritual.

I watched Orestes fold the wool around the unused labrys. He would resist sleep as long as he could, but I did not have the stamina to fight off my weariness.

Before I fell asleep I thought of Leontes. Leontes had died for me, gladly even; Aigisthos had accepted his proper death at last, and the slave was free. As I lay there I thought, over and over, What if I had managed to force them to recognize me, what if it had been Leontes, not I, who had fled to the hills after the sack of Troy? Would it have made any difference at all? I lay in the dark and despaired and longed to go back and accept the death that the slave boy had suffered in my place.

Chapter XXVII

Clytaemnestra

The sound of conch trumpets from all sides of the palace called us down to the megaron. If I had been impressed by the brief spectacle of our first meeting with Queen Clytaemnestra, I was overwhelmed now. There was an orchestra of perhaps fifty, all reed and percussion, blaring from the four corners of the chamber. There were two bulls, a black and an albino, and a pair of identical twin boys, one painted black and the other white, were somersaulting back and forth, vaulting over the bulls' backs in a way I had only heard of in tales of the ancient Minoans, who once ruled the sea. They had revived this ritual to accompany the revived ritual of the king-killing. Pubescent girls danced, slapping their tambourines to their slender hips. The men were dressed in festive finery, their phasgana gleaming; I saw many of iron, polished like silver. The women, bare-breasted, wore floor-length skirts belted with serpents of gold, and gold snakes coiled around their arms and peeked out of their hair, combed and coiffed into bangs like spearpoints and into plaits and ringlets that curled over their shoulders and bosoms. Men and women alike had kohled their eyes and dusted their faces with chalk and powdered gold. And all of them sang, words in the antique language which I could not understand.

They all milled about in disarray. Presently there came a bloodcurdling ululation from outside, and others came into the megaron, their appearance so singular that the elegantly dressed courtiers all stepped back to make an aisle for them. They were a band of maenads. Electra, who had come to stand beside Orestes and me, gave a shriek and made the sign of aversion. The maenads wore scanty clothes and had stained their arms and faces with fresh blood, but, though their hideous paean shrilled from their lips, their movements seemed less haphazard than in the forest. To my horror I recognized my mother among the madwomen, crooning as she cradled a snake in her arms. I wanted to cry out to her, but I could not bring myself to.

"They're not wild; they don't lurch about and rave as they did before," Orestes said.

Electra said, "There's more to them than you think."

The maenads swayed and moved their hands and elbows in bizarre, jerky movements. "They are dancing," Electra said. "An ancient dance . . . a dance of darkness."

Another fanfare as the queen entered the chamber. Behind her came Aigisthos in his mask. He walked slowly; the potion had not worn off, and no one had thought to look beneath the gold face of an ancient king.

A tiny pause, a collective catch of breath, as we waited for the signal from Queen Clytaemnestra . . . and then the music broke out again and the procession left the megaron, with children scattering flowers before the Lady and her

consort, with the drums pounding, with our hair and our
cloaks whipping against us in the wind of the citadel's peak.
We followed the queen's party, for we were honored guests
who had brought news that the queen both feared and welcomed. Princess Electra wore fine clothes; everyone but I and
Orestes was impressed that she was showing solidarity with
the new regime, and not appearing, as was her wont, in some
degrading and derisive guise. We followed. The street was
steep; the bulls and heifers had to be coaxed down, and there
were many longueurs as the procession stalled, but they were
all good-natured about it. Mycenaeans looked down from
tiny windows overhead and scattered perfume and precious
oils over us, and sang a refrain in the old tongue, joyous and
incomprehensible to me.

It was Electra who told me the meaning of it: "*Blessed be
the king who dies to replenish the world; blessed be the
eaters of his flesh and the drinkers of his blood. In three days
he will come again.*"

I tried to look cheerful, though the words came from a
dark time. The irony of it was that the king would not come
back this time; but I was unable to enjoy the prospect of
Clytaemnestra's fury at having been outwitted by her son.
The curse was not my family's. I could only observe and
pity. Orestes had not been delivered from his melancholy.
Only Electra seemed joyful, for she danced before us, flinging her arms in the air, her face strangely radiant, beautiful
even. But there was something of doom about it too.

The procession . . . down narrow streets as the sun rose
higher and higher . . . When the sun was at its height we
reached the palace again. The killing itself was not to be
done openly, but in the sacred bathroom as tradition decreed.
The group was narrowed down to only a few priestesses, the
royal princesses, and us guests of the queen's household.

Up the stairs; to the doors sealed with ancient inscriptions;
to a room uncannily familiar to me, for it was exactly like the
bathroom in the palace at Troy, the one where I had bathed
on the night before I was to encounter the mistress of the
dark places in the bowels of the earth. Aigisthos was led to

the tub and divested of his himation and his chiton; only the mask remained. Clytaemnestra held a two-edged axe in her hand; she stood with her back to the sacrifice as they poured over his body lustral oils and perfumed waters.

A window overlooked an outside courtyard. The crowd was gathered there. The madwomen were out there, howling like wolves as they prepared to rend the pieces of the corpse; I could not see them from where I stood, but I could hear their crying, and the crowd's breath welling up as though the sea had come to Mycenae.

Clytaemnestra's face: an ancient face. The past possessed her.

She gave a signal.

Priestesses rushed forward and threw a golden net over Aigisthos. He did not struggle as the net tightened. Clytaemnestra whirled around and rushed forward, swinging savagely with the axe. It sliced into his side and the dark blood oozed out. He was too stunned and drugged to cry out. The axe fell again and again. A severed hand slithered down the stone steps. Blood gushed now. Spurted over the queen's face. Spattered the robes of the priestesses. Fountained up. I felt a sprinkle on my cheek and dared not move to wipe it off. At last the king screamed, screamed, screamed, and still Clytaemnestra hacked away . . . until at last he screamed out a name, her name. The axe fell from her hand, her face changed from triumph to horror in a single moment. Wildly, steeping her arms in blood and flesh, she gripped the golden mask and tried to rip it off, and then at last she saw the face of the man who had been her lover these past years. She moaned.

Then screamed out, "Electra has done this!" and she began to sob hysterically, tears mingling with blood. "I loved him."

The priestesses were crowding around the body now; one by one they recognized him. Outside, the howls of rejoicing continued. Clytaemnestra rushed at Electra and began to pummel her wildly with her fists, while Electra laughed that animal laugh I had first heard coming from a treetop. Chrysothemis was trying to pry them apart now, and

Clytaemnestra was beating them both back. At last she was overcome. She sank down on the steps of the bath in a pool of blood. Her dress sopped up the blood.

Electra said, "You were wrong to rob the ancient graves to make the ceremonies more potent, Mother. You were wrong to try to bring back the past at all. The past has come back of its own accord, Mother, the past you rejected. Here is Orestes."

And Orestes stepped forward.

She looked into his eyes. "My son," she said. And lifted her arms, imploring. "I know you must kill me."

"Mother," Orestes said. He drew the iron labrys from his chiton. "Mother, Mother . . . Why did you send me away?"

"You must kill me now. It is your destiny." She spoke very calmly now; all the emotion had been drained from her. She was drenched with blood from head to toe, but she spoke softly, as though they were just mother and son together, speaking of private things, as though all the world were not listening to them.

"Where will it end?" Orestes said. "Who will kill me?"

"It will end soon." She unfastened the clasp that held her robe together. "Look, my breast. I gave you life once. Kill me now."

"I—"

"What kind of a man are you? Do as I tell you!"

He moved toward her. But he made no move to strike. No one tried to stop him. I turned and saw that some courtiers and priestesses were already deep in conversation, doubtless trying to work out some way of salvaging their positions under new political conditions. Clytaemnestra said, "You see, son? They are already abandoning me."

"I don't want to kill you, Mother." Orestes moved forward again; I could not tell whether it was to embrace or to strike.

"No. You must! It is well, Orestes. You're far too weak to fight destiny all by yourself. Killing me is the path of least resistance. The Age of Bronze is ending, my son, and darkness is swallowing the light. Perhaps you think that it is the Lady's doing; but that's not the whole answer. Now, kill me.

You know that you must. You know as well as I do that our family lives under a curse. When I brought back the worship of the Lady to our land, I too was weak; though I thought I was punishing Agamemnon for killing your sister Iphigeneia, I was really fulfilling his bargain with the Lady, the bargain that gave us an empty victory over Troy. When you kill me you will wreak Skyfather's vengeance on the Lady. You think it's all about love and hate within our family, you think it's about honor and vengeance and incest. What happens between us is just a little thing, just a domestic squabble. We are just pawns in the great war between earth and heaven, nothing more. I'm not going to plead with you for my life. Iphigeneia pleaded—it didn't move your father's heart. At last she convinced herself that she was dying for the glory of the Akhaians, that it was a noble, wondrous sacrifice for our people, not the sordid political maneuver that it actually was. She was an innocent. But I am not innocent, and in killing your father I knew that I was already placing the weapon in your hand and aiming the blow at my own heart. Ah, I've regretted it again and again. I've been tormented by night-mares. Your sister has tormented me, and wouldn't stop even when Aigisthos whipped her like a common slave. You must kill me, Orestes. You must free me. I have suffered so much. I will bequeath you my suffering; it's all I have to give you, for the kingdom is yours by conquest and inheritance, and I don't have the right to bestow it."

"But who will free me?" Orestes cried, anguished. And raised the axe and, not looking, smashed it into his mother's side.

She did not move at all at first. Then . . . she turned to me. She seemed to see me for the first time. She looked at me with the clarity of vision that is the gift of those about to die. I saw in her eyes that she knew my true name, that she could set me free. Dying, she reached out to me and whispered: "Here is the one who will set you free."

They were all looking at me now, wondering.

"Why?" Orestes said. "Who is this man to whom I have given the name of my dead friend?" For the old madness had left him, and soon a new one, far more horrible, would replace it. But in that moment of lucidity he remembered that I was not Pylades. I could feel that foreign name uncoiling itself from me. I could feel my true self grow strong.

I knelt down beside the queen. She fell into my lap; I held her face in my hands. She stared into my face in wonder and bewilderment.

I said, "Queen, you must utter my name. I can see that you know it. I can see that you have the power to free me."

But she was already dead, and I was still only half a soul.

It was Electra who spoke next. "Throw both their bodies from the window," she said. "The maenads are too maddened to know the difference. Let the flesh of both be plowed into our fields. Long live King Orestes!"

Those in the sacred bathroom looked uneasily at one another. Orestes still held the bloody iron labrys in his hand; he had not spoken since he had demanded to know my true name. He only stared wildly at the multilated bodies and at the pools of coagulating blood. Someone ran out to get help from the palace guards. Men with spears and ceremonial armor came in now, gaping at the carnage. They too did not move, until Electra urged them once more, "King Orestes has come back. Look at him. Kneel to him. He is your king, and Snakemother's servants have paid the price. Agamemnon's pact has been wiped out."

And they knelt down, the blood sticking to their knees and their hair as they prostrated themselves before Orestes; and soon they lifted up the bodies and threw them from the window, and the crowd gave out a mighty cry of bloodlust. But Orestes seemed to see nothing of all this. At last the news must have reached the people gathered outside. Again and again the shouts of "Long live King Orestes" burst into the air.

"Are they so fickle, these people, my people?" Orestes said. I went to stand beside him. "Now that my destiny is completed, I suppose the gods have no further use for me." I could tell that he was slipping once more behind that wall of melancholy with which he had always shielded himself from the world. Then he said, "I have killed my mother."

They are the most horrifying words that a man can utter.

He and I stood there for a long time. I could offer no solace. In liberating his kingdom from the rule of Snakemother he had committed the one impiety for which there can be no forgiveness, from which it was my sacred duty to shrink in utmost horror. Yet I did not recoil from him either. I saw that he was weak and that destiny was inflexible; it had not made any allowance for his weakness, his humanity. It had forced him down this road, and at the road's end it had forsaken him. We were alike, he and I, lonely men molded by implacable forces.

Presently he said, "Look, look . . . they've come at last."

"Who?" We were alone in the chamber, for all the others had left to join in the celebrations. I could hear not only shouts of triumph, but shrieks of death and the clang of bronze on bronze; I knew that the supporters of Agamemnon's government must have arisen and were even now putting Aigisthos's henchmen to the sword. As always, there was a blood price to be paid for kingship, even when that kingship came by legitimate inheritance. Gently, I said, "Orestes, there's no one here. You must go to your people."

"No! I see them! Do you remember how I used to fear to fall asleep, because of the dreams that would come? No more. It's not a dream now, it's all real. They're all around me. Everywhere I look." He pointed at the bloodstains on the wall.

"It's blood. The slaves will wash it clean—"

"Not blood alone! But women . . . snake-haired, gibbering . . . their eyes dripping black rheum . . . they're calling me . . . they're all around me . . . No!"

I knew then that the Erinyes had come for him. Though the gods had driven him to matricide, they had not spared him matricide's punishment. The Furies had come, and they would never leave his side, sleeping or waking. Orestes was lost. No man could reach him now.

And I said, "How can Skyfather allow such things to be?"

And remembered that Skyfather had not shown himself to me that day when I first came back to Troy, but only sent me his messenger, and a riddle with no solution.

At last I said to Orestes, "I cannot stay here anymore. I have to travel on."

"I too," he said. "I cannot be king until I have been purified. I will go to the court of my uncle Menelaos in Sparta. There is a woman there who perhaps can heal me. She is the daughter of Zeus. She is my aunt Helen. Perhaps she can intercede with Skyfather."

"I too must go to Helen," I said.

He said, "You too? Can you not tell me who you are, my friend? You have stood by me in these most terrible of times, and I have done you the injury of bestowing on you a dead man's name. I see now I was wrong; it was selfish of me, for I saw that some magic had bound your true name, and I longed so much for my friend to come back from the dead. Look how those women jeer and flap their leathern wings. Some will say that I have gone mad, but that is not so. I see more clearly than ever before, I see . . . something in you that I should fear, perhaps. Yet I have loved you as a dear friend." He started to shout now, as though trying to make himself heard above the cacophony of interior voices. "You will come with me to Sparta?"

"Yes. But I fear that when I find what I seek we shall no longer be friends."

"In that case, I want to know one thing. When you helped me, was it solely that you were constrained by the power of the dead man's name? Or did you feel anything at all for me?"

"I do not know, Orestes. I think I pitied you. But perhaps . . . perhaps I also loved you." It was what he wanted to hear. But in my heart I knew that all my convictions were being shattered. I had known once that Skyfather was all-powerful and good, and that Snakemother was evil; that the Akhaians were my enemies; that I must drag Troy out of its shame back into the glorious light that was its due. These truths seemed hollow now. But—as Queen Clytaemnestra had said of her son—I was not strong enough to walk away from destiny.

Thus it was I, the sworn enemy of the High Kings of Mycenae, who led King Orestes from the chamber of blood, down the great steps of stone into the megaron of the palace, past the royal supporters who were even now wiping their bloody swords on the cloaks of the slain, out of the massive portals into the courtyard crammed with cheering crowds who fell at the king's feet and clambered forward on their hands and knees to touch the hem of his robe . . . out of the darkness into the dazzling sunshine sacred to our father in the sky.

And the sky was brilliant blue that day, as though it had soaked up all the blood we had spilled, accepting it as a rich sacrifice.

And I dreamed of Helen that night, and of stars that fell from the sky and turned to pieces of iron. And woke with her name on my lips.

Book Five: The Queen of Heaven

ΑΨͲ

Occiderit ferro Priamus? Troia arserit igne?
Dardanium totiens sudarit sanguine litus?

Was it for this that Priam succumbed to the sword
and Troy to ravening fire? Was it for this
that the Dardanian shore lies soaked in blood?

> —Words of Prince Aeneas to Helen,
> during the night Troy fell
> Vergil, *The Aeneid*

Chapter XXVIII

![decorative wave border]

The Rituals of Spring

The season of ceremonies to celebrate the coming of spring had only just begun; it was proper that Mycenae, citadel of the High Kings of the Akhaians, should have first place in the calendar of rituals. Only then would the other cities in the Akhaian alliance follow suit and perform the rites peculiar to themselves.

Orestes wanted to settle the affairs of Mycenae for a few days and, though I had planned to leave immediately, implored me to wait for him. I was eager to comply. For as I moved closer to the final object of my quest, I had become ever more afraid. Would Helen too not prove an illusion? All my other goals had proved ambiguous, and my search for answers had yielded only more questions. I was anxious to put off our journey for a few sleeps. I was afraid that Helen's smile, which haunted my dreams, would prove yet another phantom.

Orestes was king in name. But as it turned out he ruled for only a single day. I was with him as he sat on the throne in the great megaron; Electra sat at his feet, I stood at his side, with Chrysothemis on a lower step of the throne, alternately wailing and fidgeting. He was richly dressed, and wore a crown decorated with gold that had been beaten into the shape of leaves, their veins filled with silver. The chamber was filled with citizens who had come to gape at their new king. They did not know whether to be relieved at the ending of Clytaemnestra's backward-looking regime or to be appalled at having a matricide for a king. It was a gloomy gathering; I was conscious of their staring, and knew that it must be far worse for Orestes.

He was trying very hard to be a king. But now and then I would see his head dart from side to side and I knew he was seeing the Furies. How could he keep his mind on the business of government? Monsters surrounded him. His private air was befouled by their stench, though the wind blew mightily as ever and the sun shed a gray light from behind thick clouds. To the east of the throne a great window opened out onto a terrace that hung on a ledge of the mountain. It was flanked with red columns.

Presently they brought before him the usual petitions and legal cases, the sort of thing any king must deal with daily. He dispensed justice in a detached, distant voice. The theft of cows . . . a gift of land in compensation. Presently a murder came up for consideration; it was the victim's daughter, kneeling before Orestes in supplication, who had brought the petition, not only demanding the death of the killer (it was some drunken argument) but claiming restitution for the possible loss to her future dowry. The girl was ten, barely of marriageable age.

"Can you be sure of the killer's identity?" Orestes said.

"He boasted of it, King, at the house of Aias the fuller." She began to weep.

"Is the man present?"

A surly man stepped forward and knelt down before the throne. "I did kill him, King, but because he was planning to sacrifice the girl to the Lady! He had some notion of making a bargain, much as—excuse me, King—your father once did."

"What shall I do?" Orestes turned to me in indecision. I could see that he wanted nothing more than to leave the citadel of the Atreidai. His soul was polluted by the Furies' foulness. Only a god could lift the curse. It was no use pointing out to the gods that he had had no choice.

I said, "I cannot tell you how to govern, King."

He said to the young girl. "It is a terrible thing to kill." He paused and went on, "But to speculate over what might have been your dowry, had your father lived, achieves nothing more. Let the man live. But let him pay three times the usual blood price against the cost of a husband." He turned to me almost as though asking for my approval.

A voice from the throng: "Of course he's lenient on killers! He killed his own mother, didn't he?" An uproar. Orestes rose from his throne. Guards closed in in front of us to prevent them from mobbing the throne.

I cried out, "Can't you see he had no choice?" But I could hear, over and over, in the crowd's cacophony, the word "matricide."

Orestes clutched his forehead and began to babble obscenities. Chrysothemis recoiled; Electra went up to support her brother. I sprang up to the top step of the throne, crying, "Leave him alone, he's raving!" For madness is an affliction sent by the gods. Orestes moaned in his sister's arms. The guards looked about in consternation. Someone had to take control. I ran down the steps and tried to shout down the mob. "It's not fair to him," I screamed. "He has come to set you free; he's done it at the cost of his own sanity. You've no right to torment him like this."

An old woman in the mob yelled back, "At least the old queen's killings were sanctioned by ancient custom!"

I dashed into the crowd. I seized the woman's arm. I heard low mocking laughter. I saw her face. I knew that face so well: from the day of my own crowning, the snake-haired woman who had taunted me on the steps of my own palace. She melted through my fingers, a dry abrasive slithering sensation, a serpent coiling into the crowd. "Snakemother!" I whispered. I was chilled. I turned to Orestes, vividly remembering the day I had become king. "You spoke so glibly of the blood price a murderer must pay to the victim's kinsmen. That is why the crowd is angry. They are animated by Snakemother. She has come to exact payment."

"But Aigisthos has paid!" Orestes said. "A king's blood for a king's throne."

"But you are the kinsman who must receive payment, and you are the murderer who must pay," I said.

Orestes said, "I can't be king yet."

He freed himself from his sister's arms. "Your embrace suffocates me," he said.

She said, "But you are the liberator."

Orestes said, "Enough. We must go." He staggered down from the throne. "Help me, stranger." Again he did not call me Pylades. "We'll go away, far away. South, to my uncle's kingdom." He looked at me. There was nothing in his eyes; it was like looking into the eyes of a blind man. He said, "Oh, if you could only see. But you cannot. Oh, I wish I were like you. You have no name. . . ."

"At last, my friend," I said, "you see that I am not Pylades." I supported him; he leaned against my shoulder as we left the megaron. The crowd parted. I could not tell whether it was from respect for the king's office or whether they felt that we were like criminals, like lepers.

In the courtyard, in the wan sunlight, he stumbled on the chipped flagstones. "Do you despise me?" he said. "I am only a king's shadow, but you have in you something that makes me feel you could be a king."

My heart beat faster. It has been said that mad people can see hidden things. "You know who I am, then?"

Orestes said, "Perhaps. I cannot say."

Electra was following us into the courtyard. She had put on robes of triumph. But the kohl on her eyes was streaked from weeping. "You didn't come to free us after all. It's the same as it was before, with or without Clytaemnestra."

"The sickness isn't in people," Orestes said, "it's in the whole world."

Then it was that I whispered the words I had heard uttered by the Pythoness in the navel of the universe: "The Age of Bronze is ending."

"What will come next?" Electra said.

"I don't know." A few curious onlookers had come out behind us. I said, "But I think I know how to stave off the ending. Perhaps it can be postponed. If we choose to live out the rest of our lives in the shadow of the war's aftermath, if we don't provoke the gods, if we pay a sufficient blood price"—I remembered the stranger I had killed in my father's palace on the day of my coronation—"perhaps we can delay the end of the world."

"If a blood price is what's needed . . ." Electra cried out.

Suddenly I realized what she intended to do. I grasped her by the wrists. She twisted free and ran back into the megaron. Orestes only stood and stared dully ahead. I ran after Electra.

The court was still in confusion. Somewhere dogs were yapping. A child bawled. Electra pushed a guard aside and sprang up to the window ledge. She screamed, "If you must have your blood price, let it be me!" I caught up with her, put my arms about her waist. The wind made her hair billow, getting into my eyes, blinding me. She struggled.

"Let me go! You don't understand. All my life I've had only my hate to sustain me. Now there's no reason for hating and no reason for living."

The crowd was shouting now. I smelled their bloodlust in the wind.

Then they parted for Orestes to come forward.

He said, "Don't." But there was no force in his dissuasion. Perhaps, hounded as he was by the Erinyes, he could not even tell what she intended.

Electra said, "Now I know Agamemnon will never come back."

"No," I said, "he won't. You always knew that."

She said, "I will smother the appetite of Snakemother with blood, and make her forget that she has lost her dominion over the high citadel of Mycenae."

I could not hold onto her. She was possessed, charged with a superhuman energy. She wriggled free of my grasp, ran to the edge of the terrace, and jumped. I winced when I heard the dull slap of flesh against rock.

"I told you I couldn't be king yet," Orestes said. He expressed no other emotion.

"What? Didn't you love your sister?" I said, thinking of my grandfather's countless progeny.

"I knew her only as someone who wrote me letters pleading with me to come home and kill our mother."

At that moment the clouds parted a little. The leaves of the olive trees on the terrace gleamed. The sky seemed to draw color from Electra's sacrifice.

"The war's not over," I said.

Orestes stood at the edge of the precipice. For a moment I
thought that he too would cast himself down on the rocks.
But he did not. He turned and flailed at the air. The Furies
must be close to him, drawing him into their serpentine
embrace. He expressed no grief. Still his eyes stared vacantly.

Members of the court were climbing up onto the terrace
now. There were boys in loincloths with their long dark hair
braided and stiffened with lamb's fat; there were women with
their nipples painted crimson and their many-layered skirts
trailing over the stones. The king's guard moved to bar them
from the king. I saw that their swords were crusted with
green; perhaps they had not been used in many years. And
their shields were frayed, the leather drooping from their
frames.

Orestes said to me, "I wish I were like you."

"Like me, King Orestes?" I said.

"Do not mock me with the title of *wanax*. I am no king of
men as was my father Agamemnon." Again he swayed from
side to side and held his arms up to ward off the invisible
Furies. "I wish I were like you. You are some kind of king, I
think? Yet you no longer have a name save what men wish to
call you. If I had no name, if I were not Orestes, then I
would escape the destiny that the Fates have attached to the
name of Orestes. That is what I want—to have my name
stripped from me."

"You do not know," I said, "what you ask." I concentrated, trying to draw the memory of my name from the air; I
could not.

"Nevertheless I will ask it."

"Who has the power to take away names?" I thought of
Memnon and of the elaborate trickery by which he had
bewitched my name into an image of clay and faience.

"The gods."

I said, "The gods will only laugh."

Orestes said, "I see it clearly now. I promised I would
come with you to Sparta. The rituals of spring are about to
begin there. Aunt Helen will be presiding over them. She is
the daughter of Skyfather. I have said that perhaps she will

intercede for me. Now I see that her intercession is my only
hope."

I ached at the mention of my kinswoman's name.

"Yes. To have my name stripped from me. To have my
soul drained from me, so I can be like an empty amphora, so
I can be refilled with a better destiny."

We remained in Mycenae only long enough for Orestes to
preside over the interment of his family. They were buried in
the old style, and in haste; to cremate them would have
abrogated the purpose of Electra's self-sacrifice, which was
to sustain the deception of Snakemother. Orestes ordered
them placed in the very tomb we had seen opened when we
first came to Mycenae. Then he commanded that the golden
mask of the Perseids be thrown down, and all the other ritual
objects that had been taken from desecrated graves. The
diggers sealed up the corpses, and we trudged up the streets
to the safety of the palace, for night was imminent and we
were both afraid of the shades of the dead.

Orestes summoned a scribe from the warehouse and commanded him to set down these words: "I, High King of the
Akhaians, at Mycenae, decree that the Lady of Darkness
has been cast down, banished to an ancient grave not of our
time. Thus it is that we close our rituals of spring for this, the
first year of my reign. The images of Skyfather are to be
brought back into the sunlight. It is in Skyfather's name that I
speak, and of no other deity."

The scribe showed him the tablet. Orestes took the reed
from him and signed his name on the wet clay:

ᛗᚼᚤᛄ
ᛡᛏ⊕

ORESTES THE KING

"This shall be my only decree as king," Orestes said as he
tossed the moist tablet to the scribe, "until the gods have

purified me of my mother's murder.'' So saying he tore his king's vestments and smashed his crown onto the stone floor.

The gold leaves buckled; the crown rolled away. I heard the echo of its clanging.

"And now we will go to Sparta," Orestes said.

Night was falling as we left.

Chapter XXIX

Sparta

Four days we journeyed through the heart of the Akhaian alliance to reach the city of Menelaos. Orestes never slept at all now. There was no reason to sleep, for sleeping and waking had become the same. He was only sane enough to know that he had gone mad.

Everywhere we went they were celebrating spring. They danced in the fields; by the rivers they sacrificed. At night, by starlight, men and women embraced, naked to the wind, praying for that special fertility that is the gift of the gods, hoping to catch a little of Skyfather's seed as it spilled on the thirsty land.

But I felt no joy in their joy. For as I came nearer to Sparta it seemed to me that my sundered soul carried a heavier and heavier burden. Though our chariot flew at tremendous speed over the ancient roads, it seemed that the news of Orestes' matricide had flown yet faster. We were not exactly turned away from the villages we passed, but we were made to feel unwelcome. We would stumble into such a place and we would find that food had been left on the thresholds of houses for us, rich food as befitted the High King of the Akhaians and his friend; but the villagers would be nowhere to be found.

Once a man talked to us; but he was blind.

We were perhaps an afternoon's ride away from the city. I asked the old man, "Where have they all gone?"

And he said, "Hurry, my son . . . they've all gone to the fields to hide from the bad luck of the mother-killer's passing."

Orestes cried out then. Perhaps it was what the blind man had said; perhaps it was because of something in that living nightmare of his. "What is he saying?" the blind man said. "Is he ill?"

"Don't give me away," Orestes said softly to me. To the old man he said, "I am someone who has no name." It was evening. A light wind, fragrant with olive oil and roasting lamb, wafted through the village.

"You're hungry," the blind man said. "And my son, who always guides me everywhere I go, has gone away to hide with the others. They are so superstitious, these people! If only they were blind like me. They'd soon see things more clearly. Hold my hand and I will tell you the way to my house."

I said, "I will lead you by the hand, grandfather."

Orestes started to protest, but I raised my hand to quiet him. I knew that he was undergoing more torment than I could understand, but I was hungry and I blamed him for my hunger. I suspected too that the old man knew more than he let on, for the blind always possess to some degree the gift of prophecy.

His hut was the farthest from the village center and the most unsturdily constructed; smoke tendriled from it through gaps in the thatch. When we entered I gagged from the stench; the floor rushes had not been changed in months, and reeked of the excrement of men and sheep and dogs. Nevertheless, having accepted the man's hospitality, we could not now gracefully decline, for his invitation set in motion an unchangeable sequence of events laid down by the gods at the beginning of time.

There was a thick darkness here. A fire burned, but its smoke concealed rather than revealed. The man moved easily, though, being blind. A dog, bigger than the old man, growled somewhere. In the dim light I saw him shift and curl up so that the man could lean squatting against him.

After inviting us to sit beside him, he said to me, "And why does this man always gasp and moan? I hear swift furtive movements, as though he were clawing at the air. He has nothing to fear here, except perhaps the foul odors of my little nest."

Orestes did not speak, so I said, treading carefully between truth and falsehood, "He suffers from nightmares."

"But he is not asleep," said the old man.

I said, "Grandfather, he can't tell the difference between sleeping and waking anymore."

"To be blind is much the same," he said sympathetically, and poured us new wine in earthenware bowls. It was cool and it took my mind off the stench. "But you will want a way to get rid of the nightmares."

"Yes," Orestes said, his voice ghostlike.

The old man looked among the dirty rushes and pulled out a loaf of bread. He broke it and gave it to us. "Miserable fare," he said apologetically. "But you are welcome."

"To end the nightmares," I said, pressing him. "You know a way?"

"You must give yourself," he said, "to the Queen of Heaven."

I watched the fire guttering and chewed on the bread. It was gravelly but full of flavor.

"We have come to see the Queen of Sparta," I said, "not the goddess."

"The Queen of Sparta shows herself only as Queen of Heaven," he said, and I realized that one must be a title of the other. "And only at the festival of spring."

"Why?" I said. "Is she no longer beautiful? Have the years since the war taken their toll? Is she afraid to show herself?"

"Ah . . . you have seen her then," the blind man said.

It was Orestes who stared at me now. I do not know if he had already divined the truth. It was possible that they both did, since one was blind and the other mad, both conditions that give rise to the ability to see hidden truths.

I said guardedly, "Yes. In a manner of speaking, I have seen the Queen of Heaven."

"Yes . . . I hear the villagers returning." Orestes and I heard nothing. "Eat, eat. Hurry. There's a wrongness about your presence here. But it's too late for me to make you leave; you are guests, and sacred because of it. And I am too old to listen to silly superstitions."

Orestes murmured, "But you know of a cure for my affliction?"

The blind man said, "Only this: to be whipped before the queen brings about a cleansing of the soul."

"Whipped?" I said, astonished.

"I know what he means," Orestes said, lucid suddenly. "My aunt Helen told me of it once." The old man did not seem surprised that Orestes had let slip her name and therefore his identity.

I closed my eyes and remembered, from a time when Troy still stood. . . .

It was in the courtyard of the princes. I knew it was a memory of my early childhood because of the sunlight, the shadows of olive branches dappling the uncracked flagstones. No place could have been farther from the blind man's hut. I was being scolded by Leontes' mother. I was no more than four years old. With every word she whipped Leontes with a bundle of flexible green twigs from which the leaves had been plucked clean. I could see red ridges form on Leontes' scrawny buttocks. "Remember! Remember!" his mother was shouting at me. When I tried to look away she stuffed my head under her left armpit so that I could not avert my eyes, and whispered, "Remember he is suffering for what you did wrong."

I do not remember what I had done. But it was something harmless like pilfering a sweetmeat or pissing on my mother's dinner chiton. I wanted the beating to stop even though I could not really imagine what Leontes felt, for none of the

slaves had ever laid a hand on me, of course. I could see the
tears well up in his eyes. Once my grandfather had said to
me, "A king must feel his subjects' pain, Little Star." I tried
to feel it. I forced tears out, but Leontes' mother did not
relent.

Until a shadow fell across the three of us. A slender
shadow and a woman's fragrance. And I looked up as my
nurse let go of me and saw the skirts of my aunt Helen.
"Don't hurt the child anymore," she said. She did not use
the imperious tone that my mother Andromache used with the
slaves. She was gentle, almost as though the woman were a
child herself. Leontes was so startled that he stopped sniveling. She took me by the hand into the shade of the olive
trees.

She said to me, "I have always hated to see anyone being
whipped."

"What a strange thing for a queen to hate," I said.

She called for a slave to fan us as she sat beneath a tree. I
climbed into her lap. She toyed with my hair, saying "Look,
it matches mine; the shade is just so." Then she seemed sad
again. It was some moments before she answered me, "I am
no longer a queen here, Little Star. The gods have made me
young again. Look, I'm only a princess."

"Young again? But you're not old."

She laughed. "Silly boy! I'm almost as old as your mother.
I've been a married woman since I was eleven years old, and
an adulteress since twelve. You don't think I'm too old?"

"I'd marry you too, Aunt Helen. Because you're so pretty."
But long after that it was the smell of her I remembered best,
apart from the melancholy smile of hers, which seemed to be
only for me and perhaps one or two of the other children of
the palace. The smell was like crushed pomegranates. It was
nothing like the smell of other women I had known.

"I'll remember that you said you'd marry me," she said
abstractedly. "I'll remember that you proposed to a woman
almost twenty years old, long past the age of marriage."

"I swear it by the stone of Skyfather."

I do not know why I said that. Nor why the memory had

not surfaced until that bleak day. But I remember that Helen became solemn and tried to change the subject, but she could not easily find one that pleased me. Until I reminded her of the whipping. "You were going to tell me why it upset you so," I said.

"It reminds me of Sparta."

Sparta seemed so distant to me then. I said, "Do you miss Sparta? We have a scullery maid who comes from there. She says that it's very mountainous and very primi—primi—"

"Primitive." She was tickling my neck now. I pretended to resist, and it brought my head nuzzling dangerously between her breasts, and I felt them undulate a little. It was a great mystery to me. "Yes," she said, her eyes far away, "they're primitive all right. I still remember the first day of spring, the first year I was queen in Sparta. They dressed me as the moon and they put a quiver and a bow in my hand, all of gold, and they covered me with veils and set me in a chariot outside the city where the fields were freshly plowed; and the young men came out and lay naked on the earth and the priests beat them with leather quirts and they writhed and twisted and turned and I could barely see through the veils but I knew that some of them were in ecstasy as well as pain. Menelaos explained it to me later. 'It's an old custom,' he said. 'We've always had it and we always will. It's from the time of Snakemother and it's never been eradicated. You see, they beat those young men into a frenzy of sexual excitement and then their mingled blood and semen spurt into the earth and bring it to life. Oh, don't be upset, Helen. You will grow used to it when you go back tomorrow.' And I said, 'You mean I have to watch it again?' And he said, 'Of course, my queen, that's what being Queen of Sparta is all about— you're the goddess, the Queen of Heaven.' I cried and he made love to me. I didn't feel anything except the pain. It was the first time. He jerked about as though he had the falling sickness and he cried my name again and again and I said, 'Why do you call me, Menelaos? I am here already,' and suddenly he shuddered and fell still and rolled away from me. And he started to snore."

I said, "And the next day you went back, Aunt Helen? To the fields, I mean. For the ceremony." I was not much interested in hearing about her and Menelaos; I had no idea what she was talking about, except that it concerned something that happened between men and women about which no one had cared to enlighten me.

She sighed. "Yes, I went back and watched the whipping some more. I was there to inspire them, you see. They hugged the earth, but it was me they imagined in their arms, not the stinking, fresh-plowed sod."

When I looked at Orestes, I realized that a similar memory had come to him. I wondered whether it had been under similar circumstances. It must have been after the war . . . perhaps after the killing of Agamemnon . . . perhaps when Orestes had already become a refugee.

He ate his bread greedily and gulped his wine and his head darted from side to side like a serpent's, and now and then he whimpered.

"Your friend is strange," the blind man said.

I heard the villagers coming back. I heard voices outside the hut: "A royal chariot . . . horses still tethered . . . they're here, I tell you, they're here polluting our soil . . . nowhere to be seen . . ."

A young man burst into the hut. He carried a torch. He was about my age. Had I not become king, I would have been like him, I thought. He took one look at us and made the sign of aversion. "Father, how could you!" he shouted. "But you are blind, you couldn't have known." To us he said, "You must leave at once."

"Do you not know who I am?" Orestes said. "I am King, High King!"

"That's why you must leave, filthy mother-killer. Oh, Father, we'll have bad luck for years to come. Our crops will die."

The blind man said, "They are my guests."

The young man was confused. But "guest" is a magic

word to any man. He calmed down and said sullenly to us, "Rejoice."

"Rejoice," I said, but Orestes, smarting at a rebuff from a mere peasant, said nothing. Quickly, to allay his anxieties more, I said, "We must be going."

"No. Leave when it is completely dark. There is no moon. No one must see you. Or they'll take their revenge on Father and me."

We sat for a long time, not saying any more to each other. Orestes rarely surfaced from his nightmares. Presently, when the babble outside had quieted, Orestes and I slipped away, found our chariot, and returned to the road.

I was so sleepy that I leaned against the side of the car and dozed. The sun was rising when I awoke. We saw the city walls ahead. A huge crowd was gathered outside. Orestes had been driving the chariot by himself. We stopped. "You must rest. Your eyelids are drooping; they must be like lead," I said.

Feverishly he said, "Got to hide the chariot. . . . I can't go in as king now. . . . How will we see Helen?"

I looked ahead. "The crowd is heading toward us. There are fields here." I heard distant music, drums, and blaring conch shells.

"The ritual of spring!" Orestes whispered.

"She'll be there." I was seized by an uncontrollable trembling.

"I know of one way we'll be sure to see her," I said. "But it's going to hurt."

"Hurt!" Orestes screamed at me in a passion. "How dare you talk to me of hurt! Let them lash me, let them whip me to death, if only it will drive these demons from me!"

"It's our only hope," I said. I still could not stop shaking, and I knew it was not only because the wind was cold.

It was because I knew that I could no longer put off the moment when I would encounter that terrifying smile from which I had been fleeing these fourteen years.

Chapter XXX

The Whipping Fields

We hid the royal chariot in a grove at the edge of the field. Already I was falling victim to the rhythm of the chanting. I could see that Orestes' eyes were glazed over, like a sleepwalker's. Drums thudded, high voices of children keened, and then I heard a sharp, slicing sound like the wind when it whips the reeds by the riverbank, only there was no wind here beneath the walls of Sparta.

There was a human wall in front of us, hundreds of people with their backs to us. They were singing and clapping their hands in syncopation with the whipping sound I had heard earlier, and jumping up and down and pounding down the furrowed earth. Conchs blared.

"Be cautious. We might not blend in," Orestes said. For the people of the city, male and female, wore only strips of wool about their loins. Their bare skins were daubed with mud. "We'd better do likewise," he said. I saw that he was making a supreme effort to resist the torment of the Furies and to appear normal.

We retired behind a tree to undress. Orestes shredded his chiton of fine lamb's wool and handed me a piece, which I folded around my private parts. I thought of removing the lion's paw that still hung around my neck, but in the end I could not; for since I left Troy I had never taken it off. A little stream ran beside the tree; we coated ourselves in the mud from its banks.

Then he and I slipped into the back ranks of the celebrants. The sky was gray, pregnant, about to burst with rain. Thunder boomed; I was glad to hear the voice of Skyfather, but the people were too intent on their ceremony to notice it. Making sure Orestes was in sight—I could not tell how long

he could pretend to be sane—I pushed and shoved my way to
the front lines. My belligerence went unnoticed, for all the
young men were elbowing their way forward at once. There
was something going on at ground level; those in front had
crouched down so as to see better. Children were squinting
from between the legs of adults. The chanting was infectious.
I did not know the words and I knew that there was something ancient and perhaps Snakemotherly about them, but
they possessed my tongue and I could not stop shouting,
shouting until my throat hurt. Slowly it dawned on me that
the ground itself seemed to be moving. No, those were not
ridges of earth—they were the backs of men who lay face
down in the sod and who had painted themselves with a thin
layer of mud, and they were making love to the earth. And I
remembered how I had endured the treacherous embrace of
Snakemother, but this was something else altogether, both
solemn and wildly joyous. Their buttocks hunched above the
furrows and thrust hard down into the ground as the crowd
cried out. But where did those lashing noises come from, that
sounded so much like the wind in the treetops of the mountains where I had once tended sheep?

I saw the source now—a row of girls, not quite marriage-
high, naked, their lips and nipples colored brilliant red with
pomegranate juice, and each one carrying a leather flail.
They were moving slowly toward us, their high voices a
melismatic counterpoint to the guttural groaning of the crowd.
Their heads were crowned with woven leaves. They danced
in a long line, their barely formed breasts heaving a little,
always smiling as they lashed the young men, who shuddered
in pain and passion with each stroke. And now the crowd
was screaming, "Fuck the dirt! Blood the mud! Life from the
lifeless clay!"

And suddenly I heard Orestes' voice from behind me.
"It's her. Look." And he pointed to something far away, a
smudge of gold against the gray walls. I saw that it was a
chariot, and that a woman stood in it, veiled, and in her
outstretched hand she clutched a bow. She stood motionless
for so long that I thought she must be a statue.

"It's the image of their goddess," I said.

"No!" Orestes cried. "No, it is Helen!"

I could not tell. I did not want to believe. Not yet.

"I've got to go to her!" he shouted.

"No. Perhaps . . . perhaps it's an illusion. . . ." But I spoke lamely. I could not deny my own longing. Even as I resisted I was already unwinding my loincloth and throwing myself into the mud and crawling forward through the slush toward the woman of gold . . . and feeling the lash tear into my skin. "Helen! Helen!" I gasped as I groped my way forward in the mud, my eyes blinded, crusty. My phallos stiffened as it slid into slick soil. The earth was a woman and the woman was Helen and Helen was the Queen of Heaven. I thrust and thrust like a dog, goaded to frenzy by the screaming and the stamping of feet and by the piquant burning of the whip on my back, my buttocks, my legs, driving me to jerk forward, to drag my phallos through the slush. I felt blood running down my back and the mud cracking, I felt the pain warming me, maddening me. Beside me a hundred others writhed and wriggled and we were a hundred gigantic earthworms, a hundred monster phalloi, we were a single sky-creature with a hundred phalloi that ravished the palpitating earth, and I saw for a moment we were no longer man and woman but one whole, one hermaphroditos, indivisible in the dance of joy and pain.

I could see Orestes ahead of me. We seemed to be in a race, swimming in an ocean of unnatural thickness. I could see him gasping as a young girl struck him firmly on the buttocks. I felt the pain myself now and heard the girl whispering softly, "What you do is sacred, hero. The red and the white will blend and turn to bronze-colored corn." Again and again she lashed me and spurred me forward. I felt greater than myself, I felt godlike, full of the power of creation. But though my passion grew and grew I did not feel the semen spurt forth yet. The chariot that bore the Queen of Heaven was so near, I had but a little way to crawl and I would reach it, and Orestes was ahead still, propelling himself forward with strong arms. The Furies must be on his back, I thought, for he moved with inhuman alacrity. The mud coating on his back was cracked, and rivers of blood ran down it to the earth.

I caught up with him; we swam side by side. The earth was more slippery here, my body fairly glided along. I heard him croak out the words "Helen, Helen," as though it were all he cared for in the world, but I myself experienced a strange detachment. I could not believe that the woman dressed as the huntress was truly Helen. I thought of that smile, brighter than the fire that had gutted my city. A terrible fear took hold of me but I crawled on. There was more pain than joy now, more exhaustion than sexual excitement.

He had gained on me. I saw him throw up his arms and heard the thunk of flesh on metal. The tires of the chariot were of beaten copper and the wicker of the chariot was coated in gold. With my last strength I reached out to touch the cart. Burning air blasted my face. I ran my fingers down the hot metal, touched the writing embossed on the gold:

$$\text{𐤀𐤉𐤕}$$

and I saw that behind the chariot, in characters of woven grass much taller than a man, the same letters flamed: it was the name of Helen.

And the woman in the chariot spoke to Orestes, ceremonial words, ancient words: "Thou art the first to reach the huntress. Thou art the first to seed the earth. Thou art Skyfather."

She set down her bow and knelt down to pull him out of the earth.

"Thou shalt kiss me as the sky kisses the earth."

Orestes murmured, "Helen, Helen."

But I already knew that it was not Helen's voice.

And when the woman removed her veil, I knew it was not Helen. How could it be? Yet she was beautiful. There was something of Helen in her face. She was young, as Helen had been when she first came to Troy; she could not be more than twelve. Strands of blond hair fluttered down from the wreath of beaten gold. Her eyes were heavily kohled, and her mouth painted bright crimson. There was something of Skyfather's blood in her, for when I saw her face it seemed that a wind sprang up from her and made her chiton flutter.

She took Orestes' hands in hers. He whispered, "Forgive me, goddess, purify me, cleanse me. . . ."

"You are a suppliant?" Her voice was gentle. But it was not Helen's. It had all been a sham. I had come for nothing.

I was furious. I felt impotent, drained. I dragged myself up from the mud and began to wipe the mud off myself in a frenzy. "It's all hopeless!" I said. I was weeping. My cheeks were soaked with sweat, blood, tears, and filth. "You're not the one! You're an imposter!" Helplessly I began to flail at the chariot car. My fists bled as they pounded the jagged metal. "You're not Helen, not Helen. . . ." So this was to be the end of my journey—to have participated in an unkingly way in a fertility rite in a kingdom far from my home. I wished I had remained a shepherd.

The girl laughed. "Of course I am Helen," she said. "I'm the best Helen they've ever had in Sparta . . . but then, it's in the blood."

Orestes said hoarsely, "Does it matter which Helen she is? She is beautiful, and I've won her by winning the race." For the first time since the terrible events in Mycenae there seemed to be hope in his voice. But I despaired.

I looked more closely into the girl's eyes then—she had used so much kohl that all I had seen at first was a black smear—and saw in them the blue of the sky. I could tell that the blood of Skyfather ran in her veins. But who could she be? Again she laughed softly. She had something of Aunt Helen's laugh. But not quite.

I said, "It's all illusion. Just as I feared. I will never find my name again. I should never have left the hills. I'm in the labyrinth without a thread. I'm lost, I'm lost."

I could barely hear myself speak above the roar of the crowd as more and more celebrants collapsed panting at the foot of the woman who called herself Helen. They were all laughing at me, all, all, all. I was a naked man covered in blood and offal and I did not even have a name to call my own. I sobbed helplessly.

"Why do you weep?" the girl said, puzzled. "Because your friend won the race and not you?"

"No!" I screamed. "Because I sought to be a hero, because I did not stay a shepherd . . . because a slave boy died in my place and stole my destiny from me!"

Wildly I looked about, knowing that what I said could not make sense to anyone.

At that moment there came a renewed caterwauling of flutes and drums. Uphill from where we stood, the gates of the city screeched open. Girls scattered flowers. Boys somersaulted and juggled flaming torches. Dogs ran yelping through the crowd. A line of chariots emerged, their metal wheels clattering against the stony road. The crowd fell silent in an instant.

Then there came a covered litter borne on the backs of warriors.

I said, "Who now has come to witness my shame?"

The voice from within the litter: "I have, Astyanax."

That was the moment when, far across the sea, the blue king began to sicken and to turn back into clay.

And the curtains of the litter parted to reveal that smile, unchanged over the years.

"My Little Star," she said. So quietly. I was sure no one else had heard her.

I started to go to her. But I had come so far and I was so tired. I did not have those few steps left in me. I fell at the feet of the daughter of the sky. Her name had not even left my lips.

Chapter XXXI

Menelaos

I dreamed of mist and fire.

I burned and was blinded. There was no sun. At the end of the dream we were all rushing toward the bank of a dark and foaming river. We were thousands in number. The mist was bloody mud, enveloping, erotic. We were thousands in our gleaming helmets and our clanking, articulated armor. The river steamed. I stirred in my sleep, cried out.

A cool hand touched my forehead.

"He's waking up." The voice of the Helen-that-was-not-Helen. I moaned. The voice again: "Fetch some more water, quick, from the well."

"The mist," I whispered, "I'm—"

"Don't try to talk."

My eyes were crusted when I opened them. I was too weak to wipe the dried mucus from them. But I saw her face. It was no longer painted. It was an earnest face, solemn, beautiful in its own way; no, her face was perfect by any human standard. I would have thought it astonishingly beautiful if I had not first expected to see the face of Aunt Helen.

"You funny little king," she said, and kissed me on the cheek. "You thought I was my mother, didn't you? As if the Queen of Sparta wouldn't have a stand-in for the spring rite, especially after all these years. You expected someone young, didn't you? Shall I call you King? Or will Astyanax do? After all, we are cousins. My name is Hermione. Of course, I'm Helen, too, for ceremonial purposes. All the queens are called Helen here."

Panicking, I tried to move. "How many know?"

"Shush." I could see more clearly now. We were in a small stone chamber; I had obviously been brought to the

246

palace. The mud had been scraped from me; only traces of it remained on my fingernails and other inaccessible parts of my body. Light flooded the room from a window open to a courtyard. I sat up on the pallet and saw the horses we had brought from Mycenae tethered to a tree, and my clothes hanging up to dry from the branches. A little boy was prodding them with a stick. "No one knows," she says, "except my mother. And Orestes and I, because we couldn't help overhearing."

"Is Orestes—"

"Yes, he's very angry, especially since you saved his life and you share bonds of guest-friendship. But he has much more to think about than you. Oh, he is suffering so much."

"He killed his mother," I said with deliberate insensitivity; I had my own share of suffering to wallow in, and no time to think of another's.

"My mother, the queen, has commanded me to take him to the sanctuary of her sister Athena in the township of Athens, north of here," she said. "There, far from the center of the Akhaian alliance, the goddess may decide to heal him. It will be up to the gods to decide. We are hoping to negotiate a truce between them in the matter of Orestes because he acted on the instructions of Apollo Truthsayer."

"If Apollo spoke true, why are they punishing Orestes?"

She sighed; she did not want to answer me. Instead, she eased me back onto the pallet and began to wipe my brow with a cool cloth. I pressed her and she said, "It seems that the gods have not yet determined exactly what the truth will be. They are in the process of refashioning the world, did you know that? And they plan to change the past to fit. We are moist clay to them; it is for them to decide whether you or I will become a drinking cup or a jar of wine or a tablet that catalogs the horses in the king's stables."

"I had a feeling the answer would be something like that," I said. I did not want to go on. Angrily I pushed her hand away.

"Are you well enough to come down to supper?" said Helen's daughter.

"I suppose so," I said, groaning as I sat up once more.

"Good. Come now." She took me by the hand.

"I have my name back now," I said. I had expected some dramatic transformation to take place when I was finally called by my true name. My ka, divorced so long from its true body, did not suddenly break free from its clay host and come flying to me. I felt even less like myself than I had before. I was disoriented, lost.

"No one will call you by your true name yet," said the granddaughter of Skyfather, "for my mother has made Orestes swear secrecy with fearsome oaths, and neither she nor I will give you away. Though I don't think you've anything to fear from my father."

"He won't have me killed if he finds out?"

"He's . . . well, perhaps it's best you find out for yourself, King." It was strange to be addressed by that title again, and not quite comfortable. There was something in me that preferred to be a fugitive. I was used to it, after all; I had been fleeing one thing or another since I was five years old.

Helen-that-was-not-Helen clapped her hands for a slave to enter. It was the boy who had been prodding my laundry in the courtyard outside. He knelt before me (though he did not perform the obeisance customary for kings, and therefore did not know my secret) and then rose to clothe me in a woollen chiton. He paused to admire the lion's paw that still dangled from my neck. It was matted now, the fur scruffy and discolored from exposure to the sun and the rain.

Seeing the slave boy made me think of Leonidas. Was he waiting anxiously for me . . . or was he keeping vigil by the side of his new master, grieving as the blue king grew sicker as my ka twisted and tugged to free itself?

The boy straightened my hair with an Egyptian comb (its handle was a silver scarab beetle) and chattered on as slaves do. "Master, your cheeks are too pale. Let me paint them a little. Or shall I pour you some wine to put the red back into them?"

"Don't fuss," I said. But it was good to be waited on once

more. Helen's daughter stood in the doorway while the slave put the finishing touches on me and replaited my hair.

At last there were no more excuses left, and I followed her down to the megaron of Menelaos's palace.

Dinner was already in progress. A bard was singing listlessly in one corner of the chamber. Guards leaned against the fat columns on either side of the entrance. By then I had seen many dilapidated palaces: my own of course, the squalid little palace at Phthia, the shabby splendor of Mycenae. This one in Sparta was the meanest of them all.

There were two vacant wooden chairs at the square table. My guide sat down in one, facing Orestes, who sat picking at a pig's rib. He looked up and nodded at me. I could tell that he was furious with me. The slave boy, who had been following behind us, scampered forward to pull out the one remaining chair. It faced the twin thrones.

One throne—a throne of wood inlaid with ivory—held an old man, whitehaired, shaggy; I had rarely seen a man who looked that old, except for my grandfather and the shepherd Philemon. His face had neither Priam's nobility nor Philemon's gentleness; it was a savage, scarred face. The man squinted at me long and hard, and finally grunted as he motioned me to take my place.

"Thank you, King Menelaos," I said. I sat and held out my hands for the slave to pour water on them. My eyes were fixed on the other throne, the throne that contained the woman and her smile.

Her face was absolutely still. She gave no sign of recognition at all. But she had spoken my name! Surely it was not knowledge that she could now repress, retract. I looked from her to her daughter. Yes, I had thought her daughter beautiful, perfect even, and I had always known that Helen must be middle-aged now, and yet . . .

Perhaps it was true that they called all their queens Helen. There was a Helen, it was said, whom Theseus abducted three hundred years ago. But there had never been a Helen like this Helen. There was a kind of eternity in Helen's face.

Yes, it was lined—just a little, far less than is normal in a woman over thirty-five. Yes, her golden hair had lost a little of its shine. But these things made no difference. In her eyes I saw the sky itself, I saw the very soul of Skyfather. Her beauty was an absolute thing; it was not in the physical arrangement of her facial features or the angle of her breasts or any such quality. She was woman incarnate; she was mystery made flesh.

I could not speak. Why did she not speak to me, not give me any sign that she knew me?

Instead it was Menelaos who spoke: "Sit down, sit down, dear boy." He clapped his hands. "Have a drink." He himself drained an entire krater in a single gulp. It dribbled onto his beard. "You are a friend of my nephew's? Speechless, I see. Well, I am not surprised. Courts can be overwhelming places, can they not? Ah, but you should have seen Troy. Troy, Troy, Troy!"

"Father," his daughter said, eyeing me nervously, "I don't think *Pylades* wants to hear any more of your war stories. They're so dreary, with their endless lists of heroes and gory hackings and slashings! You'd think we might talk about something a little less bloodthirsty for a change."

"Bah!" King Menelaos turned to me in a huff. "My own daughter tells me to shut up at dinner! You see, my boy, what kind of a king I've become? Have a drink, have a drink." He drained another kraterful. "No, Hermione, don't scold me." A slave poured more wine for him. He did not dilute it with water. "So, Hermione, you're going to marry Orestes?"

"Yes." She was defiant. The conversation kept intruding on me when all I wanted to do was to look at my aunt Helen. Was she going to remain silent all evening?

Menelaos said, "Their only purpose in life is to get carried off, these women. Then off we go after them, we men, waving our bloody swords, burning down cities and slaughtering old men. Old men! I'm old too now. Yes, old." He lost the thread of his argument and stared wildly at me and Orestes. Orestes was still fidgeting with the same bone.

"Listen to me, boy! No respect for your uncle Menelaos? How's that pigheaded father of yours? Never got over the fact that I married Zeus's daughter and he got the harpy. I suppose he sent you to spy on me?"

"Father, Uncle Agamemnon has been dead for ten years," Hermione said testily.

"Dead? Oh yes." Hermione turned to me and rolled her eyes. I was beginning to understand what she had meant about her father. "Where was I?" Menelaos went on. "Oh. Well, what about that other brother of mine, Aigisthos? I suppose he's king?"

"He's dead, Uncle," Orestes blurted out. "They're all dead, every last one of them, and I killed them, I killed them!" And he began to sob helplessly.

"There, there," said the old king, struggling to his feet, taking Orestes in his arms. "It's just a bad dream." Suddenly Menelaos retched and flailed about. A slave ran forward with a slop bucket, but it was too late. The King of Sparta had vomited all over his nephew. "Curse you!" he sputtered at the slave. "Can't you be in time to catch my puke, you tortoise? You there, guard! Take him away and whip him!" A guard came and dragged the slave away. Quietly Hermione left the table and whispered in the guard's ear. While Menelaos's back was turned, the guard released the slave and the boy scuttled away.

Orestes did not seem to notice the vomit on his clothes. He sat there staring at his food. He had taken leave of reality for a while.

In the pause I could hear the bard's voice and the twang of an out-of-tune kithara: *"Magnificent he rose in the rosy-fingered dawn . . ."* Hermione had returned to her seat.

Menelaos grunted. "So this is what it's like," he said, "to stay home and raise a family. Give me a war any day . . . the war! Rape and pillage! We are still paying for that stupid war, did you know that?" His voice rose higher and higher, cracked. "A war over a whore!" He pointed at Helen, his thin arm vibrating like a branch in a wind. "Whore! Whore!"

Helen's face betrayed no reaction.

Hermione began to weep very quietly to herself.

Menelaos noticed at last; he turned on her in a fury. "Sniveling again!" he screamed. "Well you might! Whose daughter are you anyway? Whose daughter are you?"

I could endure no more. It was terrible to see Menelaos reduced to a gibbering drunkard. More terrible still to see the grand heroic conflicts of my childhood fantasies reduced to the level of petty domestic tragedy.

I stood up. I was reluctant to stop looking at Helen, but I tore myself away and walked out of the megaron.

It was dark in the inner courtyard and I was unsure of the way. I did not care. I paced angrily back and forth. I kicked a stone wall, grimacing from the sudden pain. And saw Hermione standing in wait for me, holding a torch.

"They're still in there," she said. "Father is still raving, Orestes is staring sullenly ahead, and Mother is playing at being a statue."

"Is it always this bad?" I said.

She laughed bitterly. "You're joking! That was considerably toned down for the sake of the refined sensibilities of our guests."

"Helen acted as though I wasn't even there," I said.

"Of course she did. What did you expect? I mean . . . if my father were even to suspect that you plan to . . . I mean, you do plan to, don't you? I mean—"

"I don't have any plans anymore," I said.

"Astyanax . . ."

I felt my ka a little. A chill wind hovering around my face. "Say it again," I said, "again, again."

"Oh, I don't dare, I don't dare," Hermione cried, and began weeping again. "I wish I were strong like Mother."

"You take after your father, then?" I said, surprised by my own sarcasm.

"He's not my father!" Hermione said. "Of course he's not!"

I said, "Then his vicious accusations over dinner—"

"Well, perhaps he is. But then, it's traditional to think of

Helen's daughter as having come from the god—the wind from heaven impregnating the queen during the rites of spring."

"That's Snakemother-worship sort of talk." I reacted instinctively before realizing that it was no longer possible for me to view matters of religion in terms of black and white as I had always done before.

She changed the subject. "Will Orestes be a good husband, do you think?"

"I didn't know you were formally betrothed."

"Well, he's one of the few people of royal blood still living, you know. And he did win the whipping race. That makes him my ritual husband, if you're going by the old ways."

"The old ways . . ." I remembered what she had said earlier: that the gods were in the process of destroying the world and creating it afresh, and that when they were done they would revise the past to fit their new concept of truth. If I had journeyed all these months only to encounter silence from the daughter of Zeus, perhaps it was because we were all waiting to see what words the gods had decided to put in our mouths, what roles they had decided we were to play. How had the Pythoness phrased it? "Time is not seamless, and you are a creature dwelling in one of its cracks"?

I had resigned myself to having lost control of my destiny. "When I speak to her at last," I said, "it will be to bid her farewell and to go home."

Hermione said, "That's what your uncle Paris said."

Chapter XXXII

Helen

After the appalling spectacle of dinner and my brief, confusing conversation with Hermione, there was nothing left to do but retire to my chamber and wait for whatever might happen next. Orestes was nowhere to be seen and I did not inquire after him. I was afraid our next encounter might be an angry one.

Alone in the room above the courtyard, I paced while the torchlight flickered. It was a plain room. Its murals had faded beyond recognition; here and there I could puzzle out a face, a ship, the snout of a leaping dolphin.

"I am Astyanax," I said to myself over and over. "I am the king." At every repetition I felt my ka drift closer, though the sea still separated my twin souls.

I did not notice the girl come in until she spoke to me, and then I jumped in astonishment. "My mistress begs the King of Troy to celebrate more rituals of spring with her," she said.

"What is this? Who are you? The rites of spring are over. I've no wish to be flogged over a field of mud again."

"My mistress says these are secret rites," she said. She fell prostrate on the rushes at my feet and said, "Thus my mistress commanded me to kneel to you, King. Come quickly, she bids you, for there is not much left of the night."

"What kind of rites—" But suddenly I knew. "I'll come." I made to follow her, but the slave stopped me.

"First you must put on these clothes," she said.

She unfolded them. I looked: they were a woman's flounced skirt and a shawl of wool and a tiara. "What nonsense is this?" I said. I was in no mood for any more ceremonies designed to fool the gods.

"It's not part of the ritual, King. It's just to get you past the guards. My mistress awaits you in the women's quarters, and, as you know, it is forbidden for a man to enter there."

I stood stiffly as she dressed me. Awkwardly I followed her out, trying to imitate a woman's gait. When I stumbled, she could not resist laughing at me. "I'm doing my best!" I hissed at her.

"There's no need to mince, master. Look at me. Just glide. Softly. Like moonlight." I tried to copy her movements. We passed through several portals; each was guarded by a pair of sentinels. Most of them were snoring. I failed to see the point of the disguise.

We crossed a final courtyard and entered the women's wing of the palace. Soft, high-pitched voices in the still air . . . The slave girl stopped once or twice to glance furtively behind us. At last we reached a closed wooden door. It reminded me of . . . A wild terror struck me. The bathroom of the king's ritual death—that was what it was! I had been brought here to be killed!

Burned into the wood—it was an ancient wood, gnarled and pitted—were the three characters:

$$\textup{A Y F}$$

"Helen!" I whispered. No, I had not come here to be killed. I had come to speak to her at last. I had to be brave, to forget all the dark events I had experienced in Akhaia.

"Helen!" I said again. And a third time, "Helen." At that the door creaked open of its own accord. Light burst from it. It was dazzling as daylight. But not warm. Cold, like moonlight, only a thousandfold more bright. I stepped inside.

"Helen!" I cried. "Your name is burned into the door." My guide had vanished unobtrusively. I squinted, I squeezed my eyes against the glare. The light came from all around me, from the walls themselves.

"Why are you so sure it is my name?"

And I was looking into the face of Skyfather's daughter. She was standing there, dressed exactly as I was. I wanted to touch her, to know it was really her and not another phantom. I reached out. My hands collided with flesh, firm, burning flesh, as her hands clasped mine and pulled me toward her.

I stumbled into her arms. At first I felt like a child again; I did not feel sexual passion for her yet. It was relief I felt. For she was the one fragment of my past I had found untainted by the touch of time.

"Oh, Little Star," she said. "You must think me a frightful old woman." In truth I could hardly see her; she seemed of the same stuff as the searing light. But I could smell her; the room was suffused with the sweet scent of her that I remembered from sitting in her lap when I was a young child.

"What is this place?" I said. But I knew already that it must contain a profound magic, and I was afraid.

"Be still, be still, Little Star. I can feel your heart pounding like a wild thing. Be calm. We are and are not in the palace of Menelaos." Her words were as full of contradiction as those of the Egyptian sorcerer. "We are and are not in the world itself; we are and are not in the stream of time."

I tried to calm myself. As I did so my eyes focused more clearly and the light became less hurtful. I saw her more clearly now, though I was still more or less tongue-tied. Some moments I could have sworn she had not changed at all. Others . . . I saw the crow's-feet and the layers of paint. But her eyes, my eyes, the eyes of the sky—fiery and icy cold in the same instant. "I well believe you are eternal," I said. "That it was you Theseus abducted three centuries ago."

She said, "Time is like gold; it can be stretched and beaten and molded into whatever shape we can imagine for it." She embraced me again. I was beginning to feel desire. "There are times when I feel a thousand years old. But the mortal part of me does show its age, I'm afraid." Then, more quietly, "Are you really going to abduct me?"

At last the thought had been spoken.

"I—" But the choice had been made for me long before. I had thrown the apple.

She sighed. "Menelaos is right about me."

"He's a senile despot."

"That too. But I mean, when he said that I exist only to be carried off."

I was overcome with emotion. I began to weep helplessly, as though I were still her Little Star and I had run to her to be comforted. So long I had tried to be strong: for the Trojan people, for poor orphaned Pergamos, my half brother, even for mad Orestes. I had no strength left. I sobbed and sobbed.

"Why are you weeping, Astyanax? Because you want to be able to choose, to defy your fate, because you have

learned that there is only one path for us to walk down, and
that the bitterest of journeys?''

I did not answer her. I thought, I will vent my grief and
she will answer me with more conundrums. That's what they
all did: my cousin Hermes, the mage Memnon, my mother,
the Pythoness . . . Why does Skyfather not appear in blazing
majesty and reveal the truth? I did not care what truth it was,
as long as it was only one truth, unshakable. If it was a
painful truth, I would at least know it was the truth and
accommodate myself to it. The gods exist to give us cer-
tainty, I thought. If they cannot do that, they cannot be the
gods.

Helen said to me, "Dry your tears, Little Star." And she
kissed me on the cheek, once, twice, three times. "There are
some consolations to consider. For example . . ."

That was how we began to make love. Later that night
there would come passions that would tear me apart, burning
exaltations, cries, moans . . . In the beginning it was nothing
like that. I hardly knew it was even happening at first. I had
never in all my life dreamed that the first woman I would
ever make love with would be the most beautiful woman in
the world. Later it would be said that it was inevitable, that I
had moved inexorably toward this union from the moment I
chose Aphrodite, from the moment I came back to Troy,
from the moment I changed clothes with Leontes. Perhaps
those who said these things were right. But I did not see it
thus; I could not.

For a long time we merely kissed, our lips scarcely touching. I was so nervous that my phallos shriveled when my
tongue encountered hers. She had to have seen my embarrassment, but she only held me closer and lightly peeled
away my woman's robe and tossed it, spread wide, onto the
rush-strewn floor. I cast away my tiara and shook my hair
free. I fell to my knees with my arms around her waist, her
hips. Her thighs were slippery; my hands slid up them,
brushed too quickly against the stubble of her shaved pubis. I
withdrew hastily, but she caught my hand and held it there,
and it was moist and warm. I eased my body into place. And

she whispered, "Astyanax, Astyanax, I have been destined for you from the beginning," and I felt mighty suddenly; I crushed her to me; we fairly stumbled onto the rushes; she did not laugh at my clumsiness but smiled, and that smile drove me mad. . . .

A crazy joy visited me then. Wildly, messily we coupled. Each time she called my name I became more and more myself. I do not know how many times we made love. But in the end I remember feeling like a small boy again, and burying my head against her breasts and calling her "Mother, Mother" in a small voice. Again I thought she would laugh at me; but she only said, very seriously, "I always felt I was closer to you than your real mother."

"Don't speak of her," I said. I tried to conjure up a vision of the snake-haired cannibal women, but it was fleeting, phantomlike.

She said, "Mother, daughter, wife—I am all three to all men."

I looked at her, perplexed.

She said, "Are you still bitter about your consolation prize?"

"Bitter? Bitter?" And yet I still wept, though I had known a joy more profound than I had previously imagined. For at its deepest this joy was close to grief; I could not distinguish the two emotions. I wept and laughed and wept and laughed, and she smiled the smile that contained both grief and joy.

And Helen said, "You were born to be a hero, Little Star. I think you are the last of the heroes, the hero who will end this age and bring in the next. I know I am the last of the Helens."

"And the most beautiful. The daughter of the sky."

"What does that mean, Astyanax? I see my father every day. I have only to step from my bedchamber into the courtyard. But he has never spoken to me."

"I love you," I said.

"That is how we are human, you and I," Helen said. "The part of us that is god-descended doesn't know what love is. If you say you love me, you're also saying that it's

blood and not ichor in our veins, that we breathe real air and
not the ether of Olympos, that we have real hearts that pound
with human passions.''

I looked around me. The walls had dimmed; they were
mere stone now. The room we were in was part of the real
universe again.

"I have a gift for you," Helen said. "I had it made when I
knew you were coming."

"How long have you known?" I said, surprised.

"For fourteen years," she said.

So she too had been waiting for this moment.

She toyed with the lion's paw around my neck for a
moment; then she went into an inner chamber I had not
noticed earlier. When she emerged she carried a sword.

"Look," she said, "a lion's paw for a hilt."

I hefted it. The paw was crudely carved, and the blade was
utterly devoid of the usual markings. I swung the sword; it
whined. It was sleeker than any sword I had seen before. It
occurred to me that it was not bronze.

"Iron," I said.

"Once it fell only from the sky," Helen said, "but now
the earth yields it too. That will be my gift to the people of
Troy—I will bring them iron. They will need good weapons
for the war."

"The war," I said.

Images raced through my mind: fire . . . rape . . . my
grandfather's head flying through the air . . . the shattered
horse black and tall against the firelight and the red-hot city
walls . . .

"There will be another war," Helen said. She said it without rancor, without bitterness. "And it will be fought with
iron. That is what the gods have decided, and that is what has
brought us together."

It was not like Helen to question the gods. She was almost
one herself, after all. She did not have doubts. She had
beauty, and that was an absolute. I knew that it saddened her
to think that her beauty might be the cause of more blood-

shed. But it was something she had long since learned to accept.

"I love you," I said again, slicing the air with the sword, seeing it gleam. "I will break the sacred laws of guest-friendship for you, I will destroy the world for you, because I love you."

"Yes."

She did not say, then or later, that she loved me. I do not think she ever said it to my uncle Paris, either.

Chapter XXXIII

Another Trojan War

So it was that I woke in the arms of my aunt Helen, in a secret room in the women's quarters of the palace, in a place where it was death for a man to enter.

Sunlight on my face. I opened my eyes. We still lay on the robes we had untidily cast off the previous night. She was still sleeping. I touched her face, I ran my fingers through her lustrous hair. The light was bright, so bright; it came from a window set high into the stone wall, and when I looked up I saw a sky of such deep blue that I thought I had been transported into the past. For the sky's blue matched her eyes exactly and I knew that they matched mine too, marking us as Skyfather's.

She stirred. Sat up. Looked at me. Smiled.

"I'm not afraid of that anymore," I said.

We made love again, but without the chaotic wildness of the night. We knew each other's bodies now; we slid easily into the slow rhythm of it; we were the wind and the sea, not the fire and the forest. We swelled together; we burst together; we sang with a single voice. Or so it seemed to me. I had never been so happy.

But afterward, she twisted free of my embrace and sat by

herself in a corner of the room, and would not look at me. And I said, "Helen, Helen, why are you staying away from me?"

She said, "What are we to do now?"

And I saw, to my astonishment, that she was weeping. Quickly I hastened to comfort her. I said, "What does it matter? I've crossed the sea for you, I've found you, I've found love."

She scoffed at me, saying, "Love was not in the bargain you made with the goddess."

I said, "It's easy. We'll slip away under cover of darkness. Or perhaps while Menelaos is hunting—that's what Uncle Paris did, isn't it?" I was full of myself, full of my achievement. "The Phoenician has guided my ship to your shores, and is even now waiting for us, within sight of the beach," I went on, though I was far from sure he had obeyed me. I thought it more likely that we'd have to bribe one of the coastal towns into lending us a ship and crew. "I'll take you away from your puking tyrant of a husband and from all these ill-destined Atreidai!"

"I exist only to be carried off."

Suddenly an appalling thought occurred to me: "Was it not good, then, when we made love? Didn't you feel what I felt?" Surely that could not be. We had shared something precious, something ultimate.

She only said, "My weeping fit will soon pass, Astyanax. Think nothing of it." And she smiled again through her tears. "It is difficult to be a woman again, after having been a goddess all these years."

"Yes. You were the huntress. The one they all desired while the girls scourged their blood into the ground. But you didn't play the role this year, I notice. You relegated it to Hermione."

"That was only as custom dictated. I'm much too old to play the virgin huntress."

"Old? You are eternal."

"So long as I retain that which is godlike in me. But if I choose to be a woman . . ."

"I've been told that people like us don't have any choices."

"That is true. That's why," she said resolutely, "my tears will soon be dry. Don't worry about me. But it might upset you to know that my husband no longer goes hunting."

"We'll get him drunk, then," I said, "and leave when he's in a stupor and can't come after us."

She began to laugh. "You see, I didn't cry for very long."

"Is it so easy to choose womanhood over godhood?"

"As easy as throwing on a cloak," she said, as she scooped our clothes off the floor and shoved a bundle of them into my arms. "Get dressed."

"As a woman? In broad daylight?"

"Akhilleus lived as a woman for months. His mother hid him in the women's quarters because there was a prophecy that he would die at Troy."

"Not before he killed my father."

"Menelaos told me that Patroklos jumped young Akhilleus in the bushes one day—he was the prettiest girl in the women's wing, they say!—and he was confounded when he started thrusting like crazy and he couldn't force it in. He kept muttering, 'By the gods, this wench is tighter than an oyster,' until Akhilleus couldn't contain his laughter anymore. When Patroklos angrily demanded some recompense for having been made a fool of, Akhilleus laughed and said, 'Keep looking; maybe you'll find another hole somewhere!' and that was how they became lovers."

"Such a charming story!" I said. "This was the man who dragged the bleeding corpse of my father three times around the walls of Troy."

"But he loved Patroklos," Helen said. "And your father killed him. That's how war changes people."

"That's a dangerous, modern idea," I said. "Hector would never have gone for it. He believed that war was ennobling, that though it was evil it was necessary."

"You're going to start another war nonetheless. In fact, you've dreamed of it all your life."

I was so happy then that I did not want to inflict pain on anyone. Truly I did not want war. I did not even think it would be necessary. "Why war?" I said. "Who will come after us? Agamemnon is dead. Menelaos is decrepit. Odysseus has not been heard from in years; I've heard that the storm took him. And what of their sons? Telemachos is wandering the world in search of his father out of some forlorn hope that he may not be dead. Pergamos . . . he's only a twelve-year-old boy, and he's my brother. He'd rather die than hurt me. And as for Orestes, who by rights should lead the Akhaian expedition against me . . . I saved his life. He can't touch me without violating the sacred bonds of guest-friendship."

Helen said, "I am a woman in a world that men imagine they rule. This has given me the chance to observe men very keenly. And I tell you that men always say such things before they declare a war."

"But I want you, not war."

"It is not yours to choose," she said sadly. "And though you may think I am yours, you must remember that part of me belongs to the things of eternity."

"I'm not greedy," I said. But in fact I was. I did want her, all of her. I really thought there might not be a war after all. It was my desire that convinced me, that made me blind.

In my women's clothes, veiling my face completely, I managed to return to my room without incident. The next thing that had to be dealt with was the afternoon meal; I had barely a moment to myself when a servant arrived to summon me to it. Fortunately, I had concealed the clothes under my pallet. I tried to act normal as I entered the megaron.

It was even worse than the evening before. Menelaos was already raving, and Orestes was still staring at his food. When he looked up and saw me, the madness seized him and he had a hysterical fit. He jumped up from his seat and began to prowl about on all fours, growling like a wolf. He attacked me. I dodged him, threw myself under the table. Three or four dogs pounced on me and started to lick my face. I felt Orestes grab my legs and try to pull me out. I prayed he would not reveal my identity, but he could not. The oaths he had sworn were too powerful.

He had a madman's strength; I could not resist. I wrapped
my arms around the intricately carved table leg. I could feel
it all collapsing under the strain. An amphora clattered to the
floor and I felt the wine soaking into my chiton. Orestes
tugged me and the table, and the rushes were covered with
roast fowl and figs. He let go abruptly and returned to his seat,
where he resumed his sullen silence.

"Ah, the spring," Menelaos said. "It does things to a
young man. It drives him wild, eh, Helen?"

I sat down as the slaves scrambled forward to replace the
table and its contents. A cupbearer poured me wine with a
shaking hand. I overheard him whisper to another servant,
"We're done for; he's going to have us all whipped for
certain." I put out my hand to steady the slave's; it was
trembling. I looked from Menelaos to Orestes to Hermione to
Helen.

Helen once more was playing the role of statue.

Menelaos rambled on. "Spring, ah yes, spring, nephew.
You know, my brother Agamemnon used to love spring. We
would go raiding all the way to Boiotia. We would sail to the
islands and terrorize their inhabitants. We would hunt boar,
deer, lion. Ah, hunting—hurry, slave, I'm dribbling again!—
ah, hunting . . . Ah, nephew, we've done nothing to enter-
tain you since you've come to visit." Orestes did not look as
though he wanted entertainment at the moment, so Menelaos
went over to him and began poking him with an arthritic
finger. "Hunting, my lad! That'll get you over what's ailing
you."

"You haven't been hunting in ten years, Father," Hermione
said testily. "I don't suppose you could tell a quiver from a
boar's tusk. Oh, do stop all this nonsense."

"A hunt!" Menelaos said. "Yes, a hunt!"

My heart sank. I remembered the hunt that I had insisted
on organizing for my guests. "I think it's a terrible idea," I
said.

"Nonsense!" the king roared. "It's a splendid thought.
Look all around you. Do you think I don't know I'm rotting
away alive, that I'm drowning in my own puke? You think I

don't know how far our world has fallen? We must have splendor! We must have spectacle again!''

Those were the very thoughts I had had when I had insisted on taking Memnon hunting. And I too had been drunk. I felt helpless, trapped, as Menelaos went on and on about the glories of the hunt.

It was then that Helen spoke. The whole court fell silent. Even the bard stopped in mid-melisma and let his plucking die away.

She said, ''Why not, my dear? The fresh air will invigorate you. Shall we say tomorrow, at dawn?''

And she looked straight into my eyes.

I saw that I was doomed to repeat all that had happened here twenty-five years before. My abduction of Helen would be, like Uncle Paris's, wholly without honor; it would be a violation of the sacred obligation of guest to host. I suppose I had known it all along. But now I was appalled at the sordidness of it. I was even more appalled by the fact that I did not care. I wanted Helen, and to me her complicity was a kind of proof of love.

Just before he staggered from the hall, Menelaos turned to glare at me. He said, ''The sky is very blue today.'' He made it sound like an accusation. Had he somehow divined our secret? But he said nothing else. Perhaps he had already accepted his fate: that he should have as his wife the daughter of Zeus, and that he should forever be a cuckold.

I did not even wait for the slave to fetch me. Helen was waiting for me in the room that night. We made love until sunrise. Though our lovemaking was never less than glorious, it seemed that there was always a part of her I could never reach. Perhaps it was because the more naked she became, the more she seemed to clothe herself in light and shadow; it was this that inflamed me the most. The more she fulfilled, the more I found to desire.

At last, as dawn filtered down through the high window and heightened the blush of her pale skin, we broke apart.

Once again she left me and went to sit alone in the corner.

It was as though she lost part of her ka and needed time to call it back into herself. Once again I went to her and tried to comfort her.

"Leave me alone," she said. "We must both make ready for the grand hunt. And it would not do for us to arrive at the palace gates together."

I said, "Didn't you take pleasure in what we did?"

She said, not looking at me, "Rejoice, Astyanax, that you have loved a goddess. Do not ask that I feel pleasure. Did you not feel, when we made love, that I was somehow the thing that made your self complete? That is what it is like to love Helen. It is to become whole. As for Helen's feelings . . . that is not why Helen exists."

How could she speak this way after all we had done together? It was as if she were two different people in one body. I said, "But to give you pleasure would be the final consummation of my desire."

She said, "Do not ask for that. That is the one thing you cannot give me."

For a moment I thought I detected longing in her eyes. There must be a part of her that wanted love. But even as I gazed into her eyes it was as though the life drained from them, and they became like windows to the empty sky, bright and soulless.

Chapter XXXIV

The Return of the Lioness

I did not see Helen until the court gathered for the hunt, and then she gave me no sign of recognition. As the chariots and supply carts were lined up outside the gates of the city, the sun blazed; the grass was vibrant, the stones in the walls burned with reflected sunlight. When Helen emerged we all gasped; she had assumed the identity of the goddess with her bow and quiver and her raiment of gold.

Orestes and I had been assigned nondescript chariots with the usual unskilled charioteers; Menelaos stood in the royal chariot, propping himself up against the side. I did not think that the procession would ever get going, but after some perfunctory music, and after the hounds had been rounded up, the expedition began to move downhill. Though I had thought my Trojan hunt a pitiful thing for a visiting dignitary to see, my shabby spectacle so far outclassed this one that I did not even have the heart to laugh at it.

I decided to put a good face on this fiasco. I stood straight and manly, with my new iron sword strapped to my side. It gleamed in the sun and I was surprised that no one remarked on it.

We moved unevenly south, across a plain. The brilliance of the daylight made our little troupe seem even sorrier, for it mercilessly lit up the bedraggled wicker of our chariots, the manginess of the dogs, the dented, discolored weapons of the guards . . . and most of all the unkingliness of the two Akhaian kings: Orestes alternately shrinking in terror from his private hauntings and maniacally raving; Menelaos quaffing and babbling and gesticulating with palsied hands. I myself did not resemble a king, but then those who knew I was one were all keeping the knowledge to themselves. It spared me a certain embarrassment.

After an hour's riding we reached the forest in the foothills. Helen and Hermione lagged behind; their purpose was essentially decorative. In front, with the dogs barking and jostling between our chariot wheels, we three rode abreast: the mad king, the senile king, and the king unknown in his own country. Music blared and warriors ran ahead to search for prey. I did not believe there would be any, for hunting thrives only when the forests are properly cared for and their stocks replenished by trained beastmasters.

Suddenly Menelaos cried out: "Halt! Everyone halt!"

The group stumbled and shambled to a standstill.

"Music too!" Menelaos wheezed.

The background music spluttered and faded. All we could hear now was the lifting of the boughs overhead in the hot wind. And then . . .

From the shadows, a menacing vibration, like a purr of a cat but deeper, louder. "Ha! My ears can still hear, can they not?" Menelaos said. "A lioness, by the gods!"

There was some scattered, desultory applause. It had not sounded like a lion to me. But without warning it sprang across our path. A lioness, lean, a splash of gold against the shadows. And it was gone.

The dogs became agitated now, yelping and running aimlessly, clogging our chariot wheels. "After the beast!" said the King of Sparta. In confusion the hunting party surged forward. I urged my charioteer on, but he was too frightened; so I seized the reins myself. I could see that Menelaos's wheels were stuck. I tried to edge the horses over to him. Three or four dogs had become tangled up in my axle and the spokes of one wheel, and I could not go on without crushing them. In frustration I tugged the horses in the opposite direction, where the lioness had gone. The driver was still shaking, so I said, "Get off the chariot, boy! Go over there, pull the dogs off me." I kicked him off the car and went after the lioness.

Darkness fell suddenly on me. It was as though I had entered a private forest. I was moving in perfect silence. I could not even hear the chariot wheels bouncing on the stones. There was not even the slightest breeze. I realized at once that the gods had cloaked me in this darkness, that no one would see me. It was time to act.

The lioness leaped across the dark once more. I swerved to avoid her. Instead I found her running straight toward me. In silence she sprang. I gasped. She had no paws; but where there should be stumps, her legs merely melded into the blackness around us. I touched the paw that hung from my neck.

"No!" I cried. "It can't be!" I could not even hear my own voice. But the lioness had been killed! In Troy, on the other side of the sea! It had to be a sending from the gods

. . . but from which side, darkness or light? I looked back but I could see no refuge. The forest darkened steadily until I could see only the eyes of the lioness, and I felt the chariot bounce and she pounced into the car. I felt the fetor of her breath and then saw that the eyes had become . . .

The eyes of Helen. And I embraced the darkness and felt fur dissolve into flesh and hair and moist lips . . .

As we broke out of the darkness, I whipped around to see the citadel of Sparta far behind us, almost at the horizon.

"Helen!" I said.

She said, "You have chosen me. I have come."

"Your love for me has triumphed." That was what, in my innocence, I still believed.

She did not affirm it, but instead said, "The ship, you say, is waiting? Where?"

"I don't know exactly," I said.

"It doesn't matter," she said firmly. It was her confidence that terrified me the most. "The gods have decided that this thing is to happen, and therefore it will happen."

"What should I do?" I said.

"Just drive."

Did I delude myself? Or was the chariot moving at unnatural speed? And were those horses whose hooves pounded the road before us, or were they lions or serpents or dragons with flame-flared nostrils? Shocked, I let go of the reins, and still we moved, and I saw the landscape race by but I felt no motion at all. Against the blurring, shifting terrain the only thing I saw clearly was Helen, still wearing the attributes of the goddess, bare-breasted and bearing the weapons of the virgin huntress. Her lips and her nipples were crimsoned with a paste of crushed rubies. Though the sunlight streamed down on us, she seemed to stand in a swath of moonlight, as though the fragment of space in which she stood had been snatched from a different universe. I loved her and feared her. I thought of turning back, but the fragrance of her made me mad.

"Faster!" she said. I took a deep breath and quirted the flanks of the creatures, dragons or horses.

As suddenly as we had begun, we stopped.

And we were by the sea. And the sky was darkening with each passing moment.

I felt the wind rushing. The smell of salt and seaweed. I saw waves crashing against rocks shaped like legendary beasts. I did not know what shore this was. I knew that Sparta was more than a half-day's journey to the sea. Where could we be? The wind was wild, the current restless, the crags foam-flecked and steaming.

Helen gasped. And murmured, "Father, Father." She did not think I heard her. I knew she was talking to Skyfather himself. Far out to sea I saw dolphins leaping. Delicate filaments of lightning burst over the cloud banks.

"Father!" Helen said, addressing the lightning. "Where are we to go now?" For the first time she seemed not to know what would happen next; I saw the woman beneath the goddess for a moment.

"There's no ship!" I cried. As I expected! Phalas and his crew had betrayed me; doubtless they were carousing in Tyre. The wind roared now and I could barely hear my own voice.

And Helen leaped from the chariot. And before her feet touched the ground she had once more taken on the lioness's shape. I could not see whether she had paws, for her feet were buried in the sand, which the wind whipped up in my face, my eyes.

"Helen!" I dashed after her. I screamed her name again and again. I lurched forward, my hands grating on the beast's rough skin.

She was bounding toward the waves, and the roar that left her throat gave birth to lightning in the gray sky. I could not let her slip away, no matter what form she took. There was a dark magic in her that seemed to come not from the sky but from the earth. But I no longer cared to distinguish light from dark or good from evil. I only wanted her in my arms, though she were as thousandshaped as Proteus.

As soon as she touched the waves she began to shift again. I threw my arms around her flanks. As the brine cascaded over her, her fur seemed to dissolve and I was holding onto a slippery thing, sleek and streamlined, and a high-pitched chattering sound came from her throat and I saw that she had become a dolphin. Desperately now I hugged her to me as she plunged into the sea. Water clogged my nostrils. I could not breathe. It was a deception! I thought. Snakemother has lured me into death by drowning!

We surfaced. I was astride the dolphin now. Waves towered over us and the wind whined and whinnied and I was slipping down the dolphin's slick skin into the water and darkness was closing in. . . .

I called on Skyfather's name. With my last strength I shouted out the litany of my ancestors, the seed of Skyfather. At least I was dying with my soul intact, for I could feel my ka about me like a swarm of locusts.

"Skyfather!" I could not spit it out. Water was running down my nose, invading my lungs. And still the dolphin streaked on, until . . . my head banged against something hard. The thud vibrated through me. I was beyond feeling pain.

I clutched whatever the object was. Barnacles sliced into my hands. The object was bobbing up and down. I felt the dolphin thrust me loose, I saw the dolphin stand upright in the water and leap high high into the air, and I followed the arc of its leap and saw where it was landing. I saw the dolphin clearly for the first time: golden, lion-colored, with eyes richly blue as Egyptian faience. I saw the dolphin only for a fraction of a moment before it transformed itself once more into the daughter of Zeus, standing tall on a floor of wood.

I had collided with a ship.

Book Six: The One-Eyed King

自丫

"Her lips suck forth my soul; see where it flies!"
—The words of Faustus upon kissing Helen
Christopher Marlowe, *Doctor Faustus*

Chapter XXXV

The Open Sea

The storm ended as suddenly as it had come. Thus I knew that its purpose had been entirely magical. There was a power that intended us to escape from Sparta; but what that power was I could no longer venture to guess.

We were unusually far out to sea, for I could barely see land. As the storm subsided I looked at Helen, who seemed untouched by the dramatic transformations she had undergone. A little moisture clung to her lips, and her ceremonial robes of the goddess were plastered against her skin. Her breasts moved against the cloth like serpents in a bowl of wine.

If anything she had emerged rejuvenated from the water. Those little signs of encroaching age that I had first noticed in Sparta seemed less evident. Perhaps she had worn her age only as a woman paints her face; beneath it she remained ageless, true to Skyfather's divinity.

The clouds broke; the sunlight burst out on the deck. The crew were all staring at us both. I recognized some of them; the old men who had shipped with us were no longer there, but some of the adolescent boys still were. But in a few months they had grown muscles, and the sun and the wind had bronzed their faces.

"But where is Phalas?" I said. "Did I not bid him bring the ship here, and wait for us?"

They did not answer me.

But one by one, as the ship drifted serenely away from the shoreline, they crept forward and fell prostrate before Helen.

I was not pleased. "Do you not know me?" I said. "My name may now be spoken; I am Astyanax, your king. And I

275

command you to set sail for Troy, for Troy must greet its former princess and new queen.''

They did not acknowledge my words at all. I accosted one of them, one I had been fairly friendly with on our voyage from Troy; he gazed at me—right through me—with glazed eyes.

"They are bewitched," I said. "Helen . . . help me, tell them who I am."

Helen said to them, "This is the King of Troy. It is true, what he has said."

Suddenly, as though by a signal which I could not hear, the oarsmen returned to their positions. They had no drummer, but seemed to know the ship's movements so well that they did not need the sound of pounding.

"Which way are we going?" I shouted.

Helen said, "It seems, Astyanax, that they aren't listening to you. I am the only one who seems to have registered on their consciousness at all."

"Is this some trap?" I asked her. "Did you lead me on for some nefarious purpose of your own?"

She said, "You must know me well enough now to know that I do not do such things. There is no deceit in me. I am Helen. That is all there is to me."

"You exist only to be carried off," I said, bitterly mimicking her words and Menelaos's. "But these sailors are the victims of some spell, I know it. I've heard of the dead being waked to life for use as slaves." Where had I heard that story? From Memnon. Another unsolved mystery. "Are the Egyptians behind this?"

"There are those who believe that I never went to Troy with Paris; that what he carried off was merely a phantom, given to him by the goddess to fulfill her part of the bargain—"

"Misdirection!"

"—and that I was safely kept by the King of Egypt until the war was over. Do you think that it's true?"

Bewildered, I said, "Surely you must know the answer to that."

But Helen said only, "Sometimes it's difficult for me to

tell when I am real and when I am merely the product of someone else's fantasy.''

"Are you real right now?" I had to know.

"Only you can know," she said. And kissed me. Her cheeks were moist, and tasted of salt, but I do not believe it was from tears. Her body was like fire. I embraced her. I could not let go.

"You have to be real," I said. "Or what would all this mean?''

"Misdirection?''

"You mock me!'' But her words had contained no hint of mockery.

She left me then, and went to sit beside the boy who held the rudder. She sat looking back, to where the land would have been if we could only see it. I had never sailed beyond sight of land, and was unnerved. The fact that the crew would not speak to me did nothing to settle my mind.

The wind blew steadily, fiercely; unnaturally so. The crew hardly rowed. When they were not straining at their oars, they sat like statues. I thought they might be like Memnon's ushabti, but their skin did not have the blue cast that characterized the king who had been ruling Troy in my place.

As I stood confused, they piled up in front of me those articles of mine they had salvaged. Some of these they had found floating on the water; some had been attached to my clothes and had clattered onto the deck in the first moments of my arrival on board.

There was a small leather pouch with a few jewels and a lump or two of gold—the gifts I always carried with me in case someone rendered me a service that I could not in honor repay later. There was a short bronze dagger, its blade inlaid with a sequence of hunting motifs.

There was the sword of iron. I would never grow used to the way iron gleamed. While unpolished bronze shows patches of blue-green, the color of grass and sky, the patina of unpolished iron is the color of human blood. With a bronze weapon you must scrape off the memory of life before you

use it to deal death. But iron is always dead; you remove the
aura of death only to bathe it in more death.

Bronze is magical and iron is not. Iron kills without magic.
You do not need skill to kill with iron.

My thoughts were heavy as I hefted the sword once more.
I had heard often enough that the Age of Bronze was coming
to an end. Perhaps my Trojan War would be the first war of
the Age of Iron. And I would be an iron king, a king with
strength but without magic. Yet magic had brought me to the
lands of the Akhaians, and magic, it seemed, was transport-
ing me thence. I could not fathom these contradictions. I
wished for a revelation from some god; but I also feared such
a thing, for each new meeting with the divine or semidivine
had engendered only more enigmas.

I went to where Helen was.

She sat over the edge with her hand trailing the water. She
was unbearably beautiful. I could not speak.

In the evening we ate apart from the others. The ship was
well supplied with roast pig, wrapped in leaves, and a
hearty, resinated red wine. The sailors ate salt fish and dried
figs, and did not speak with us.

Becoming a little drunk, I walked over to them and began
to yell at them. "How dare you not even speak to your
king?" I screamed. "How do I know we are even going in
the right direction? Where is Phalas? He was the one with
skill at navigating, not you untrained boys . . . unless you've
been pirating up and down the Aegean Sea during my absence!"

I tottered back and forth, berating them; but they said
nothing.

"Has some sorcerer robbed you of the power of speech?"
I said. I turned away. I stumbled into Helen's arms.

She said quietly, "If magic has stopped their tongues, your
railing will not unstop them, Astyanax." And she led me
back to where we had been sitting.

The men started to drift into sleep at their oars. And still
the wind held high and we moved steadily.

"It seems we are being pulled in a certain direction," Helen said, "and there's nothing to be done."

"Maybe you're used to being carried off," I said, "but I don't like it."

"It's a knack," she said. "After a while you learn to accept anything that happens. A man comes, a beautiful young man from the east, with Skyfather's blood in his veins. A man comes; the wind comes; the ship comes; the wind takes the ship and the man and me; we make love. Day follows night. Perhaps you won't believe this, but Menelaos was young too once, even beautiful, though not like you and Paris."

"Do you think I am beautiful?" I said.

"No one could argue otherwise."

Still she did not say she loved me; but I was young enough to believe that one could not see beauty without loving it. Her words awoke desire in me again.

And we made love for the third night in succession. Under the stars and the steady wind, in rhythm with the rocking of the ship. The moonlight silvered her hair, her face, her whole body, even the beads of sweat and semen on her thighs. I was bolder than ever before. I had not come by stealth, wearing a woman's dress, into the forbidden quarters of another king's palace. The sea was not Sparta, but a kingdom outside Troy and beyond the Akhaian alliance. There was brine on her lips, and sometimes her skin seemed dolphin-slick, her hair like a lion's. As we climaxed, I seemed to relive our journey through the sea. I grasped her body desperately to me; I felt myself drowning, drowning, and yet I wanted to yield myself utterly to that drowning, to the death that was joy.

But at that ultimate moment, I heard a whispered chorus that I thought at first to be waves shattering against the side of the boat. But it was so regular, so rhythmic, it could not be. And the whispers were forming into words, faint but perfectly distinguishable: "Piggy-fucker! Piggy-fucker!"

I had heard those words before . . . on the island of the priestesses of Snakemother. Where were they coming from?

It had to be an illusion brought about by my innermost fears. I froze, turned over onto my back, as Helen murmured my name, "Astyanax, Astyanax."

"Listen!" I whispered, my voice hoarse.

"I don't hear anything."

"Shush. It's on the wind." I sat up. Were the men completely asleep? I groped in the darkness, for the moon had hidden itself behind a cloud. "The moon," I said, "come forth."

I had unwittingly invoked an attribute of Snakemother. I made the sign of aversion.

The moon emerged a little; there was a pale starlight too. I could see that the crewmen were not where I had last seen them. They were sitting cross-legged on the deck around us in a circle.

"Piggy-fucker, piggy-fucker . . ."

Wildly I looked at Helen. "Surely you must hear something!" I said. Angrily I stepped naked out of the circle. Was it the men who were chanting those words? But their eyes were not open, and their lips did not seem to be moving. Or were they? It was too dark to tell.

I came back, took Helen in my arms; but I could feel no more passion. We crept around to a different part of the ship; I threw a cloak over us, and we slept in each other's arms, but chastely, huddled together.

The chant woke me in the morning. Helen was already up. She was stopping her ears and squeezing her eyes shut. I shook her. "It's me," I said. "How long has this been going on?"

We both looked around. The sun was rising. Where the sun was was the direction of Troy. By that reckoning we must be going north.

The crewmen were chanting the words over and over, monotonously, and rowing in time to them.

"They've been back to the island," I said. "And those priestesses have done something to them, I know it."

"Priestesses?"

"Of Snakemother!"

Enraged, I stalked over to the boy I had questioned unsuccessfully before. I pulled him away from his oar and dragged him up. "Now talk!" I shouted. I slapped his face hard. His nose began to bleed, but he said nothing. "I am Astyanax, your king, and you'll speak to me!" I screamed, slapping him again and again. Suddenly something was dislodged from his right ear. It was a small object, pebble-shaped. The boy became terrified when he saw it; he managed to extricate himself and he dived after it as it began to roll down the aisle. I raced after him. He put out his palm to cover it. I stamped on his hand. He cried out.

"So you aren't deaf!" I said.

I pried his fingers off the deck. Underneath was a lump of something soft. Wax.

"So you made yourselves deaf on purpose!" I said. "Do you know who I am? I am Astyanax."

The crewman heard the name and heard the truth in my utterance. Abjectly he fell to his knees before me. "He commanded it, King. He said you would use wiles on us, that you'd use magic to drive us mad. He told us not to speak to you at all, and if we were fearful, to speak the sacred words—"

"Sacred words?" I said. " 'Piggy-fucker' is a sacred word?"

"Sacred to the Lady."

"Who has sent you?"

"The One-Eyed King."

Some of the sailors had spied us. They were chanting louder than ever now. "Bid them cease!" I said. "Make them unplug their ears! Let them hear my name spoken so that they may know their king!"

The chanting grew faster and louder. The oars plunged more swiftly into the water. At that moment I heard Helen's voice: "There is an island, Astyanax . . . an island dead ahead."

I let the sailor go and turned to look.

"How can this be?" It was as I had feared. But it was impossible! We could not have reached the island of the pigs in this short time. And was the island not much farther to the north?

"I know what you are thinking," Helen told me. "But this ship is not the leaky wineskin in which you sailed to Akhaia. And you were not making love to the daughter of Zeus as you crossed the ocean from the east."

"Do you mean . . ."

"Much more time has passed, Little Star, than you knew; each night that you lay in my arms, night after night passed in the world outside. For time begins and ends in me."

"Then we may not have outrun your husband's forces—"

"Do not think of them. Not yet."

We had reached the island where I had refused to make love to the high priestess for fear of being trapped in one of Snakemother's spells.

Yes! It was coming back to me now. Phalas the Phoenician had taken my place in the arms of the priestess. He had boasted of it to me, had berated me for not making love to the living goddess myself.

Having mated with Snakemother—if the custom here was the same as had once prevailed in ancient times over all the world—Phalas must have been made king! *He* was the One-Eyed King! For I well remembered that the Phoenician had had but one eye.

Chapter XXXVI

The Island of the Pigs

No sooner had this revelation come to me than I saw the men diving one by one into the water and swimming for the shore. The sand was bloodied by the dawn's light; I saw shadowy figures standing, watching. They were pulling the ship toward the beach. There was a look in Helen's eyes which I was now beginning to recognize; it was when the divine in her overcame her humanness, and one could no longer understand her utterances.

Helen and I stepped into shallow water; I saw the Phoenician almost immediately, but I did not know him at first because he was dressed as a king. A throne had been brought out by the sea; its legs were half buried in sand and wound around with seaweed. It was old wood, rotting, pitted; the Phoenician's face seemed the same.

"Phalas!" I cried. "What is the meaning of this?"

He spoke to me. It was the old voice, gruff and dour, though he spoke Skyfather's tongue perhaps more grammatically than before. "Much has changed, I see," he said. "We have both become kings . . . you for the second time, I'm told."

I said, "My kingship comes from long descent. I am the six-times-great-grandson of the sky. What gives you leave to claim to be a king? Though this island of pig-fuckers isn't much of a domain."

"My kingship is as justified as yours. I am wedded to the ancient earth. I am the Lady's consort. I could just as easily accuse you of being an upstart, since your way of reckoning your ancestry goes back only seven generations! But I am not as rude as you, you see."

He clapped his hands. Two attendants immediately stepped forward. One bore an amphora of wine; the other, a platter piled with bread, figs, and pigmeat. I looked at them in dismay. It was true that he had only followed the correct protocol for dealing with kingly visitors, but I did not want to accept his food and drink. I had incurred too many problems in the past by binding myself to guest-friendship before I had known what I was letting myself in for. And this king was a man who only recently had been a criminal in Troy, about to be executed for cheating in the marketplace! I hesitated, long enough for Phalas to notice.

"You disdain my hospitality, properly presented according to your rank and place, King!" Phalas said scornfully.

"Don't eat—" I tried to stop Helen. But she had already torn off a piece of the loaf and had put it in her mouth. . . .

"Too late, my abortive abductor!" Phalas jeered. "She has partaken! Perhaps you would care to parley, to compromise? You know the story of Persephone and Hades, I suppose, and the six pomegranate seeds? Perhaps you'll suggest six months of the year in sunny, gold-rich Troy and six months in this barren, desolate island of—as you, oh, so tastefully put it—pig-fuckers?"

"What do you mean to do with us?"

"Perhaps you mean, what does the Lady mean to do with you? For you have been in the Lady's power all this time. Did your journey to our island not seem almost instantaneous? The Lady was in your sails. The Lady was in your ship. The Lady has been your lover." He got up from his throne and fell prostrate in the wet sand . . . in front of Helen.

Helen turned to me. I could not read her expression at all.

"O Goddess," said Phalas, "thank you for returning to our island. We have been in mourning for so long."

The conversation switched to another language. I knew its sounds, though I did not understand a word of it—it was the old tongue, the hissing tongue of the people of Snakemother. I was about to protest when two men seized me and tied me up. I was ignominiously thrown down to the wet sand. I breathed salt water. I choked. I heard the voice of the Phoenician: "Learn your place, grandchild of Priam! A king must kneel to his goddess: his mother, wife, sister."

"Helen . . ."

They ignored me. I could not rise; they held my face down in the sea. Helen and Phalas continued to converse in the tongue of Snakemother. I cried, "They've got you in their power, Helen, they've bewitched you. Don't listen to them!"

The islanders laughed. I thanked Skyfather that I did not hear Helen's laughter with theirs.

"Helen—"

She turned to me. Her expression was the same as the one she had worn at the moment I told her I was going to abduct her: I could not fathom it. She said to me—the words were untinged with any emotional coloring—"He has told me that I have been brought here to be the new living goddess. The old one has passed on; she did not have time to name a successor, and the priestesses could not agree on one. An emissary was sent to the oracle; the Pythoness told them that you were about to lead me away from Sparta. They prayed to the Lady. They say that she has brought us here, that I will be set up as the living goddess here in the island of the pigs.''

"But Helen," I whispered, "how can you go with them? Didn't you come with me because we loved each other?''

"I came because I am Helen."

"What does that mean, 'I am Helen'? We made love, we felt passion. I did not know until I saw you, touched you, what my uncle Paris felt. Now I know why our peoples went to war for you. You consumed me, you burned me up. Are you going to discard me now?''

"I do not discard you," Aunt Helen said. "I did not choose you."

Phalas said to me, in my own tongue, "He has loved the goddess, and it has driven him mad! But that is a fairly common consequence of having sex with gods.'' And he laughed uproariously.

"What will you do to me?" I gasped. They still held me fast, and when I struggled to free myself they pulled the rope tighter so that I could not breathe. I managed to say to Helen, "These are barbarians! Even if they set you up as their goddess, they only have a miserable little village and no temple. How could you bear to be here and not among those who speak a human language?''

"You fool," Phalas said. It was hard for me to credit it, but there was compassion in his voice. "The gods need no temples. But we are building one, and it is the custom, in those lands that worship the Lady, that a royal warrior be buried alive under the threshold of such places. Your arrival is . . . timely, King of the Trojans. We're a poor people, and we have few princes, and they are all needed to administer this island and to serve as judges and leaders of raiding parties; you see, we simply can spare no one of royal blood. But the earth needs blood, and the blood of a king is the richest offering a people can provide.''

"Save me, Helen!" I turned to her.

She only smiled at me, the same smile I had fled those many years ago. I thought of Aigisthos, of Agamemnon, kings cut to pieces to appease Snakemother. I remembered how I had feared the sacred bathroom in King Priam's palace. I had always been afraid of dying this way. But to do so in a land of barbarians was even more ignominious.

"I had great deams once," I said accusingly to her. "About bringing back the age of heroes, about restoring the color to the sky."

There was no answer from the daughter of the sky.

"We have never left the age of heroes," the One-Eyed King said, "and you are about to become one of them."

How could my dreams end thus? In vain I gazed at Helen. I wanted to weep, but I would not do so in front of barbarians. I reined in my emotions. If I was to die I would die without doubts, I would die with my true name and my two souls and my integrity and my kingship intact.

Four bearers lifted up the throne of the One-Eyed King on their shoulders. Others brought in another throne for Helen; it was of old, smooth wood. They took Helen in their arms as though she were as fragile as the egg from which her mother Leda hatched her, and placed her on the throne. Then, beating their drums and chanting incomprehensible words, they began to march toward the village.

Armed men prodded me with iron-tipped spears; I staggered forward. They pushed me along. I and my guards brought up the rear of the procession, like a battle trophy. The island was not bleak as I remembered it, though there were still pigs everywhere; the paraders were constantly kicking them out of the way or shouting at them when they scurried underfoot. But the houses were adorned with spring flowers of every kind, and the doorways were hung with the skulls of pigs and men, their eye sockets decorated with fresh blooms and with sprigs of herbs.

It was getting toward noon. Though I had tried to stifle my despair, not wanting to display it in front of these people, yet it had been growing inside me.

We trudged past the village itself. We were going uphill. There were caves ahead. The procession wound its way up a narrow steep path; it was slow going, for we were continually interrupted by suppliants. Children ran forward to lie at the feet of the living goddess, careless that they might be trampled. Young women with flounced skirts and bare breasts ran gaily ahead and strewed the path with flowers; in the back of the group, I came across those flowers crushed and blended into the mud.

I was exhausted but still they pushed onward. The first of the cave mouths lay ahead. Priestesses emerged, chanting and scattering more flowers. Many had serpents coiled about their necks, their arms, their waists. At the entrance they took me away; I did not see Helen and the others enter the makeshift temple. I gazed after her, but they came and dragged me away.

Inside the cavern—fires burning, altars, smoke and haze, broad red columns and walls painted with images of bulls and serpents, the smell of incense and roasting pig's flesh. I tried to see what they had done to Helen, but I could not see her at all; I saw only the throne, bobbing up and down over the heads of the suppliants as they carried it farther and farther away from me. . . .

"Helen . . ." I said softly.

One of my captors slapped me in the mouth. "You must not speak her name," he said. I tasted blood. I was too weak to struggle. I resigned myself to the fate of Aigisthos and Agamemnon. Snakemother had won the war after all; the plan had been hers the whole time. I had only deluded myself in thinking I was carrying out the will of the sky. That was what the Pythoness had told me. Why had I persisted in believing in the things of my childhood, against all the evidence of the outside world? I said nothing more, but I thought: It's over, my fantasy of a return to the age of heroes. My father is dead, and Troy has been razed, and there will come an age when heroes are no more.

Perhaps there would be no more gods either. Perhaps the gods had already begun to die.

Chapter XXXVII

The Lady's Temple

I was immediately aware that the labyrinth of caves into which I was being led bore an uncanny resemblance to other caves I had seen on the mainland—the caves in which the Pythoness dwelt within the bowels of Mount Parnassos, at the navel of the world. There, as here, it seemed that I had entered the entrails of a living creature, a part of Snakemother herself.

The tunnels became narrower and narrower. At last we came to an opening in the side of the passageway, blocked by a great round stone. In the flickering light from the torches that hung in brackets on either side I could see that the stone was chiseled, in a spiral pattern that wound from the edge to the center, with words in the old tongue of Snakemother. Only here and there could I read a syllable or two in succession, and they were nonsense to me.

The stone was rolled away and I was thrust into a cavern. A torch was thrown in after me; the stone was rolled back. I slid on moist rock. The air was dank, close, smelling of human excrement. I scraped my body painfully against the walls to fray my bonds a little. I could see almost nothing. When I had most of the ropes loose I crept over to the torch and stood up, feeling for a bracket.

It was a tiny prison, barely long enough to sleep in. But steep. And, far over my head, there seemed to be a light source. Some straw and some firewood lay heaped in one corner. Despite the smell, there were no other prisoners. At least none living . . . for when my eyes grew used to the dimness I saw vague shapes—skeletons, perhaps? I did not look too closely. Perhaps they were the shades of the dead, for did I not still have the vision of my celestial ancestor, and could see the dead, sometimes?

For a long time I lay still, despairing. I wished they had killed me immediately. I knew they planned my death; they wanted my angry shade to guard the threshold of their temple. I did not think that death could be worse than the waiting.

I called on the name of Skyfather. But not even Hermes the jeering messenger appeared to make light of my torment.

In time I became obsessed with the light source overhead. I tried to climb up the walls. I slipped against the slick stones. There were footholds, but I kept sliding. After a while I noticed that there was a circle of dryness around the torch. I thought, I'll make all the moisture go away by burning something. I crawled over to the firewood and straw, heaped it into a pyramidal pile, and ignited it with my torch. It blazed up. The sweat began pouring down my brow. For a while I watched the fire, thinking, I have built my own funeral pyre . . . and remembering how they would not let me see them burn my father and how Pergamos had tried to seem brave at the funeral of his murdered brother.

I felt the wall behind me. It was hot, barely tolerable. But drier. Shadowshapes, crimson-tinged, danced on the rock. But yes, there were footholds, and there was an opening of some kind—a circle of bluish light. I had seen such a light before: in the necropolis outside Troy, where I had first grappled with Snakemother. The memory chilled me.

I climbed higher. I was dizzy and faint. But as I reached the top the air became more fresh, and the stones less slippery, for they were blanketed with moss. I slid through the opening—it was barely wide enough to admit me—and found myself in a low cavern lit by its own cold light; the walls glistened. Here and there were human skeletons manacled to stalagmites or lashed to the rocky ground. They were richly dressed; they wore coronets of gold and tunics of the finest wool, and they held aloft spears of bronze. A faint putrescence laced the air. I was in a strange state: I still believed I was going to be killed, but I had buried the fear of it deep inside myself. Instead I felt a kind of light-headed curiosity; I marveled at the wealth that surrounded me—the rhytons of silver and carved ivory, the caskets of jewels. Yet the islanders were not a rich people. How could they have come by such magnificent treasures, and what were they doing within these caverns?

From very far away, the bubbling of an underground stream. Was this one of the places where the Styx welled up to touch the outside world? It would not have surprised me.

The blue light beckoned: it came from the end of a twisty passageway. I followed. The haphazard scattering of human remains gave way to an orderly sequence of biers on either side of the tunnel; each bore a skeleton in repose, dressed in a flounced skirt of the antique style, holding in its crossed hands a clay serpent.

I knew where I was now. This was where they buried the women who served as the living goddess. As I surmised, the biers of skeletons gave way to biers of fresher corpses. The last one was a face I knew: the priestess I had last seen here, who had invited me to make love with her . . . whose embrace I had fled.

She was dead now, and decay was just setting in.

Treasure lay at her head and feet. I knew some of the treasure. A gold ring on her putrefying finger was a ring I had seen on the hand of my grandmother Hecabe.

The gold of Troy! I had seen it everywhere—even in the tawdry palace of Neoptolemos! Anger came to me, blind and terrible. I no longer cared. They were going to kill me anyway. I kicked the corpse of the priestess; I ran enraged through the tunnel, smashing skulls, hurling treasures against the walls.

Then, in the midst of my passion, I heard voices. My onslaught of emotion dissipated all at once. I listened.

The tunnel went on, becoming narrower. The voices were

nearer. I was crawling now. But the light had grown brighter, and it was not all coming from the walls.

I emerged into another cave. Ahead was an irregular patch of brilliance. I squinted. Crept closer. Tried to peer at the light. There was a slight breeze. There was an opening, perhaps a way to freedom. . . .

No. The opening was barricaded with wooden bars. I could look out, but I was still in a cage after all. The entire escapade had been fruitless.

Numbed, I pressed hard against the bars and stared out.

I was overlooking another cavern, a huge one. Beyond it was light: the entrance to the outside world. The walls of the cavern were painted with images of bulls and snakes, and the smell of incense wafted up. This, then, was the interior of the temple, which I had only glimpsed before.

At the entrance, some men were digging a trench into the cavern floor. There were stone slabs piled up where they were working. A shaft of sunlight fell on them from outside.

A throne was set up in the middle of the cavern. It was the throne of Snakemother, and Helen was seated on it. I could barely make her out; but even from here I could see that her face was passive, immobile. There were worshipers in the temple, all prostrate before her, and a pile of offerings. I recognized my sword, the sword Helen had given me herself.

"Helen!" I cried out. I shouted with all my strength but my voice could barely be heard. She did not even look up.

One of the worshipers rose. I saw that it was Phalas.

He began to laugh at me. His laughter echoed. It seemed to be coming from right beside me, even though he was a tiny figure in the cavern below.

"So, King of Troy," he said, "you have climbed and struggled and pushed yourself gasping up the slope . . . only to find yourself more captive than before. Do you see what we're creating down here, just for you?" He spun around and pointed to where the diggers were working. "It will be a grave fit for a king. We will crown you and drug you and lower you into the cavity and then we will tenderly cover

your body with those slabs of costly stone—stone brought
here all the way from Egypt—''

"Pirate!" I shouted. I knew that the island had nothing it
could trade for such fine stone.

"That all depends on your point of view," the One-Eyed
King said. "I serve the Lady and bring her treasure. You and
I are only men. We are like the flowers and the crops, born
for death and war; but the Lady, being a woman, is mysterious and eternal. If I should risk my life at sea for the Lady,
many would call this noble."

"I would not!"

"But you are going to perform the noblest act of all, my
fellow king," said Phalas. "I have only given wealth; you
will give your life."

"No! I won't die to serve your perversion of truth. I'll die
taunting you, not mouthing your precepts."

"But that will be good. The angrier you are, you see, the
better. You'll make a fine spirit to guard the threshold;
besides, better you than me."

"So you've made some kind of bargain with them!" I
said.

"To be honest with you, I didn't relish the notion of
filling the hole you are about to fill, Astyanax. But the Lady
in her wisdom provided me with an alternative. She has little
love for your kind, Trojan or Akhaian; both of you have
sought to take her power from her. Now, in the wake of the
new darkness that is about to fall upon the world, it is her
time to return."

"The new darkness . . ." I thought of the mysteries that
Helen and I had celebrated in a room bursting with radiance.
Could the new darkness have begun even at that moment? I
did not dare to think of it. I was overcome by misery. I
turned my back on the window into the temple. I sat leaning
against the bars. I stared at the corpses of the dead priestesses. I thought of my own death, and of Helen's death;
when she died, she would join these others here. I gazed at
the one most recently dead, her skin greenish in the pale cold
light.

I thought of making love with Helen, and I thought of how I had almost made love with this other goddess, decaying in the darkness before my very eyes.

I drifted into sleep. I dreamed of making love to Helen, of her body rotting, falling apart under my passionate thrustings.

For a whole day (as far as I could judge the passing of time) I was hungry. At length I climbed back down to the bottom of the pit; I found food waiting beside the great stone that blocked my escape. They had not meant to starve me. It was fine food—roast pig and thick loaves and figs—served from vessels of silver. Was it night by now? Far away I could hear the obscene chanting. I ate. There was a jar of wine too. It was cold and I was thirsty. I drank, hoping to forget.

I passed into a torpor. Too late I realized that the wine must be drugged. They always used drugs to dull the senses of a king they were going to kill; I remembered the slave in the cage in Mycenae.

The fire I had built seemed to dance, to drift, to be stretched out into a skein of gold-red streaks. I was drowsy. My fingers, my toes, felt warm; the warmth flowed into me, and my phallos tingled as though in the afterglow of love. When they killed me I would be unable to shout curses at their Snakemother!

I threw the jar into the fire. Blue-green sparks flew from it. I was not going to let them siphon my soul from me, my soul only newly joined again—once I heard how the Egyptians extract the brain from the body through the nose with a special instrument. It was this vision that haunted me as the potion took effect. I was in a half sleep; nightmares seemed real. Once I thought I saw the Furies, and I cried out, "No, I am not Orestes; Orestes has gone to Athens to be purified. You have come for the wrong man." Another time I thought Hermes stood before me, with his beautiful, scornful eyes and his feet aflutter. But it was only a tongue of flame.

I did not drink the wine the next day, but poured some out, and climbed once more into the gallery of dead goddesses. I spent the day gazing at the activities below. Most of the time

Helen would sit in state and receive offerings. Usually there would be sacrifices: pigs or cattle usually, but once there was a small creature, in a basket, that might have been a piglet but whose squeals sounded distressingly human. Did they sacrifice babies? They were a barbarian people. I shuddered. I would not have put it past them; I had heard rumors of what went on to the south of Troy, where they worshiped Snakemother under the name Ashtart.

If I wait long enough, I told myself, I will find Helen alone. Alone she will not be the same.

But it did not happen that day or the next. Always she was surrounded by priestesses and suppliants. In the mornings there were chaste dances; in the evenings, wild singing and sexual dancing. Helen presided, but I did not hear her say a word when she sat enthroned.

The days passed. I grew weak from thirst; now and then I had to drink the drugged wine, and a timeless apathy fell over me. In this state I did not even want to return to Troy. I felt nothing at all; I was already dead, like one of Memnon's zumbi creatures. I was not even interested in climbing the wall to watch the rites. But I knew that the grave they had dug for me was almost complete.

At last they let me out, trussed me up, dragged me into the chamber of the goddess.

They threw me at Helen's feet; they knocked my head against the hard ground. Blood ran down my eyes. I looked up at her. Again that inconstruable smile. She had never been more beautiful. They were gone completely, those lines of age that I had seen in Sparta. She was as she had been in Troy. They had dressed her in the old style. Her bare breasts were firm as a young woman's. A snake coiled about her arms, around her neck. I almost choked on her sweet fragrance. I was about to speak to her, but they pushed my face back onto the floor.

I heard Phalas speak. "Welcome, young king. I do not wish to see you in any more pain than is necessary. Shall we proceed directly to your burial?"

I looked up. He stood before the throne. I could see the

pile of offerings; my iron sword was still there. They had
polished it. Humbly Phalas knelt before his goddess and said,
"We will celebrate the sacred marriage now, Living Goddess."

I managed to gasp, "Don't listen to him, daughter
of Skyfather!" Phalas kicked my jaw. I tasted blood. There
was not much pain, because I had been unable to avoid the
drugs completely.

"Her father may be the sky," Phalas said derisively, "but
what do fathers matter? I suppose you subscribe to that
strange notion of the father's seed implanting itself in a woman's womb? That is a myth—a myth your people created to
supplant the truth! Fucking does not create life! Woman
creates life!" He punctuated each exclamation with another
kick. He must have thought I was completely drugged, that I
felt nothing at all. In reality it was all I could do not to cry
out. But I did not want to give him the satisfaction of
knowing I could be hurt. He went on with his absurd denial
of what every child knows: "It is woman, woman alone who
possesses the mystery of creation. Man is dust, but a woman
is Queen of Heaven."

I could not answer this madness. He continued for a while,
but his enthusiasm abated when I did not respond. At last he
said, "We had best get on with it." Then, as they raised me
up and started to drag me toward the entrance to the cave, he
said, "Don't think I've no misgivings about this at all, King
of Troy. But you held power over me once. No man likes to
be a slave, even under a just master."

Those words were his only concession to our old relationship. I stood at the brink of the pit they had dug for me. It
was as deep as a man is high, and narrow; I could lie down,
but only barely. Phalas came to watch as they lowered me
down.

"Have you no . . . last requests, King of Troy?" he said.

I said, "Let me not be buried without my sword. I have
tried to be a hero. And let Helen kiss me goodbye."

He laughed. "Infatuated to the last. You're too young to
know women, boy! You think that sex equals possession!

How wrong you are. Women possess themselves, boy, themselves alone."

It was dark in the pit. The stone amplified the sounds
above; people walking boomed in my ears. I could only see
legs around the edges of my grave: the legs of the diggers,
sweaty, scarred; Phalas's legs. Now a face: a curious child
who had crept up close to see the burial of a king.

Phalas left and returned. He threw the sword down to me.
It clattered against stone. I thought it would slice me. In-
stead, it rasped against the ropes, loosening them slightly.
Not enough to twist free.

"As for a kiss," Phalas said, "you will have to make do
with a vision. The kiss you shall imagine."

I could hear them lift up Helen's throne. They set it at the
brink of the pit. I saw the old wood clearly. And Helen. Had
her expression shifted a little? Had I seen pity cloud her eyes
for a moment? I could not allow myself to think so. They
were all under Snakemother's ancient enchantment. The bargain that Agamemnon had struck with the huntress still held
true. The ancient ways were fated to come back. That was
the meaning of the new darkness.

She watched me. I thought I saw compassion. But by then
I was beginning to understand that men saw what they wanted
in Helen; she was all things at once. I thought I saw love. It
was only then that I realized she had never said she loved
me.

They began to shovel earth into the grave. It fell on my
arms and chest first. A clod struck me in the mouth, but
Phalas cried out angrily, "Not the face! Let him gaze on
Helen until the end! It's the least we can do." But I knew he
wanted to protract my pain. The sound of scraping earth,
magnified by the rock, screeched in my ears.

Suddenly I heard a sharp cry of pain. A crushing weight fell
on me. It was one of the gravediggers. He had an arrow in
his neck. Blood was gushing everywhere. Scuffling sounds,
crashing through the walls of stone. The corpse pinned me
even more; I could not move at all, I could not even jerk my

head to shake the blood from my eyes. What was happening?
Blood ran into my mouth, my nostrils. . . .

Someone else had leaped into the pit. The corpse of the
digger was being pulled off me. They were sawing at my
ropes, yanking me loose. The iron sword was thrust into my
hand.

A voice: "Can you stand?"

"I think so." I wiped my eyes with a fold of my chiton.
Blood everywhere. My hair was matted.

"Come. We might have to fight our way out. I haven't
brought that many men."

I felt arms now, pulling me from the pit. The first thing I
saw was Helen. Blood had spattered her robes, but she still
sat motionless. There were armed men fighting. A priestess
flung herself at me; before I knew it I had swung the sword
and sent her severed arm flying into the pit.

I turned to my rescuer . . .

"Orestes!"

"Not now. Just fight. Here. Back to back. With me."

Phalas was bearing down on us now. He had gathered his
men behind him. I saw corpses everywhere. A man jumped
at me and I plunged the iron into him. The sword cut right
through flesh and bone like magic. *This* was what fighting
with iron was like!

I whispered to Orestes, "Have you come to kill me or to
save me?"

"I must save you first. I owe you my life. After that I will
be free to kill you."

"Did Athena cleanse you of—"

"Yes. I am purified." He stopped talking to swing at
Phalas.

We fought on. We staggered about the cavern, killing,
killing. I did not know or care who the corpses were. The ease
with which iron could kill brought out a madness in us.

I found myself exchanging blows with Phalas. At last he
gasped, "And if you kill me? Who will get Helen? You or
Orestes?"

"I don't know!" I screamed. Sword struck sword. Sparks
against the smoke of incense and sacrifice.

"We should let the goddess decide," Phalas said.

I was overcome with exhaustion. I had been fighting in a
kind of drunken frenzy; now I let the sword drop, not caring
whether I lived or died. And turned to see Helen rise from
her throne. . . .

At this, though she had spoken not a word, every weapon
clattered to the floor of the temple.

Helen said, "We have desecrated this place enough."

I looked from Phalas to Orestes. The three of us, carefully
stepping over the corpses heaped around us, walked slowly to
where Helen stood. Though her clothes were bloodstained,
she seemed untouched by the battle, just as she had been the
last time I had seen her in Troy, radiant among the drab,
bedraggled wives and mothers who were soon to become
concubines and slaves.

Orestes said to me, "Now my debt to you is paid, Astyanax.
My life; your life. And Athena has interceded with the Erinyes
for me, so that the madness has left me. Oh, Astyanax,
sometimes I think it would have been better to have stayed
insane!"

I said, "Isn't there a way for me not to kill you, Orestes?
After all we've been through together."

"But you had another name then."

We were silent, expectant; it was for Helen to make the
next decision. "I exist only to be carried off," Helen said,
echoing Menelaos's drunken joke with deep seriousness. "And
now there are three of you, and you all plan to carry me
off."

Phalas said, "You must choose, Goddess."

Orestes said, "And when you choose, you will also choose
for us. You will choose between war and peace; light and
darkness; love and hatred."

"But not between life and death?" Helen said. A weary
sadness emanated from her. It was as if the entire world had
grown resigned to the end it knew must come. "Ah, but I see
all of you have chosen already. Oh, tragic Orestes, mis-

guided Phalas, Astyanax who hoped for so much . . . do you think I would not choose life for all three of you? But you have wrestled that choice from me. You have all chosen death. Extinction lies at the end of all those choices, my three kings.''

Chapter XXXVIII

The Judgment of Helen

She said, "So now I must choose."

"As I chose," Phalas said, breathing heavily from his exertions. The three of us made no move to threaten one another. We knew that what happened next was in the hands of fate; we would wield no influence over Helen's choice. Phalas went on, "I chose between obedience and defiance, and I made myself king. I chose to be true to the old faith, to the Lady. It is because of that faith that I claim you. You are the daughter of the sky, but also of the earth, and it is proper that you rule here."

Orestes said, "I chose between two conflicting duties, revenge or respect for that which gave birth to me. I was true to the new faith, but I reaped the punishments of both alternatives. I claim you because you belong in Sparta. You are queen there. You are my mother's sister. I claim you for Menelaos because his is the legitimate, just claim." The calmness that I sensed in him was new. Athena had given him strength; she had been able to do what Skyfather could not do directly. For the gods—and especially the king of the gods—are bound by laws that existed before them; it would not do for Skyfather to plead with the Furies to mitigate their wrath at Orestes' matricide. Yet it seemed that Athena had done well, and the madness had left him. The Orestes that stood before Helen now was no longer haunted. I almost missed his brooding lunacy; now he seemed colorless, as the world itself had become after the end of the Trojan War.

"As for my choice," I said, "it came when I was asked to pick the fairest of three goddesses, and I found that my choice made little difference. It had been made for me already. I was offered fortune, I was offered bravery and wisdom; but it was love that I really desired. It is by virtue of that choice that I claim Helen."

"How can I choose?" Helen said. "I have never chosen before. It has always been you, you men, who have chosen to carry me away. And I have gone where you have taken me; I have been the woman you saw in me; I have thought the thoughts you imagined in the heart you imagined me to have."

"Do you want the three of us to fight each other now, in front of you, and the survivor to win?" I said bitterly. "Is that what the will of the gods has come to?" This could not be the woman with whom I had made love in the flesh, in my dreams. Yet she was more beautiful than ever.

"No. That is not the will of the gods." She turned to summon a priestess, who threw a shawl over her naked shoulders; she drew it down over her breasts, as though suddenly aware for the first time of their seductiveness. I realized that it was getting cool; the ceremony that was to have culminated in my living burial had begun at midday, but it was now almost evening.

"We will go down to the sea," Helen said at last. "This temple is not neutral ground. The shore, where sky, earth, and water meet, is where I will decide."

Priestesses and armed men fell in beside her. One of them gave a sharp command; four of them lifted their living goddess onto the throne and raised it up. It was as though the whole thing had been rehearsed. From behind us, the temple women began to sing in their alien tongue. As we left the cave, I felt the evening breeze; it lifted Helen's soft golden hair, and the setting sun's light spangled it with artificial stars. The wind blew stronger, drowning the stench of death with the smell of brine and seaweed.

We went downhill. The path to the sea led through the village. Children crept out of houses and joined us. Couples and old men and women dropped their work and filed in. It seemed almost by design. Now someone would raise his voice and join the chant, picking it up in mid-phrase; a child, not missing a beat, would add his wavery treble to it. And so the music swelled. I noticed as we reached the beach that there were drums and pipes and kitharas, but I could not tell when they had become part of the music.

Helen raised her hand. The music stopped. Even the wind was hushed.

Three kings stood facing her in a semicircle. Behind her was the populace of the whole island. Even the pigs were there; they too were silent. As I have said before, they seemed ensorcelled by Snakemother's power. Perhaps it was true that these pigs possessed the souls of luckless adventurers who had chanced upon this island.

Helen rose from her throne. The wood of the throne was black in the crimson dusklight.

The ceremony was impressive. But for me there was something lacking. I remembered the judgment in the temple of Skyfather. Here there were no manifestations from Olympos.

I looked out to sea. There were several ships there, Akhaian ships; they must have come with Orestes. At a word from him, warriors dived from the decks of the ships and swam to shore. They clustered behind Orestes, standing knee-deep in the water. All were armed with iron.

"I see you're all ready to take me back to my husband, Orestes," Helen said, with neither enthusiasm nor disdain. "Just as Phalas has his followers behind me, waiting to set my throne up once more in the temple. Only you have nothing, Little Star." Though she called me by my childname, there was no tenderness in her words. If I had hoped to hear the slightest sign that she remembered our lovemaking, I was disappointed. "How shall I choose? Astyanax, surely I cannot choose you. You don't even have a ship to take me back to Troy. . . ."

I looked down at the sand. I could not believe my ears.

"As for Phalas, you hardly figure in this at all. Orestes comes as emissary of my proper husband. . . ."

"No!" I cried out. "I won't let you go back into the arms of that spent old man whose breath stinks of wine and old puke! You and I are kin, we are both pieces of the sky, we belong together."

Phalas laughed. "The Lady belongs to no man," he said. His people swayed forward. Their shadows, long in the sunset, reached into the sea.

Orestes said, "Think of your honor, Queen of Sparta."

Phalas said, "Think of your divinity, Living Goddess."

Again I burst out: "The gods made me choose too, when there was no choice! Do what I did, Helen! Ask them how they will bribe you. Ask them what gift they'll give you if you choose them! Show them how cheaply a goddess can be bought!"

"Yes." Helen's face was still a mask of serenity. "Obviously that's how it must be done. My judgment to counterbalance your judgment, Astyanax. Only then can there be harmony in heaven and earth."

We waited.

"You will speak in turns," she said. "Each one of you will say what he will give me if I choose to come with him."

Phalas spoke first. "That's easy, Living Goddess. Only here can you be all divine. I stand for the golden past. Women ruled once and they will rule again."

Orestes said, "In Sparta you can be a link between the human and the divine. Your kingdom will be far more magnificent than this barbaric island. The Trojan War is over. Let it slide into the past. Let's have some kind of future now. I killed my mother, but Athena showed me that I can be forgiven. Things are going to be different now. We don't need a world ruled by men or by women; we need compromise and compassion. A future, Helen."

So Orestes had not been cured of his insanity after all; it had merely taken on a more insidious form. "The gods have not decreed any future for the Age of Bronze," I said. "You know that, Orestes. I don't stand for the future or the past.

The future's an illusion, Orestes. As far as the gods are
concerned our age of heroes is already over; we exist in a sort
of half world. The universe is not always as tidy as the gods
would have it. I stand for the crack in time, as the Pythoness
called it. I'm nothing at all. I don't even have a ship. You
won't be a goddess. You won't even be a demigoddess as
you were in Sparta. You'll only be human. Human as I was
when I kissed you, haltingly at first, fearful of adultery and
my own unproven virility, and then with more warmth,
because you answered my kiss with another more passionate. I didn't think grand thoughts of honor and godhood
while we made love, Helen! Making love was all there was
to it, and it was everything, and it was enough.''

"Absolute power over the life and death of your subjects!'' Phalas said. "Sacrifice and prayer and immeasurable
wealth! Immortality!''

"Glory!'' said Orestes. "Honor! The living symbol of
Akhaia's hope! The rebirth of our ravaged civilizations.''

"Frailty,'' I said, "love, and perhaps death, and perhaps
the destruction of the Troy I have labored to rebuild.''

Slowly she looked from one to the other. Both the others
bore expressions of utter triumph; each thought he had won. I
wanted her. My dreams, my illusions, had all been stripped
from me. But there was Helen, Helen whose body I had held
in my arms, whose lips I had tasted, salt and sweet and
bitter. She was my last illusion. "If you felt anything at all,
you would come with me,'' I said, despairing. "They've
offered you things I can't give, things I can't possess . . . but
they haven't offered you *feeling!* Yet you've felt nothing
through all this. You must envy the love I feel, even though
you're incapable of feeling it, because you're at least half a
god, and the gods don't feel pain, they don't understand
love. For you I'll throw away past and future. I'll throw
away civilization. I'll throw away Troy, Akhaia, the Age of
Bronze, everything, everything.'' I began to walk away. I
did not want any of them to see my tears. My quest had
foundered so many times. I wanted to end it once and for all.

I began to walk into the sea. I had some wild notion of

walking, walking toward the setting sun, until I could breathe no more, until the brine poured into my lungs and drowned me.

I heard her voice: "True, Astyanax, you don't even have a ship."

I paused a beat. Her words must be a refusal . . . they had to be.

Then she said, "But I must give myself to the strongest among you three."

I continued walking.

"Orestes: you came on a mission from a king. Justice shored up your claim. You sailed to the island with retainers and ships. Phalas: your ancient faith sustained you. You too had ships and men. Astyanax alone came to me with nothing, without even his name." I stopped again. Chill water splashed my chest, my neck. "He did not have faith or justice to support him. His power came from himself alone. That's why I must choose him. No man has ever dared to offer me the choice of becoming human."

I could hear the people on both sides gasping. I spun around, waded back to the beach. Consternation had broken out among the Akhaians and the islanders.

"If I choose to be human," Helen was saying, "I might no longer be beautiful. I am old enough to be your mother, Little Star. I will soon be forty. Will you make love as passionately if I'm dry and withered and bad-tempered?"

"It still doesn't make any difference! I still don't have a ship!" I cried. I was still reeling from her decision. "How can I—"

At that moment some of the women screamed. I saw both my kingly rivals gape in astonishment. I had not yet reached Helen, not yet embraced her. I whirled around, for they were pointing out at the sea, at some distant object.

The patch of brilliance on the horizon, outshining the twilight, making my eyes burn . . . the tiniest outline of a ship, drawn in lines of dazzling gold.

"There's only one ship in the entire world that sails in perpetual sunlight," I said.

And I felt her hand in my hand, trembling, like the hand of a frightened girl. She does love me, I thought. Perhaps one day she will come to say it. But it doesn't matter.

"Do you know whose ship it is?" Helen said.

Against the twilight fell a rain of golden ankhs.

"Yes," I said. "It is the ship of A-A-A—"

The heretic king! I could not say his name. But of course, all of us knew who he was. I would remember the name soon enough, once I set foot again in the domain of Memnon the dark mage.

Chapter XXXIX

Figures in the Sand

The light . . . masking the sunset, the ship of the nameless king burned on the darkling sea. The others were staring dumbfounded. The memory of the ship was mine alone. This was how Skyfather chose to speak to me.

"I have a ship now," I whispered.

The vessel of the pharaoh came closer. It glided on the water like a golden swan; the rowers had raised their oars. At last I saw Memnon, his arms outstretched toward me, a man of ebony suffused with radiance.

Faintly I heard the shouts of the navigator. A smaller boat was being readied. I saw Memnon's litter being lowered, and four blue men with him, their skin glazed clay, their loincloths linen.

"This is trickery, black magic, shameful," Phalas said.

"Misdirection," I said softly. Only Helen heard me. She had not let go of my hand, though it had stopped trembling.

Ankhs drizzled from the gray clouds. They sparkled, dissolved before they hit the sand. Some of the crowd, emboldened, were running about, trying to catch them. One seemed to collide with my face; it was cold and tickly, like a snowflake.

Suddenly the bearers were close by, wading to the shore. Memnon sat in state: he wore a wig of woven gold; his oiled, bare chest was covered with gold ornaments. It is always so with the Egyptians; even their ministers and mages were more richly caparisoned than any king of Akhaia, for they come from the place of the sun.

Many of the people, awed, had prostrated themselves.

"No need, no need!" Memnon said. He seemed amused at the attention. "Though I've lived a couple of centuries, I'm just a humble magician. The king, as some of you may know, never comes ashore anymore."

"My old friend!" I cried out. I was not sure whether to be overjoyed at his coming, but I wanted to make sure that these people knew that the mage was my acquaintance.

"Astyanax." The bearers sank down to their knees. I was now face to face with the man to whose magic I owed all the adventures and misadventures that had befallen me. The sight of him, black and beaming, made me remember so much. While I wandered with only half a soul, my knowledge of myself and my place in the world had been slowly seeping away from me. When Helen called my name for the first time I had begun to feel whole again; now I realized how much of my soul still remained to be regained.

I went forward and, leaning over the kneeling litterbearers, embraced him. He had a faint smell of sandalwood and of embalming fluids. Laughing, he said, "You seem to have a little problem?"

He was looking at Helen, but I spoke. I panicked, thinking she might change her mind. "Helen has picked me. She wants to cast godhood aside completely."

"Is this true, daughter of Zeus and Leda, perfect union of earth and sky?"

She neither affirmed nor denied it. But Memnon nodded thoughtfully and said, "Can the woman who chooses this truly be Helen? There have been many Helens, many phantoms."

She said, so softly that we had to strain to catch her words,

"I am the true Helen. I am the child of earth and starry heaven."

"Then these are truly the last days of our great age. But I rejoice," he said—though I could see no joy in his eyes—"for when the cataclysm comes my master and I will find freedom. The rift in the ages will come suddenly . . . and my ship and its crew will sail into eternity through the crack in time. A difficult concept, no?"

"But familiar," I said, for I had heard the Pythoness say much the same thing.

"Then, Astyanax, I must give thanks to you."

"Why?" I was puzzled, for I had done him no favors.

"Because, my young king of the last days, you are the gods' instrument of ending. You are the most important figure of your time, though in the next age few will remember your name."

"I've found, Memnon," I said, "that your words always carry at least two meanings. You're the master of misdirection—you yourself taught me its importance. What are you up to now?"

"Dismiss the others," he said, waving his hands at the mob. They obeyed him without question, not waiting for a command from Helen or from any of the kings. Somewhat sulkily, Phalas too started to leave, and Orestes to follow him.

"No. The kings shall remain. And, of course, the goddess."

Almost instantly the crowd seemed to have vanished. Darkness was all around us, except for the ship that shone in the mid-distance. But Memnon looked up to heaven and held up an ankh that he wore around his neck, and a ray of light pierced the cloud canopy. It fell over our group, so that we stood in a pool of silver radiance; beyond us, the gloom deepened.

At the center of the light was the throne: gnarled, rotting, the seat sunken from centuries of living goddesses.

We waited.

At last Memnon said, "Now I will do something I never thought I would do again."

And he stepped from the litter and stood unsteadily on the
sand. "There!" he sighed. "Wasn't so hard. Oh, I feel
wobbly, though."

A tremor . . . Was it thunder? Or had the sand heaved
beneath my feet? Wildly I looked at the other kings. They
had felt it too. "But . . ." I blurted out. "You told me,
Memnon, you told me your feet could never touch the earth,
because you draw your power from Skyfather, and Snakemother
is always ready to drain it away from you—"

"I lied."

"Memnon—"

"And I did not lie." He tottered as he stepped toward us.
In his hand he held a rod—it was the same wand with which
he had woken the blue king to life. "The earth is sapping me
of power. And yet it must be so. Because the magic I am
about to work is a new kind of magic. It draws in equal
measure from earth and sky. The things you thought were
opposites, Astyanax, are really one. That is the great lesson
you will have learned, when you finally come to stand on the
brink of never and forever. It is time for my latest and my
greatest masterpiece of misdirection."

So saying he began to scratch something in the sand.

"What is he doing?" Orestes said.

I saw three symbols:

$$\Upsilon \qquad \mathcal{A} \qquad \mathfrak{h}$$

"Astyanax," Memnon said, struggling mightily against the
earth's pull as he finished the last of the three characters, "do
you see what these letters mean?"

"I don't know," I said. "But I'm reminded of the time I
was a boy, when Hermes came down and made me choose
between three goddesses, and I discovered—"

"Enough. All the world knows the story. It's not the first
time it's happened," Orestes said. "The three signs are the
initials of three sacred names: Υ stands for Athena, the
goddess of war and wisdom. You and your uncle rejected
her. $\mathcal{A}$ is for the Queen of Heaven, Hera, whom you also

disdained. ϟ is for Kutherian Aphrodite, who won you over with a promise of sexual fulfillment.''

"You're a bright lad," Memnon said. "But then the insane so often are. It takes a special effort to be utterly, gloriously mad. I congratulate you."

"Athena has wiped away my madness," Orestes said.

"Perhaps she has cured the symptoms," Memnon said, "but ah, the sickness itself . . . it is an ancient thing. You are the last and maddest of the Atreidai, I'm afraid." He turned to me. "But there is another interpretation of the three symbols, no?"

Suddenly I saw. "The three mortal women . . ."

"Yes. The celestial trinity has its earthly complement."

"Ͳis for my mother, Andromache," I said.

"Then ϟ must stand for *my* mother, Clytaemnestra," said Orestes. "Both Clytaemnestra and Cytheris are written with an initial KU."

"And the third?" Memnon turned to Phalas, who had been watching the proceedings uneasily.

"That is easy," Phalas said. "The Ᵽ represents the living goddess, Helen. It also stands for the Queen of Heaven— the two are identical. Helen." But he seemed dubious.

"Now, my queen," Memnon said. His voice was fading, and the four blue litterbearers hovered anxiously around him, waiting to lift him up if he grew too weak to continue. "You must stand beside the throne."

She did so, resting her fingertips on one worn arm.

The tide was coming in. It was dissolving the symbols of the feminine triad that had ruled my life.

With bold strikes of his wand, Memnon wrote one more word in the sand in front of the throne:

Ᵽ Ψ

E-ra. Hera, the Queen of Heaven.

Helen was about to speak, to protest. He shushed her with a finger to her lips. "The sea," he said. He motioned me to stand next to the water. "You must be ready," he whispered. "Don't forget the sword."

"I—" I obeyed him, slinging the iron sword over my shoulder.

"Be silent!" he commanded. He returned to a pose of the utmost concentration. The water was lapping at my feet now, the wet sand prickly between my toes. To Phalas he said, "I will satisfy you easily enough." Phalas had said nothing since uttering Helen's name. Memnon turned to Orestes. "Alas, I will not be as much help to you. The Phoenician is firmly anchored in the far past; him I can satisfy with an illusion. But you, Orestes, have cast yourself adrift; I can give you nothing." Orestes was silent, waiting; Phalas stood dazed. The magician had worked a spell on him already.

"What are we waiting for?" I asked him at last.

"Silence!" Memnon said again, with such annoyance that I felt like a scolded child.

The water was ankle-deep now; it was spreading to the foot of the throne. . . .

Suddenly I saw what was about to happen. The waves were racing toward the writing in the sand. I was about to cry out when the dark water touched the second syllable of the name and began to erode the etching, and even as I watched I saw the thin scratch marks melting away and the symbol 𐤅 transform itself into Ψ.

I could not contain my excitement. I shouted, "You've changed the writing to *E-re-* and now it's ambiguous; it could be the beginning of Helen's name or something completely different. You've confused the names and now the gods will be confused too— "

"Be quiet!" Memnon hissed. "How do you expect it to work if you give it all away?" He reached out a hand to Helen. "Quickly, quickly now, before everyone realizes what's going on."

He yanked Helen from where she was standing. "Up!" he shouted to his bearers. He staggered to his litter. They seized him and thrust him ungracefully into his seat, and began unceremoniously to retreat into the sea. "Hurry up!" Memnon said. "We can't fool them for long!" He hauled Helen up. She sat at his feet, awkwardly straddling the poles.

I could not stop talking. I was shaking with excitement. "You're going to put Helen's divinity into the wood—just as you did with me and the clay figurine. You're making her fully human." I was too awestruck to move at first. Then I saw the anger building up in Orestes' face. I hastened after the litter. I was up to my waist in water now. But I had to look back. I had to see what Memnon's magic had wrought. . . .

The wood of the throne was pulsating, throbbing with an eerie parody of life! It was twisting, forming into a vaguely human shape . . . and Phalas was prostrate before it in adoration.

Orestes was running after me. He held his own sword up. "I couldn't kill you before—because you saved my life. But now I can!" he shouted. "And I have to—for the sake of my uncle's honor! You'll curse the day you rushed to rescue a madman from the madwomen of Mount Parnassos."

"Honor—" I wanted to tell him it was useless, that we were all in the hands of powers greater than ourselves, that we should feel no rancor toward each other. We had been friends after a fashion. I had not chosen the name he gave me.

He gave me no time. He swung the sword wildly, impotently. I parried. The blades whistled in the air, missing each other. "Hurry up!" the mage urged. The bearers paused. The water was up to their necks. It occurred to me that they could walk completely submerged. They did not need to breathe, being men of animated clay. I threw my arms around the poles of the litter. I grasped Helen's ankle, I held onto the wood, I pulled myself up.

The bearers were running toward the ship. I saw the mage's face. He seemed tired, so tired. I had not known he could feel exhaustion. "You should not have touched the earth," I whispered.

He only smiled, half sadly. "Rules are made to be broken," he said. And then, "So are people."

I heard Orestes' shout, "We'll come to Troy! Maybe we

won't have a thousand ships. But you don't have Hector and your fifty uncles anymore. We'll beat you down again, just as we've always done. Heracles destroyed Troy in ancient times, and my father razed it in our own time. I'm going to finish the job! I'll dash your brains out myself against the stones of the city walls!''

I looked back. He was standing on the shore again, trying to gather his men. A scuffle had broken out between Phalas's guards and his. Orestes' ships were anchored not far off. The men on board clamored and waved their weapons, but they were too fearful of Memnon's magic, and they must have guessed that Skyfather's power was in the Egyptian ship.

"Look, Helen!" Memnon was saying. "Look at the last vestige of your divinity!''

"No, I will not,'' Helen said, staring resolutely out to sea. "I cannot look back. I'm afraid that I will be afraid.''

But I looked, and I saw that the throne had become a statue, and its face was not the face of Helen, soft and beautiful, but a cruel face with sneering lips and hard eyes, set on a formless mass of wood so knotted as to resemble scar tissue. The statue seemed to erupt from the black, foaming water. I could still see Phalas worshiping it. I could hear him thanking the Lady for returning to him. Memnon had created a phantom Helen.

But I possessed the true Helen. Not a goddess but a human.

Almost inaudibly she said, "Will I grow old now?"

"Not for me!" I said. "You'll always be the Helen I loved. As a child, as a man.''

"But for me . . . there will be mirrors.''

"I'll have all the mirrors in the palace melted down if they displease you.''

She turned to stare at the Egyptian ship. Her eyes watered. The brightness hurts her eyes, I thought, wondering at her transformation. This was not going to be the same as the other abductions. She had gone through the others unchanged, because she had been a principle, not a person. "You've begun to live, really live, really to live, at last.''

"It means I've begun to die, too."

"I don't care!" I said passionately, selfishly perhaps.

Tonight, I thought, we will make love as a man and a woman for the first time. But I still do not think you will say you love me. That will come with time. If there is any time.

Book Seven: Kings of Iron

⳦⳪⚑⳨⚁⊕
⋈Ψ⊏

Ζεῦ ἄλλοι τε θεοί, δότε δὴ καὶ τόνδε γενέσθαι
παῖδ' ἐμόν, ὡς καὶ ἐγώ περ, ἀρπρεπέα Τρώεσσιν,
ὧδε Βίην τ' ἀγαθόν, καὶ Ἰλίου ἶφι ἀνάσσειν,
καί ποτέ τις εἴποι: πατρός γ' ὅδε πολλὸν ἀμείνων,
ἐκ πολέμου ἀνιόντα, φέροι δ' ἔναρα Βροτόεντα
κτείνας δήιον ἄνδρα, χαρείη δὲ φρένα μήτηρ.

"O Zeus and all the gods, grant that my son
may be as great a prince as I among the Trojans,
as valorous and strong; that he may rule
in power over Troy. When he comes home from battle
may men cry out: 'He is greater than his father!'
May he kill his foes and bring home blood-drenched spoils
to gladden his mother's heart."
> —words of Prince Hector to the infant
> Astyanax on leaving for battle
> Homer, *The Iliad*

Chapter XL

𝕈𝕈𝕈𝕈𝕈𝕈𝕈𝕈𝕈𝕈𝕈𝕈𝕈𝕈𝕈𝕈𝕈𝕈

The Ocean Between the Worlds

The sea is no longer new to me, I thought, as the ship of the sun glided away from the island of the pigs. There was the wind: warm, moist, heavy with the scent of kelp; the sea, dark as a well-aged wine.

The rowers' oars struck the water with stark, inhuman precision. Their skin was the color of the sea and the sky, and glazed. I knew them for ushabtis, products of Memnon's magic. As was the blue king, waiting for me in Troy, still clinging a little to my captive ka.

For a long time I stood facing the misting shoreline. The heat was overwhelming. Above my head fell the endless rain of ankhs. The oarsmen chanted in the Egyptian tongue, words I could not understand; I turned to ask Memnon what they meant. But he and Helen had wandered toward the prow, and were reclining on rush mats, resting against cushions of linen stuffed with crushed rose leaves. In the perpetual brightness that enveloped Akhenaten's ships, Helen's hair shone, burned almost. Perhaps it was only the brightness that brought tears to my eyes.

I walked toward them. The ship rocked; the boards squeaked. I whispered her name and she turned, Helen the woman, to see me coming. Memnon, laughing, pointed me to a place beside her. "We were reminiscing," he said, "about old times." One of the blue men poured us wine.

"Old times?" I understood suddenly what I had known intellectually all along—that the war was to me a memory of chaos, a blur of images in a child's consciousness, but to them it was concrete, less idealized.

"Do I suddenly seem ancient to you, Little Star?" Helen said. I waited for the smile—the smile that had made me

317

reckless enough to make myself king, and having become king, to abandon kingship in search of her—but it did not come. She sensed what I was waiting for. She said, clasping my hand in hers, "I am human now. Does that upset you?" She did smile then, but it was not that smile. It was an endearing, affectionate smile; it concealed no enigmas. "Still, I am what you are going to war for. Maybe you won't think I'm worth it anymore. My divinity is a magnificent prize. Perhaps my womanhood is not so. That's what Ariadne discovered when Theseus carried her off from Crete." She ran a slender finger up and down my iron sword, which lay on the matting at their feet.

"You can cite all the myths you want," I said, "to prove any point you want. We're making our own myths here, and the old stories have lost their power." I looked at the sword but did not pick it up. "New metals mean new magic."

"Wisely said," said Memnon. There was perhaps a hint of irony in his voice. I did not want to pursue the subject. The past clung to them, an aura I could almost reach out and touch; I felt inexperienced, sheepish.

Another strain of the oarsmen's song, guttural and monotonous. "What are they saying?" I said.

"A hymn to Skyfather. It was composed by the king who sits below. Is it not time you paid your respects to him?"

"Yes."

"Come."

The brightness dissolved. We were suddenly in the bowels of the ship. I recognized a sarcophagus, the very one in which I had pretended to die so that Memnon could work his magic. I gasped.

"Eventually one gets used to these supernatural modes of travel," said a voice behind me. It seemed to be coming from far away, echoing through limestone caverns. I turned around. The mummy-king was sitting on his throne. He was crisscrossed with light and shadow, for the throne was directly beneath a wooden grating. His pectoral ornaments and his gold crown glimmered. He held his crook and flail against his chest. They were absolutely motionless, for, being a mummy, Akhenaten did not breathe.

"We meet again," King Akhenaten said. His gesture included Helen too; I wondered when they had met before. There was so much I did not know about Helen. "I am glad to see you, sister."

"I'm human now," Helen said, "and no longer an anomaly, half mortal, half divine. I've made my choice."

"We will see," said the pharaoh. "In my experience, choice has always been pretty much an illusion for humans."

There was one question I desperately wanted answered. Perhaps he would now. "The war!" I said. "Will it come to pass?"

The mummy did not speak. The king stiffened. Perhaps he had turned to stone.

"You shouldn't have asked that question!" Memnon said harshly. "You stupid boy!"

"Memnon, don't patronize him," Helen said. "What he has done—will do—is a sacred thing."

"Sorry." But Memnon did not seem apologetic, and began to pace the narrow chamber, his face set in one of those enigmatic expressions the Egyptians are wont to assume.

At last the heretic king said: "It is a good question." I waited for him to answer me. "As always, there is no simple answer."

"How can there not be?" I said, perplexed. "Yes or no?"

"The dead cry out," the king said.

"For vengeance? And I am the only instrument left to them?" I said. And thought of Hector's smashed body dragged through the gravel and the burning grass.

The king said, "You are more than an instrument for the dead. You are also an instrument for those who are not yet dead and who, perhaps, long for death; I mean—"

"Yourself, King?" I said softly.

"And all the others."

"What others?"

But again the mummy stiffened and would not speak. At

last Memnon said, "You've disturbed him enough. He doesn't like to think about these things."

"What others?" I demanded again.

Helen touched my hand. My emotion subsided. We were back on the deck again. And Memnon, glowering, was pacing furiously, his lionskin cloak whipping in his face. I sat back down on the woven rushes, moving the sword to one side so that Helen could lean her head against my shoulder.

Though we were wrapped in brightness, I could tell, through the veil of light, that the sun was setting on the water. I twisted around to get a view of the land but I saw none. The oarsmen chanted and heaved. I stood up. "There's no land at all," I said. "Are we going straight across the sea?"

"You know this is no ordinary ship," Helen said.

I panicked. Around us the sea seethed, though we floated in a circle of utter calm. In the distance dolphins breached; the air was full of the clicking of their speech.

"It's strange," Helen said. "I can barely understand them anymore."

"Did you once?"

"I think so. I don't remember."

"What do you mean?"

"Knowledge is fleeting. I remember there are two ways of knowing a thing. To know with your heart—that's knowledge that comes at birth, that you don't ever remember having learned. But to know with your mind—that's a painful thing; it involves getting acquainted with things, gradually learning their names, their attributes. I haven't forgotten anything I learned with my mind, Little Star. But what I knew in my heart . . ." And she wept, and would not be comforted.

I said, "But why? You must tell me why so I can make it better."

She said, "How can you ever understand? As a goddess I knew so much; as a human . . . Oh, it's like being blinded and having your tongue cut out and your ears stopped with wax. I can't tell what they're saying anymore, except, here and there, a word, a phrase." She made a piercing, inhuman sound, high-pitched, energetic. "I think that is a word for death."

They leaped, black against the sunset, dolphin upon dolphin.

"No shoreline at all," I said. "Are we going straight over to Troy? Are we men or fish?" I was dismayed; no voyager likes to lose sight of the firm earth. Not to see land is to drift from reality.

"This is a magical journey," Helen said. "I don't think we are going to see much that is familiar."

"I don't know. Days and days of uncertainty. Perhaps it will drive me mad."

"Fool!" Memon said, coming up to me. His anger seemed directed against the elements themselves, not me. "Not days and days. A single day and a single night it will seem to you. We will not go to Troy over the wine-dark sea you know, but over the ocean of chaos—the ocean between the worlds, between life and death, past the future, truth and illusion!"

"That is why he is so moody," Helen said. "He must make a powerful magic if we are to make it through the night. And—"

"And for you I touched my feet to the earth of Snake-mother!" Memnon cried, brushing me aside and beginning once more to pace. He uttered a few syllables I could not understand. The rowers redoubled their rhythm; the ship sliced through the turbulent sea like one of the dolphins that danced against the sunset. "Oh, my magic," he mumbled, "my magic, slipping through my fingers like rain."

I held Helen close to me. My heart beat fast. I felt a dull dread, like a throbbing headache. The pain grew suddenly. I trembled. I was feverish. I was dimly conscious of Helen, saying over and over, "Don't be afraid, Astyanax, we are only passing through a space between worlds," and the air around us seemed on fire and I closed my eyes but could not shut it out. The pain came in waves now, battering me. "Helen," I whispered, for through my closed eyelids I seemed to see her still, and her eyes glittered like cold stars. "We are through, we are through!" she said at last. "Look."

I dared to look then. We, the ship, were still bathed in the soft radiance of Skyfather. A circle of light surrounded us, but beyond it I could see a storm gathering. The waves towered about us. Jagged rocks jutted from the sea, their edges frothing. The rocks had the faces of demons. Lightning writhed in the black sky, lightning in the shape of serpents. The oarsmen rowed implacably.

"It is all illusion!" I heard Memnon's voice booming as the wind's whistling rose to a roar. "Back I say, back!" He stood at the prow now, holding the darkness at bay with a staff. "Oh, it's all different now; the world is splitting at the seams."

The wind was propelling us toward the darkness. Against the horizon I saw two pillars of rock; between them a whirlpool churned. I heard a groaning sound, like the closing of city gates. "Charybdis!" I said. These were the clashing rocks of legend. The ship moved inexorably toward them. The rocks towered over us. "We're going to be killed," I cried out.

But Helen only smiled.

And Memnon screamed and waved his staff and shouted to the oarsmen to row faster. . . .

We were between them now. Blackness on either side. I cowered in Helen's arms. The pillars touched over our heads and clanged and rock slammed into rock. The wind roar grew strangely silent, masked by the thickness of stone. "Helen—"

"Shush, Little Star." Her voice was suddenly clear; the air had become as close as in a cavern. "Watch the illusion."

And I looked up and saw that the pillars were the legs of a giantess, that the cavity into which we were being drawn was formed by the lips of a vast vagina. Her pubic hair was a forest of moss and seaweed. Darkness was falling. I looked up and saw the hair streaming in the sunlight like the hair of Helen. "Scylla is Charybdis," Helen said softly. And the great light was doused, and the ship was sailing in a place that was not a place. The air was permeated with the smell of a woman who is about to make love.

And Helen touched my face, my chest, my limbs, her

fingers barely skimming them, making me tingle. She whispered, her lips moving tenderly against my skin, "We have moved beyond the world, beyond the Trojan War; we're within the Great Mother. The Lady is the flesh of the universe and her bones are the stones and her blood is the endless ocean."

"Snakemother!" I said, starting violently. "How can you utter such an abomination? Have you forgotten who your father is?"

"Snakemother is what you have made of her," said Helen, "because you are afraid." I could barely see her eyes. I could hear the rhythmic ripple of the waves as the oars struck in uncanny unison. She said, "Once I could change my shape."

"I saw you become a lioness . . . a dolphin."

She laughed. "Tricks of the eye." Then, more seriously, she said, "But I'm exhausting my supply of tricks. By the time we reach Troy, I will have been quite drained of them. Do you know that?"

"Do you regret it?"

She played with my phallos with her tongue. It was too dark to see, but . . . could her tongue really coil around it like a serpent? Her body seemed hot, burning hot.

"You're making me . . . you're arousing me."

"Love me. Love me. Now. Now."

"Here?"

"Yes!" And she crushed me to her. And it seemed that she changed her shape again and again, that I was making love sometimes not to a woman but to a lioness who clawed me and whose fur was prickly and abrasive . . . to a dolphin . . . to a thing of fur and scales and feathers and smooth skin, and I clung tight to her, not wanting to let her go for fear she would not regain her human shape, and we made love again and again until it seemed that she had become the sea itself with her smell blending with the scent of seaweed and her body rich and pliant as the deep. And I thought, I am making love to the last shards of Helen's divinity, I am draining the godhead from her as a vampire sucks away the essence of life, I am killing her even as we celebrate this eternal mystery. She cried out; her voice was like the keening of distant whales. I slid down her sweat-slicked skin from darkness into deeper darkness.

And then we climaxed and I knew that I now held woman in my arms, woman mortal, frail, capable of growing old; what I clasped to my bosom was the final moment of a myth, and that moment transformed into flesh. And I said, "Now you have thrown away everything."

And felt her tears on my lips.

And we burst out of the womb of the Lady and entered the world of light once more, and I heard a voice cry out, "Phrygia!" over winds that were even now subsiding. The sun was rising over a strip of dark land. The waves whispered. As the ankhs rained down from the mast, they tinkled and sparkled.

"It is Troy," I said. "It is gold-rich Troy with its walls built by Apollo, Skyfather's son, our cousin." I wept as I spoke those empty bardic epithets and remembered Troy as I had left it, its walls mere rubble and its treasuries empty. "It is Troy, and you are Troy's queen."

"Yes," she said. "Once more I am no longer Helen of Sparta but Helen of Troy." Her eyes shone. "Oh, Little Star," she said, "I want so much to bring it all back again!"

But she still did not say she loved me. And I dared not ask.

Chapter XLI

The Guardian of the Blue King

"Now," Memnon said, "get back into the sarcophagus."

He had had it carried up to the deck. "Why?" I said. I had been woken from Helen's embrace; I was naked, save for the lion's paw. I was irritated at the mage's intrusion.

"It is time to make the exchange," said the mage, "and it must be done skillfully, with the utmost precision."

The lid was lifted. I touched the cold stone. "You know this resting place!" Memnon said. "You have lain here before, feigning death like a coward."

Helen turned away.

"Don't you dare look at him?" Memnon said. "Are you afraid this death is going to be more than a mockery?"

"Don't taunt her," I said. I remembered how Clytaemnestra had driven the axe into her husband's body, gleefully, confident that it was only a slave. I knew that even death's name was a powerful magic and not to be invoked in vain. I remembered the many times I had died already. I knew that I was fast approaching reunion with my other soul. But would it truly know me, after all this time immured in the clay and faience of the blue king? I looked at the blue men, each in his linen loincloth, each one firmly muscled and with glaze-glistening skin. They swayed forward; I felt as though they were closing in on me.

"Lift!" cried Memnon.

Four of them grasped the corners of the lid and raised it. An oblong shadow fell over us; it was a patch of unfamiliar cool after the incessant sun. I looked inside the sarcophagus. It was as I remembered it.

"Just climb in," Memnon said.

"What? No magic words, no arcane rituals?" I said.

"Why bother? You're already supposed to be dead. You're supposed to have been in there the whole time. Nothing that has happened to you since the blue king took the throne is supposed to have happened. But if and when you sit once more upon the throne of Troy—then, yes! The past continually revises itself, my young king, according to the whims of those who tell it, and what more mighty teller than a king?"

"I see." I swung myself over. "You have a plan."

"Of course I do! Do you think the ushabti will yield up the throne to you without a fight? It is possessed by your ka, your soul—it *is* you. Would *you* yield up your power to a pretender?"

It was cold in the coffin, so cold. Was this death? I could hardly open my eyes; my lids were heavy, as though they had crusted them with gold and lapis, like the mask they were lowering over my face. The eyeholes were narrow; through them Memnon seemed diminished, distorted. And beyond him I saw a tiny Helen, still with her back to me.

"But you weep!" Memnon said to her. "How easily tears come to those no longer blessed with godhood."

Angry, I shouted, "Why have you become so full of taunts, Memnon? Leave her grief be!" But the mask muffled my words.

Memnon continued, his voice charged with a bitterness I had not seen in him before this latest journey: "Are you thinking, Queen Helen, of the Trojan husbands you've had, all dead now? Perhaps of Paris, the handsomest of all men . . . dead at the hands of Neoptolemos? Of Deiphobos, his brother, to whom Priam gave you after Paris's death, as a matter of state policy, because the war could not end with the abductor's death, because it was the will of the gods? Are you thinking this sarcophagus is a prescience of what may happen to this little king, this nephew-husband of yours whom you seduced with all the wiles of Snakemother?"

"That's enough!" I shouted. I reached out of the sarcophagus and tried to throttle him. Helen stood facing the shore, a shadow against the wavering heat haze. He threw me back with such force that I hit my head against stone and felt blood ooze down the nape of my neck.

Then he said, "Are you thinking of your husband who still lives, the senile, puking Menelaos? Do you think he will come for you this time? But if Astyanax dies violently, still young, he will never be like that; he'll never embarrass you at dinner by vomiting all over the guests." I could hear Helen sobbing passionately. I could not move. "The lid!" he shouted to his blue servitors. It crashed down. The seal was perfect. There was not even a crack of light. My hands felt the outlines of hieroglyphics on the smooth granite. The mask was stifling and stole the breath warmth from my lips. I banged on the lid until my fist was raw. Presently it was jerked open, and

Memnon was peering down at me. "Oh, I forgot," he said rather offhandedly, "you'll need this."

He dropped my iron sword down into the cavity beside me. I grasped the hilt and tried to wield it, but the lid was already being lowered again.

"I hope you're not too uncomfortable," Memnon said. "It's only for a few brief hours."

"Oh, don't worry about me," I said angrily. "I'm getting used to being buried alive every other day." It slammed shut over me, and I am sure he did not hear the end of my sentence.

But by a curious magnifying power present in the stone, I was able to hear their conversations not less, but more clearly than before. The words of those outside my coffin sounded hollow and metallic, but they were quite distinct.

First I heard Helen's weeping. My heart went out to her, for she had once been a goddess and her choice was now irrevocable. And Memnon continued to vent his rage. She was not its real object, I knew; something else was troubling the mage. I realized what it was: he had floated in a world outside time for so long, and now he saw that world coming to an end. He must be afraid, I thought. For centuries he has delayed his own journey into the dark world, the world where he must be weighed in the balance. He must be afraid of paying the price that all magicians must one day pay for playing with ancient forces, and for knowing the true names of things.

If he was this afraid, then it must be true that the Age of Bronze was ending.

And I was its last hero.

Presently I felt the sarcophagus hoisted up, then lowered, then moving slowly uphill; the bearers must be wading to shore. I rolled; my head struck the side of the coffin, and I felt pain again. An eerie chanting started up. The surf pounded in my ears, and I heard the wind, though the air in the sarcophagus was deathly still. Had Helen come with us, or had she remained behind? Was Memnon giving commands from his litter? Yes; I heard his voice rasping ahead in the procession, and then I heard Egyptian music—wailing flutes and brittle kitharas. Wildly I thought, What will my people think when they see a funeral procession moving toward the Skaian Gate? The coffin moved on, up and down, up and down. We were on dry land now, for the bearers' feet did not sink into sand with every step; it made a palpable difference to me. I clutched the sword to my chest. Although the stone itself was cold, the air inside was becoming foul. The sides were clammy from my condensed breath. The procession trudged on; eastward I presumed. The ground seemed more uneven now. They must be reaching the edge of the city, about to climb the steep rocky pathway into the citadel proper.

Uphill now: I felt myself sliding against the foot of the sarcophagus. I jammed the swordpoint against the bottom and propped myself up. The chanting grew louder. To my astonishment I heard other sounds of grief too: the heartstopping thud of many women beating their breasts and shrieking their wails of mourning; drums and conchs sounding from every direction. I put my ear against the stone. The songs of sorrow reverberated, pounding my skull, bludgeoning away the pain of my concussion. It was intolerable. Once more I battered the lid with my bare fists, I pushed, I tried to pry the seal open with my iron sword. I screamed; but my cries were trapped in the stone.

After an hour of this slow progress I felt the angle steepen even more. I realized that this must be the final leg of the journey; we must have entered the palace grounds themselves.

We stopped. I waited for the lid to be opened, but it was not.

Instead I heard a voice: my own voice. It had been weakened by some disease, but it was unquestionably my own.

The voice said: "Memnon, my old friend. Let me embrace you."

"You know I may not come down from my litter, King."

It was the false Astyanax! And he was greeting my Memnon

as though he were his personal mage! I raged, I beat against the lid once more. They seemed to hear nothing.

"I have brought the sarcophagus from Egypt, King," Memnon said, "the one you ordered."

"Yes," said the blue king.

A trick! Whose side was Memnon really on? I could not tell. Presently the blue king said, "Who is that woman? The one draped from head to toe, and veiled? Another of your illusions?"

"The woman!" Memnon said. "Ah, in due course, Astyanax. She is here to help in the ritual."

"Ah, women . . . it is true that we have had to make compromises as king. My body has weakened inexplicably over the past few months. I have had recourse to the ways of the Lady. I have had to bring snake-haired women into my very house."

"Do not fear, Astyanax. You will soon be whole again."

The blue king had betrayed Skyfather. He had invited Snakemother into the palace. I did not feel anger. The blue king was a thing of clay, and clay comes from within the earth. I understood him, understood his pain and his reluctance to die; after all, we were the same person. It was a terrible sadness that seeped through my thoughts, not anger. What did Memnon mean when he said, "You will soon be whole again"? Who would be whole? Me, or the half man made of clay?

"Already I feel stronger," the blue king said. "It is as though my soul were coming back to me." Though his voice was weak, he spoke with authority; he was as strong as I. "Well, let us get on with the ceremony, then." A pause. "Have the lid lifted."

"You must command it yourself, King. And you must get into the sarcophagus; you must pretend to die. Only then will the earth be fooled." Where had I heard such words before? A master of misdirection! Were these words a clue to me? There were three raps on the side of the coffin; my ears rang from them.

"Lift the lid of the sarcophagus," said the blue king.

The lid was slowly raised.

I saw . . . the megaron of the palace. The blue king, ashen, the veins pulsating on his sunken face. I was wearing a deathmask and clasped the sword; the mage, hovering over me in his litter, threw a cloak of black wool over me so that the mask was all that could be seen.

The blue king whispered, "So this is my face in death. Gold like the face of the sun."

"Say the words," said Memnon.

At the periphery of my vision I saw Leonidas. He was standing behind the king. He was so full of concern; his eyes were fire-red from his weeping. Had he forgotten? The paw of the lioness still hung around his neck, but it had become desiccated, the fur worn to the bone. He moved closer to the sarcophagus. I wanted to call him but I could not. I thought, Do not weep over a man of clay, you foolish boy! Your real master has come home. But the boy did not hear my thoughts.

We were bathed in sunlight from the ship of the sun; but there were guards with torches, and I knew it was really evening. From far away I heard murmurs of grief; my populace had turned out for my funeral.

The blue king seemed to hesitate. "This charade of death," he said. "It is beginning to unnerve me. Mage, are you quite certain . . . that it is an illusion?"

"Astyanax will not die," said Memnon. "I can assure you of that."

I took heart at those words.

Then Leonidas spoke. His voice had changed. I wondered how long I had been away. "King," he said, "let me die in your place. It's the only proper thing to do. Or at least take me to the underworld with you."

The blue king said, "No, most faithful of servants. The burial of servants with their king is a barbaric custom. We don't do things like that anymore, do we now?"

Leonidas wept.

Memnon said, "Hurry up! There's only so much time."

The blue king said, "I go then to my death."

I felt a nudge against my shoulder. Memnon whispered

harshly, "Cut off his head! Then seize the ka before it flies away!" Aloud, he said to the ushabti, "Do you speak these words of your own free will? Do you accept your fate as a king, proudly and with joy?"

"I do."

"Then step into your sarcophagus," Memnon said, and he waved toward me with a flourish.

The blue king stepped up beside me.

I sprang up. I flung the cloak about my shoulders. I heard scattered screaming. I must have been a terrifying sight, wearing the mask of death and with the black cloak flying and the huge sword of unfamiliar metal. I swung the sword and struck the blue king's neck. There was a sound of cracking stoneware. The head flew off. The blue king's torso seemed to harden.

"My ka!" I shouted. In the air, hovering over our heads . . . a phantom, a double. It flitted back and forth, a shimmering outline in the haze. "Come to me!" The ka drifted. "No!" I leaped from the coffin now and tried to grasp my soul in my hands, but it siphoned through them and whirled away.

And Leonidas was upon me, shrieking, "Murderer—you killed my lord," and pounding at me with his fists while I flailed about trying to wrest my shadow out of the wind.

The head of the blue king was clattering across the flagstones. It came to rest against the lion-footed throne. The head was not dead; its eyes stared furiously. The ka was spinning in the air, distended from our tug of war. "Traitor!" the head rasped. Its voice was like the quaking earth. It was bright blue now, and its features were becoming more and more frozen into those of an Egyptian figurine. I held the wriggling boy in my arms, trying to fend off his blows. "Leonidas, Leonidas, don't you know me?" I cried. "It was I who gave you your freedom, I who gave you your name."

I managed to disentangle myself from him. Hysterically he ran toward the severed head. Could he not tell that it was only clay? But we are all clay from the wheel of Prometheus the primal potter. He clasped the head in his arms. The mouth moved soundlessly, emitting a wheezing whistling sound as the wind rushed through its cavity. What was keeping it alive? I realized suddenly that it was Leonidas's loyalty, his love for me, for the thing he thought was his master Astyanax. That was why the ka could not decide. I ran toward the boy. Green, sticky blood oozed down his chiton from the stump of the blue king's neck.

"Leonidas . . ." His devotion, misguided though it was, moved me to tears. I wanted to embrace the boy, but he backed away, still clutching the head, now a hybrid of clay and flesh.

At that moment the cloak Memnon had thrust over me fell from my shoulders. And Leonidas saw that I was wearing the lion's paw around my neck.

"That's not yours!" he shouted, pointing accusingly. "Someone capture this assassin, put him to death."

But there was doubt in his eyes now. I advanced toward him with my arms outstretched. "Don't you know me? Don't you remember why we were given these lion's paw amulets?" I said. His eyes widened. I saw the head in his arms stiffen; it was weeping, and its tears were tears of faience glaze that hardened on its cheeks.

Leonidas looked from me to the head, back and forth.

"Come on, Leonidas!" I cried. "Does a severed head talk? Only by magic. But I'm not here by magic; I'm not an illusion. I've come back from the land of the Akhaians."

"You never left," Leonidas said dubiously.

I looked about me. The court was gathered in full force. I saw Phoinix and Leukippos standing side by side. To my dismay I saw that there were snake-haired women among the courtiers, and they did not tremble at being in the presence of Skyfather's many-times-great-grandson. I saw Helen standing behind Memnon's litterbearers; she was still veiled from head to foot. Behind her the great window overlooked the city; from beyond there came continual sounds of mourning.

Then I saw Philemon. "Come, old man," I said. "You were always like a father to me." He crept forward on bended knee; I could almost feel the hardness in his joints.

"Don't kneel to me, Philemon. You gave me bread and shelter when I was only a child."

The old man came to me. He touched my face.

"The other king never acknowledged me," he said softly. "He was a proper king; he knew he was above me. But you, you . . ."

And Leonidas too was kneeling at my feet. And there came Phoinix and Leukippos too, shuffling forward fearfully, for they had encouraged the false Astyanax to exile me from Troy. The whole court, following their lead, fell prostrate. And I spoke to them, quiet, authoritative words such as I had heard my grandfather speak so long ago; and I felt my ka slowly infuse itself into me and merge with my ba.

I said, "Tell the people to cease lamenting. I am the king, and I have come home." I lifted my iron sword. "I have earned a new sword now; perhaps I will always be unworthy to wear Hector's armor and wield his weapon, but the gods have given me one of my own." And then I beckoned for Helen to come to me. "And I have a new queen. Or rather, I have brought Troy's proper queen home to her people."

I heard them whispering now; some of them looked up from their prostration. I looked at Memnon. His face had lost all trace of the fury he had shown earlier; he only smiled sadly, like a man who listens politely to all of a story when halfway through he has already guessed the outcome.

Leonidas laid the head gently down in the sarcophagus.

I placed the mask over it, almost tenderly. The head was shrinking now. The body was already nothing but clay; it was no more than two handspans tall. Leonidas had found it and threw it in beside the head. Then I laid the dark cloak over it and put on the kingly robe which the blue king had been wearing, and which lay in a heap on the floor.

The head uttered a few more words, in a tiny voice, no more than the buzzing of a fly; I think I was the only one who heard them.

"Do you think you are so different from me?" said the smashed ushabti. "Do you think you too are not born of the earth? But I'm only a broken statue, you think, and have no thoughts. Nothing but a broken statue. You're wrong, King, wrong, wrong, wrong.''

"Seal the sarcophagus," I said.

The lid slammed shut.

"And now," I said, "I will show you your queen."

I tore off the veil that covered Helen's face.

She stood there: bright-eyed, radiant. The court was stunned. "Rise, I say, rise!" I said. "Once we were crushed by the Akhaians, but the time has come for us to become great once more!" I spoke with passion, desperately wanting to believe those words, even though in my travels I had lost much of the dream.

But they all wanted to believe too. I could see their eyes light up, I could see the joy in the tumult as the court rose to its feet and began speaking all of them at once. I led Helen to the window. I looked out over my kingdom. The streets were lined with those who had come to mourn. The doorways were jammed with onlookers. Children played, leaping over the gaps in my sundered walls. The light from the distant ship filled all the sky. When they saw me they began to shout; when they saw Helen their shouts redoubled, for the old men remembered her and knew all that she stood for. The noise was overwhelming. I held my new queen close to me, trying to think of future greatness, of a great city rising upon the ruins, gleaming with marble and granite; of the landscape flooded with the brilliant colors that had been in the age of heroes; of the sky blue always and the land forever green.

Helen said, "I always dreamed of coming back. You don't know what it was like when I was mistress of my husband's cold gray palace. When I was a little girl I heard the bard sing songs of gold-rich Troy. And now—the broken walls, the people bereft of hope until our coming back . . ." She was trembling.

I closed my eyes.

And closing them saw blood: a wall of blood; the blood of heroes, the color of sweet new wine.

Chapter XLII

The Three Dreams

The night: at last I was in the king's bedchamber with the queen in my arms and Leonidas and the dogs asleep at our feet. After we made love, I fell untroubled into sleep; I knew I was home and master of my kingdom. Deeper and deeper I tumbled; it was as though I had entered once more that great cave that was the entrance to the womb of the great goddess, the tunnel through which we had passed during our sea crossing.

It was during that first night of my return that the three dreams returned to me once more. I had carried them vividly in my mind during my quest, for I had seen them as precognitive, as emblems of my grand destiny. Now some of the events they prophesied had happened, in ways I could never have predicted. But still their meaning eluded me.

The first dream was the wedding. At first it seemed that I stood in the dark tholos of the necropolis. I was about to strip away the veil of the goddess. I was afraid, for I knew that her face would be that of a skull. Had that not been the dream before? The crowd gathered around me, lurching forward; they were all dead men, bleeding and putrefying, like the zumbis, the living dead that Memnon had once described to me.

"It must be done," I said in the dream.

I tore away the veil. I saw the skull, pallid, fiery-eyed . . . but there grew flesh upon the skull, and the fire was subsumed in the blue of Skyfather's heaven, and hair sprouted in filaments of gold, and the leering rictus was covered by lips moist and slightly parted as though to say my name. And when I whirled around to see the monstrous throng, they

were no longer ghosts but my own people, laughing, cheering, chanting a victory paean. And my bride was my own
Helen, and she was whispering to me, "You cannot forever
sunder the light from the darkness. For they long to be one,
and they seek each other out, and they yearn to become one
flesh, as do a man and a woman."

In the dream we kissed under the brilliant sunlight, for we
were in a tomb no longer but at the very summit of the
citadel, between the mountains and the glistening sea.

And in the dream we made love feverishly, causing the
fields to blossom and filling the earth with color. At last
in the dream I fell asleep, and dreamed a dream within the
dream; it was like the second dream of my prophetic dreams.

I was doing battle with the serpent once more. It was
many-headed, and like the hydra it grew two heads for
every one I severed. The severed heads lay thick on the
ground, dripping a dark rheum and sending foul fumes into
the air. But the serpent was coiling around me now; I hacked
and slashed and could not free myself, for my sword was of
iron and lacked magic. I do not know when I began to make
love to the serpent. But I suddenly realized I had been doing
that all this time. And the serpent's face was Helen's face;
and Helen said to me, "There is a woman in the serpent, and
a serpent in the woman. That is the fathomless mystery that
the Lady has bequeathed to us. When it is a mystery no
longer, men will no longer believe in the gods."

I could not protest. I saw a truth in it, though it was
contrary to the truths my grandfather had taught me. In any
case there was no protesting left in me. The serpent squeezed
me, and she had the limbs of a woman, and her breasts were
hard, and she was slick with sweat and with the fluids of
desire.

As I climaxed, I was vaulted into a third state of dreaming,
and I stood in the house of the Sky my ancestor, watching the
skystone. The sky was serene. Perhaps a war was raging beyond
my walls, but here I stood untouched, I and the shades of my
ancestors. I knew now that the stone that had fallen from the

house of Skyfather contained the makings of iron. Iron was
the way of the future. It was the will of Skyfather. But I
remembered also what I had thought to myself, the first time
I dreamed that dream: "I have killed my father, yet I rejoice."

Could it be that Skyfather, by making iron fall from heaven
and making me come in possession of the iron sword, was
naming me the instrument of his own destruction?

Could the gods die?

It was this thought that drove me upward from this dream.
The dreams were layered, one beneath the other; I seemed to
crash through the roof of the sky into the world where I still
fought and loved the serpent woman, I broke through the
serpent level to the dream where I was being wed to Helen
and the goddess. At last I surfaced. I was breathing heavily.
The room was still; the air was close and humid. I reached
for Helen and found her place empty; only her fragrance
remained, clinging to the cloak that had covered us both. I
sat up.

"Leonidas," I whispered.

"King . . ." The boy's voice was sleepy, indistinct. He
got up, kicking one of the dogs out of the way. "I dreamed I
saw the queen leave, King."

"She's gone." A wild thought: it had been an illusion, all
of it—the sea journey, the palaces of Akhaia, the island of
pigs, everything. "Where could she be?" I did not want to
rouse the whole palace to seek her out; even in my confused
state I realized that I would seem absurdly possessive, and
my court would laugh at me.

"King, she murmured something about 'my father's house,'
and took one of the torches from its bracket. I heard footsteps
echoing, far away."

"Bring me my chiton."

I found my way to the temple of Skyfather. It was not
quite dawn. I told Leonidas to stand watch by the entrance,
though there was nothing to fear. The temple had never been
roofed. A smear of brilliance at the eastern horizon showed

that the ship of the heretic king (whose name I had once more forgotten) still remained in the vicinity. Columns surrounded the sacred precinct, their paint cracked. Grass and weeds grew in even greater profusion than before; I knew from this that the worship of Skyfather had not been kept up. There was the stone. A ray of light from the east, bursting through a gap between columns, fell on the stone and made it glow, and I saw what my dream had predicted. The stone was black no longer, but had the glint of metal. In the beam of light, by the altar, stood Helen. Her torch burned from a broken pillar. I did not call out to her. I hid in the shadows, feeling like the child who had hidden here years ago when the Akhaians burst in and killed the king.

She knelt before the stone and embraced it and whispered, "Father, Father." I did not know if Skyfather would appear to her. I knew he would not come to me. I thought of the choice I had made between three goddesses, the judgment I now knew to be a mockery of judgment.

A flame sputtered on the altar but was almost invisible against the light of the distant ship.

She appeared to be deep in conversation now. But I could see no one else. I could not catch her words; some of them seemed to be in a harsh, ancient language. She importuned; she wept; at times she appeared to be angry. At last the conference ended; she kissed the stone three times as though in parting, and she turned to leave.

I stood a few paces away. She saw me, but it was as if she saw straight through me, as if I were a ghost, like the shade of Leontes. I called her name. She did not seem to hear me. She walked toward me. I could hear her muttering to herself again and again the words, "Father, don't leave me, don't leave me."

She left the temple; I heard the quiet echo of her footfall down the steps of stone. I went to the stone. A wind rose up and fanned the flame; but it was not the wind of godhood that burns and freezes all at once—it was a spiritless wind, a mere movement of the air.

I knelt. I kissed the stone. It was cold with the new metal. I prayed, my eyes closed, full of bewilderment.

"Skyfather," I said, "when I was a child I swore vengeance. I sought revenge, but the fire left me in Akhaia. Can't you give me a sign?"

The wind blew out the fire.

A shadow fell over me. I turned. It was Leonidas.

"Come away, master," he said. "The magic has gone from the holy places. We've all known it for some time now."

His words had the ring of truth. I was bitter in my disillusionment. I felt anger, ugly and uncontrollable. I struck at the boy and he fell against one of the columns. "I've given up so much, to bring the magic back!" I raged. "And this is how the gods repay me!" Leonidas was sobbing quietly, still endeavoring to hold the torch upright and light my pathway. I was stricken with remorse, remembering how loyal he had been, how he had struggled to defend the clay figure that possessed my ka. "I'm sorry, boy," I said. Then I added, "I think it's time I officially announced your freedom."

"Yes, King." But he did not dare approach me. Lifting the torch, he walked several paces ahead of me, out of range of my fists, all the way back to the palace.

Dawn had come. It was time for me to sit in the megaron as king.

I gave a few commands. First, that the ushabti that had ruled the city for so long be pulverized and that the powder be ground into the earth at the next plowing. I wanted no interference from Snakemother, and I knew that she was most appeased by the blood of kings.

Second, I declared Leonidas free and gave him the rank of basileus, as though he were as nobly born as Phoinix and Leukippos; and I gave him dominion over the land containing the village from which his mother had come, for that leader had died of a wasting sickness in my absence. It raised a few eyebrows, but it seemed clear that I was not to be thwarted. Leonidas trembled as I raised him up. He said, so I alone heard it, "I will still be your servant boy, Astyanax."

Next came Memnon. "I have come to say farewell, little king," he said to me.

"You are leaving?" Even though his recent behavior had been incomprehensible, I found it hard to believe that he was abandoning me.

"We will meet again soon, as will all the principals of this great story, when it all ends in blood and in fire. You cannot know how great a service it is that you will render my king. He is so tired, so tired. I must tend to the final preparations. But I will not be far. Perhaps I can be summoned."

"I don't know what you mean," I said uneasily. But I dispatched Leonidas to lead them safely to the gates of the city.

I watched as he clapped his hands and his bearers lifted his litter and marched slowly out of the great portal of the megaron. Almost as soon as he left, the great light from the east grew dim. He had probably reached the ship already. I knew he traveled by supernatural means. I wanted to call out after him, but dared not show weakness in front of my people.

Then came Helen. A gasp ran through the court. I bade the guards carry in a second throne and to place it one step lower beside me. She walked slowly. She was simply dressed; she had applied almost no kohl to her eyes, and her hair streamed freely down her shoulders except for two perfectly braided plaits that fell to one side.

I heard someone say, softly, "No wonder they went to war for such a woman." I could barely contain my pride. She took her seat.

"Welcome, Queen Helen," I said. She seemed to remember nothing of our meeting in the house of Skyfather; indeed, she acted as though she had only just come from her bed.

She smiled—a smile for the whole court as well as for me—and said, "When your uncle Paris brought me to Troy, Troy made me younger; in Sparta I was a queen, but in Troy

I was only a princess. This time I don't seem to have grown younger at all.''

I introduced her to old Philemon, saying he had been a father to me in my exile from Troy.

She said, "Then you are my father too, for my own father no longer speaks to me."

I introduced Phoinix and Leukippos, whose arrogance I had so frequently suffered before. They seemed subdued by Helen's presence. They knew I would not be bullied by them anymore, for Helen was a visible memory of Troy's ancient greatness. She smiled graciously at them.

Phoinix said, "We will gladly fight to defend you, Lady."

Helen said, "Why do you speak of fighting?"

Leukippos said, "Isn't that the whole idea? To start the Trojan War all over again? For us to drag ourselves up from the dust and rubble and to cry out Skyfather's name in triumph?"

"I don't want war anymore," I said, thinking bitterly of who my opponents would be: tragic Orestes; youthful Pergamos, my own brother; spent Menelaos. "Not if it can be helped."

At that moment there came a commotion from outside. "Make way!" It was a boy's voice. Leonidas was elbowing his way through the crowd. "There's another ship, King!"

"What ship?" I shouted, rising from my throne.

"They're here," Helen said very quietly. "Remember, Astyanax, that Memnon's ship sailed in a little circle of eternity; it seemed to us to be a single day. Who knows how much time has elapsed in Akhaia."

Leonidas prostrated himself at our feet. He was shaking. "King, as soon as we stepped out of the palace I heard people talking of it. A runner has come up from the ship—"

"How many ships?" I said, thinking of the thousand ships of legend. "More than one, surely."

"They say there is only one. The runner is waiting outside to see you. He gave me this seal." He held it up to me.

Helen stiffened; her breasts heaved against her queenly robe.

"Who could it be?" I said. "Orestes? Pergamos? One of the other young heroes?"

"I know that seal ring," said Helen.

I called for a clay tablet. I pressed the ring into the wet clay. There was an image of a lion; beneath it were the signs:

𐀞𐀩𐀷𐀠

"Menelaos," I said to myself. "The old, decrepit fool—"

"Was young once," Helen said. "Perhaps he dreams of ancient glory. As you do, Astyanax. Chasing after what can't be anymore."

"Let us hope," I said, "that he dreams of a diplomatic solution."

"Will you admit him to your very house?" Phoinix said, alarmed. "After all, he is our sworn enemy."

"Why not?" I said. "War has not yet been declared. And he entertained me with due honor at Sparta, even though he did not know my name." I did not add that he puked all over the dinner table. "Well, Helen, are you up to seeing your old husband?"

She said, "I've given up being a goddess. Don't you remember? That means I've given up being abducted. I don't want to symbolize anything; I just want to be myself."

She rose and kissed me on the cheek. There was no eroticism in that kiss, but there was desperation. Skyfather had not spoken to her. She wanted to belong somewhere.

I said, "We will prepare to receive the King of Sparta with royal honors. Leonidas, repeat those words to the runner and bid Menelaos welcome in my court."

Chapter XLIII

The Embassy of Sparta

"We must put on a good show for Sparta," I said. "And if they plan to put on a decent show themselves, they can't get here until midafternoon." I was racking my brains, thinking of ways to greet my cuckolded ex-host with the proper pomp. "A feast . . . Leonidas, get someone to manage it. Phoinix and Leukippos, you had better see about coming up with some kind of military spectacle, some token show of might."

"It's short notice," Phoinix grumbled. "Why can't we just jump them and kill them?"

"They have sent a runner. We have become their hosts, and custom provides that we must extend them diplomatic immunity," I said.

"Ha!" Leukippos said. "Is that what you said when you ran off with the Queen of Sparta?"

But Helen said only, "I am Queen of Troy now, kinsman and underling," in a tone so laden with authority that Leukippos stepped back as if stung.

"What am I forgetting?" I said, trying to smooth things over. "Food, spectacle . . . gifts! We must have gifts! Send down to the potters' quarters. And the stables. Surely there's a chariot or two in running order!"

Helen said, "I will supervise the gifts," and smiled sadly. "It's the least I can do in return for the gift my former husband unwillingly gave you, Astyanax." She had a knack for taking over, I noticed; but I could not chide her. After all, she had been a queen before I was even born.

I ordered a chamber readied for Menelaos. I retired to the bath, and Helen to her toilette; I commanded that they bring out the best finery that remained in our treasury. The room they aired for my rival turned out to be the bedroom of my childhood, the one I had shared with Leontes. There was some hidden irony in this, but I did not care to think of it; our preparations were too hasty for such niceties.

I found Helen in the royal bedchamber. She was pacing while a maidservant quaked in prostration. She cursed and wailed disconsolately. Three chests of cedarwood lay open. I saw the cause of her distress when I looked at the meanness of our treasures. "Has it come to this?" I said. I lifted a bracelet from the pile; it was broken, and its hinge, cunningly worked, was smashed. A gold neckpiece inlaid with lapis lazuli seemed fine from a distance; close up one could see that its joints were faulty. "What can I do?" I said. "The Queen of Troy can't look like a—"

"Whore! You were going to say whore, weren't you?" And she would not look at me.

"No." But that word had been about to escape my lips. "Well . . . I meant nothing by it; you know that."

"You foolish boy!" she said. "To think of appearances now, when our world has long since been consigned to perdition. Do you think Menelaos will care about a few paltry toys? He has looted ten times that much from this very palace."

I knelt down by the chests, dug my arms in, trying to find something that could be repaired in time. "What shall I do?" I said in despair. "Do you think I should rob the necropolis?"

"Do you think there's any dark magic left to stop you?" she said. But I balked. At last she said, "Once there were those who said I needed no ornament." And she tore her robe from her body, and I saw her in the midmorning light. She unfastened the pins that held her hair and tossed her head so the hair, finespun and glittering, fell on her shoulders and covered her breasts. Were they perhaps sagging a little? "Oh, Astyanax, I have learned something new since I became human—I have learned vanity!" She shook her head and let her hair fly. "Is it frazzled yet?" she said. "Does a rank smell rise from my pubis, does it no longer exude the fragrances of heaven? I hate mortality. One day I will be like Menelaos, puking and putrid.''

"You are what is in your heart," I said softly.

And I clothed her myself in the queenly raiment, and I placed the broken neckpiece around her shoulders, and clasped the bracelets on her arm, twisting the gold wires until they stayed on; she gasped in pain, and I saw that they were pinching her flesh a little, but then she set her face and told me to go on. Her servingwomen began to paint her face with a paste of crushed chalk and to mix the kohl for her eyes. "Only a little," she said. "I'm not an old hag yet, after all, am I? After all, I'm still beautiful enough for men to abduct, to go to war over. . . ." Did she say it to reassure herself? I thought so.

I escorted her back to the megaron, where a steward was directing a group of slaves as they moved furniture. At the foot of the throne, Leonidas was throwing his hands up in the air. He saw us coming and said, "King, what are we going to do? Not a thing matches!"

I saw what he meant. The rushes were strewn with vessels of baked earth. There was not a perfectly round one among them, and the designs, whether painted or reliefed, were crude imitations of the style of pottery decoration current during my childhood. "A king can't eat off such inferior crockery!" I said, though I knew full well that most of the fine vessels had been smashed during the sack of Troy and that the art of pottery had suffered ever since for lack of discriminating patrons.

"Why not?" Helen said sharply. "You were happy to eat off ugly dishes in Sparta."

"Troy isn't one of your provincial principalities. You know that. And besides . . . I was distracted in Sparta."

"By my beauty, I suppose." I could tell that she was still pouting over what she imagined to be her fading radiance.

"And I didn't exactly come as a visiting monarch."

"No, your manner of arrival was decidedly ignominious," Helen said. "But it worked well." She laughed suddenly. "For Skyfather's sake! I would never have imagined making such a fuss about Menelaos while I was married to him, the old—''

''Hush! Music in the distance!'' I said. The bustling in the megaron halted abruptly. Slowly it died away. Yes, there were drumbeats and raucous reedy music quite unlike the funereal chantings of the previous evening. ''For better or worse,'' I said, ''they are coming up the hill.''

Helen seemed subdued suddenly. She went to her throne and sat, her eyes downcast; she appeared almost submissive. I wondered whether she planned to give herself back to her husband as easily as she had given herself to me.

As the slaves cleared away as much of the mess as they could, some warriors entered. From all the way across the hall they looked impressive. Their weapons were, I noted, made of iron. At my signal Phoinix and Leukippos led armed men forward, and they rattled their swords against their shields in greeting. A herald stepped forward and cried, ''Menelaos, King of Sparta, greets his fellow king and kinsman Astyanax of Troy!''

I raised my hand to salute the stooped figure that entered.

He was tired from the long journey uphill; his whole body sagged. ''Offer him wine!'' Helen whispered to me. ''Anyone can manipulate him while he's drunk.''

''Helen,'' Menelaos mumbled. ''Helen, Helen.'' He staggered forward. ''Fancy seeing you here again. Well, well. The war's over now, and the troops have given you over to me for judgment. I suppose I should kill you right away. . . .''

To my horror I realized that Menelaos had lost his mind. He was reliving that other war. I could not blame him, for the world of the past had all that our own world lacked: heroism, idealism, magic.

Gently, the herald went over to him and whispered in his ear. Menelaos nodded, appearing to understand. He came nearer. He looked at me belligerently. ''Aren't you that friend of young Orestes'? Weren't you at dinner the other night?''

''Yes, King,'' I said, as gently as I could.

"I see you've been fucking my wife."

Consternation in the court; even the slaves turned to gape.

Suddenly Menelaos was shouting, his voice hoarse with anger and age: "You've been fucking my wife, you bastard! Just like all those others!" He lurched over to Helen and shook his fist at her. Before he could say another word, Helen spoke for him.

"Whore! Whore!" she said, cruelly echoing his rasp. There was not a drop of feeling between them. "When the Lady ruled, men would not have dared to call me such names. I'm only a woman now, a woman in your universe that has no place for women except as chattel and merchandise. Only in such a universe am I a whore. Go away, you pathetic old man."

I was distressed at this exchange, for Menelaos had come to Troy as a guest, and I did not wish to violate the sanctity of guesthood. And the Helen who was no longer a goddess seemed to have lost a measure of compassion in the transition. I felt another piece of my dream waft away, and I grew a little angrier.

Keeping my voice calm, I said, "Menelaos, I have prepared a feast in your honor."

I had them show Menelaos to his place. I myself sat between him and Helen, to ward off any possible conflict. I was uneasy; I had thought in terms of war for so long, and I was rapidly discovering that diplomacy is far thornier than fighting. I poured wine into Menelaos's cup, krater after krater. He did not say anything about the misshapen vessels; I wondered whether it was tact or whether he was simply too divorced from reality to notice anything at all.

"Well," he said at last, as the steward served him a roasted sheep's head on a platter, "you've given me a fine welcome. But tell me, did you enjoy it? Fucking my wife, I mean."

"Must you resort to such vulgarity?" I said. "Let me cut you a piece of the shank; it's very tasty."

"I'll have an answer!"

Helen said, almost inaudibly, "At least he had the courtesy to ask me whether he had pleased me."

I tried to change the subject, but word was already going around and the court was in an uproar. Some talked about the insult to my virility; others were openly jeering at the cuckolded king.

"I don't care," Menelaos said at last, disconsolately. "You know, I really am not as senile as I act." He burped. "My mind's sharp . . . sharp, I tell you, sharp as an iron dagger!" He pointed at Helen. "I know the war was over years and years ago. I'm old, you know! It's good for me to take refuge in fantasies. How can you begrudge an old man? What I mean is . . ."

Everyone had fallen silent, even the Spartans. Apparently they were unused to this level of lucidity from their king.

". . . I have traveled here, on a single ship, with a minimal escort of warriors, to tell you you can keep her! Just don't let's have another war; let's just enjoy the twilight of our heroic age as best we can. . . ."

I was breathing heavily. "You mean, Menelaos, that you're not seeking revenge?"

"Revenge! I'm not young anymore. My brother's dead. He pushed me into it anyway. Why should I care about a war over a whore? It was the other members of the Akhaian alliance who demanded vengeance. I had to go along with it. Oh, I'm not a strong man, I never have been. . . ." He was weeping copiously into his wine. I regarded him with a strange mixture of respect and revulsion.

I was beginning to believe that the war was not going to happen after all. Piece by piece my dream had been taken from me—why not the dream of a new Trojan War that would vindicate me and my people? I could find no hatred in my heart for this man. The Akhaians may have looted our treasury and forced me to serve my guests on ugly dishes— but Troy possessed the greatest treasure of all, the goddess-woman who had confused all the known world for almost two generations. "Perhaps you're right," I said, "perhaps it is time for us all to retire from all this posturing."

At that moment there came, from outside the palace, a fearsome babble. Amid the commotion, a messenger arrived. He knelt before me.

"What now?" I said.

The messenger was panting heavily. I could barely make out what he was saying. "King, another ship has arrived! They demand an immediate audience! Otherwise, they say, we're all going to drown in a sea of blood!"

"Whose ship?" I cried, rising from my seat.

I had no sooner spoken than my question was answered, for the ship's warrior escort was already filing into the megaron. They were a flabby, middle-aged lot, these fighters, but their screeching paean was bloodcurdling and unforgettable; even Helen winced, and Menelaos cringed visibly into the back of his chair.

"Myrmidons!" I heard the whisper running through the gathering. I saw terror in their faces. The Myrmidons advanced toward the banquet table with uncanny precision, throwing their swords in the air and catching them as they screamed their warcry. Then, as one man, they stopped and stood stock-still, like statues.

Silence fell. We waited.

Chapter XLIV

리리리리리리리리리리리리리리리리

The Embassy of Phthia

He did not know me, of course. He saw Astyanax, the marauding king of a distant country, his mother's other son, mysteriously reappeared from the dead to reawaken nightmare memories of war. He did not see the nameless wanderer who had held him, frightened, in his arms the whole night long in a chamber full of dead men, who had shielded him from the incestuous attacks of his mother . . . my mother. He saw the brother he had never seen before, the brother he must now call enemy.

We stared at each other from across the megaron. He was taller now. He looked so much like Andromache; there was something of me too in his face. Yes, he was taller, but he was still not quite a man. But the old Myrmidons seemed to cherish him; there was a proud ferocity in their faces—after all, the boy they served was the grandson of Akhilleus, who had humbled Troy's greatest hero, my father, his mother's husband.

He did not meet my gaze. No one spoke. He stared instead at Helen. Perhaps she had not yet lost her magic for him. I did not know if he had ever seen her before. The tension became so unbearable that I had to speak.

I said, "Pergamos."

He was approaching. I beckoned the slaves to bring a chair for him, so that he could sit across the banquet table from me. "Do you know me?" he said, as he sat. Only a platter of roast lamb and a mixing bowl of wine separated me from my brother.

"You don't remember?" I said.

He looked at me long and hard. He knew. He said, "It was you the whole time."

"You said, 'I wish it were true, I wish we really were brothers.' Well, you see, it is true. Have you come to declare war on me?" I said. "Brothers should not declare war on each other. Pergamos . . . I love you. When I saw you at Neoptolemos's palace, it almost broke my heart. You were so brave, standing there at Pielos's funeral, making sure the sacrifices were done right, even though the madwomen had overrun the stronghold. Don't come to say that we must fight."

Pergamos wept. And my heart did break then; for Pergamos was all the family I had left in the whole world.

Menelaos looked up from his wine then, and said, "Don't, nephew. I've given her up, the whore. She can fuck whom she pleases. No more wars, no more death. We're old now.

Even your aunt Helen is old, though she may still look to you like the most beautiful woman in the world! Have some wine.''

"Wine.'' Pergamos stared dully at the cup that had been poured for him.

Helen said, "Menelaos is right, you know. We can't drag this thing on forever. I'm not Sparta's, I'm not Akhaia's, I'm not Troy's, I'm no man's. In the years since the war you've all come to believe that the war was fought over me. How insufferably simple! A man's point of view: honor, blood, glory. Nonsense! Do you think Troy's wealth meant nothing to Agamemnon and his followers? There's no wealth here now; it's all been long since looted. Do you think they didn't know that Troy lies at the junction of trade routes that crisscross the world? There's absolutely no reason to have another war and you know it.''

"There speaks Helen the woman,'' I said, "not Helen the goddess.''

"With me no longer divine,'' Helen continued, "there is not even any symbolic reason for you to fight over me.''

Pergamos looked at the three of us—Helen, Menelaos, and me—and sighed. "I knew there was something about you, even when you had no name,'' he said to me. Then, turning to the queen, he said, "Aunt Helen—'' His voice cracked. Helen reached across the table and squeezed his hand.

"So, my boy! I suppose you'll fuck her too! After the Trojan princeling is done with her!'' Menelaos said in a gruff, jocund tone which I knew concealed a profound personal tragedy.

"I can't covet what is his. He is my brother,'' Pergamos said. There was even defiance in his voice. "But it's Orestes. He's gone mad, you see. He has visions.''

"Yes,'' I said. "Not visions. I wonder whether Athena has cleansed him completely.''

"He's gone completely mad . . . completely! He imagines he sees his long-dead sister Iphigeneia, whom Agamemnon sacrificed when he made that terrible pact with the Lady!

Sometimes Electra appears and whispers in his ear, her broken neck making her head hang at an impossible angle. He
told me all this. But it's Iphigeneia most of all. She's always
at his side, always telling him about bringing back the dead
past. Oh, I'm afraid. I've just visited Orestes at Mycenae,
and he's preparing for war. He's sent out his embassies, he's
been drumming up support, playing on the other chieftains'
nostalgia and their frustration at the decline of the world. He
even sent a dispatch to Ithaka.''

"Ithaka . . . But poor Odysseus is lost at sea," Menelaos
said.

"Maybe not," Pergamos said. "For a while there were
rumors that he had taken up with the high priestess of a pig cult,
one that adheres to the old religion, on an island. . . ."

"No, Pergamos," I said, "I've seen that island. He is not
there. Perhaps they killed him. They claim to have the power
to turn men into pigs. I nearly became the guardian spirit
under the threshold of Snakemother's temple."

"Then there are other rumors that he is living with some
other priestess of the Lady on yet another island. . . ."

"Forget him," Menelaos said. "It is true that he fashioned
the horse with which we won the war . . . but I don't think
the Trojans are going to fall for that one again. He is lost.
You young people tell stories to keep yourselves from facing
the void of death. You don't want to be alone. 'Don't leave
us,' you say, though we are old and tired and long for rest.
Odysseus is doubtless as dead as Agamemnon and Akhilleus
and all the others who fought in the war."

"But you're not dead, King Menelaos!" Pergamos said.
He had a great deal of respect for him because of his age; it
is true that few men can live beyond fifty years, and the
depredations of age upon one's face and limbs are a prodigy
that all remark upon.

"I'm not dead," Menelaos said, "because I'm a coward."

"There *is* going to be a war," Pergamos said at last,
slowly. "Astyanax, I can't fight against you. Phthia will
remain neutral. But Orestes is drawing them all into an

alliance. I don't know how many ships he can command—
nothing like the first war, of course—or who will come out
and say that he is allied with a matricide. But on the other
hand, there's honor to think of."

"Honor," Helen said. She laughed out loud then. "Oh,
it's true that men never change. They have a great yearning
for death, and they call that yearning honor."

"That's why I've come, Helen," Pergamos said. "I'm
linked by blood to the Akhaians as much as the Trojans. I've
come to ask you to return home. Otherwise there will be
war."

"It makes no difference," Menelaos said. "She won't
go." He turned to me. "I repeat, I give her to you. I wash
my hands in wine." He plunged his fists into the krater. His
hands came back out dripping. Like blood.

Helen said: "I made a choice, Pergamos."

Pergamos cried out, "You're putting me in an intolerable
position! He's my friend, my brother. He stood by me, he
grieved for my brother whom he didn't even know. I don't
want to be his enemy."

"That is a choice you must make, little king," Helen said
gently. "As for me, I've made my choice already. And
women too have their own kind of honor. They are not
fickle, like men. They are strong, like the earth, not change-
able like the wind and sky. If I am a whore, it is what men
have made me. I am content with what I am. I need no name
for it. It is men who feel that everything must have a name."

What she said chilled me. Every child knows that all power
resides in names. Hers was a radical idea, one that challenged
all we knew to be true.

I was torn by my brother's torment. I thought of sending
Helen home. But in the end I remembered my grandfather
being killed on the altar of Skyfather, and I remembered my
oath before the stone that had fallen from heaven; and I knew
there was no going back.

"I must be going," Pergamos said at last. He had eaten
nothing at my table. This was a dangerous omen, for it

absolved him from the obligations of guest-friendship. "I've spoken my warning; and I give my promise to remain neutral in the war. More than that I can't do. I can't stop Orestes. Madness comes from the gods."

I got up. I wanted him to stay. I wanted to show him I was proud of him, to do him honor. He turned and walked across the hall, and his Myrmidons followed. Their walk was an eerie mime of war. They clenched their fists and screamed out a bloodcurdling paean. They stamped their feet in thunderous unison. They tossed their weapons in the air and caught them. Their swords clanged against each other. It was the dull scrape of iron on iron, not the heroic ring of bronze on bronze. I moved to restrain Pergamos.

At the doorway he stopped. "No emotion," he said. "Or I'll start weeping and lose all dignity. Don't shame me, Astyanax."

"Would it be too forward of me to ask my own brother for a farewell hug?"

He shrugged. I embraced him. He was not yet a man. He slipped into my arms; he seemed no more substantial than the ghost of Leontes. I saw that his eyes were brimming with tears again. I said nothing of it. I knew he wanted to look like a hero. I understood that feeling well; I myself had wanted it all my life.

But now I saw the falsehood in it. And another piece of the magic was stolen from my dream.

We stood apart from each other, neither daring to touch the other again. I said, "You are a king now, Pergamos."

With those words I stripped my young brother of his boyhood and consigned him to the role the Fates had made for him.

I watched him pass through the doorway of the megaron. Then I turned back. The feast was almost over. Soon it would be time for the bards to come in and sing to us the stories we had all known since childhood. The stories that had molded us and made us what we were.

Chapter XLV

Hittites and Amazons

It was time to think of fortifications and of reinforcements. After I bade farewell to Menelaos—I could not find it in my heart to hate him—I purified myself for three days, keeping myself from Helen and consuming only a piece of bread dipped in wine three times each day. On the third day I surveyed the city to see how much needed to be done. I tried to tell myself it was not hopeless, but it was difficult. My only solace was that the Akhaians could not be in a much better position than we were ourselves.

The outer walls were in disrepair; there was no sense in even attempting to rebuild them now. If the Akhaians managed to reach the outer gates, the outer circle of the city was lost, and I had to reconcile myself to that prospect. The inner city, however, could be salvaged. It was almost impregnable; if the Akhaians had not resorted to the trickery of the wooden horse, the war would have gone on until the end of time. I gave orders for the inner walls to be strengthened; rubble from the outer city was used to fill in the gaps. It was difficult work, and my people complained of it, for the harvest was barely done and already they were being made to labor again. But each evening they saw Helen walking along the battlements by my side. Though some said she had aged, others saw her still the Helen of legends. She was what a man wanted to see in her; that was her mystery. And when she showed herself, smiling in the dying sunlight as they toiled, I could hear them saying among themselves, with a kind of desperate urgency, a kind of hope, "We will be great again."

By day I sat in my megaron dispensing justice and listening to reports that came in from seafarers. It was said that Pergamos had made good on his pledge to remain neutral; he and his Myrmidons would have no part in the war. It was said that Menelaos was in two minds, despite his promises to me at the feast; that one day he set out with armed men for Mycenae, and the next he turned back, thinking harsh thoughts about Helen; the third day, moved by a dream in which his dead brother appeared to him, he set off a second time, but on the way fell into a drunken melancholy from which he could not be roused. I pitied him. Sometimes, nights, Helen would tell me of their life together, and I knew why Menelaos had been selected to be custodian of the world's most beautiful woman. It was because all the other Akhaian leaders had perceived in him a certain dullness; Menelaos was simply too colorless, too boring, to cause trouble. I suspected that the other chieftains had all entertained thoughts of abducting her at one time or another, and had thought Menelaos the easiest of them to be cuckolded.

Other news, too. Now and then we heard a rumor that Odysseus had returned to Ithaka. I dreaded the very idea; the architect of the wooden horse could just as easily dream up some new treachery. But the stories were always full of contradictions, and with things so fanciful that I knew them to be impossible: encounters with such creatures as cyclopes, which have not existed since the gods conjured them up to construct the first great walls around Mycenae and Tiryns and Troy. It was said that his wife Penelope was weaving the entire story of the universe on her loom as she waited faithfully and chastely for his return; conversely it was said that Penelope was a whore and had slept with a thousand men in her husband's absence. I did not believe any of the tales, except for one, which was that Odysseus's son Telemachos had been seen in Europe, where he had gone to search for his missing father.

Another rumor was that the sons of Idomeneus King of Crete had rallied to Orestes' call. Some said that Idomeneus had sacrificed his best beloved son to Poseidon to ensure victory; others that the victim had been the king's daughter. This latter was particularly disturbing, for it recalled Agamemnon's sacrifice of Iphigeneia to the goddess before the Akhaians had set out on their first campaign—a pact between him and Snakemother which gave him victory at a most terrible cost: his own death, and his kingdom ravaged by the wild women who served the goddess, and the whole world plunged into shadow.

It was too cold for war now, but in three changes of the moon the warmth would return. That was when I expected the Akhaians to arrive. There was little time, and we did not have heroes such as my uncles had been. Phoinix and Leukippos were eager enough for war, but they were hardly Hector and Deiphobos and the rest of Priam's fifty sons. I realized we would have to do something unprecedented; we would have to find warriors among those who were not noble. I was ashamed to have to go to the shepherd villages to recruit men to defend our city; yet I knew that they would not have to spend years learning the craft of war. For we had iron now, and the coming of iron made of war something crude and ugly, a thing at which even a commoner could excel. Helen had prophesied that the war would be fought with iron, and that this was to be her gift to me. I was only now beginning to learn how ambiguous that gift was.

Only now, too, did I learn that iron had a quality apart from its superior strength; I learned that iron attracts iron. For the young recruits that began to flock to Troy during the cold season brought weapons of iron with them. Many did not know where they had obtained it; when questioned at length, they could only say that a woman had brought it to their village.

I sent out messengers to the lands that had once been my grandfather's allies, with presents—as rich as I could afford—for their kings, entreating them to come to my aid. If they came, it would not be because of Helen, but because the trade routes were at stake; in the few years since I had resumed the kingship, we had been able to maintain a

tenuous stability and to discourage brigands, and it was in no
one's interest to see Troy once more laid low. At first only a
few responded; minor chieftains who sent a score or two of
green young men—boys who had never seen a city all of
stone, who stumbled gaping through our streets, too dull to
know that ours was but a shadow of Priam's gold-rich Troy.

From the citadel's height I would watch the men training
in the plain below. If clumsy, they were young and eager,
and they thirsted for a past that the storytellers had already
made a hundredfold more glamorous. I had raised to the rank
of basileus perhaps a score of young men. Phoinix and
Leukippos each had a squadron of their own retainers. Leonidas
I made master of the king's chariots; all day he could be
found by the tumbledown warehouses, salvaging what he
could. There were not enough chariots, and I commanded
that the necropolis be opened and despoiled of its wealth.
The thought would have terrified me once; but now, as the
vengeance I had sworn grew closer and closer in time, I
became ever more heedless of fate. For the Pythoness had said
that our time was but a crack in the seam of time; it was
already clear to me that the future age that was coming upon
us would have its own rules, and that what we knew as magic
would no longer hold true.

I grew bold. I heard it whispered among my people that I
had grown heartless. But still they obeyed me, for I had
Helen, and Helen symbolized all that had made us great.

Our winter was unnaturally cold, as though the very elements had become confused about the nature of time. Once
there was even snow in the citadel, and wolves, seeking out
the relative warmth of our fires, prowled the steep streets.
The snow was a wonder; I do not think any of my people had
come so close to snow before, though they had seen it
cloaking the peak of Mount Ida.

"It is an omen," I said to Helen before we slept. The dogs
shivered and moaned at our feet; Leonidas crouched uncom-
fortably on the wet rushes. "But of what?"

Helen said, "They say that the land reflects the king's heart."

"That can't be so," I said.

She said, "Perhaps not. But you should search your heart, Little Star. Are you as compassionate as you once were?" The torchlight shadows flickered across her face. Her lips gleamed with pomegranate juice; I wanted to taste the sweet and sour of them. I leaned over her to kiss her. But she said, "Look at Leonidas, shaking in the cold, huddled with the dogs. Would you have let him suffer like that in the days before Helen touched your life?" Perhaps that was true. All I could think of was making love with her. I had purified myself by denying myself for three days; when I returned to her it had been as a drunkard returns to his wine after a forced abstinence, and each time we made love I had become more obsessive. Helen said, "I have heard them say you have grown cruel, Astyanax."

"But war is coming! And we need unity and discipline."

"War is coming. And glory. But since the Lady relinquished her rule over the earth, and men became powerful, women have not shared that glory; we have existed only to be raped and to have our children dragged from our breasts and to become concubines of the brutish conquerors. Not so? But we have endured. We will always endure, as the earth endures; but men are like wind and fire, fickle and easily smothered."

I sat up. I hugged myself against the bracing wind that sang through the tears in the shutters of the stone windows. "This is a bad time," I said, "to start protesting against war. I just want to make love."

She said, "Since I laid by my godhood, I have thought more and more of mortal things. Do you think your war will be as magnificent as the great war Hector fought? No; it will be sordid, bleak, squalid."

"I did not bring you here so you could think such mundane thoughts. I brought you here because you could fire men's hearts."

"Yes," she said. She closed her eyes. I could tell that she was remembering something. What? Perhaps the women, chained up like wild animals beside the Akhaians' tents? Oh, I remembered too. The terror had not touched her; she had seemed strong then. While my mother and the other Trojan women had seemed so pitiful that I was almost ashamed to have sprung from their race . . . I remembered even now, vividly, how my mother had not recognized me, then or ever again. I wondered whether Helen would speak of that time, and about the smile that had set all this in motion. But she only said, with her eyes still closed, "I'm getting older every day. Perhaps I may even die." I could not bear to think of it, and I made love to her angrily, inconsiderately. And I gave no thought to shivering Leonidas, or to any other of my people.

The snow lasted only a few days, and when it was melted, the Hittites came. It was evening, and they came from the east; dinner was interrupted as the whole court streamed out to the battlements to watch. It was a long black line that stretched into the twilight, segmented, like a great worm. The rumble was not like distant thunder, for it was continuous. Here and there armor glinted. Faintly I heard the squeaking of metal chariot tires against the still icy road.

"Ready some chariots," I said to Leonidas. "We must go to them." I did not know yet whether they were allies or enemies. I had to find out before they reached the gates. "The queen will preside over the rest of the evening meal," I shouted, and I left the megaron with Leonidas and several of my men. Old Philemon came with us, for I needed the appearance of wisdom that only an old man could provide. We strode through the inner and outer courtyards, Leonidas running ahead to alert the stablehands and to have the chariots brought forth.

They were yoked and ready as we reached the citadel gates. I mounted. A slave brought me the iron sword, newly sharpened, and threw over my shoulders a cloak of kingship, so that I should be properly attired to receive them if they were of royal blood.

We rode out, away from the sunset, against the chill wind.

In the air we heard a faint paean, in a language no one could understand. We urged our chariots on. Presently, as the road bent back on itself, we saw them emerging from a dark forest at the foothills. There were chariots drawn by asses, in which stood archers, and men on foot with spears. It was too dark to see how many. They were moving toward us, chanting their marching paean. I ordered my herald to lift his great conch and to sound the royal greeting. The noise filled the air. They stopped; a single chariot came toward us now, moving with the solemnity required by ceremony. I was impatient, and bade them sound the call once more. Another answered, its notes alien, haunting. "Who?" I cried out.

Philemon replied, "King, they are Hittites. They were your grandfather's allies."

"Then I shall go to them." And I too moved forward, alone, with Leonidas as charioteer; I left the others behind for fear of committing a diplomatic solecism.

The Hittite was fantastically dressed, with armor of leather and a helmet of iron and a cloak with clasps like mating serpents. He wore a kilt edged with purple, an earring in the shape of a rampant lion, and his eyebrows were painted and dyed with henna and seemed to sweep up in a curve to meet his hairline. Though not young, he had no beard, like a boy. At first I thought he was a eunuch. But his voice, as he barked a command to his lieutenants, belied that illusion. We halted. His asses pawed the ground and bellowed and breathed clouds of cold steam. The sun was setting fast. We left our chariots and walked toward each other with agonizing dignity. I saw that his sandals were pointed. All the while I was thinking, The Hittites have come, and others cannot be far behind, and we will have a magnificent war after all. . . .

"I greet the messenger of the King of the Hittites," I said.

The Hittite paused; a dwarf—dressed in a grotesque parody of his master's warlike garb—leaped down from the chariot, and the Hittite bent low so the dwarf could whisper in his ear. At length it was the dwarf who ran to me and cried out, "I am the voice of Prince Anbar," in a high-pitched, birdlike squawk. "The King of the Hittites is plagued by an evil dream. When he received your message he sent me." The prince said a few more words in a language that had the cadence of the true speech but many bizarre, guttural words; it was the Hittite language, which declines and conjugates much like our own but which has adopted many features of the ancient speech of the east. The dwarf translated: "Anbar was not always my name. I had a fair name once, a name that boded well for the future of our kingdom. But King Arnuwandas dreamed of a shadow that swallowed up the world, and an ending in fire and blood. And the shadow was in the shape of a great horse, and the death star of the world shone through the eye of the horse. In despair he revoked the name of his favorite son and gave him a new name, Anbar, which in the ancient tongue of Akkad means 'iron.' A name from the past for a weapon of the future. In iron, says the king, the world will return to the ancient darkness. And the king said, 'My son will be a sacrifice. Take this prince and these men, both in token of the pledge of friendship which our two kingdoms once shared in the days of glory, and as a symbol of my mourning for the end of the world. I know it will come soon, and my son has agreed to become part of it, to inscribe his name upon the tablets of blood.' "

"Can you not take back your name?" I asked him.

"It would dishonor me to let the name be spoken, now that my father has marked me for a different fate."

But the dwarf cried out, "Suppiliulimas!"

And the prince said, "No!" and struck the dwarf in the face with a little flail he kept tucked in the belt of his kilt.

"Then I will not call you by name either, Prince," I said, knowing full well the anguish he must be feeling, "until you tell me that I may, son of Arnuwandas."

The dwarf retrieved a wet clay tablet from the chariot, and a wedge-shaped reed such as the easterners used for their script. The prince took out his sword and made a small cut in his wrist, not even wincing. He let the blood run onto the clay. And he made a motion to me, that I should do the same. I hesitated; Leonidas cried out, "My lord, you must not—" But I knew it had to be done. Unsheathing the iron that I wore, I sliced across the flesh of my palm and pressed it hard onto the moist tablet, mixing our blood. I too tried to show no sign of pain, for that seemed to be part of the ritual. Then the dwarf inscribed cuneiform characters into the clay. And the prince smiled grimly. I knew that he felt no joy at the sealing of our pact.

I said, "I am sorry your father has had an ill-omened dream. I can only say that I hope it will be otherwise for us, and that your coming will not be a cause for grief among your people." To see a deathstar in a dream is a terrible thing; but we had seen no such thing in our own heavens, and I hoped it was only an illusion.

Through his interpreter, Prince Anbar said, "They have already grieved; my father has already held my funeral. All of us have given away our wives and children, and have accepted the decree of fate."

"Then we must defy fate!" I cried passionately. For I saw in him something I might myself have become, had it not been for Memnon's magic and his artful misdirection of the gods.

"Perhaps we shall," Prince Anbar said. For a moment there was fire in his eyes; perhaps it was only a reflection of the sunset, for soon the luster left those eyes and they became as vacant as the eyes of the undead zumbi of which Memnon had once spoken. . . .

I turned to Leonidas. "Send a chariot back to the citadel at top speed," I said, "and tell them that we welcome friends into our gates." A messenger was dispatched; after a seemly interval, I invited the Hittite prince to board the royal chariot, and we drove back.

As we passed the shards of the shattered horse, the prince gave a terrible, death-seeing cry, as an infant left on a hillside to die cries, knowing that the wolves will come with the sunset.

And I thought: Perhaps I should have the fragments cleared away. It is too painful a memory.

At dinner the prince repeated his tale of his father's dream, while his men performed a war dance, full of abrupt gestures and angry grimacings. The prince added; "And now my father sits and waits in the palace of Hattusas, twice devastated by rebels from the east and west, and will not eat or drink, and longs for death; and he cries out, over and over, 'The deathstar comes not for a king, but for a whole world.' "

Since the departure of Memnon, we had been without a mage or astrologer, a condition unthinkable in the days of Troy's glory; no one could construe the dream. But Helen said, "Perhaps it is not a star of death. Perhaps it is only my brother Castor, whom, they say, my father has newly taken into the sky, and who mourns for his mortal brother Polydeuces."

We were ready for diversion after the coming of this gloomy prince, so Helen told us all the fanciful story of her birth: how Skyfather had seduced Leda in the shape of a swan, how she and Castor and her half siblings Clytaemnestra and Polydeuces had hatched from the selfsame egg. But she added, "It's a silly story, something my nurse invented to explain why I was beautiful and Clytaemnestra was ugly. . . ."

We all laughed. Helen charmed them with more stories, such as the one about how she had never been to Troy at all, but that it was a mere phantom whom Paris had abducted, and that the real Helen had remained in Egypt all the time; but she added, "Your Paris felt pretty real to me!" and then again, "I am tired of being only what men see in me."

After dinner, before the prince retired, he spoke to me. He had spoken little during the meal; we had all been rather uneasy. Through the dwarf he said, "Is it true, King Astyanax, that the sky-god's messenger came to you, and returned into your hands the famous panoply of Hector?"

"Yes," I said distractedly. "But why think of it? It is made of bronze, and bronze is worthless now."

"Yet I would see it, King."

There was nothing for it but to take him to the storeroom where Hector's armor was kept. I had not set eyes on it since leaving Troy in the hands of the blue king. But since I was his host I could not refuse him. I took him and his translator with me; Leonidas preceded us with a torch.

The room was small and bare. The armor was stacked unceremoniously against one wall; it was crusted with green now. The great phasganon, which I had barely been able to lift as a boy, leaned on the shield, nicked in a dozen places.

I thought to myself, This armor is not built for a giant, as I used to think. It seemed puny and ineffectual. As though the magic had been bled from it. It was true. Beside the gleam of deadly iron, the gracefulness of Hector's weapons seemed almost effeminate. They were strange thoughts to be thinking when my ambition had once been to restore the age of heroes.

But the Prince of the Hittites fell prostrate before my father's armor and prayed in his own language. It was the first time he had betrayed any passion since our meeting.

"What is he saying?" I asked the dwarf.

"He sees hope for the first time," said the interpreter.

"It's only old armor," I said bitterly. It did not seem to me that I had changed; only that, in my many adventures, I had acquired wisdom, and had learned to distrust the surfaces of things. It did not occur to me that I was no longer being true to myself, or that, as Helen had told me, my heart had grown cold. It was merely, I told myself, that I had been forced to become pragmatic. I had to win the war. Feeling oddly vulnerable, I left my guest to his fervent prayers and went to seek out the embrace of Helen.

In the days that followed, the Hittites were much marveled at. They trained without rest, without passion; each was already resigned to death. While on the one hand I welcomed reinforcements, on the other I was afraid of what their presence would do to my own men. At dinner the prince was a dour, glowering figure who did not speak. His dwarf

seemed livelier; within a single moon-change he was sneak-
ing each night into the women's quarters, and I had to
present him with one of the female slaves in order to preserve
propriety in the palace. By day the Trojans and the Hittites
trained together, and we learned new methods of warfare that
had been perfected in the east: group maneuvers in which
men acted not as heroes but as pieces in a giant machine. This
kind of warfare was alien to me, but I did not object to it,
believing it would give us the advantage.

The Hittites had been among us for many sleeps, and the
cold was giving way to warmth, so I knew the Akhaians must
come soon. One day, before the dawn, I was awakened from
my bed by Leonidas, who cried, "King, more allies have
come. They are here beside the sea . . . not human. . . ."

"What do you mean?"

"Centaurs, King! That's what they're saying."

I did not know whether we were to deal with gods or men.
It seemed best to investigate before I summoned all the men.
Once more I found myself mounting a chariot; this time we
were speeding away from the sunrise. Rounding a cluster of
boulders, we came suddenly on the beach. I saw them then,
dark against the rosy sky, half in, half out of the sea. Their
bodies were sleek. Their hair, dark as the twilit sea, was long
and unkempt. They neighed and whinnied, and mixed with
those bestial sounds were human voices, hoarse, high-pitched.
Leaving my chariot, I walked toward the sea, trying to hide
my fear.

They were running out of the sea now, and . . .

One of them seemed to separate into two entities! There
was a horse and a woman, and the woman leaped up onto the
horse's back, screeching a shrill paean, and then she sprang
up, somersaulted, stood on her hands on the horse's haunches.
Leonidas, beside me, gasped, "How can it be? How can a
human being ride on a horse itself, as though the two were
one?"

"I have heard of acrobats that perform such death-defying
tricks," I said. "The barbarians of Thessaly, it's said—"

"But King, you have never seen it," Leonidas said, reading the awe in my eyes.

They rode toward us. There were fifty, perhaps a hundred of them. They were all women, all naked. At a shout from their leader they all stood up on their horses' backs and leaped from horse to horse, all the while shrieking out their battlecry.

"They are Amazons!" I said, astonished.

"But Amazons have not been seen since—"

"Since Penthesileia, their queen, was slain by Akhilleus, who lusted after her so much that he violated her corpse after he had killed her." But I felt hope in my heart. For the Amazons had been our allies, however briefly. No one knew whence they came. But, as my grandfather had told me once, they were an ancient race, and knew many secrets that the rest of the world had forgotten.

They were near now. I smelled the sweat of horses, mingling with the odor of kelp and brine. Their leader jumped headlong from her horse and cartwheeled to a stop in front of me.

And cried out: "Heyah! King of the Trojans! We come to stand beside you at the end of the world!"

In a single, bloodcurdling voice, the Amazons screamed: "Heyah! Heyah! Yahey, hey, hey!" And they shook their bows at the sky.

Scattered by the pounding of horses' hooves, flocks of sea gulls streamed into the sky, chattering and keening. They dappled the sand with shadows. I held out my hand and shouted, "Rejoice!" in greeting.

"I am the last of the Hippolytes," said the Amazon leader. "I am the daughter of that Hippolyte slain by her sister Penthesileia, who expiated for her impiety by fighting on the side of Troy. It was then that the Amazons learned your language, for our own tongue is as the speech of horses. We come to you as a gift from the far past. We are priestesses of the Lady, but we come from the time before the worship of the Lady became laden with darkness. We are survivors of the world's dawn, come to witness the last days. A dream sent us here. Heyah, heyah! We will fight by your side, we will herald the coming of the end with the bloodsong on our lips and the deathjoy in our hearts!'' She swept her hair back from her breasts, and I saw that every inch of her had been artfully scarified: her body was a very mural of whorls and triangles and streaks and interlocking designs. In some of the scars a bright blue pigment had been rubbed. She seemed more a mythical beast than a human, yet I knew her people to be an ancient one, survivors of the Silver Age, knowing still (as Helen once had known) the speech of birds and animals.

"You are welcome," I said.

At once there came renewed the women's wild clamor. At first I was seized by a fear, remembering the snake-haired women who had torn Neoptolemos in shreds. But had she not said that they came from a time before the goddess worshipers had turned to darkness? And had they not come at the rising of the sun?

Another cry. And the sky was thick with arrows, arcing away from the sea, toward the sun. And the women whooped and made their horses paw the sky, and the air was steamy with their pungent breath, and they rode forth along the beach, sometimes clinging to their horses' bellies with their feet to scoop up the scattered arrows from the sand. It was a sight of fierce, elemental beauty. They had subjugated nature, yet they had set it free. I was overcome with the same joy that I had felt on first making love with Helen, the joy that could not be distinguished from pain. They did not have the constrained discipline of the Hittites, but their movements had a fluidity and a music that could only have come from hard, incessant practice.

"Arrows!" cried the leader. "Arrows tipped with iron!"

Once more I felt the great truth: iron attracts more iron.

And now we moved toward the city. As we approached, the Amazons became subdued; they whispered among themselves, and their horses seemed restive, unnerved. People were emerging from their houses, some to stare, some to jeer; many thought, as I had, that these were centaurs, and hid in fear. But as the sun rose higher they saw clearly that the woman did not grow from the steed, and they became bold. Indeed it was the Amazons who seemed fearful, especially the younger ones.

The leader, who had called herself the last Hippolyte, said to the others, "Be calm, daughters. This is a city. This is the kind of place men live in. They cage themselves from the wind and the sea and think themselves powerful. Heyahey! They are scum."

At last the outer walls could be seen clearly. The sunrise burst over the haunches of the shattered horse. Its eyes glowed, as in the day when I had first imagined that it spoke to me. As they caught sight of the pieces of the horse, the women began to wail and to beat their breasts. In alarm, I said. "Why do you mourn? Our city greets you as friends."

"Ai! Ai! We see the fragments of our father!" cried the one who was known by the hereditary title of Hippolyte.

"Rebuild! Rebuild!" the women chanted.

"The one who sent us the dream, the one who brought us to this desolate place," said Hippolyte. "But we will rebuild our father."

"Your father?" I said, looking up at the woman who rode beside me, her thighs clenching the horse's bare back in an almost sexual fashion.

"The horse is the sea and the sea is our father," she said.

The others repeated the words in a singsong litany: "The horse is the sea and the sea is our father. The horse is the sea and the sea is our father."

I knew what they meant: that the horse is sacred to Poseidon, god of the sea, and it was reputed that the Amazons coupled with their own horses and conceived without the seed of a man, as women did centuries ago before the way of Skyfather was known in the world. They must not know, I thought, of the trickery that brought the horse into the city. They saw it only as the image of the god.

"Here," said the queen of the Amazons, "in the city

where my mother died, we will rebuild the image of our father, the sea. It is the sea that will wreak vengeance on those who killed Penthesileia. The great horse will come to life and strike them down with fire."

"You are mistaken," I said sadly. "It's only the broken shell of a war machine. There is no power in it, except for the power of human treachery." And again I wanted to dispose of the thing that most reminded us of our shame.

"Foolish man!" said the Amazon queen. "There is magic staring you in the face, if you only knew how to harness it!"

But I knew better, or thought I did: that even as we spoke, the magic was being drained from our world. It was a heavy truth, and I did not want to utter it aloud. It would not be wise, I told myself, to offend my newfound allies. I was in love with their innocence, and I did not want to taint it with my disillusionment.

Thus it was that the pieces of the shattered horse came together once more, on the eve of the war. Prince Anbar watched the rebuilding, silent as stone; he thought, I knew, that it sealed his doom. But then he had already consecrated himself to death. I did not know whether the horse signified that history would repeat itself, or that it would be a new covenant between Skyfather and his people; but when it was done I was proud, because the horse, towering over the outer wall, dominating the hillside, showed that we were determined to negate the Akhaians' treachery, to turn back time and defy the will of the gods. What gods? I told myself angrily. Skyfather had never shown himself to me, and as for Hermes and the three goddesses—the memory was fading. Fading! I told myself, furious that I even considered it at all.

And men came from distant nations to see the horse and to see the living goddess, daughter of the sky, who daily showed herself from the parapet of the palace; and Helen concealed her new humanity with kohl and powdered chalk and poultices of clay and herbs, and the people believed that the grace of Skyfather was with them again; they even tolerated the capricious cruelty of their king, accepting it as the necessary discipline of a warrior people, never divining that he had lost his faith in the gods, and with that faith compassion.

Chapter XLVI

The Akhaíans

They lost no time in coming. Scarcely one moon-change from the time the weather grew warm, in time to interrupt the ceremonies of spring.

They came openly, brashly, their ships always within sight of the coast, for the reports preceded their coming by many days. I sacrificed at the stone of Skyfather, and I waited. One morning they summoned me to the beach and I saw them for the first time: a line of dark smudges to the northwest, against the gray horizon. Their oars beat the water; at this distance the ships seemed like an army of bugs crawling on the sea. I could not tell how many of them there were; surely not a thousand! I stood and watched them for a while, hardly believing at first. Philemon estimated they would beach by the end of the day; they would not attack until the next morning, and even then not until Orestes and I had the traditional altercation that always precedes such battles.

There was something hypnotic about that sight. I had to strain to see them, perched precariously on the great water; death-bringers though they were, they were beautiful. It was hard to tear myself away, but there was no time to waste. I and the others rode our chariots hastily back to the city, and I convened an immediate meeting of the leaders.

I was in the throne room of my grandfather. Before me, such as they were, were my tributaries and allies. Once or twice, as a child, I had wandered into such meetings and found them dull. What I remembered most was the circle of men, intent, each one more glittering than the last, for they wore their polished armor and had shields of bronze, and they stood arguing endlessly about tactics until my grandfather would silence them with a word or even a mere raised eyebrow. Now I took the place of Priam, and I found myself trying to ape his gestures, his imperious demeanor. Though inwardly I felt awkward, I found that the gestures worked well enough; for kingship itself commands authority. And though I had found myself believing less and less in the gods, yet all knew that I had the blood of Skyfather and that what I said must contain divine inspiration. I felt both foolish and insufferably proud.

The Prince of the Hittites stood in the heavy panoply of his people. The queen of the Amazons stood naked save for a loincloth, but with such dignity that one dared not think of her as a sexual creature. My own kinsmen wore their finery. There were barbarian chieftains who had owed Troy allegiance once, and had come for the sake of Priam's memory, each one more outlandishly dressed than the next; some—the Ethiops—had skins dark as bark, polished until they shone, wearing necklaces of gold and ivory and bones that pierced their ears. When they spoke it was in a babble of exotic tongues, and everything I said was repeated by interpreters such as Anbar's dwarf.

"Strategy—" I began. But the Amazon interrupted me almost at once.

"No strategy! We sweep down from the hill! We slice them to shreds!" she said.

"No, we should not yield the high ground," Phoinix said.

He had a point. But before the argument could proceed, Philemon cried out, "The king should decide on a plan."

"A plan. Yes." When you fight a war with bronze, you need no plan; each man is a hero and fights as a hero, singling out some worthy opponent on the field and taking him on, making sure that he observes the etiquette of war. Bravery counts more than anything else. With iron a plan was necessary; iron is the metal of cowards. As I looked around the room and felt the responsibility of all these disparate lives, I felt more and more attracted to the coward's viewpoint. I began to outline some of my thoughts.

The hall fell immediately silent. They all turned to me, their king. I held their lives in my hands.

*   *   *

I stood just beyond the outer walls, in front of the Skaian
Gate. It was an hour before sunset. Beside me was Leonidas,
his hand on the chariot's reins. Behind me were the chieftains
in their chariots. Armed men were hidden behind the pieces of
the wall; though I was prepared to parlay, it was not my
intention to be caught by some trick. The sun was behind the
hill; we were almost swallowed up by the shadows of the
broken walls, lengthening toward the sea. I wanted to give
the command and have my entire army come bursting down
the hill, racing toward the Akhaian ships, setting fire to their
tents; I kept my impulse to myself. One more day of honor, I
told myself, before the madness is let loose.

We heard the chariot thunder. Distant, at first, at the
threshold of hearing. Then, from the direction of the sea, we
saw the dust. Slowly, serenely, it floated skyward. Birds,
startled by the commotion, streaked across the gray sky. An
alien scent on the wind: a choking, gritty odor of churned-up
earth and the sweat of men and horses; faint at first, then
overpowering. All at once the dust cloud was upon us, and
we could hear inhuman shrieks. The cloud stretched all the
way across the horizon, obscuring the line where the cliffs
met the shore and the ocean . . . .

Phoinix was trembling.

"Are you afraid?" Hippolyte said scornfully. "You have
never seen blood, except the blood of your own slaves at the
whipping post. You are afraid to see your own?"

"No!" Phoinix yelled. "I—"

"Be still!" I said. "All of us feel the dread. It is an
illusion. The earth is shaking from the traffic of chariot
wheels, not from terror." It made me feel better to say it.

One of our horses reared up, whinnied, tried to drag its
chariot away.

Hippolyte walked over and stroked the horse's neck, soothing it with words in a strange language, half human, half
equine; perhaps the horse understood, for it settled down and
was no trouble.

"*Kurur esir!*" whispered the son of Arnuwandas.

The dwarf shrieked, "The prince says they are hostile!" and let out an abrasive cackling.

The dust began to settle. I saw the Akhaians now; their chariots were lined up at the bottom of the hill, where the slope was least unfavorable. Three chariots had detached themselves from the group and were coming toward us. Even at this distance I recognized Orestes in front; he was dressed in black, and he had the distracted appearance of the death-haunted. But Athena had cleansed him of his crime! Orestes had told me so himself when he rescued me from the pig worshipers, freeing himself of his obligation to me so that he could make war on me without impiety. Yet Pergamos had told me he was still mad. Something was not right here.

As Orestes' chariot drew nearer I looked at the other two. One bore an ancient man, his hair white and shaggy, dressed in the ornate fashion of a Cretan. Without introduction I knew that this must be Idomeneus, King of Crete. He wore a necklace made of boars' tusks; tusks dangled from his cere-monial leather shield. He was a veteran of the first Trojan War; as rumor had it, he had joined forces with Orestes, not content with the one war. The other chariot bore Hermione. It was startling to see her; she was dressed as on the day I first saw her, in the garb of the Lady, with her golden bow and quiver and her hair immaculately plaited and her face elegantly painted. Was the sight of her intended to arouse me? Or perhaps to remind me of the day Orestes and I entered Sparta, exiles both, utterly dependent on each other?

"Give back Helen!" Orestes shouted. "And we will pack up our tents and go back to our native cities." His voice sounded tiny against the background clatter of iron and horses' hooves.

Since he had come forward with two companions, protocol demanded that I go to meet him with two. I beckoned my kinsmen Phoinix and Leukippos to ride forth with me.

"No!" I screamed. We were close now; there was no need to shout. I drew up alongside his chariot. For a long time we looked into each other's face.

What did he see in mine, I wonder? I know what I saw in
his eyes: confusion. Guilt. Madness.

He turned away. He was talking to the empty air. "Yes,"
he said, addressing some phantom. "We mustn't give in,
must we? Don't worry, dear sister. It will be all right, I
promise you. Don't tilt your head; keep it straight, Electra. . . .
Iphigeneia, why is your breast bleeding? Oh, I'll stanch the
blood with my chiton. . . . There, the fabric is black so no
one will see the red, you see, and they'll think, she's untouched by the knife, she's been saved by the grace of the
Lady. Ai, ai, ai!" In a fury he turned back to me. "Look
what you've done, you evil king! You've upset my sisters."

I turned to Hermione. "What's happening?" I said. "Orestes
has gone completely mad . . . yet they follow him. . . ."

She whispered, "They say that the gods have touched him,
that in his madness he can do no wrong, that he's a
prophet. . . ."

I said, "But the goddess purified him!"

She said, "Yes and no. Pursued by the Furies, Orestes
sought refuge in Athena's shrine. The goddess, speaking
through her priests, said, 'You have killed your mother, and
yet you seek my pardon! Very well. Let those that torment
you no longer be called Furies but Eumenides, the kindly
ones.' And the priests said, 'The goddess has spoken. He is
cured; the Furies no longer haunt him.' But it wasn't true!
She had only changed how others perceived him; Orestes'
heart was untouched. And because the Furies were now 'the
kindly ones,' to him they became illusions of his dead sisters.
Do you see Orestes as mad? Your sight is truer than that of
most men."

"Yes. I have Skyfather's eyes," I said, not without irony.

"You should not mock your gifts," she said sadly.

"Why not? They have brought me only bitterness."

In the impasse that followed none of us spoke, save Orestes
alone, who argued with spirits, gesticulating wildly, crying
out, cursing, threatening, entreating. At last he repeated his
demands to me. "Helen," he said.

The wind whipped up more dust. I smelled dread in the

air. I said, "I would release her gladly, Orestes. But I do not think she will come. For the sake of the friendship we shared—no matter that it was through ignorance of each other's true identity—do not make war. We cannot undo what Helen has decided to do."

"Let me hear that from her own lips!" Orestes shouted.

Idomeneus spoke, his voice worn and brittle: "Why are we wasting words? I have so little time left to fight." I looked at the old man, with his pitted face and his extravagant white beard. He seemed feeble. But his eyes were wild. This Idomeneus had once single-handedly burst through a wall of men, his boar's tusk helmet striking terror into their hearts. Could this be the same man?

"Do not contradict me, old man," Orestes said sharply to him. "It is Mycenae that gives the orders, and I am Mycenae."

A look of defiance crossed the face of Idomeneus; but it yielded to resignation.

"I say I will hear those words from the lips of the faithless queen," Orestes said again.

"As you wish," I said, and dispatched Leukippos with a message to the citadel.

We waited.

Orestes was deep in conversation with spirits. Hermione looked beseechingly at me. Idomeneus railed at us all, his voice a whining parody of what must once have been a great, resonant, persuasive instrument. "I knew that the war was not yet over!" he said. "I knew it when our ships left Troy so many years ago, when Skyfather and his brother the Sea sent the storm that wrecked my fleet, a hundred strong, the pride of Crete. Adrift, clinging to pieces of wood, I called on Skyfather, but he did not appear to me, though I am the son of Deucalion Ark-builder, the oldest of all men, who survived the great Flood with which the gods ended the Silver Age. No! Skyfather did not come to me—"

"Nor me," I said, angry.

"I called on the darkness instead . . . and the threefold goddess said to me, 'What will you give me if I let you live?' Oh, but I fear death by water—often my father would dandle me on his knee and tell me of the Flood that destroyed the world—the one thing that I feared. I said, 'Anything, dark goddess, I will give you anything!' and she said, 'You will sacrifice to me the first human being who greets you on the Cretan shore. How could I have known it would be my firstborn, my own daughter? With my last conscious breath I screamed assent, and I was borne to shore in the embrace of a great serpent that was also a woman.''

"You struck a bargain, as Agamemnon did," I said. "A child's blood to feed the mother of darkness." I remembered that I too had struck a bargain: I had given the golden apple to the fairest of three that were one. We were doomed to tread the same paths over and over again. I wanted nothing more now than to break free of the circle, even if I had to tear apart the fabric of fate and time.

Idomeneus said, "For that impiety I was dethroned by Leukos, who took my own wife Meda to his bed. That was my reward for defending the whore's honor. My kingdom taken from me, my hands stained with my own child's blood. I am consecrated to the goddess now! I only want to die, to die bathed in the blood of Trojans—"

He stopped for breath. He was shaking.

Phoinix cried out, "He dishonors our queen! Let him be killed, now, and let's get the battle started."

But I could not hate this man; I had seen too much of the Akhaians' viewpoint, in the days when I had involuntarily carried the name of Pylades upon my soul. I pitied him. I did not believe that the Deucalion who was his father was the selfsame Deucalion or Ut-Napishtim or Noah who had survived the Flood; more likely the name was hereditary, as Helen's was. But I saw that the old man truly believed that his was the one true link with our mythic past. I said, "The Silver Age was destroyed by water; it is said that the Bronze Age will die in fire. So I have dreamed, and so has dreamed King Arnuwandas of the Hittites. Do not attack us blindly, King Idomeneus. I have too much respect for your age and your lineage to harm you, yet there are others who might.

Would you have it said that your family, which survived one world catastrophe, has not the strength to weather a second?''

But no one was listening.

For Leukippos had returned with Helen.

They all stared past me. I looked too. Did they see something I did not see? But none of them had possessed her. I saw the hunger in their eyes. Had I once felt so desolate a longing, I who nightly knew her in the most intimate way that one can know another?

It was Hermione who broke the silence first, saying, "Mother, stop this nonsense. I implore you. Come home. Maybe then, at last, my husband's madness will go away. . . .''

Helen stepped from the chariot. Her feet were shod with sandals of gold and leather; they glinted, ruddy, in the sunset. They were carelessly fastened; her ankles, through the gold lacings, had the sheen of ivory. With a swift, subtle gesture she straightened her skirts so that they fell over her feet and obscured them from sight, drawing the men's gaze upward to her bare breasts, still firm, the nipples painted and scented with rose-water. Then to the neck, moon-colored, smoothed with a poultice of gypsum. I knew that neck was sometimes wrinkled; I knew those lips were sometimes cracked, and the eyes edged with crow's-feet. But the others saw none of these things, for they saw only the Helen of dreams, the daughter of Zeus, whose eyes were windows to the sky.

And Orestes said, very softly, "I have come to take you home, Queen.''

In the distance, the neighing of impatient horses; the line of Akhaian chariots had become ragged as the drivers struggled to restrain the animals. The air was steeped in the stench of dread now. Queen Helen shook her head, slowly, with such compassionate regret. . . .

"I will take you home!" Orestes cried. "We can't have our honor violated, our traditions of guest-friendship trodden upon. We took this man into our homes, and he repays our hospitality with excrement!" He shot me a look of hatred and, perhaps, pain.

Helen said, "Why don't you just tell me I'm a whore, that I'm worthless? Then you can go home!"

"Honor—" Orestes screamed.

"Honor and dishonor," she said, "love and lust—these are distinctions men love to make. As for me, I no longer have any choice in the matter. I must remain."

"Mother," Hermione said, leaving her chariot and kneeling down in front of the queen, "I'm begging you on my knees. I'm pleading with you."

"You have your own Helen, do you not?" Helen said to Orestes, ignoring her daughter.

"She is Helen but not Helen."

"What is it about me, I wonder?" Helen said softly. She turned back; Leukippos assisted her onto the chariot. "Take me back, Leukippos," she said. Although I had given no command, Leukippos obeyed her instantly. She was gone almost before I could open my mouth. Behind us, my men parted to let her through.

The sun was almost gone now. Men with torches came forward from either side. Orestes' face, eerily lit, seemed phantomlike, inhuman.

Orestes sighed. For a long time we looked at each other, knowing full well the absurdity of it all. "Perhaps she has no choice, as she claims," he said. "But you and I . . ."

Was he truly going to turn back? I saw the resignation in his face. I had been his friend after a fashion. I had stood by him when he plunged his sword into the breast that fed him. I knew how haunted he was. Did he truly think this war would expiate for all the sins of the House of Atreus? He wavered.

For a few heartbeats I thought: We can avert this thing. No star of death hangs over us.

Then I looked from Orestes to Idomeneus. The Cretan king seethed. "You foolish children!" he shouted. "I killed my child for this war. I need to die. Don't steal my death from me. If you will not start the war, I will!"

Before I could say anything he had seized a spear from his charioteer and thrown it straight at me. Stupidly I stared at it, not understanding. It was Leonidas who grabbed me and thrust me hard against the side of the chariot and caught the spear for me. In his side. Blood and water gushed out. He fell into my arms.

I thought of his brother who had taken my death upon himself, who waited for me by the river of death . . . the body grew limp . . . rage took hold of me, blind rage . . . I struck at the horses with the flat of my sword, and the chariot hurtled forward . . . I swung the sword wildly at the old man . . . the iron sawed through bone and tendon, sliced through flesh and slippery blood, and his severed head flew up toward the last rays of sunlight . . . screams of panic, as my horses and Orestes' became entangled . . . my hands were shaking, I dropped my sword, it banged against the side of the chariot, and the body of Leonidas was hanging out of the back, his face dragging in grass and mud.

"Enough!" Orestes cried. "Blood has been shed. We have a war." And he transfixed me with a look of sorrow as his charioteer managed to disengage our chariots. "Darkness is falling. Tomorrow we will meet on the field between the city and the sea."

I stared in horror at what I had done. The old man's head lay on the ground. His headless body flailed about in its chariot as its driver set off behind Orestes.

The head stared back at me. I cried, "You got what you asked for. You wanted death and I gave it to you!" Behind me, I could already hear the keening warcries of the Amazons and the guttural paeans of the dark barbarians and the relentless chanting of the Hittites. It seemed to me that the head was weeping blood. I had never seen a red so bright as those droplets of blood. Nor, it seemed to me, had the grass of the plains been so green, green as jade from the east. Was it not the blood of heroes that made the sky blue and the grass green? Even the sunset was brilliant, its hues of scarlet and burnished copper making my eyes smart.

I could not think of the coming battle. The sight of the head of Idomeneus had dredged up the most terrible memory of my childhood: the sight of the head of King Priam being tossed across the flagstones of the temple of Skyfather in the burning city, the implacable face of Neoptolemos, myself a small child vowing vengeance, clasping the cold stone from the sky, alone, so much alone.

I was not an innocent anymore. I was just like Neoptolemos. I was barely out of boyhood, and I had killed a king whose ancestry stretched back beyond the beginning of our age. I was no better than the man who had killed my grandfather; worse, perhaps, for Neoptolemos had paused, in the midst of his mad butchery, to show compassion toward me, whom he had thought a mere slave boy.

It was then that I realized that I no longer cared about honor. Honor was a futile affectation. I was going to win the war. I was going to throw aside valor and piety and compassion; I would win the war by cowardice and cunning if need be. For I had seen into the future, and the future was going to be an Age of Iron, and there could be no room for honor in such a future.

Book Eight: Kings of Bronze

ᛏ⏀ᛀᛏ⊕
ᛝᛉᛐ

"Women like you, wives and mothers,
cannot know
what men may feel with me . . .
Intolerable desire, burning ecstasy.
All prices paid, all honour lost
in this bewilderment.
Immortal, incommensurable
Love such as this stretches up to heaven,
for it reaches down to hell."
        —Helen's words to Hecabe and
        Andromache on the eve of
        Troy's destruction
        Sir Michael Tippett, *King Priam*

Chapter XLVII

~~~~~~~~~~~~~~~~~~~~~~~~~~~~~~~~~

The Night

From infancy I had heard descriptions of the eve of battle. I had heard tales of chieftains regaling their men, firing them with words; of bards reliving ancient deeds to fill men with desire for blood. It should have been a time of togetherness; for me it was a night of alienation.

The funeral of Leonidas was a dismal thing, but I could not think of the impending battle until I had taken care of it. And so a small group of us gathered in one of the minor courtyards, whose walls had never been rebuilt, and I consigned him to the fire, the first casualty of my war. Phoinix and Leukippos, who had always envied Leonidas for my favor, found excuses to be absent, saying they had to get their men ready; in truth the funeral was a luxury I could ill afford, for the time for planning was swiftly dwindling. Helen came; for that I was grateful. The Hittite prince was there also. But the Amazons, Ethiops, and other allies were not present.

The bier was my old pallet. The pyre was not fragrant cedar, but firewood from one of the storage rooms; some of the servants would be cold that night. I thought of the funeral of Prince Pielos, my half brother, in all its gloomy splendor, and how it had been interrupted by madwomen.

Leonidas was no relative of mine, but I cut off a plait of my hair for him. I could not sacrifice horses—we needed every one of them for the battle—but I freed a brace of doves and killed a lamb, and saw to it that he was lying with the lion's paw that matched mine strapped tightly to his neck, for I wanted him to know me in the underworld. And I placed a nugget of silver in his mouth to help him over the river of darkness. I called in no mourners and no musicians; in silence we stood.

It was Helen who said, "You must feel terrible, Astyanax.

385

He took the blow that was meant for you. His death has once more tricked the earth, and made the war possible. . . .''

"I don't believe in such things anymore!" I said, walking resolutely away from the fire.

She held my hand. "Astyanax."

Prince Anbar said, "We must prepare ourselves, Queen Helen. Your husband cannot give up his soul to grief, not tonight, not until the Akhaians are driven into the sea."

She said, "I will stay and weep for Leonidas."

I could summon up no tears. It seemed to me that I had ceased to be human.

The prince, the dwarf, and I went to the outer walls. The great horse reared up beside the cracked stones. The Amazons had remade it so that it seemed never to have been shattered; they had oiled it, and in the moonlight it glowed. Just outside the gate, the charioteers were unloading tires of copper from oxcarts and covering the holes in the chariot cars with makeshift patches of cowhide. My chariot, made of figwood inlaid with gold, had been stolen from the necropolis. The fact that a tomb had been violated for me left me completely unmoved; my hand did not shake as I reached out to feel the finely stranded wicker wedded to the sturdy frame. They were repairing the axle and hammering the tires into shape around the wheels. From the hillside, round about us, the clang of awl on metal pelted the night. Here and there were fires, around which the Amazons slept with their horses, for they disdained the comforts of the city. The stars were out. The great horse peered over piles of rubble and sections of wall, against which men leaned, conversed, sharpened their swords upon their grinding stones.

"It could have remained a great city," the prince said softly to himself; at least, I fancied that he said that from the few words that I knew of Hittite.

"It is, and will be," I said defiantly, looking up at the citadel, ghostly in the moon.

The dwarf, sensing discord, hurried to translate. "I do not mean your city; I mean my own, threatened by the Mitanni

and those Luvians who are not under your suzerainty." I
knew I should feel sympathy for him, for he was far from
home and his father had taken away his name because of a
dream. But the war preoccupied me.

We half walked, half stumbled downhill. Some of the
Amazons were up; one was wrestling with Phoinix. A group
of men surrounded them, cheering one side or another.
Hippolyte broke away as soon as she saw me. "Laggards!"
she shouted.

"Do you never sleep?" I said.

"Why? We drink up strength from the moon."

We sat down on the ground. There was a mound of earth,
an anthill. "That is your city!" said Hippolyte, laughing.
"You are like ants, you city people, never knowing the night
as she truly is." She scratched in the ground with the point of
an arrow. "The sea." Another line. "The River Skamander."
Another. "Look: the way east, from the Dardanian Gate,
toward Hattusas."

As she spoke, one of her kind, painted black from head to
toe, appeared as though by magic, startling me by crawling
up beside me. I jumped. The Amazon laughed and said,
"The camouflage works well!"

The messenger said, "I've been down to the shore."

"How many ships?" I said.

"A thousand?" the Hittite said, mocking the myth.

"No," said the Amazon in all seriousness, "but there may
be as many as a hundred. They are camped"—she pointed to
Hippolyte's schematic construction—"beside some rocky outcroppings that would seem to shield them from direct assault."

"But if your camouflage is as effective as this, and if
under cover of night . . ." I began, my plan of attack starting
to become more and more clear to me.

"I see what you're saying," said Leukippos, joining us as
the wrestling match between Phoinix and the Amazon broke
up, "but is it honorable to—"

"Honor!" the Amazon shrieked, and she leaped up and
uttered a shrill ululation that was echoed by others across the

hillside. I shuddered; the others too were touched with unreasoning fear. "Honor, he says!"

Emboldened, I said, "We can dispense with honor now." I lifted my iron blade, firmly gripping its lion's paw hilt, and waved it at the moon; it flashed and the sight drew hearty cheers from around me. "We are warriors of the future, warriors of the new way."

Quickly I outlined the strategy I had conceived. They nodded, seeming to think me wise; I became bold and told them that if all proceeded as planned I was convinced of victory. For Orestes, maddened as he was, thinking in terms of the noble code of warfare under which our fathers fought, would hardly be prepared for a ruse. And he did not know we had the Amazons.

As soon as we finished our discussion, the Hittite went off to talk to his men. From their encampment I heard shouts of *"Hurtantes!* They are accursed!"

Hippolyte made a sound like the cry of a frightened mare, and those of her people who had been asleep jumped up, alert, and began running up to the great horse. They began to climb upon its flanks and to fling their bodies against the slick, oiled wood in a sexual frenzy, moaning and whinnying, while others danced around. "What are they doing?" I said.

"They're invoking the sea. They've been doing it all evening," Leukippos said. "They're mad, these women! But absolutely fearless," he added, not without envy. He was as frisky as a hunting dog about the coming battle.

I watched as the women continued their orgiastic ritual, half fascinated and half repelled.

"What I wouldn't give to be that horse!" Leukippos said, laughing.

"Not much!" Phoinix panted, coming up behind. "They'd tear your arm off."

"I take it you lost the encounter?" I said.

"She went at it like a lioness!" he said. "But I was more graceful." I doubted that. "I'm glad they're on our side," he said, and I had to agree.

There came a message from the queen, and I hastened
back as my two chief warriors jeered at me for a lovesick
fool. I detected a certain wistfulness in their voices, though,
and I knew that, though all of us were going to war, only I
made love to the queen. Was it unfair? I mused.

But only briefly. I ran all the way to the palace. I passed
the courtyard where the ashes of my dead friend smoldered. I
had no time to stop.

I ran into my chamber and threw myself into Helen's arms.
We made love as though it were the last time. I remember
forcing myself to think, The war will have been worth it; I
have loved the daughter of the sky. How selfish I was. I did
not think of her at all; I plunged my phallos deep into her,
thrusting until anger exploded into pleasure. She cried out
like a wounded creature, and still I plowed her. In the end
she closed her eyes and became limp and I did not know
whether she was even conscious, and it put me in mind of the
story of Akhilleus and Penthesileia: how he had been unable
to rein in his lust, how he had performed necrophily upon her
lifeless body, fucking her while the blood spurted from the
death wound he had dealt her. Again and again I cried out,
"Are you dead, woman, dead?" and she did not answer me,
and again and again I pounded against her, despairing of
evoking any feeling in her. Abruptly my emotions were
spent. She lay beside me. Moonlight streamed in, illumined
her soft features; I felt nothing.

I heard voices from outside. I should have rested, but I
could not; I got up and looked over the courtyard. Leukippos
was shouting, "King, King, they've seen the star of death!"
And someone was running across the paving toward the
megaron, on his way to summon me. I seized a torch from
the wall, dressed myself, ran downstairs.

We were sprinting now. I had not put on any sandals, and
pebbles bit my feet. I was heedless of the pain. We passed
the inner wall and reached the edge of the city; the Hittites
were clustered around the wooden horse.

"First it was the Amazons," I said, "and now it's the

Hittites. The horse seems to mean so much to all these foreigners. . . ."

Prince Anbar, arms upraised, was wailing.

A slave came to me, carrying a bulky object in his arms. He was trying to hand it to me, but I was too preoccupied to notice him. "What is he saying?" I yelled at the dwarf, who had slunk away from the gathering and was sidling up to us.

"Do you not see the deathstar? It is what King Arnuwandas saw in his dream: the star flowering from the shadow of a great horse."

"What are you talking about?" I said.

"Look! Through the eye of the horse—"

"Master," said the slave, who was still trying to give me something, "you must take this—we salvaged it from the field. It's yours by right of conquest. . . ." Abstractedly I took it from him. I continued to look upward at the horse. I could see no star.

I saw a creature of polished wood; I saw empty eyeholes filled with the luminous blackness of night and moon. But there was no tailed star such as prophesied catastrophe. . . .

"Am I blind?" I said. "I don't see anything."

But they all pointed and clamored and seemed moved.

"Once the horse spoke to me," I told the dwarf, "but now it seems dumb. Or have I merely become deaf?"

"You are the six-times-great-grandson of Zeus," the dwarf said—I do not think he spoke with irony—"and you if anyone can see the truth behind illusions."

"If that is so . . ."

"The horse is speaking to all of them," the dwarf said, "except you."

"Once I saw Thanatos in the palace; the night before they razed the city."

The dwarf shrugged; his arms were stubby, and the gesture made him seem even more grotesque than usual. "As I said, you have the sight."

"But now the common people are seeing things . . . and I am not!" I said. "What can this mean?" But I thought, I have relinquished my divine ancestry; I have no right to see hidden truths.

"Ah, but perhaps truth and illusion have become reversed," the dwarf said. I was sure he was mocking me this time. "They want to see a hairy star, do they not? They want their shattering apocalypse. All is illusion, all is—"

"Misdirection," I whispered, thinking of Memnon.

At last I looked at what the slave had put into my hands. It was the helmet of Idomeneus, cunningly made from the tusks of boars; it was an object so famous that in the stories they told of the war it had been enough to mention the helmet and the audience knew the man. But I had killed the man. The gray, dispossessed king who had come to Troy to seek death.

"I don't want to wear it," I said. The dwarf shrugged again. I felt helpless. I knew they would expect it of me. Reluctantly I put it on my head; a roar of approbation burst from the crowd.

"Some are saying you are as great as Hector," the dwarf said. "Others that you are greater, for you brought back Helen and the gift of iron and you slew a king with a single blow."

"A grizzled king, feeble, asking for death," I said.

"Soft! Do not underestimate the value of propaganda!" said the dwarf. "We have only a few hours till sunrise. The Akhaians will attack then. Your Amazons are already moving. A few hours can make all the difference in a matter of morale." He seemed to speak from experience; perhaps he was reliving some conflict between the Hittites and their many enemies.

I stared up at the wooden horse, trying to see the tailed star in its eye. Nothing. It was just as well. I did not want the horse to speak to me. The past no longer mattered.

I stood, hardly moving, while they dressed me. They did it with great care, for if I was to die, I had to look beautiful in death. They plaited my hair and brushed it and slicked it with olive oil so that not one strand stood out. As they handed me the sword, freshly sharpened and scraped clean of Idomeneus's blood, rosy-fingered dawn broke out behind the eastern hills, and already I could feel, at the threshold of perception, the earth tremor, the premonition of chariot thunder.

"Attack." Had I really said it, or had the word just come tumbling from my lips of its own volition?

At once came warcries from ten thousand throats, and the braying of asses and the neighing of horses, and the clatter of swords upon shields, and the crack of quirts, and the clatter of rattling chariot wheels as we came rushing downhill.

Chapter XLVIII

The Burning Ships

It was barely day. In the half dark we charged them. They faced us in a long line. I was already choking from the dust. Clouds of it obscured the blood-red sun. I wore the helmet of Idomeneus. My new charioteer had been a stablehand, a protégé of dead Leonidas. He was very young, no more than twelve. But that was how old Neoptolemos had been, it was said, when he killed his first Trojan. He was anxious to please, fearful of making an error on his first day of battle. He locked his face into an expression of profound concentration and held on to the reins for dear life. His long unplaited hair, windswept, blew in my face as I bent down to draw my sword. "Tomorrow," I said urgently, "cut some of it off." He nodded, all seriousness.

We were almost upon them. I saw Orestes. I could tell it was Orestes from the black clothing he affected. But his face was completely covered with a grotesque mask—a monstrous face of beaten gold, a deathmask such as Aigisthos had worn when Clytaemnestra struck him down with the two-headed axe. Seeing him I forgot about the men I was leading, about the cacophony of warcries and rumbling chariot wheels. He saw me then. He began to move toward me. The mask glittered in the red light, taunting me. Suddenly I realized it was a female face, and that face framed with serpents of gold. What madness could it be? Why had he come for me in the guise of Snakemother? Everything was a blur except Orestes, his horses galloping toward me in a strange slowed time. "Go straight at him!" I shouted. The chariot veered to one side as we skidded over something—the first casualty of the day, the torso of an Ethiop, black and crimson, the spear sprouting from his chest and swaying. The car flew into the air, slid through mud. Suddenly we were hurtling right into each other and I raised my sword just as he raised his; I held it straight out and waited to strike.

My horses reared up! We swerved again, and Orestes was flailing at the empty air. I turned to see Prince Anbar assailing Orestes' flank, jabbing his javelin again and again at the car, his asses butting and pawing at the wicker, upsetting the quiver that was attached to the side of the car so that arrows spewed out into the mud.

A shriek from my charioteer. We were surrounded by Akhaians now. I had to control my panic, for I suddenly remembered how they had burst into my room when I was a child. Anbar and I had Orestes trapped between us; Mycenaean chariots were circling us and poking at us with their thrusting spears. Recklessly I thought of killing Orestes and ending the war on its first day. An arrow pierced the wicker of my chariot. "Control the horses!" I shouted to the boy. I slashed at the air with my sword. Meanwhile Orestes turned first to one side then the other, speaking to his invisible dead sisters. . . .

"The chariots are jammed together, King," the charioteer shouted. "I can't get free."

"Ai!" Orestes screamed, and raised his arms as if to invoke some magical force. Behind me the sun was rising. It reflected off his mask; for a moment I was blinded. There was a great wind. I tried to scramble up the side of the chariot to get a better angle for my sword. My eyes were smarting from the gold dazzle. The cars were next to each other, the reins tangled, the horses whinnying helplessly against their yokes, and Orestes was in easy striking distance as he danced. The light again! I squeezed my eyes shut and slashed and slashed, but as I opened them I saw . . .

He had vanished! In his place, slithering across the narrow space between our chariot cars, was a golden serpent. Orestes had called on the power of Snakemother. I knew now the nature of the sacrifice of Idomeneus. Wildly I sliced the serpent in two. A half snake coiled about my sword, a head lashing at the air, blood oozing down the iron onto my fist. I looked across Orestes' empty chariot and saw the body of his charioteer slumped over the side. Anbar had run him through with a spear. I heard a scream from beside me and whirled around to see my charioteer pointing hysterically. It was Orestes . . . balancing on the back of one of my horses, dancing, prancing, screeching the laughter of Snakemother's madwomen—laughter I had heard from my own mother's lips. He hopped from horse to horse. No human could do a thing like that. The eyeholes of his deathmask were blank. I realized that Snakemother herself had come to the Akhaians' aid. But I did not call on Skyfather, I who no longer trusted in magic.

At that moment the driver managed to jerk loose and we careened into a line of Akhaians, both in chariots and on foot. The screams burst upon my senses, for I had been concentrating so hard upon Orestes that I lost all sense of the battle. "Forward!" I shrieked, and the Hittite and I rode relentlessly into them. My iron ripped through leather, flesh and bone. An Akhaian tried to climb into the chariot, wielding a comrade's severed arm as a club. It still clutched a sword. He had been unable to pry it free. I kicked him down with my foot and ignored his muffled screeching as chariots trampled him into the mud.

I saw Orestes in the distance. Where had he appeared from? He still danced, perched on a fresh chariot, his mask glittering like a second sun. "Follow!" I said to my charioteer, trusting that if I showed bravery, my men would come rushing after me. We had to push the Akhaians back to the sea. The others were rallying behind me. I saw Phoinix hacking his way on foot out of a cluster of Akhaians. He saw me and was trying to work his way toward an overturned chariot. A stream of men ran between us. The blood was running into the mud, making it ever more slippery and treacherous. He vanished from view; I could not tell if he had been killed. There was no time to find out.

It was almost midday now, and already scorching. Sweat was running into my eyes. There was Orestes—again barely out of reach—taunting me. A strange serenity possessed him as he danced. Surrounding his chariot, ululating and cavorting like demons—were they gorgons or humans? The snake-haired women I had expelled on my return from Akhaia—they had come from the necropolis, they were gleefully running about, striking down my men. One had a half-chewed human heart in her mouth; another was stooping to extract the brains of a dead hero with a huge rock. Rage exploded within me. I took a thrusting spear and hurled it at them with all my might. The woman stopped, shuddered, vomited the heart onto the grass. My gorge rose. But I was too angry to give vent to emotion.

I was at the front of a solid wall of Hittites and Trojans now. The Hittites cried, over and over, "Death to the Ahhiyawa!" which was their name for the Akhaians. They had gathered into a tight formation, three men thick, and were marching stolidly toward the enemy. The ground shook with their footfalls. I was astonished at how they fought; for they were not as heroes, each man picking his own foe and stalking him, but like some superhuman machine. And this, I saw, was to be the future of the art of war. I told the charioteer to lash the horses; Prince Anbar's chariot wheels had caught on a clump of corpses and could not be budged, and he had climbed out and was trying to dislodge the car. Disregarding him, I turned and saw Orestes once again.

And then, behind him, that the sky was beginning to turn gray. And I knew that the Amazons, who had slipped down to the shore under cover of darkness, had begun their sabotage. Yes! On the horizon, a tendril of smoke, and another, and another—we were setting fire to their ships!

I knew then that we were winning the battle. With fresh

vigor I urged the men forward. The Hittites were running toward the horizon now, holding out their shields in a solid wall, heedless of the raining arrows. The Ethiops were leaping, somersaulting over corpses, shrieking shrill paeans at the Akhaians. . . .

I had caught up with Orestes once more. We were within shouting range. I cried out, "I have sent centaurs to burn your ships!"

Some of the Akhaians had broken loose from the host and were sprinting back toward the ships. "Drive them into the ocean!" I shouted. I felt greater than myself; I felt the killing joy race through my blood like undiluted wine. We were giving chase now, and the Akhaians were running back toward the wall of smoke that was the sea. . . .

The way was rockier now. We were nearing the stone outcroppings where Leontes and I had played once, the place where I had seen the women penned up, so many years ago, concealed among the boulders, where Helen's smile had first terrified and ensorcelled me. That scene was far from my mind. The sun was high now, and shafts of light pierced through the dust and smoke. I could hear the shattering surf, and the patter of horses' feet on the sand. My chariot hardly touched the ground, and when it did a fearsome pounding shook my whole body. There were the tents . . . fire everywhere. The Akhaians were dashing toward their ships, any ships. Everywhere I heard the cry of "Centaurs, centaurs!" and then I saw the Amazons at last, urging their horses onward, throwing their flaming torches at the ships. I saw Hippolyte at their head, whooping as her horse sprang from ship to ship, and the ships' pavilions roofed with fire.

We drove a wedge through the mass of Akhaians. It was a rout. My charioteer took me straight onto the beach, and I saw Orestes, still surrounded by his bevy of madwomen, but he was no longer in the grip of Snakemother—he was in a state of panic as he urged his horses into the sea.

"Give chase!" I said, leaning out of the chariot to strike down an assailant, cutting his arm off at the elbow as he moaned like a hungry dog. The wicker of the chariot was punctured by arrows. I had only just noticed that my arm was bleeding profusely, that it must have been wounded some time earlier, for the gash was beginning to stink. But the battle madness had stolen all feeling from me. I felt invincible. We followed Orestes into the sea. A score of ships were on fire, and the air was pungent with charred wood and flesh and leather. Orestes had sprung from his chariot and was clawing his way up the side of an unburned vessel. The mask had come off and he was clutching it to his chest. A dozen other Akhaians were clambering on board too. But an Amazon leaped wildly from the next ship and was tossing them back into the sea with her thrusting spear. My sweat was hot and salty, and burned my eyes. I collided with the boat and half fell, half staggered out, wildly waving the sword at where I imagined Orestes to be. The tip of the sword struck flesh. I saw him clutch at his arm and scream as the brine scoured the open wound.

He had climbed on board. I shouted to warn the Amazon, but it was too late. He ran her through. The Akhaians she had been holding off jumped on. Some rushed for their oars; a few threw themselves upon the woman's warm corpse, whether to mutilate it or to perform enraged necrophily I do not know. I did not look or want to look. I heard Orestes shout at me, his voice muffled and metallic; I knew he had donned the deathmask once more.

"You think the Lady is so easily defeated?" he said. For a moment I thought he had spoken to me in the very voice of Snakemother. "I will return in forms infinitely more terrible. Do you think you can rout me with humans disguised as centaurs? I will answer your deceptions with real beasts, real monstrosities."

Water was rushing into my chariot car and the horses were nervous and would not obey, but broke loose from my driver's grip and started to gallop toward the shore, pulling in different directions. The charioteer gasped as an arrow whistled by and grazed his cheek, gouging a deep furrow of raw tissue. "My lord . . ." he said, trying hard to swallow his pain.

"There now," I said, as gently as I could amid the noise,
"we've done enough . . . we've defeated them . . . for a
time."

I looked out over the beach. Fighting was still going on,
mostly on foot. A heap of broken chariots burned in front of
the tents. At sea, a convoy of ships had detached itself from
the mass that was still flaming. I saw Orestes standing to one
side in his deathmask, and once more he was performing the
ritual of Snakemother. Was he trying to appease the sea? But
the sea-god is the brother of the sky. Surely Orestes knew
that. To my distress the fleet did not go north, but was
heading southwest, into the open sea, in the direction of the
island of Lesbos. What pact did they have with the people of
that island? Were there thousands more of them waiting
there? Was today's attack but another sample of what Memnon
called misdirection, a way of testing our true strength? Angry, I glared at the departing ships.

Riding toward the shore now came the Amazons. They
were shaking their weapons and rending the air with their
keening warcry, and their horses thundered on the water. On
the sand, the men were stripping the slain, piling the weapons and the armor up against the rocks. Some of the Hittites
emerged from the burning tents; they carried a woman, kicking and biting, and they threw her back and forth like a sack
of wheat. I knew she would get no mercy; I daresay she
deserved none, for she must have been one of my subjects
who had sought to curry favor with the would-be conquerors
by offering them her body. I forced myself to watch as the
men lined up to rape her. After all, I was the king; if I did
not have the stomach to countenance this rough justice, I had
no right to be king at all, and I would shame those who
called themselves my allies. My driver and I abandoned the
waterlogged chariot and waded to the dry land. Now that the
battle was more or less over, the boy had begun to chatter.

Presently Prince Anbar approached. The dwarf was with
him, capering up and down and jeering at the prisoners who
walked forlornly behind, their wrists bound with twine and
their bodies stooped and scarred. "My lord," the charioteer

cried out, "they are only children, all of them, and a few old men."

"Thus," squealed the dwarf, "do the Akhaians eke out their meager army!" He was throwing pebbles at them. One of them started to weep. She was only a girl, perhaps another of the villagers who had provided their previous night's entertainment. One of the Hittites cut her free and led her away to be raped to death.

"Only children!" I said to my stablehand. "But you are one yourself, and you don't seem to mind storming into the thick of battle."

"But, my lord, I serve the king," the boy pointed out.

He coyly looked at the ground, though, when the Hittites began slicing off their noses and tongues and ears and extremities and phalloi.

"So tenderhearted," the dwarf said.

"And why not?" I said hotly. "Such atrocities were not done in the last Trojan War. We were civilized then!" For the bards had not sung of children being sliced in half amid raucous laughter, or of the flocks of scavenger birds that were swooping down to pluck the eyes and other tidbits from the dead and the near-dead. They had rhapsodized, instead, of heroes and heroic exploits. Yet, I remembered how Akhilleus had dragged my father's corpse around the city walls. And I knew that even that great war, which had been declared over a point of honor and which had been waged, on the whole, with nobility and dignity, had eventually degenerated into pettiness and treachery . . . and the shameful deceit of the wooden horse. I could not contemplate these things without anger. I knew that I needed the anger so that the war would feel worthwhile, and so I reveled in it, wallowed in it, curled my lip and frowned. I had already decided, had I not, that this war was to be without honor? That it was to be a celebration of the coming of iron, harbinger of a new age of cruelty and darkness? "We have lost our innocence forever," I said, for myself alone. I did not weep for the child who had clasped the stone and sworn vengeance in the presence of Skyfather.

"We must have a feast," said Phoinix, who came toward

me in an Akhaian chariot, who wore a new, ill-fitting suit of armor. "Am I not splendid? I tore this armor off the body of one of the sons of Idomeneus!"

"No feast," I said. "They are coming back soon."

"But we burned their ships!" And he swept his arm over the sea in an extravagant gesture.

"Yes, we have burned about twenty of their ships," I said. "But the Akhaians have not gone home. They have gone . . ." I pointed. They were still visible—the ships, smudges of brown and white—halfway toward the horizon. One could hear, very faintly, the rhythmic splashing of their oars; and the confused beating of a hundred drummers pelted the eardrums like faraway rainfall. "They'll be back," I said grimly, "and sooner than we would like. We have to make ready for another onslaught. And this time they'll be prepared to be taken from behind."

That night I slept with Helen. I staggered myself with my own virility. For a few brief moments I was like a god. I did not consider Helen's feelings at all; they were no longer important.

They told me that many more had seen the star in the eye of the wooden horse; that its tail had grown longer; that the deathstar cast an eerie luminosity over the Trojan night. Still I saw nothing. I had rejected divinity, even that piece of divinity that is common to the lowest of humans.

Orestes' last words haunted me, night after night, day by day, as we labored to build wooden ramparts by the shore and to train more fighters for the next stage: "I will answer your deceptions with real beasts, real monstrosities."

I told myself: Without Skyfather's vision I will not be able to see any supernatural creatures he may unleash upon us. And if I do not see them, they cannot exist.

Chapter XLIX

The Pig Women

For several days we labored, felling trees in the foothills to build makeshift ramparts. I even set a watch by the Dardanian Gate, which faced our eastern supply lines. This was a sign of the new barbaric times, for during the first war the Akhaians had never sought to invade from the east, deeming it dishonorable to attack us from the rear. They had had honor almost until the end.

The Amazons prayed to the wooden horse. The Hittites prayed to their gods. My people invoked the name of Skyfather. I alone did not pray, but gave myself more and more into the dark madness that my love for Helen had become. I no longer cared whether she felt anything. One night, after a bout of lovemaking almost as brutal as the fighting between Trojan and Akhaian had been, she whispered to me, "When the magic is gone completely from the world, the forces of nature will be even as you and I were. The wind will not arise from a god's anger or from lust for the wild mares of the mountains. The sea will carry no messages from the brother of the sky. Do you know that? Instead they will have all the feelinglessness of our lovemaking; mountain, ocean, tree, sky will no longer be sentient things, but dead things, soulless. When I lost the power to understand the speech of the dolphins, as we crossed the ocean between worlds to reach this place, I wondered whether it was because I had relinquished my godhood, or whether it was that the dolphins had actually ceased to speak. Do you understand what I'm saying, Astyanax?"

"Only that you're endlessly vain to think that your decision to become human somehow triggered some power that robbed the animals of their powers of speech."

"I am not vain," Helen said. "Well, sometimes, when I paint my face to let the people imagine that their world has not collapsed entirely. But the truth is that I am the soul of this age, this Age of Bronze whose inhabitants are no longer godlike yet not entirely human; I am the center of their bewilderment. Did I decide to become human, or am I only the symbol, the living essence, of the world's decision? Understand me, Astyanax. Choose for me."

"No," I said coldly. I seized her. Outside, the wind of spring gusted and the dogs howled at the full moon. "I don't feel like trying to understand anymore."

"But that's what I mean," she said. "It's not that we've stopped understanding. It's that it's not there to be understood anymore. There was a time when I could feel the soul of a sword, when I could almost call the bronze by name and almost hear its answer. Do you think that once, in the Silver Age, men could speak to inanimate objects? They say that Skyfather made love to Danaë, the mother of Perseus builder of Mycenae, in the form of gold, glittering gold. Have you ever tried to make love to a shower of metal? Once, it seems, there was feeling even in metal, in stone."

"It's useless to meditate about such things," I said. "Even if it were true, it's not important anymore."

"And what is? Killing as many of them as possible—"

"Before they kill me?" I pricked my ears. I thought I heard something move in the room. For a moment I remembered how I had seen Death himself once. But that had only been my imagination. Of course.

"Do you hear something?" she said, sitting up in alarm. Moonlight on her face; golden hair mottled by shadow; a slight tremble of her upper lip. She was so pale and paler in the pale light. I felt a flash of . . . something aside from anger . . . but I pushed the feeling deep back down inside, for anger was all I needed now. She was listening now.

"Only the dogs," I said. "Go to sleep."

"No, listen. Listen." The howls were so soft and so subsumed in the sighing of the wind that they seemed almost like songs of distant whales. "There are voices. Voices."

"Oh, you and your voices. Don't tell me of voices, of visions. We've lost all our powers. I never had them anyway. And you—can you prove it wasn't all illusion?" I turned from her, not wanting to hear.

Quietly she whispered, "This is what I hear: women chanting in low voices. Not the wild screeching of the maenads: subdued. I think I can make out the words. They are 'piggy-fucker, piggy-fucker, piggy-fucker.' "

"Don't make fun of me!" I jumped. I started to call for Leonidas. His death still had no meaning for me. Instead, another slave came, one whose name I did not know. He carried a torch and stood in the doorway. He had put his chiton on backward. "Do you hear it?" I cried to him, anguished. In my mind I could hear the chant swell up as on the day they were going to bury me alive in the temple of Snakemother. . . .

"No, master!" He looked at me in alarm.

"I haven't gone mad," I said. Inwardly I laughed bitterly. I knew that were I truly mad he should be glad; for the mad make far more believable leaders of men, as witness Orestes. Only the mad have conviction, I told myself. I, who had become sane at last, knew that we had been nurtured on falsehoods and fired by illusions. "Piggy-fucker! Piggy-fucker!" I shouted wildly. I stopped. Was there not an echo from outside somewhere? Madness, madness!

"What, King?" Other voices in the corridor now. I had posted armed men in all the hallways since the Akhaians left, for I feared treachery. I heard someone say, "The king's raving." Another: "Fuck the king."

"Who said that? Have him beaten."

"Yes, King." He looked perplexedly about him. Perhaps it was I alone who heard the man speak.

"Piggy-fucker!" I screamed.

And it came! I stared furiously about me as the men who had piled into the chamber all stopped and listened. Helen, drawing a cloak decorously over herself, came to stand beside me. The chanting was quite audible now. "It's within the palace!'' I heard a voice, Phoinix's perhaps. "No," said someone else. "Outside. From . . . from the east.''

"The Dardanian Gate!'' I heard someone shriek out those words. At once another voice cried, "No, it's from the sea; I'm sure of it.'' A clamor broke out, hysterical, as I tried to push my way out of the room. And again I heard someone cry out, "The star of death—it's brighter now, its tail is slicing the night sky.'' Instinctively I turned to look, but saw nothing, as I knew I would.

I laughed. It was not mocking laughter; it was laughter devoid of any feeling, like the clatter of stone on stone.

Dark. Scuffling in the streets. I sent a runner down to the Amazons' camp and another to rouse the allied leaders who slept in the citadel. From the courtyard I looked up. Helen's face was in the window. Yes, it was bright. Surely it was more bright than the moon could make it. But I saw no deathstar. She smiled at me, a vacuous smile; I turned away and did not look back.

Men were assembling now. Were the Akhaians attacking from both sides? I had to decide. "Phoinix,'' I said, "you and Anbar had better go to the Skaian Gate with your followers. The Dardanian Gate will be easier to defend, since it's not as damaged.'' There was already fighting going on to the west. I could hear faint swordclashes, like rain against stone. And the shrill warcries of the women.

"Cowards!'' he said, spitting. "Always attacking by night. It's just as it was last time. We won't fall for it again.''

"It's bright enough to fight by,'' I said. "Come on. Archers,'' I added, "let the archers come with me.''

Stealthily we crept down the sloping street eastward. The city slept. We passed the horse; the Amazons had taken wheels from the chariots of the vanquished and attached them to it, and had burnished the copper of their tires, and in the moonlight they burned against the street striped by shadow. The word was being spread. Men and boys crept from the tumbledown warehouses where many had sought refuge from fear of siege. Our thin line of armed men became a host, cramming the narrow passages. The chanting of the pig worshipers was faint as though from a great distance, yet at the same time palpably close, as if an invisible sprite were whispering into my ears.

There had been steps with polished facings once, all the way down from the palace to the east portal. They were broken now. Roofless buildings leaned against the side of the hill. We had to climb down, hanging precariously on ledges, our shields tucked tightly in our armpits. We were quiet. The men sensed how close they were to death.

"The gate!" I said. It loomed up. The surrounding walls were not shattered, for in the first war the horse had been dragged in through the Skaian Gate, leaving the east entrance intact. But there was a vast amount of rubble from houses that had burned during the sacking and never been rebuilt. The rocks had piled up so that it was impossible to open the gate all the way; men could squeeze through one at a time. The parapet was still accessible; ledges, many wide enough for more than one man to stand on, hung out over chasms in the earth. I motioned for some of the archers to assume topmost positions. Others hugged whatever footholds they could and passed supplies up, hand to hand, quivers full of arrows and throwing spears. There were arrows tipped with iron, and other arrows dipped in pitch that we could ignite from braziers that were being set up on the ledges.

"There they are!" said someone softly. I looked up, re-membering . . . how I had stood as a small child with my head level with Hector's knees, squeezing myself into the gap between the crenellations. There had been so much sunlight then, had there not? And I had seen them, halfway across the plains, tiny men and tiny chariots, like segments of a golden centipede. What was there now? Tall grass, the thin blades silver-tinged black in the moonlight. Where the Akhaians once had stood there was . . . there was . . . I did see something! Something moving slowly toward us. A chain of shadowy things . . . Shields—that was what they were. They were hiding behind their shields; all I could see were shields.

They had painted them black and joined them, shield to shield to shield, as they shifted slowly toward the city.

"Wait until they come into range. Then fire," I said to the archers.

They stood, poised. In the background I heard the chant of the pig worshipers; it was not coming from the plain, but somewhere else entirely, perhaps high up in the air. Perhaps it was another illusion. The first priority was to destroy the wall of moving shields.

It was closer now. Closer. I could imagine the Akhaians hunched up behind them. They stopped. "Use the fire arrows!" I said. "Now!"

All at once a thousand points of fire whistled through the air. I looked out. It was like a rain of meteors. Shields caught fire; I caught a whiff of burning leather as the line was broken. The fire was spreading. I heard no outcries, no sounds of death. Something was wrong.

"Move out into the plain," I said, as the fire fanned out across the wall of shields—a wall of scorching yellow light now. I could hear the leather crackling. But never the sound of a man's dying.

"We are bewitched!" cried one of the archers.

"No!" I said. "Magic is dead!" And leaped down from the foothold where I stood, pulling out my sword of iron with its hilt shaped like a lion's paw. And led my men, screaming our war paean, beyond the Dardanian Gate into the field.

I saw what had happened. A shield, propped up by a staff, was almost consumed with fire. Others had toppled. The wind rose, whipping up the flames, making the smoke spiral upward. Through the fuming haze the moon was girt with circles of pearly iridescence. Another shield, tossed by the wind, rolled down the plain like a fiery wheel.

"They've tricked us," one of the men said.

All at once the air rang with the chant of the women of the Lady's island.

"To the Skaian Gate!" I screamed. The smoke seared my eyes, my nostrils. I was weeping from the stench.

We had no chariots, no horses. To go around the walls would waste time. So we turned back, some squeezing through the gates, others going over the wall with ropes, and made our way through the streets once more. The noises came louder and louder. I was angry at having tried to outsmart the enemy, angry at myself for not being in the thick of the fight at that very moment. We ran now, squashing and jostling in the streets, and more and more came to join us. They carried spears of ash and swords of iron and makeshift staffs and clubs. Many were not dressed, but had been roused by the shouting. The moon shone ever more brightly. We were drunk with the moonlight. We ran, as maniacal as the maenads.

At the Skaian Gate a battle was raging around the horse. Amazons were clustered around it, fighting off the Akhaians with their arrows. Darts of fire sang, their voices blended in unearthly harmony. As I reached the horse, I saw Hippolyte, who cried out, "They've stampeded the horses!" And I saw, on the plain, the horses of the Amazons in confusion, rearing and pawing the air, whinnying, riderless, and Akhaians in chariots driving them toward the sea with burning torches.

Maddened with rage, I ran straight at the enemy, not thinking about whether my men were behind me. Flames rose up before me. The heat blasted me. My anger took away all feeling from me, and I hurled myself at the wall of fire. I burst through, singeing my hair and my chiton. My shield smoked. In front of me stood Orestes. He was still wearing the mask of death. But this time the women he was talking to were flesh and blood. They looked at me. Their breasts were pale in the moonlight. Their skirts were elegantly flounced in the ancient fashion. I knew who they were.

I was standing in a circle of fire. And the women were priestesses of the island of the pigs. And they whispered, over and over, that incantation both absurd and menacing.

The noise of the battle faded. Now and then came a faint death rattle, a barely audible warcry, a tinkle of metal against metal. We seemed to be outside the war, outside the world itself.

I said, "Why have you lured me here, Orestes?"

When Orestes spoke, his voice was quiet and full of menace. "Remember what I told you. That next time I came I would bring real monsters. Not your imaginary centaurs, but true man-beasts. The moon is full, Astyanax. What is it that separates a man from an animal? The boundary is thin. In fact, it exists purely in the mind."

I had my sword in my hand and I thrust at him. He laughed. He hardly seemed substantial; I think that my weapon passed through him. Or perhaps he was not where I thought he was, for my eyes were smarting from the smoke. "Are you real?" I said.

He laughed. "Astyanax." For a moment it seemed that the features of the mask itself shifted, that the brow of beaten gold became furrowed, that the slits that were eyes shed tears of quicksilver. "Sometimes I know I am quite real, Astyanax. At times I'm certain I'm the only reality left in this metamorphosing world. Can you believe that?"

I said, "There's no point in discussing such things with a madman. Even the friendship we shared is meaningless now. You've abandoned yourself. No sacred bond is desecrated by my killing you."

Again he laughed. "I'm astounded to see in you such concern for the niceties of conduct, King of Troy!" he said. "You who stood by me while I killed my mother!"

"Do you blame me for the irony of your own fate?"

"No." He shrugged. "I have come only to unleash monsters."

He lifted his arms and swirled. He seemed to become a living whirlpool. At once the wall of silence broke and I was engulfed in the clamor of combat. Wildly I thrust at the air and the fire. The women continued their chanting. I was drowning in their harsh music as in a dark ocean. Again and again I sliced the emptiness with my iron. From behind the whorl of flame that was Orestes another man stepped. "Phalas!" I cried. "I should have known!"

"Yes, I the king and consort of the Lady." His single eye glowed. Pus oozed from the vacant socket of his other eye. "You thought you were rid of me, didn't you? I have come now. And you will see the power of the Lady. I will have you yet for the guardian warrior buried beneath the threshold of the Lady's temple! Listen, King of Troy! The power of your Skyfather is the power of naming. You have named everything in the world, and you imagine that naming is power. But the Queen of Heaven has the power to take away names, and to confuse them. Your god is the god that says, 'I am,' and thus *is*; but the Lady *is* without saying, 'I am.' With your god, some things are true and others false; but with the Lady, all things are true and false at the same time. And lo, the moon is full, and the Lady's powers are at their fullest; so when I change you will understand that it is no illusion.''

As he spoke he had already begun to change. Tusks were jutting from his jaws, and his nose was lengthening into a snout. A musky, animal odor emanated from him. I could still hear the priestesses chanting, but I could not see them. Orestes had become one with the circle of fire, and that too was dissolving into the thin dark air. Brown hairs were erupting from Phalas's arms and chest. He was collapsing, becoming squat. "Now you will see what this silly 'piggy-fucker' chant is really all about!" he rasped. The last few words were not even human, but barked out. I was afraid. Childishly, instinctively, I made signs of aversion. Then I backed away, uphill, for the flames had gone. The boar reared up, its bristles glistening, silver on black. It roared. Answering roars came from all over the hill. And the chant went on. I raised my sword. The boar was poised to leap. I dodged. My sword grazed something. Then the boar was upon me, knocking my sword out of my hand. I rolled on the grass. A sharp splinter jabbed into my shoulder. I howled with pain. The boar butted metal—a shield that lay on the grass. I found the sword and slashed. Blood fountained up, hitting me in the mouth and eyes. The blood was black and oily in the moonlight. The boar turned on me and with a growl made for higher ground, where the Amazons were still fighting off the Akhaians, backed against the wooden horse.

I was slipping in blood as I climbed. But the boar ran

easily. As I watched, the Akhaians above were also being transformed. Was it a trick of the brilliant moonlight, making me lose my hold on what was real? The boar's blood mingled with mine flowed down my face, and I saw what happened next through a wine-colored mist: a crowd of boars rushing at the women, tearing into them, pushing them to the ground, raping them, and devouring them alive.

I ran, despairing.

I saw Phoinix and Leukippos ahead. Back to back, they were fending off the angry animals. I was suffocating in the smell of human guts and animal excrement. I rammed my sword into the side of one. It squealed and began to change back into human shape as it died. "Phoinix!" I shouted. My kinsman had been unable to hold his bladder. His legs were covered with piss. He and Leukippos were hacking desperately at the wild pigs.

As I managed to reach them, the boars broke away and made for the Amazons, who were being slaughtered as they clung to the wooden horse. More pigs were charging up the hill, intestines wreathed about their snouts, trampling over corpses and weapons, their paean a hideous gurgling.

"We're being beaten—by an army of pigs!" Leukippos wailed, overcome by the ignominy of it.

"Honor . . ." Phoinix clutched a gaping wound in his abdomen where a boar had mauled him.

"They're going to break into the city," Leukippos said. "The Hittites can hold out against any mortal men, but not monsters, not infernal beasts of Snakemother . . . No, no." Unselfconsciously, pathetically, he began to weep.

"Do what you can to delay it," I said. "I'm going up to the citadel. For Helen."

I left them then. I scrambled past the horse. Women's bodies were piled up against the wheels, and the boars were gnawing, rending, violating the corpses. I saw Hippolyte pressed against the flank of the horse, flailing at a boar that was shifting to human shape. I watched for a moment, hoping that she had killed it. But it was stabbing savagely into her vagina with its tusks, and her face was contorted with pain. I remembered how I had seen Leontes' mother raped against a stone lion so many years ago.

I tore myself away. Soon Hippolyte would be beyond pain.

At the gate I shouted my name. I climbed in through the guardsmen's hatch. The streets were crowded. Few noticed their king. The populace was streaming toward the gates of the city. I could hear the ululating of lamenting wives and the bawling of infants from every doorway. Some, seeing the glint of the sword, fled from me. I elbowed my way uphill. And came upon the temple of Skyfather.

From the entrance I could see that the altar was lit. I was glad that the proprieties had been observed, even though I had not come here since I had lost my trust in the power of the gods.

I stood, in my warlike dress, inside the temple hall, still open to the elements. I saw Helen.

She came to me. We kissed, a feelingless, comfortless kiss. In my arms she seemed a stone. For the first time I realized that it was because I had been treating her so these past months. She was, as she always said, what men saw in her. Her face was haggard; the kohl around her eyes had been smudged by tears and sweat. She smiled at me, a vacuous smile.

I said, "We're going to lose the war, and the whole world is going to be swallowed up in darkness."

She said, "Is that what you've come to tell me?"

"No." I strode toward the stone of Skyfather. A beam of moonlight illumined it while Helen and I stood in the shadows cast by the pillars in the firelight. I cried out, "Why must it be this way? If this destiny was shaped by the gods, then the gods understand nothing and care nothing."

"Yes," Helen said.

I did not know whether she agreed with me, or whether she was answering some altogether different question. I shouted again, "Let there be magic! Let time be turned back and the course of the war reversed! Let my ancestor heroes return from the dead lands and fight themselves!"

Helen looked at me, uncertain.

The fire on the altar rose. My heart almost stopped beating. "Hermes?" I whispered.

It was another's voice that answered, a rich, deep voice that could belong only to one man. "What you ask is not impossible," the voice said. "But you must want it very badly."

I whirled around.

"Memnon!" For that was who it was. The litterbearers' blue torsos glistened as they knelt down so that the mage could look me in the eye. He had lost none of his arrogance of demeanor. He wore an Egyptian wig of heavy cloth of gold. About his loins was wrapped a linen kilt whose clasp was an emblem of mating lions. I said, "I thought you were gone forever."

"The universe is a circle," the magician said.

Helen said, "All of us will be gathered here, in one place, all the protagonists in this story. I foresaw it long ago, when I was still blessed with the gift of true sight." Wondering, I looked at her.

Memnon said, "You said, 'Let the dead heroes return and fight beside us.' Is that not what you said?"

"Yes!" I screamed. "I've failed to do it alone, I've failed my oath."

"And what could you give me, if I were to undertake to bring them back?"

"Anything! Anything!"

"Now, listen to me, little king, and listen most carefully." He motioned his bearers to bring him closer. He looked down at me. His eyes and teeth shone in the moonlight. I hid my trepidation and did not back away. "You offer me this 'anything' of your own free will, do you not?" He transfixed me with his glittering eyes.

"Of course I do!" I shouted over the screams of the dying.

"You must say, 'I do it of my own free will,' " said the sorcerer.

"I do it of my own free will."

Memnon smiled.

I knew that smile. It was the smile that Helen could no

longer smile. It was the smile of the gods, who do not have compassion, and who alone can kill without feeling. The smile faded. But I knew I had not imagined it.

He said: "Good. I have never concealed from you, Astyanax, that it was an ulterior motive that impelled me to serve you with my magic. Since I have known you, little king, I have waited for those words to come uncoerced from your lips. They are the words that have been destined from the beginning, the words that will destroy the old universe and set the new in motion."

"But I meant no such—"

Too late. I remembered now how Memnon had told me the tale of the zumbi, the first night he was in Troy. I remembered how he had brought Leonidas back from the dead, how the boy had come to life unchanged, yet not the same.

"So be it," I said.

Chapter L

The Return of the Mage

In bewilderment I looked from the mage to the woman. Wildly I imagined the victim of their evil collusion. "My own free will," I said again. But I knew I could not retract those words. The wheel had been set in motion. "How did you come here? And where is your king, your lord A-a-a-a—" I could almost utter the name. The magic was weakening.

"I have been here all this time," Memnon said. "Why, did you see me leave?"

I had not. "And yet—"

"Misdirection." He shrugged. "But to answer the second part of your question, my king and lord, look, over the citadel, far away, toward the Skamander. Do you think that the moon alone is reason for this unnatural brightness in the air?"

I went out through a gap between two smashed stone columns. I saw the light, to the southeast of the city. The Dardanian Gate was bathed in it. Beyond, across the river, was the necropolis. There, as we all knew, was a path to the world below; for once I had stood in the labyrinth of Snakemother, holding on to our world only by a thread from Leonidas's chiton. "You have brought the ship upstream?" I said. "It floats in the river by the city of death?" Already Memnon's reasoning was becoming clear to me.

"I suppose," Memnon said, "that I should confess that I have not always told you the whole truth. But you knew all along that I serve the king whose name cannot be spoken, and that my master's greatest wish is to end his voyage forever."

"To die."

"Yes, if that is what you want to call it."

I laughed.

"Listen, King, and understand my master's injunction to me. The name of my king has been erased from all the monuments of Egypt; that is why his name cannot be uttered, why he cannot enter the dead lands. To free him we must annul that magic."

"But the magic of names is the strongest magic in the world," I said.

"Yet magic disintegrates," said the mage. "Did you think that this earth, with its gods and men, is eternal? Did you think that Skyfather, having displaced the Lady from the high place and sent her into the bowels of the earth, will be enthroned forever? Ah, no. The words that will cause the end of all things were ordained at their beginning, little king, and you have uttered them; you, the littlest and last of Great Kings, have wielded the mightiest power in the universe."

"And all unwitting," said Helen, almost whispering.

"Yes," Memnon said. "The world-destroyer must be innocent of foreknowledge; that too is preordained. But we must proceed to the waking of the dead."

I said, "But what's the purpose of this for you? And why did I have to ask you to do it?"

The mage said, "When all names shall cease to have the power of binding, then the dead return. But—if the dead walk, could not the walking die? The moment I create shall be the crack in the seam of time through which King A-a-a- will slip to freedom and to death. It was forbidden to me to work for my master's salvation of my own volition. But the calling up of the dead heroes is an inviolable command which you, Sacred King, have laid upon me. For I am but a magician, and I exist only to serve kings."

"You serve yourself by serving me!" I said, disillusioned.

Memnon inclined his head in a smirking obeisance. Despairing, I turned to Helen. As we looked at each other, it began to rain. "The altar!" I said. The fire sputtered.

"Hurry," said Memnon. "Soon the earth will be soaked. They'll be slipping and sliding in mud and blood, your armies, while the pigs wallow in their own element and rampage through the city itself. Do you think the gates will hold all night?"

"What must I do?" I cried.

"Sacrifices . . . sacrifices, and . . . yes, you will have to die once more." Another ritual death then. I had rehearsed my passage through the gates of death so often I could not help thinking that my real death would be a letdown.

"Don't come with me," I said to Helen, kissing her. "Go to the megaron. Sit there enthroned. Surround yourself with handmaidens. Array yourself in the most splendid vestments in the treasury."

"We should be together," she said. And drew me toward her with her gaze. But we both knew that we had our roles to play.

"If the end should come," I said, "and the Akhaians should reach the palace, they will come upon you, a queen, proud and beautiful, and not"—emotion choked my voice—"a suppliant clasping the knees of a stone image, begging compassion of the gods. Feel no terror, for the Akhaians will feel no pity."

"I will in all things do what is seemly, my husband and my king," Helen said, her voice very small. I embraced her.

In those brief moments I rediscovered my love for her. It burned me like the thirst of a dying man in a desert. Our lips touched in the rain—her fragrance all but drenched in the downpour—but already Memnon was urging me to leave.

We slipped out by the Dardanian Gate. There were a handful of women with us, robed as mourners; among them came Dione, who had once come to the necropolis with me disguised as my bride. There came also two priests, and sacrificial animals: goats tethered to the well in the central square, doves we had been saving for important funeral rites, a heifer we found loose in the megaron, nervously butting her head again and again into a column.

Just outside the gates stood several chariots of Egyptian design; by this I knew that Memnon had already presumed what my response would be. Never had I felt more manipulated. Mud clogged our chariot wheels; there was a delay while the charioteers, all blue men, quirted the asses until they pulled the cars loose. Memnon's litter was placed in an oxcart. We passed the wall of shields, smoldering in the rain.

Almost instantly we reached the riverbank; Memnon had not lost his knack for unorthodox travel. The ship of the sun nested against the far bank of Skamander. The sun-disk atop its mast still glowed, but more dimly than before. The shower of glittering ankhs was more of a drizzle. But the ship still cast a perfect circle of light around it, and when we stepped into the circle the rain ceased and the screams of the dying no longer reached us across the Phrygian plain. The light played over crushed grass and crumbling monuments and the mouths of desecrated graves.

I waded to the boat while the women began their lamentations. I left Memnon on the bank, but when I climbed into the ship he was already there, and the king himself, whose name I now remembered, sat beneath the awning on the deck. The throne was gold and bore a relief of the sun, and beneath it a pair of arms outstretched to receive its warmth and radiance. The king moved jerkily in his mummy wrappings, lifting his hand in benediction as his servitors fell prostrate before him. I alone did not kneel, for I too was a Great King and his brother by destiny.

"Embrace me, my son, my salvation," said King Akhenaten. I went forward. The bandages were stiff as stone, and beneath them I felt no heartbeat. He was covered from head to toe with ornaments of gold and lapis lazuli, jasper and faience and whitest ivory.

"First," said Memnon, climbing down from his litter, "we will bring down the sun." He gave a gruff command to one of his servants. The blue man ran to the mast and climbed to the top with abrupt, mechanical movements. He grasped the sun-disk and put it under his arm. The circle of light became dimmer; its shape, distorted.

"Bring it to me," he said. "Hurry!" The blue man came forward. "I said faster!" As the man reached us and prostrated himself, Memnon struck him furiously with his flail. The man splintered as he touched the deck; all that remained was the sun-disk, an ember in a heap of potshards.

"Hold up the disk," Memnon said to me. "Look at it carefully."

I did so. "I see a bronze disk with characters inscribed in a spiral," I said. "The figures make no sense to me; they're in the old tongue, the tongue—"

"Of Snakemother, you were going to say." He took the disk from me. "Ah, but this disk contains the spell that gave the sky and the sun dominion over the earth and moon; it is the very essence of the Bronze Age. That is, if you start at its center and read it outward, syllable by syllable, until you reach the edge. It is the very name of the idea that to name is magical. Do you understand that? But to read the syllables in the opposite direction—"

"It would take away the idea of naming from the universe! And render up the cosmos to eternal chaos!"

"Eternal! That word again! Oh, you make me laugh, you children of dust and clay, whose lives are over in a moment, with your obsession with eternity. What futile fantasy."

"In the future names will be just air and nothing more?" I said.

Memnon said, "I think you understand now how we are to enter the underworld and bring back the ancient heroes?"

I knew. The knowledge numbed me. But I was bound by my word, the word of a king . . . though the act I was about to perform would take away forever the sacredness of the king's word.

I grasped the hand of the mummy. I turned to the bank and saw that the women were wailing and that the priests had begun to slaughter the animals. Blood was running into the water. "The powers that reside in the earth are distracted," Memnon said. "Quick, now!" I squeezed the dead man's hand. It was cold, searing cold. I wanted to snatch mine away but there was no time to lose.

"Your name is Akhenaten," I said. "Your name is Akhenaten."

"Step from the boat," the mage said. He raised the sun-disk aloft.

"Your name is Akhenaten." I pulled the king forward. His dead weight gave me no help. I pried him firmly from his throne. "Akhenaten," I repeated. I could not let the name slip from me, I could not . . .

"The magic cannot stop it from being spoken anymore!" Memnon cried. He had already begun to recite the spell backward, syllable by syllable, all nonsense to my ears: "GLA—BRA—ZE—KAI—RHOI . . ." Already he was getting into his litter.

"We haven't yet left the ship!" I said, fearful of forgetting the name when we left the waning circle. I resumed my chanting as we reached the prow. Blue men leaped into the water and crouched down, their faces in the water—of course they did not need to breathe—making a bridge of glazed backs that spanned the river toward the necropolis. I pulled the king down with me, though he seemed to become heavier and heavier as less of him remained in the ship. "A-a-a-a-a-" I chanted.

"Don't lose your resolve! The magic has no power!" the mage shouted after me, beating his litterbearers with his flail, urging them to follow us into the water.

"Akhenaten!" I managed to blurt out. The circle of light was fracturing in a thousand places. When I looked up, the moon seemed to be weeping blood. "Akhenaten!" I screamed. The river seethed, the river itself was blood, the blood of my butchered people. "Akhenaten!" The frothing water shattered the circle of light, but Memnon continued with his spell.

When we reached the water's edge he jumped down from his litter. His face was frenzied; his eyes seemed to bulge from their sockets; he was sweating.

"Your feet touch the ground once more!" I said, remembering how he had worked the magic on the island of the pigs by giving up a part of himself.

"What does it matter?" he said. "I celebrate the end, I rejoice!" And he stooped to kiss the rain-splashed earth before urging us onward.

Once more I was at the edge of the pit where I had once gone to try the might of Snakemother. As the circle dissolved the rain lashed at us. Rocks cascaded down from open tombs. The wind roared; over the wind came the sounds of the battle, frighteningly close. What am I doing here? I thought. I should be out there, dying, with my people. I gripped the mummy's hand tighter and continued to cry his name. At first I could utter it only with difficulty. But as I went on, the name came easily from my lips; truly it seemed to have lost its meaning. "Down into the chasm," Memnon said, "don't falter!" Rain was running down my face, flooding away the drying blood. The mummy's body bounced against the steps. The women continued their lamentation, their voices sweet against the rain's percussive pelting. Farther and farther we descended. Surely the steps had not led so far into the earth before. I let go the hand. At once his arms closed tight around my neck, as though I were pulling the drowning heretic from the sea.

I do not remember when I ceased to feel the rain. But there came a moment when I knew we were no longer in the world above. The sounds of grief, of war, even of the driving rain, were cut off. Instead we were surrounded by gray. It was how I imagined our world would be like when the color was drained from it completely. There was no sky. Mist swirled; here and there a tree, denuded and black, emerged out of the gray. At first I was conscious of no noise. But there came a sound like the stridulating of locusts. It was the gibbering of the dead. For here and there the fog formed a shape like a contorted human face before it swirled away. Somewhere I heard water lapping against a shore.

"Good," Memnon said. "So far they haven't stopped us. Now, what is the king's name?"

"Akhenaten."

"Good, very good." He paused. "It all seems to be working very well." He was not addressing me but the king his master.

Akhenaten said, releasing me from his strangling grip, "Thank you, Astyanax."

He embraced me for the last time. He was no longer stonelike, but frail, light, like a child. He straightened himself, and allowed Memnon to rearrange his wig, his pectoral ornaments, the many amulets he was hung with. "One must keep up appearances," he said, "even in the final judgment."

And Memnon said, "Now you, little king, must face the Lady herself, here in her place of exile."

He threw me the sun-disk, which had ceased to glow completely. I caught it, not knowing why he had thrust it at me. Anguished, I cried out, "Is this the world of the afterlife? Is this what will come to us after all that we dream for, hope for, strive for?"

The pharaoh said, "Courage, my son and brother king. You do not see yet with the eyes of the dead. What I see here is quite different. And yes, it is what I have longed for."

For a long time I stared at the emptiness. I saw more and more now, for death was seeping into me. The gray was filled with insubstantial people. Now and then I thought I saw someone I knew. Was that not Leontes? I cried his name. I thought I heard him answer me, "My lord, you are here before your time; go back, go back before you are doomed to stay. . . ."

And there . . . Was that not my grandfather and grandmother, sitting, sunken, shrunken, in their thrones of mist? Could they not see me?

And the void parted to reveal a throne whose arms were the paws of lions, and whose sides were their flanks, and whose back was the heads of two lions facing one another. And on the throne sat a woman who was Helen and not Helen. Sometimes she had only one eye, and a serpent writhed in the empty socket. Sometimes she was my mother in the throes of her madness. Sometimes she was Clytaemnestra, the mother of Orestes, her eyes blazing as she brought the two-headed axe crashing down again and again into the body of the man she thought to be a slave. And also she was the three goddesses who were as one. And she was the Pythoness who had first caused me to question the order of the cosmos. But I knew her by another name too: Persephone, Queen of Death, the most dreadful and puissant form of the Mistress of Darkness, she who had once ruled the universe before Skyfather banished her to the gray country.

I stood before her, uncertain and afraid.

I turned for support to the pharaoh and the mage, but they had vanished while I looked away.

Chapter LI

The Dead

"Come forward, my young king," said the Queen of the Dead, and flames spurted from her lips when she spoke. I moved toward the throne. Handmaidens hovered about her. Their faces were skulls and their hands, protruding from shroudlike robes, were the hands of skeletons. "Don't be afraid."

I moved forward. I did not answer her. But I could not

help thinking: My ancestor the sky has never appeared to me, and yet this one, his mortal enemy, has done so. . . .

She said, "Would you like some food?" A skeletal slave knelt before me with a tray. "Perhaps a pomegranate?" I recoiled. "Ah, but you know better than to fall for that old trick!" She laughed. I did not expect such laughter—the giggle of a young girl caught in some prank. "But, Astyanax," she continued, "I already know the favor you will ask me."

Still I did not speak to her, and I avoided her gaze, for I had heard that Snakemother could send her venom directly into a man's eyes. Then I heard, "You're still angry at me, aren't you, for not being able to tell you from Leontes when he lay dead on your father's shield."

"Mother!" I screamed, and rushed at her. I caught a glimpse of the face of young Andromache, just as I remembered it from that day on the ramparts of the city . . . but the face was already melding into the face of the Mistress of Darkness.

She laughed again. I expected a witch's cackle, but her laughter was without malice. "Poor Astyanax. Forgive me. I am old, old, old; you have just relieved me of my old age. You unmade the spell of naming; you unfastened the bonds of the cosmos. Soon even I will be no more. But come, I know your request before you ask it. And I grant it, insofar as I am able. For a while yet, before it all disintegrates, I may have some little power in me. And I cannot refuse what you ask, for you carry the disk of the sun on which is written the beginning and the ending."

I prostrated myself, for though she was the hated one, the enemy of my ancestor, yet she was still a goddess. Though her form had become monstrous, there was majesty in her. And I knew now that the antipathy between Skyfather and Snakemother was not entirely of their choosing; it was the very substance of our universe. "Yet, my son," Persephone said, "you no longer believe in magic. . . ."

"I have seen, Queen, the magic pass away from the holiest objects."

"And yet your judgment is perhaps premature?"

"Memnon and the pharaoh—"

"Instruments, nothing more. They have been admitted into
the dark country; they no longer concern you, High King of
the Trojans. But for now"—she rose from her throne and
touched my cheek, lifted up my head—"we shall celebrate
the coming of the end." At last I looked into her eyes, and
she said, "For I too am Helen," and I saw that Helen's
cast-off divinity reposed in the eyes of the Goddess of Death. I
was terribly afraid. But I fell into her chill embrace, and felt
her hands caress me, clammy and oozing coagulating blood,
and kissed her lips that were mere rags of flesh strung upon
bone. And she cried, "You do not know what you ask, for
without their names, what are the ancient heroes but dust and
maggots? Yet I will give them a semblance of life." And all
the while we made love. And I answered, "I've given my
word. It is set in motion. I can't go back." And we made
love among the serpents, on the steps encrusted with blood.
As our bodies came together, flesh grew over her bones. At
first her face was withered and her hair white, and I knew her
as Hecabe, my grandmother. Then her cheeks filled, new
blood rushed to them, and I saw that she was my mother
Andromache; but I felt no horror at this incest, for the laws
of the universe were being wiped away, like scratchings on
wet clay left out in the rain. At last I saw that she had the
face of Helen. And I crushed her hard to me, no longer in
cold anger but with all the passion that I had first felt when
we first made love in Sparta, and she cried out again and
again, a joyous shout that seemed to rive the very mists that
shrouded us.

And when we were done and she returned to her throne, I
saw her shining, resplendent, beautiful.

I fell prostrate once more, for though I had made love with
her I knew that I did not and never could possess her.

She said, "Return now to the world, before the gray takes
hold of you forever. Your sacred ancestors will follow you.
But you must not look back at them until you have reached
the top of the abyss. And remember that they are no longer

bound by names, and that what you will see will be as much dictated by what is in your heart as by what they really are."

"I accept the conditions." What else could I do?

The throne and Persephone blurred; their images drained into mist. Behind them was a winding uphill path, as though to the citadel of a great city. Behind me I heard the rustle of distant chariots . . . the hot wind of their approach. My heart lifted. I dared not look back.

I held the sun-disk in both hands as though it were a torch to illumine the way to the land of the living, and I ascended. I heard once more the voice of Persephone, clear through the dissipating mist, "Remember never to look back. You have already seen much, child of dust; you will see much more, too much perhaps, in the last moments when the world is devoured by fire."

"Master, master . . ." A child's voice. "Master, it's me, Leontes."

I hardened my heart and walked on. The air became light as I neared the surface.

Again, more faintly now, I heard the voice of the goddess: "Do not strip away the illusions of the others."

I continued. At last, hearing the voice of Hector calling to my mother, I was tempted. I gripped the disk so tightly that the incised characters cut into my palms. For I well knew the story of Orpheus, who had faltered at the brink of the gateway, and lost Euridice a second time.

The faraway clatter of chariots became a rumbling. I heard the pounding of the man-tall body shields against firm earth. Still I looked only ahead, at the steps of the subterranean citadel, passing through gateway after gateway guarded by lions of basalt and sphinxes of marble. Though I was still walking in a tunnel, I saw fleeting vistas of ancient worlds before our own, worlds with primordial beasts and shining limestone-faced ziggurats, of cave dwellers worshiping the Lady and warring with unwieldy weapons of flint and bone. For the fabric of time had become unpinned.

Presently I saw the surface up ahead. When I emerged, there was a crowd of people gathered at the riverbank. The women broke off their mourning cries when they saw me return. A man sprang from his chariot and hastened to embrace me, shouting, "Brother, brother, I've come—"

"Pergamos." How tall he was now. "Whose side have you come to fight on?"

"Oh, Astyanax, I haven't come to fight. But I couldn't stay in Phthia, sitting in the grand hall listening to the grandiloquent verses of the couriers with their news mixed with hearsay. I had to come. The fighting is terrible. I passed it by and came upriver, seeing the light at the necropolis." He stood before me. The rosy dawn illumined his fresh features and made his bronze helmet glow. I had seen him first a frightened boy and then an adolescent bitter over lost innocence. Now he was beautiful and strong. I was full of pride that he had sprung from the loins of Andromache; I had long forgiven him, that his grandfather had killed my father and his father my grandfather.

I said, "You are welcome, brother." Emotion stopped me from saying more.

Then it was that Pergamos cried out, "Look! Across the river! Gathered upon the plain!" I did not dare look, for I still feared Persephone's injunction. Instead I listened to Pergamos: "They are standing there . . . hundreds upon hundreds of them . . . ancient heroes with glittering panoplies. Their chariot wheels are aflame in the dawn light. Oh, Astyanax, is this the miracle you've wrought by harrowing hell?"

The chariot thunder burst at last upon my senses. I looked over the water. Pergamos's men were already fording the river, shouting with joy. But I saw no hosts of glory.

No. I saw dead men with empty eyes. I clutched at Pergamos, but he was outstripping me, dashing across the water like a young deer, running toward the dead men. Yes, they were the ancient heroes all right. But they had been separated from their names, and they were only earth . . . animated skeletons, corpses ridden with maggots. The stench of them was in the air. "Pergamos, don't . . ." I called after him. But I remembered the command of the Queen of Death:

"What you will see will be . . . dictated by what is in your heart. . . . Do not strip away the illusions of the others." I saw what might have been my father, staring vacantly and wielding a broken spear. His body was a mass of congealed blood. I saw the wounds Akhilleus had inflicted on him. He could not speak, but the wind whistled through his corpse as through a limestone cavern.

And Pergamos said, "Look . . . it is the shade of your father, Hector, bold and magnificent in his armor. His shield is so bright it hurts my eyes," and tears of joy were spurting down his cheeks. He was blinded by splendor I could not see.

For I was not innocent: I knew that the world was ending; I understood illusion to the core.

The others too were crying out: "The shade of Hector has returned at the head of the hosts of Priam . . . to lead us to victory."

Persephone did not need to warn me! How could I bear to tear down those glorious illusions? I myself had been sustained by them all through my childhood . . . until the world grew too confusing to hide in. "Zumbi," I whispered, knowing full well what I had brought up from the ground. "Zumbi." But no one heard me. Already the chariots were racing toward the city, toward the sunrise.

We reached the hill of Troy. The whole city rose from a bed of fire. The earth was so soggy and piled high with corpses that we had to abandon our chariots and fight our way up on foot. Amazons were sprawled in the mud, having their entrails devoured by the wild pigs.

The army of dead men charged the hill. Pergamos said, "Look, look . . . there's Deiphobos, there's your uncle Paris with his golden bow, there's Troilos, Helenos, all your uncles . . ." But I saw only rotten corpses shambling, staggering, flailing at the wild pigs and the humans, who were fleeing in terror. "They seem almost immortal!" Pergamos cried. "They take blow after blow and don't turn back;

there's no fear in their eyes at all!'' But I saw that they could not be killed because they were dead already.

Side by side, my brother and I ran uphill, tripping often over the dead, hacking at anything that came close. I did not know or care if they were allies or enemies. It made no difference anymore. From the parapet above there came shouts of triumph. Was I the only one who saw the dead men as they really were? Was I the madman, was I another Orestes? But I had brought them here. . . .

We ran through fire now, through the smoke of charred flesh, through black pools of boiling blood. A horse was being disemboweled by a pack of angry boars. But corpses swooped down on them and began to rend them limb from limb. Pergamos gave an exultant shout. I looked away. His elation was such that he did not notice my pain.

We reached the Skaian Gate. We pounded at it with our fists. It was opened enough for us to squeeze through. The Hittites were there. Leukippos lay wounded in the front courtyard. His left arm had been ripped away. Phoinix hovered over him. The heat from the burning fields blasted our faces. Akhaians were surging at us, but the zumbi warriors were seizing them and tearing them to pieces. None of the Hittites seemed to see what they really were. Prince Anbar shouted at me, "Astyanax, you've brought reinforcements, wonderful reinforcements!" and I greeted him by his true name for the first time: "Hail, Suppiliulimas, who will be King of Hattusas to come!"

When he heard this he knew that the spell had been broken. And his face darkened. Perhaps he was beginning to see what the glorious heroes really were. But he, too, kept his knowledge to himself, for he saw the longing in his warriors' faces, and knew that they dreamed of things that could be no more.

I saw one of the corpses—perhaps my father—seize the Phoenician Phalas and hold his struggling body in the air and throw it down on the stones of the street. His face was only part human. The boar's tusks jutted from all too human jowls. I was glad of his death, for he had caused me much grief, and he had never attained the stature of a hero.

I saw another corpse on fire, still marching inexorably forward until he was a charred skeleton, collapsing at last. So they *could* be stopped, if they were destroyed by fire, if there was nothing left to go on.

"Come. Let's watch the battle from the ramparts of the city." We raced to the palace through streets already jammed with singing women and dancing children. Victory was in the wind. It infected the others; they ran in a frenzy of joy. Only I saw otherwise, and perhaps Prince Suppiliulimas.

We reached the outer courtyard. People were already streaming in. They parted when they saw me coming. I ran to the parapet, Pergamos beside me cheering like a small boy.

"What do you see?" I shouted into the wind, as we looked to the west. There was blood even here, trickling along cracks in the flagstones, reddening the moss; it seemed that the stone itself was bleeding. Beyond the inner city, houses were burning.

"The heroes have taken the tents of the enemy by storm," Pergamos said. "They're burning the ships; all the ships are burning on the water—I can see the flames on the horizon. Look now! Their chariots have made it through the mud, and they're crashing into a wall of Akhaian body shields! Look! Hector has speared two enemies with a single thrust! Paris is shooting arrow after arrow into the army of pigs! Watch them squirm, watch them die in their own vomit!"

The Hittite and I looked at one another. I was convinced now that he saw what I saw.

"Fetch the queen," I said to one of the men.

"They're smashing down the gates!" someone cried. "Why?"

Pergamos said, frightened suddenly, "Astyanax, I could have sworn I saw . . . something else . . . just for a tiny moment. . . ."

Illusion, mirror of our dreams, was cracking.

Another man said, "Horrible . . . I saw . . . a walking corpse wielding a broken axe. . . ."

"They're not stopping with the Akhaians!" Pergamos said. "They're trying to storm the inner city!"

Of course they were. These walking pieces of earth had no Trojan identity, though their names might once have been Hector and Paris and Deiphobos and Helenos.

It was then that the pounding began. Each crash came like a peal of thunder. We looked at each other. "They're going to enter the city!" Pergamos said. "We're lost, we're lost."

Voices came from the crowd. A runner, panting, had sprinted up from the gates. "They're putting everyone to death, indiscriminately. They're monsters, hellish monsters in broad daylight!"

"They're massed at the gates; it's only a matter of time before they burst through," said a warrior.

"Nothing will kill them!" someone else shouted.

"Fire will," I said softly.

"And the end of the Age of Bronze will come in fire," said the Prince of the Hittites, echoing his father's dream.

And then I knew what would have to be done. It came to me all at once. The idea was so beautiful that I had to stop to catch my breath. The Fates had brought all of us to this place to witness the ending, but it had fallen to me to give the final order.

"Where is the queen?" I said at last. The sun was high in the sky, and the sounds of joy from the city and the fields were already being transformed into cries of bafflement and terror.

"Here," said Helen.

And the crowd parted and she stepped forward. So beautiful did she seem to them that they fell to the pavement and worshiped her. But I saw only my aunt Helen. As she came forward four girls—her handmaidens—ran ahead of her, strewing the bloodstained parapet with flower petals.

"You're radiant, you're overwhelming," Pergamos said. He rushed forward like a puppy and kissed her on the cheek. Did he see in her the same awesome magic that I had seen at first? But it was no longer there for me.

"Rejoice," she said, greeting me.

"Rejoice," I said.

"You have summoned me from the palace, where I sat waiting, enthroned."

"I know who you are now," I said.

"Yes."

"You are Zeus's daughter, but your mother was the earth."

"I am a child of earth and starry heaven."

We embraced formally, as noble kinsmen embrace. "The tragedy is almost over," I said. Resolutely I turned away from the ramparts. "Come. We must go now to the wooden horse."

Curiosity was in their faces now. But, stony-faced, I led my people down to where the slaughter was raging.

Chapter LII

The Conciliator of Dreams

I called for silence, though the Skaian Gate resounded with the pounding of the dead men and the screams of the dying. We stood in front of the wooden horse: I, Pergamos, Helen, Prince Suppiliulimas, and a small gathering of vassals and curious townsmen. I was no longer afraid.

"Fire will stop these monsters in their tracks," I said. "We'll give them fire."

They waited.

"I want you to gather wood from the nearby houses. Stuff the horse with dry branches. When I give the signal—"

At that moment a wailing broke out from the few Amazons who survived. They saw what I meant to do, and knew that it would destroy their god.

I held my hand out. We were a small island of concentrated silence in the midst of the cacophony of bloodshed. "They're all trying to break down the gates. Eventually the gates are going to give," I said. "Before that moment . . .

we will fling them open. And the horse, flaming, will roll
down the hill toward them and stop up the Skaian Gate. The
zumbi warriors will not flee, for they cannot reason. They
will march blindly to their death." I was calm as I spoke.
"As for the city, perhaps it will perish in the conflagration.
Perhaps it's just as well. I don't want to see the next age, the
Age of Iron. I don't want to live in so dark and treacherous a
world. That wasn't the future I dreamed of."

A young woman came forward, beating her breast, and
cried, "Oioioi! As the god dies, so will I, fighting the
darkness!" She was the new Hippolyte, who had replaced the
one raped and killed by pigs: she seemed young, appallingly
young.

"The firewood," I said. Men sprang to obey my wish.

I watched the horse and listened to the battering at the
gates. The earth was shaking, as though generations of the
dead were bursting from their graves. The horse stood, sleek,
oiled, its tires polished to burning brilliance. "Speak to me!"
I shouted, shaking my fist. But its eyes were empty. The god
had deserted me. The others saw something—a certain wildness in my eyes, perhaps—and backed away. My men
continued sullenly to pile the wood. It was better than sitting
huddled in their houses, waiting for death. The Amazons
danced around the horse, rubbing against it with their blood-
spattered bodies and singing in the old tongue. As their
dancing grew more and more impassioned, first one and then
another flung herself against the horse's flanks, bruising
herself, anointing the god with blood and bile and gall. One
woman fell dead onto the spokes of a wheel.

I wanted to speak with Helen, but I could not bear to yet. I
turned to the Hittite prince. I said, "Tomorrow you must go
home."

"Yes. My father sits and waits in the palace."

"I don't think we will destroy all of the hosts of darkness,
but perhaps we can check their advance."

The prince nodded. "Yes. But I fear they will move east.
My father's dream foresaw an end in fire for my city too. If it
were only an attack of Luvians or Assyrians, I could hold

them back. But when Death himself pursues us with flaming breath, I can see no escape."

"Soon you will be a king," I said to him. Somehow I knew that his father did not have long to wait.

"Oh, I am angry," he burst out. "Am I really the descendant of that Great King Muwatallis, who with a force of twenty thousand men crushed the might of the Pharaoh Ramses? Do I not shame the name of my noble namesake who was king five centuries ago? Is this to be the end of the great empire of the Hittites?"

"The Akhaians' power will be gone too," I said. For I had traveled in the lands over which Mycenae had once held sway, and I knew that the citadels were crumbling everywhere. "Perhaps a new people will arise one day," I said without conviction.

I still could not look at Helen or speak with her. My rediscovered love was a painful thing. I had not known before that love could be born of grief as well as joy. Putting off the moment, I called to my brother Pergamos.

He came to me.

I gave him the sun-disk with the fatal inscription. "You will live through the end of the world," I said.

"But I want to stay with you."

"You will live. You will see beautiful things in the new world, things I cannot see, because you are still young. Take this, the spell of beginning and ending. On the way home, stop in Crete and tell the sons of Idomeneus that I am sorry I killed their father. Tell them . . . that I give them this disk, that I ask them to lay it to rest in their land, the country in which this age was born."

He kissed me and took the disk from me. We embraced. If he had seemed strong and beautiful before, he now seemed frail as when I first knew him. It was like hugging a shadow. I knew from this that I was already marked for death, for the living were losing their reality.

Once again I looked at the horse. Evening was drawing near. The clamor at the gate had not abated, though I willed myself not to hear. In the eye of the horse . . . was that not a comet? No, I told myself. I'm imagining things. Because the end is so close at hand.

Was that the horse's voice? Only the wind, and the whisper of hissing fire.

And Helen's voice: "Astyanax, it's time for us to talk now."

I whirled around. I crushed her to me, kissed her with a desperate, clinging passion. I loved her. I did not want to relinquish her. But I tore myself away and said, "You must go back to Sparta."

"I will not, my husband and my king."

"You have to! You're the goddess of the Spartans. You should be with them now. . . ." The words were specious and I knew it.

"Pergamos!" she said sharply. My brother had gone off into a crowd; I think it was because he feared I would see him weep, because when he returned his eyes were rimmed with red.

"Aunt Helen," he said. "Queen." He knelt before her.

She stroked his head very softly, barely touching his hair. I remembered that she used to do that to me when I was very young. He began to weep openly now. There was no time to think of seemliness.

She said, "I have to ensure that you'll live on too. So I'm going to give you a mission as well. Go to the island of the pig worshipers. There will be nothing to fear there. In a temple in a cave, you will find a statue: a gnarled, wooden statue of a woman. Whatever divinity I once had resides in that statue now. Take it to Sparta, King of Phthia, nephew and brother. My husband says that I should return there; and so I shall . . . at least, that part of me that is worth returning. And as for me . . ."

She gazed longingly at the horse.

Once again I thought I saw the deathstar in its eye. But it flickered and was gone. All the others saw it too, for they cried out.

"No!" Pergamos said, trying to restrain her.

Sadly she looked at all of us. She seemed shrunken, spent,

exhausted. A wan smile lingered on her lips for a few moments. She said, "All our dreams are in this wooden horse. Oh, Astyanax, you dreamed of so many beautiful things. The Amazons see their god. The first time I saw the horse, those many years ago, I thought, not without regret, I have been rescued; no man will take me from my lawful husband again. I was wrong, but now I will make it right. I will become the conciliator of your disparate dreams. The Akhaians sent warriors in the horse, to burn down your city; now you must send me out of the city in the horse, to burn down the Akhaians."

"That's not what I planned!" I cried out. But there was truth in her words, and I could see that the others were moved. "You must not do it. The horse will destroy, whether or not you are inside it."

Helen reached out her hand and clasped mine. Her very touch seared me; it was as though she were already on fire. "No. It must have a soul, and I will be that soul. I am the child of the union of earth and sky. For a thousand years earth and sky have been sundered. Blindly you have worshiped first one and then the other. Do you not understand that they are not mortal enemies? You in your blindness have made them so. The wheels of the image of the horse will touch the earth, and the flames will link it to the sky. And my burning will be the act of love that will bring an end to the strife between the Lady and Skyfather. May my death consummate the universe in a burst of joy. Open the horse."

At her words the doors on the horse's back were opened. The belly of the horse rested on a bed of logs. Now the men were filling its interior with branches. "I will sit enthroned on the wood, like a hatchling in its mother's nest," Helen said. "But do not kindle me until the last moment, when the stars have begun to rise and the dark warriors can no longer be held back. For night will lend them strength."

And then her hand slipped away from mine. I felt as if life itself had been drained from me, as though I were one of Memnon's clay statuettes, void of ka and ba. She said, "You can't stop me, Astyanax. I'm going to my father, my first lover. The world must begin anew.''

"I suppose it must," I said, feeling awkward.

The sun was beginning to set. I had caged my mind against the death-cries, but I could do so no more. They assaulted my ears. The keening over the clang of iron on iron was strangely musical. I watched Helen walk away from me, not yet quite understanding, too stunned to weep, though my brother and others in the crowd had already begun the formal grief-song.

When she reached the horse she turned and said, "Go now, High King of Troy, and be a king; sit on the great throne of Priam.''

Heartsick I turned from her. I walked back to the palace alone. My vassals remained behind to watch the burning of the queen. Bitterly I thought: It was never me they loved; it was Helen, symbol of their lost greatness. It was never me they fought for.

I walked through empty courtyards and down torchless corridors. The grief-song grew faint. Even the battering at the gate was no more than a distant thud.

I reached the megaron of King Priam's palace.

A king sat on the throne.

"Draw your sword," the king said. I did. Orestes did not move. He was masked; this time he wore a male deathmask, such as the one I had seen on his uncle Aigisthos. A sword of iron lay at his feet.

"How did you get in here?" I said. "Guards!"

"They won't come," Orestes said. "The war is between you and me now. What a fool you were not to watch your Dardanian Gate!" He laughed quietly. "I know that you saw the Great Mother in the bowels of the earth . . . that you roused the dead against us. . . .''

"Who gave you this knowledge?"

"My sisters whispered it in my ear," he said, and gestured to the left and right as though I should see someone. But the chamber was empty save for the two of us. "Now fight me. That is all that is left to us.''

I drew my iron sword and ran at him, trembling with rage.

Chapter LIII

Skyfather

He stooped, seized his weapon, and parried. Our swords ground against each other. I withdrew abruptly to throw Orestes off balance. He toppled from the throne. I sprang on him. He rolled away, stood up, brought the iron smashing down on my shield. It buckled. I leaped behind the throne, shielding myself.

"Don't run away, don't hide," he said. "We hear each other, we see each other . . ."

And climbed up on the throne, bent over the top, poked at me. Wood splintered and gold shavings flew. I stabbed, but struck emptiness. He laughed. "The god has deserted you," he said. I looked up and saw his mask. Crimson light from the west played over the gold. It flamed. Blindly I swung at it. I heard the clang as the sword bit the soft gold. And I saw tears of blood ooze from the left eyehole. Still Orestes laughed, the cackling echoing in the empty throne room.

"Kill me, kill me," he taunted.

I ran at him. I brought the flat of my sword crashing down on his. His sword splintered. He reached out his hand. Horrified I watched another sword form in the air. "Thank you, my sisters," he said. And to me: "You see how powerful the earth is still."

We fought again. Back and forth, back and forth over the stones of the megaron. We fought without passion, with a kind of mechanical coldness; we knew that it was our duty.

"Why do we resist?" Orestes said. "We are here to kill each other. Why do we go on when we know that we must die?"

And still we fought on. I no longer knew or cared why we fought. We were as chariot wheels spinning as the car rushes headlong down a mountain, though the charioteer is dead and the warrior slain. Shieldless I parried, edging closer and closer to the doorway of the inner chambers. Exhaustion overwhelmed me, but I still fought on. We left the megaron and fought up and down a staircase of cracked stone. In my tiredness I could almost see Orestes' sisters and smell their decaying bodies as they stood, one on either side of him, whispering encouragement. I could almost hear their voices. Perhaps it was a trick of the dusky light, or the wind wuthering through the corridors above the wails of violated women. I could see the snakes twisting in their hair and feel the icy fetor of their breath. "They're not your sisters," I said. "Orestes, you are deluded."

He struck at me; I feinted, caught my breath, sprang over the balustrade. He leaped down after me. Again I shattered his sword. "Iron is brittle," I said.

He grabbed another from the air. I saw it clearly now, the bony hand that pulled it from a shroud of smoke and thrust it in his hand. He said, "They've found a new way of making iron now. They mix it with charred bones. Burnt warriors' bones are best . . . the new iron is irresistible." He ran at me. I backed away down the corridor. I knew my sword would give way soon. Iron does not yield as bronze does; it is far harder, but when it breaks it does so all at once. I felt my weapon weaken. I ducked into a storage chamber, prying Orestes' mask loose with the tip of my sword.

I gasped when I saw what room it was.

In that moment of indecision I felt Orestes' blade clang against mine, I saw the shards of iron fall to the floor. Stupidly I stared at the paw of the lion, all that remained of the hilt. The golden mask was on the paving stones.

Orestes stopped. I saw his face.

I saw the sisters clearly now. I was being pulled into his world. I resisted, but in vain. They stood there, like the zumbi heroes who were pounding at the city gates, their eyes staring vacantly ahead.

"We have to go on," Orestes said. "You know it and I know it."

"We were friends," I said.

"You deluded me."

"I didn't choose to. You picked the name yourself, and magic bound me to it. But the magic of names has been undone."

"What room is this?" Orestes said.

"It is the room where Hector's panoply is kept," I said. It was all there against the wall: the bronze armor, green from lack of polishing; the great phasganon I had been unable to wield; the gorgonfaced shield; the helmet . . . "I had it put here, because of—"

"Because of the coming of iron." Angrily Orestes reached out for a new sword. A hilt formed in the air as one of his dead sisters drew it forth. He waited for me instead of closing in for the kill. Something kept him from attacking; the ancient honor, tugging at his heart at last.

"I have no weapon," I said, "except . . ."

And I knew then why destiny had led me to this room. "Orestes," I said, "I will not fight you with iron. I am of the Age of Bronze. I will not embrace the new things, but celebrate the past with joy in my heart. Even if it means death." I was afraid of death, terribly afraid. I had barely lived, after all. I had gone through so many mock deaths. I had seen the face of the death-goddess. But death itself . . . "Celebrate with me," I said.

"Celebrate?" He waited, suspicious. I thought he would strike me down at any minute. But the war weighed on us both. His eyes held not vindictiveness but a timeless melancholy. "Look," I said, "perhaps the magic has gone, but we still have the remembrance of it. And memory is a kind of magic." I took the bronze armor and fastened it around my waist. I strapped the shield to my arm. I put on the helmet and I hefted the sword, which seemed for the first time to be almost molded to my grip. I said, "Will you fight me, Orestes? Will you fight the High King of Troy, Astyanax the son of Hector the son of Priam the son of Laomedon descended from Dardanos whose father was the sky?"

Orestes said, "You are beautiful, Astyanax." The sadness lifted from his face. He had the features of a king.

"I'm not beautiful," I said. "Death has already laid his hand on me. I'm wounded and worn. But my father was strong and comely and full of Skyfather's grace. And when he fought the sky shone brilliantly and the grass was green and his blood red as the finest wine."

And even as I spoke I felt those things stir deep within myself. "Fight me, Orestes," I said.

It was at that moment, I think, that the madness left him at last. And he said to the dark spirits that hovered about him, "Go now." And the walking corpses that had attended him dispersed and became mere wind. And I saw another figure behind Orestes. A charioteer perhaps, or a page, or a cup-bearer. His chiton was of the stuff of rainbow, and his hair was finespun gold, and his eyes were unmistakably those of my ancestor the sky. I knew who he was, for though he stood still and utterly solemn, and did not speak, yet there was laughter in his eyes. And his sandals were winged.

It was my cousin Hermes. This time he had come as messenger of death.

He plucked a shining phasganon from the air. And he crowned Orestes' head with a helmet of burnished bronze.

"Yes," said Orestes, "I will fight you."

"We are the last heroes of the Age of Bronze."

My sword against his sword. The bell-like clang and its plangent afterecho . . . the sounds bronze made, the sounds I had not heard for so long . . . sounds of heroism.

We fought with fresh vigor now. The High King of Mycenae glittered, and I knew that I did too. Our swords rang, and with each clash I saw the colors of the world grow more intense. The murals were exploding with vibrant blues and reds. Joyfully we ran back to the megaron, toying with each other, letting the bronze blades whistle within a hair's breadth of each other's face, not yet daring to draw blood.

"The open air!" Orestes shouted. We felt the wind of evening on our faces as we rushed out to the parapet. Again and again the swords hissed and the shields resounded and the red of the setting sun turned to resplendent gold.

We reached the ramparts' edge. I heard the sighing of the gates and knew that they were being swung open. I heard the roar of the flames. "They've set fire to the horse," I said, dodging the blade. Not fast enough. Pain sliced my arm and my blood welled up. I felt as though I were on fire. "The blood of a king will keep the sky blue and the grass green," I cried out. And thrust, and drew blood, and gave a sharp cry of surprise and pain and perhaps joy.

"Look . . ." Orestes said, standing unsteadily between crenellations. "Look . . . the horse . . . from earth to heaven . . . she stands . . . in the fire . . . Helen, flaming, beautiful . . . the hosts of the dead, shining, their chariots fiery-golden . . ."

I saw only the horse on fire and the blackened corpses charging onward. "You don't see those things!" I cried in fury. "Your madness has come back. The illusion has taken hold of your mind again." Was I to be alone then? I could not bear it. We fought on. Orestes was weeping so hard that I knew he could not see which way his sword was slashing. And behind him stood the god, bright-eyed, betraying nothing.

We fought with wild abandon now, our weapons seldom striking anything but the air. The heat from the burning horse was blasting my face. The fire was spreading into the city. I saw people run screaming from the gates, I saw the zumbi warriors flailing, charring, I choked on the smell of their burning flesh. Brighter and brighter rose the fire. We were both wounded. But I felt no pain, though I had already perhaps received a deathwound.

"She stands above the fire!" Orestes screamed.

But I saw only smoke.

The horse seemed almost alive as the wood twisted and buckled. I thought of Helen being burned alive. Of the fire riving her flesh and making the blood boil and spatter and blacken. Helen whom I had feared, loved, worshiped, loved, hated, loved. "I see her," Orestes said, "standing astride the horse with her arms touching the sky.'' But all I could see was the wooden horse glutted with writhing corpses.

Orestes could fight no more. An ecstasy possessed him. I envied him what he saw. I could bear it no more. I felt no anger as I ran him through; indeed, I felt a profound and abiding love for him as my sword pierced first the tough bronze and then the soft flesh, and his blood gushed out. He spread his arms wide and came toward me as though to embrace me. The blood spewed over me. It warmed me; I was drunk on it. I felt my sword work its way between his ribs and through his body and penetrate the leather covering of his back as he moved forward and hugged me close, like a brother, like a lover.

"You must pull it out now." He was gasping for breath between each word. "So . . . I can . . . die."

With terrible regret I began to ease the sword from him. He moaned a little. "Am I a hero?" he said softly.

"Yes. You are a king."

I kissed him gently on each cheek, once to forgive him and once to beg his forgiveness. "Our blood is the blood of kings, and it gives life back to the thirsty earth," I said. "We replenish the soil. We renew the world for the last time." And I began to sob like a child, for my grief at Helen's passing, which I had pushed deep within myself for fear of shaming myself before the populace, could not be held back now, and burst forth, as a river bursts its banks in the torrents of spring.

"Is the world . . . coming . . . to life?"

"Yes." The sword was free now. I cast it away; distantly I heard it clatter on the stones.

"Take me to the edge. Tell me what you see."

I cradled my enemy in my arms. I dragged him to the wall. I said, "The horse is burning. In its eye you can see the harbinger of the world's end, the star of death." Only then was I certain I could see it. "Next to us stands our cousin Hermes." And he was there, beside us, looking at us with wide bright eyes. "His hair is golden as the tall corn." I could almost touch the god, who did not smile or frown, but stared at us intently, with a kind of earnest, childlike curiosity. I told Orestes of the encroaching night; for the first time I saw how rich-hued it was. I told him of the fire. But his body was limp and lifeless. For a while I continued, as though my telling would bring him back to life. But it was useless. I mourned my fallen foe in silence. Then, with Orestes' god-given sword, I cut off a handful of my hair and laid it by his body. Carefully I arranged him facing the sunset. The city would be his funeral pyre . . . a costly one, but he was the last High King of the Akhaians; he was the last of the splendid, doomed Atreidai. As I was the last of the children of Dardanos.

I stood up and looked over the edge. This was the wall they were going to dash my brains against, so many years ago, I thought. My life was bought with the life of a slave boy, because I could not convince Neoptolemos that I was the Prince of Troy.

I knew what must be done now. The end of the world must be made perfect. I must return the life I borrowed. There was no more magic in the old names; I must make new magic from within myself. I stood and watched the burning horse. It seemed that it and I were alone together, and that the war itself was an illusion.

And the horse said, "They have come again with their thousand ships."

And I said, "Only a few dozen this time."

"Are you glad?"

"I think so."

"Are you still angry, are you still thirsting for revenge?"

"Hatred has been purged from me. I'm at peace now."

"Then you don't need me anymore," said the horse, beginning to collapse on itself.

"What are you?" I cried out. "Are you a god?"

The star shone, a pinprick of light that bored into my eyes. Behind the horse, far into the deep blue sky, was the trail of the deathstar's tail. And behind that, thousands upon thousands of stars, many-colored, so thick that the night sky was awash with light.

"A god?" And there came a sound like laughter from the heavens. "But the gods are immortal, and lo, I am burning to death."

The horse spoke no more.

I remained at the edge, tuning my heartstrings to the slow rhythm of the world. Chaos still raged far below. But I knew this anguish to be the first pangs of birth.

I am the child of Skyfather, I said to myself. And now I will appropriate to myself the death that was ordained so long ago, the death that once I cheated.

I will cast myself from the ramparts and fulfill my destiny.

And being the son of the sky, I will thrust myself into the earth my mother as a man's seed seeks out the womb of a woman, and my death will be the world's last act of love.

And from this love-death the world will be reborn in joy.

I stepped away from the world into the void.

I fell.

And falling I saw the vast plains shaking with the thunder of horses' hooves and gold-clad chariots. I saw the hosts of glory in the sunlight. In those last moments I regained my innocence. They were zumbi corpses no longer but radiant heroes, for I was a child again. I saw Helen riding the back of the great horse, her arms touching the gates of the sky. I was filled with wonder. "Rejoice," she said in greeting. She smiled at me with her eyes. I was no longer afraid of that smile. The dreams of all men were one great dream. I ran ran ran toward her smiling, trembling with joy.

I fell and fell and the falling was forever.

Book Nine: Games for the Dead

丅𝄞𝌀𝍖⊕

IRIS.—Zeus, le maître des dieux . . . s'en rapporte donc à Hector et à Ulysse pour que l'on sépare Hélène et Pâris tout en les ne séparant pas. . . . Ou alors, il vous le jure et il n'a jamais menacé en vain, il vous jure qu'il y aura la Guerre.

IRIS: Zeus, the king of the gods . . . therefore enjoins Hector and Ulysses to separate Helen and Paris without separating them. . . . Otherwise, he swears to you, and he never makes empty threats, he swears to you that there will be war!

— Jean Giraudoux, *La Guerre de Troie n'aura pas lieu*

TRUTH

Chapter LIV

The River

I do not know when I ceased to fall. I only remember waiting for the impact, for the jolting terrible pain that never came. The wind of falling battered me, redolent with rotting flesh and burning; but it eased into a breeze, fragrant as a field of corn after a thunderstorm.

The sensation of falling was gone altogether. In vain I looked for the figure of Helen, whom I had seen striving skyward from the flaming hulk that had been the shattered horse. I floated. I saw that I was in the dense gray fog of the underworld, and I thought: Soon I will see Persephone again, and be with the dead people, gibbering. But the mist was shot through with lines of translucence that grew into shafts of light, warming me. There was music in the air, slow, meditative melismas turning inward on themselves.

And I saw, as from a tremendous height, a great roaring river, a river made of light. And beyond it rose a city faced with alabaster and crowned with gold. And though there was no sun, the stones themselves gave light. And by the river stood people, thousands upon thousands of people, solemnly watching my approach. I do not know how long I drifted; but after a time that was not a time I came to rest on the far shore, looking across the water at the city.

A man came forward to greet me. He was not borne on a litter, but trod the earth. The light suffused his features and made them soft.

"Memnon," I said.

"Rejoice." He greeted me as an old friend. I embraced him, thinking that he would be insubstantial, as the shade of Leontes had been when I had first met him in the ruined city; but he was firm, his muscles oiled, his smile bright.

447

I said, "I did not expect this. Am I dead?"

He said, " 'Who knows, my friend, whether in the dead lands it is not the living who are considered dead, and the dead living?' Those are the words of a great poet. But he has not yet been born."

"Where is Charon? Where is the gloomy Styx? Where are the ghosts that haunt the dark places?" I said.

"I thought I just answered that question," Memnon said laughing. "Shall I show you the other world, the world you have departed?"

He pulled a silver mirror from his kilt. I looked and saw myself. And behind me the rubble of a charred city. And dour men, skeletal, always angry, their faces downcast, going about their business. Darkness and fire. Gray, gray, the whole world endlessly gray, for as I looked in the mirror the view shifted; it was less a mirror than a window into the country I had left behind.

Another voice: "Would you like to see me as I really am?" I turned to see King Akhenaten robed in all the finery of Egyptian kingship.

"We have come to take you to the necropolis," Memnon said.

"That city?"

"You do not see things the same way anymore," the king said, "now that you have crossed the boundary for the last time."

I recognized the ship that came for us across the water. A blue man stood at the prow, calling out commands to the oarsmen in a sweet, high voice. The water tinkled as the oars touched it. A canopy of white linen overhung the central pavilion, and in it sat young girls with lyres and double flutes and finger cymbals, and they sang a lilting melody over the sound of the waves.

Two children were playing by the riverbank. I knew them before I saw their faces. They looked up as they saw me. One of them wore a suit of toy armor; the other, a young man really, was garbed as a charioteer. They were playing with a small wheeled terra-cotta horse, pulling it along the pebbled sand with a rope.

"We waited for you!" Leontes said. He laughed. "We didn't want to cross without you." There was in his face none of the anger and none of the melancholy that I had seen in him on earth.

"I was so bitter that day," I said, "because you slid through my fingers like the wind, and I couldn't hug you." And after they had prostrated themselves, I raised them up and kissed them and told them that there was no more need for such obeisances; death had made us equal.

"But even in death there is degree, my lord," Leonidas protested.

I smiled. We waded to the ship. The water was bracing; I thrilled to the sensation of wetness. It seemed more real than any wetness I had felt before, and when the wind blew on my wet thighs and arms I felt each hair stand up, one by one, tingling. All the while the children laughed and splashed each other, and the musicians played. And the Egyptian king and his black-skinned mage moved slowly, majestically, over the water, their feet barely skimming the surface; for the river and the sky and the great city and all the world I moved in were woven from dreamstuff; all were mutable.

We crossed the river and reached the city.

Chapter LV

The Elysian Fields

Memnon and King Akhenaten left me and my two companions on the other shore, and returned aboard the ship of the sun. I cried out, "Will you not stay with me?"

But the king said, "I have another kingdom to go to. But we will see each other often."

They were calling my name as I entered the city, strewing

the streets with petals as I climbed, street after street, step after step carved into the rock. The children went ahead, frisky as lion cubs. We reached the palace; it was and was not the palace of Priam. At its gates waited Queen Helen.

Of my sojourn in the city I can say but little. It was a time of contentment. Nights we explored the palace, Helen and I, wandering from room to room like children. In parts of the palace my grandfather still ruled. I would see him and become a child again; I would sit on his knee and he would tell me how the world began out of the primordial waters, and I would tell him how it had begun again in fire.

During the day we waged war, for this city, like my old city, was besieged. Hector and Akhilleus battled with weapons of bronze; joyously they fought, and each time they were slain they rose again. Each noonday the sky was filled with raucous warcries and with chariot thunder. The colors were bright. The whole world shone. There were times when I felt that no greater happiness could be achieved.

But though it was a joyous time, it was not simply a city of ideal personages; it must not be imagined that we had found utopia. This was no poet's idyllic fantasy. I ruled as a king rules, and my subjects were flesh and blood. We fought hard and heroically in the wars. Often we were killed and we died in terrible agony; but then we rose again laughing. The sight of my father in his armor stirred me; the gorgon shield still frightened me at times. Sometimes I was still angry at my mother. And time passed in the city, though at a rate far slower than mortals measure time.

Memnon sometimes came to visit us. Over elaborate formal dinners, bloated with wine and roast pig, we would talk of the past, and sometimes the future. Once Helen asked him about Pergamos, and he pulled out the silver mirror and propped it up against two winecups, and we saw into the world above . . . into the Age of Iron that seemed so gray and bleak to us.

"Look!" said Helen. "He's taken the statue to Sparta just as I told him to."

"What are those funny-looking youths?"

"They're Spartans! But so different. Look, they are whipping each other in front of the statue. But I don't think it's to fertilize the crops. I think it's some test of manhood," Helen said.

"They have forgotten what the statue means," I said softly.

"I am content," she said. "Even my divinity must end."

Another time Memnon showed us the disk of the sun, buried in the earth in Crete. There were men scratching at the earth with monstrous machines, plucking the artifacts of our time up, shard by shard, scrutizining them with careworn eyes.

"Oh, don't worry," Memnon said, perceiving my alarm. "I don't think they're going to discover the secret. The old tongue is lost forever."

"Words are even more transient than divinities," Helen said very softly. I felt her hand on mine, below the dining table.

Once in a while there came suppliants from the world above. They recoiled from us in horror, speaking of blood-stained bodies and putrescent flesh; when they asked questions of us they looked at the ground and dared not meet our gaze. I had been such a suppliant once; I remembered how the dead lands had seemed to me. But now it was the mortals who seemed dismal and featureless. I tried to speak kindly to them; but in their eyes my voice was transformed into the growling of an ogre, and I knew that my appearance was as unprepossessing to them as theirs was to me.

At last, after a time that to many might seem forever, I knew that I had come only to the periphery of the great land of the dead. Though I had every fulfillment, I had grown restless; Helen sensed it first of all. I knew that my quest must take me further . . . into the heart of this country.

I bade her farewell. There was no sorrow in our parting.

I continued on my way. The quest I undertook was far greater than my earthly quest, for I traversed countries so huge that they were to the world of Troy and Akhaia as an entire city is to the hut of a peasant. My adventures were complex and my labors mighty. Sometimes I wandered alone and sometimes in the company of others; at times I encountered people I had known from the other world. Once I laid siege to an emerald island in an alien sea, for the demon that ruled it had abducted Helen. We all had different names, and the gods were thousand-armed and garishly colored.

At last I came to another river. . . .

Chapter LVI

Metempsychosis

To find the final river . . . I drifted. The world had grown ever larger, grander, richer. But there came a time when even all this magnificence palled; it was then that I entered a realm of light, and in that country, the river-of-forgetting, Lethe.

By the river stood millions upon millions of souls. For many ages I stayed with them, conversing, deepening my knowledge. There were many gods here too, for even their immortality was an illusion. They greeted me as one of themselves, for I had been the agent of the Bronze Age's end. . . .

And finally, at the very edge of the river, I came upon a company of men and women who were seated at a banqueting table. One of them called me over, saying, "Look, he is here at last, the one we've all been talking about!" He was a lean, white-bearded man whose cloak was fastened with a brooch of strange design.

"Do I know you?" I said, sitting down beside him. A slave—perhaps Leontes—was instantly by my side, pouring sweet nectar into a kylix carved from crystal, rainbow-fringed.

"No," he said, laughing, "you cannot know me yet; but all of us know you. At least, we know you at the moment. But . . . when we pass over the river . . . we will not, perhaps, retain that knowledge."

"Why not?" I said, drinking deeply of the cool, lustrous liquid.

"Ah, but you know this is the river-of-forgetting. Do you know what happens beyond that river?"

"No."

"But some dissatisfaction has driven you here, has it not? Paradise bores you at last?"

I admitted it.

The old man said, "Beyond the river is rebirth. I call it metempsychosis, the transmigration of souls; at least, I shall call it that when I arrive in the mortal world and become known as a philosopher."

"You remember the future?"

"For a span, my son, the future and the past are one. We will pass through the river. We will forget the future; we will forget even that we have forgotten; we will forget even that we have remembered that we will forget."

Another voice, laughing, joined in the conversation. "You and your endless semantics, Pythagoras!" I turned. I saw an even older man who cradled a lyre in his arms. Like many bards, he was blind; perhaps his parents had blinded him so as to make him see more vividly with his inner eye.

"A song, Homeros!" said the philosopher. He patted me on the back. "Give the boy a rousing welcome."

And the bard sang.

The song was of many-gated Troy and of the conflict with the Akhaians. Of noble Hector and godlike Akhilleus; of Priam, of Andromache, even, briefly, about myself. I wept when I heard him speak of me and my parents as we over-looked the field of battle, how I had been afraid of my father's shining panoply. I wept even more when the poet spoke of my grandfather coming to the tent of Akhilleus and begging for my father's body, clasping the knees of the killer and crying, "I have kissed the hands of him who slew my son." The others at the symposion looked at me; I knew they were gauging my reaction. And after the long recital fin-ished, and he had sung of my father's burial rites and of the great games celebrated in his honor, they all turned to me as though for approbation.

I said, "Is is beautiful." They waited. I could see that one of the rules of this gathering was that each should speak in turn, and give a brief discourse on the subject at hand. So I continued, "I did not see my father's funeral, and I cannot tell if the song was true to life there. But you tell of many things that were not so. Don't you know, for instance, that chariots are meant for fighting, not for driving to and fro from the battlefield? And as for iron . . . it was I who brought iron to Troy; my fathers did not fight with it. And your gods are just the same as humans: they bicker and complain and change sides constantly. Your Zeus is not Skyfather, the incommensurable, the terrible. Your tale is beautiful, but it is not what happened."

Homeros said, "You will tell me what happened. But I will extract, out of the sordid details of your lives, something eternal. Men need the memory of heroes, not of those who brought the Age of Heroes to an end. As for the gods, each age fashions them in its own image; and we will be imperfect mortals of the Age of Iron, not demideities of the Age of Bronze. How shall we poets tell your story, Astyanax? Better that it should end with you, an infant, crushed to death. Know, King of Troy, that when I come to set down these words you have heard, centuries will have passed, a dark age will have come. But my words will be harbingers of a bright age; for I will dredge up from the time of legends memories of greatness that will make my own people great. And they will strive toward the light, because they will know that their people began in light."

The philosopher said, "I agree with the poet, King Astyanax. There are as many truths as there are men; the secret is that they all are true. You know this; for when you began your quest, you thought that the world was divided into the powers of light and the powers of darkness, and that you were taking part in an eternal struggle between good and evil. But you learned, in the end, that it was not so. When you chose to end your life in the manner that you did, you acknowledged the truth of the myth, for you made your life conform to what you perceived as destiny. But destiny is no more than a conceptual order that we impose on the chaos of existence; for men delight in patterns—''

"Ideals," said another man, also, I think, a philosopher. "Which exist independently of the physical world." The others turned to frown at him for interrupting, but he only said, "Since I am the inventor of this genre of dialectic, surely it's permissible for me to break my own rules!"

We stopped while the first philosopher proposed another toast. "To the young king," he said, "who stands between the generations." And then he said to me, "Before you came, Astyanax, we were discussing how the next age might end. What do you think?"

I said, "I have never thought of it. But we have already had water and fire."

Another man, wizened, but with twinkling eyes and a bright smile, said, "It was iron that ended your age; what will end the next age must be to iron as iron was to bronze, a weapon exponentially more terrible. I fear that it may be I who will unleash it."

"What could be more terrible than iron?" I said, wonderingly.

"I don't know yet," said the man.

"You and your doomsaying, Monolithos!" said another man. I noticed that these two were both absurdly dressed, in thick clothes that conformed tightly to the shape of their bodies, and with separate tubular coverings for each leg. They must be very uncomfortable, I thought. And what a strange name—Monolithos—but I perceived that these must be barbarians, and that this name must be a rough translation of the name's meaning in their own tongue. The second barbarian said, "After all, it is clear that there is a place, somewhere, where the Bronze Age has not ended. Astyanax will tell you so himself. There is a place where the Trojan War is still being fought in the old heroic way." I nodded, remembering the citadel and the river, the first place I had been to in the dead lands. "What passes for reality in the worlds above is merely a chance phenomenon; it could as easily be any of the other truths, which all exist. Astyanax dead as an infant, Astyanax dead as a young man. It is all true and not true at the same time.''

"Nonsense!'' Monolithos said, pounding his fist on the table. "God does not play dice.''

"Please,'' Pythagoras said, "let us continue in a civilized manner.''

I said, despairing of an answer, "Will my story always be forgotten then? Will the future see me forever as a little child thrown down from the walls of Troy? Were all those events merely phantom happenings? But I felt them; I felt Helen in my arms, warm and firm-fleshed, and smelled her fragrance; I saw the burning city. All this I saw and touched and smelled and felt in my heart.''

"No,'' said a man who had not spoken before; he was another of these barbarians from the future, and he had a name that seemed to mean something like "Victory-Mouth-Joy.'' "Your story will one day be told, perhaps. But not in a manner that you can conceive; it will be every man's story, the true nature of myth. But first many things about the psyche must be discovered. It will be my lot to explore the dark corners of the soul; only then can your truth be told.''

Bewilderment flooded me. "What is truth?'' I cried out.

Another man answered me, one whose name meant simply "Young.'' He said, "You know the answer to that already.''

And involuntarily a word escaped my lips: "Helen.''

And the man, a healer of souls, said, "Helen, always Helen.''

I imagined her standing on the river's other shore. The vision was so vivid that I thought I had seen clear across the expanse of water. Her godhead had not departed after all; for as she stood, her hair whipped by the wind so that it seemed a corona of golden flame, she smiled at me, and it was the same smile with which my story had begun; but I no longer wanted to flee from it. No. I ached with a new and passionate longing; I felt it pulling me nearer and nearer to the water's edge, though I knew that the water meant forgetfulness.

The darkness always passes in the end, I told myself. I had gleaned so many tantalizing hints about what was to come in the cosmos. I was eager to be reborn. How many times had I played at the game of death and rebirth? First when Leontes took my place; again when I cast my soul into a figure of clay; again when I lay in a sarcophagus, waiting to trap the blue king; again when I entered the underworld to speak to the Triple Queen. I had had so much practice that it should be easy. Just to slip away . . . to drink forgetfulness . . . to burst into the blazing world above.

I gazed across the water, mirror-still and highlighted in gold. She was there; I knew it now. I could almost taste the salt moisture of her lips. And I saw that many were breaking free from the throng, running toward the river, leaping open-armed into the embrace of oblivion. Others were egging them on and cheering. I heard celestial music. I felt Helen's presence, smelled the fragrance of her breath.

"You are my soul," I said softly, understanding this for the first time. "Always you lead me upward into light."

I grew impatient. I yearned for the water and what lay beyond. My friends at the dinner table watched me as I sat fidgeting, trying gracefully to make my excuses.

At last the first philosopher said, "My friend, we cannot keep you here." And he bade me farewell, his eyes sparkling with kindness and gentility. "Rejoice, Astyanax."

"Rejoice," I said to the assembled company.

"But we have not yet determined who *will* tell your story!" said one of the others, who had not contributed to the conversation before.

"Perhaps I will tell it myself," I said, and slid away before they could call my name. . . .

My name? A moment later I could not even remember it, though once it had seemed so important. . . .

I entered the water and the water was a woman. Smiling she took my hand. Our feet were planted in the earth, but our arms stretched up up up to the height and limitless sky.

Appendix

The Historical Context of *The Shattered Horse* and Other Stories

More than three thousand years after it happened, the Trojan War is still the most famous war in the world, the mythic prototype against which all wars are seen. Each age sees in it what it wants to see. For the Homeric bards, whose words were written down perhaps five hundred years after the great Mycenaean civilization had collapsed, the Trojan War spoke of a time of dimly remembered glory. For the classical Athenians it was part of ancient history. Sophocles used it to illustrate the changeless truths; Euripides, in *The Trojan Women*, to condemn the present and to show men's cruelty and frailty. By Roman times, it had become more distant, but Virgil was able to draw on it to celebrate the magnificence of the Augustan Empire. The Middle Ages added their own apocrypha to the Trojan War: the story of Troilus and Cressida, for example, is a medieval myth, and Cressida's name a misinterpretation of the accusative form of Chryseis, the young captive girl over whom Achilles and Agamemnon argued in the *Iliad*. Successive ages saw the war sometimes as pagan, sometimes as pastoral. As the scientific age came upon us and people became more preoccupied with *facts* and *things*, we have the romantic Schliemann, determined to dig up the physical Troy and the physical Mycenae. It was important to know things, to measure things and to grasp them in our hands and minds.

But science has changed now. In a world where science is less and less concerned with the physical existence of things, where Heisenberg's uncertainty principle is at the root of knowledge and where we accept that things can be both true

458

and untrue at the same time, I felt impelled to evoke a new vision of the Trojan War. Because we are an age preoccupied with the end of the world, it seemed important that the Trojan War occurred at the cusp of two great ages of man—as, perhaps, our own time does. Because we are an age that has elevated the idea of uncertainty to the status of ultimate truth, I felt that the book should deal with things that are said not to have been, with events that might have slipped through the cracks in the quanta of time. Because we are an age in which mysticism and science have gradually drifted closer and closer to each other, I felt that equal emphasis should be given to myth and reality: that, while writing about the nature of myth, I should try not to compromise the growing body of what is known, surmised, and believed about the culture, history and worldview of the inhabitants of the Bronze Age. The problem of choice and freedom is at the root of my book, and it was certainly at the root of the compositional process, for far more is known today about this period than at any other time, and yet the number of mysteries has not decreased.

Nevertheless, for those unfamiliar with the mythos as it was recorded during the Historical Age, perhaps I should briefly summarize the "official" version of the story and note the points of deviation in my version. They are not as many as might be imagined. The outline that follows covers most of the events alluded to in my novel.

At his birth, it was prophesied that Paris would be the cause of his father's death. He was ordered killed, but (as in all stories of this type) those entrusted with the execution had mercy on him, and gave him to a shepherd. While still a shepherd on Mount Ida, Paris made his famous judgment and won Helen as his prize. Unfortunately, Helen was the Queen of Sparta at the time. Paris was reunited with his father and, while on a diplomatic mission to Sparta, abducted Helen. Her husband Menelaos called on his brother Agamemnon, the High King at Mycenae, to honor the pact that all the kings of Akhaia had agreed to at Helen's wedding. War was declared. The Greeks gathered at Aulis, but could not set sail because of a lull in the wind, apparently caused by the pollution of the sacred grove of Artemis. Agamemnon sacrificed his own daughter Iphigeneia, tricking his wife Clytaemnestra into sending her to Aulis by claiming that she was going to be wed to Akhilleus. The wind sprang up, and they set off for the war, which lasted ten years. The story of the wrath of Akhilleus and that of Odysseus's Trojan horse are well known. The destruction of Troy happened much as I describe it in the first chapters of this book, and dead characters and heroes mentioned are more or less "officially" correct.

After the sack of Troy, Astyanax was hurled from the battlements. Polyxena, his sister, was sacrificed to Akhilleus, who had fallen in love with her when he saw her contribute her jewelry to the ransom for Hector's body. Hecabe became Odysseus's slave, but was later transformed into a dog. Andromache was given to Neoptolemos. Cassandra was taken by Agamemnon as a concubine.

But Agamemnon's triumph was shortlived, for he fell victim to the curse of the House of Atreus. Clytaemnestra, now living with her adoptive brother-in-law Aigisthos, slew him and Cassandra with an axe as he bathed. She sent her son Orestes away, but he eventually returned and, with the help of his sister Electra, killed his mother and her lover. For the matricide he was pursued by the Furies until he was purified by Athena. Even then his troubles were not over, for he had to rescue a wooden statue of Artemis from the land of Tauris, where it was the object of human sacrifice. It seemed that Iphigeneia was not dead after all, but had been snatched away by Artemis and had been serving as the priestess in this temple the whole time. Just as she was about to sacrifice her brother and his friend Pylades, however, he revealed himself and they escaped successfully.

The classical Greeks believed that the Trojan War was a historical event, and that such characters as Agamemnon and Priam actually existed. Clay tablets written in the Linear B syllabary, which was deciphered and shown to be Greek by Michael Ventris in the 1950s, show such personal names as Orestes and Hector; there is no reason to doubt that the movers and shakers of the late Bronze Age possessed such names as are found in mythology. The date of the war was calculated to be about 1190 B.C.; it is now known that this date coincides, approximately, with the destruction by fire of that layer of archaeological Troy that is generally known as Troy VIIA. Whether that was *the* Trojan War or not is uncertain, for there are traces of other wars and also of an earlier destruction by a violent earthquake. What is clear is that the Troy destroyed by fire was resettled almost immediately, though with a certain loss in the quality of life.

I have tried to remain as faithful as possible to the archaeological record and also to contemporary paleoanthropological thought. I have set my novel on the traditional date of the war. But wherever there is doubt, wherever there are any cracks in the seams, I have been able to speculate more freely than a historian could. Indeed, it could be said that my entire book derives from a single phrase in Robert Graves's comprehensive and trailblazing *The Greek Myths:* "Some say . . . that Astyanax survived and became King of Troy after the departure of the Greeks."

In the official version to which most of the classical mythographers adhere, however, the boy Astyanax was cast down from the walls of Troy shortly after the destruction of the city.

Helen is thought to have been a vegetation-goddess of the Bronze Age whose worship was localized in Sparta. In the myth, she was abducted twice: once by Theseus and Perithous, and a second time by Paris. Since the periods in question are mythologically separated by more than a generation, and archaeologically by perhaps three hundred years, I have made use of the theory that her name was a title of the priestess who may have played the function of the living goddess. The whipping ceremony described in the Spartan section of the book was, in historical times, rather different, taking place as it did before a wooden statue of the goddess Artemis and being more a test of manhood than a fertility rite. Nevertheless, the Spartans believed in a Bronze Age origin of the rite, and the statue itself was said to be a survival from ancient times. I have extrapolated the rituals from such evidence, and essentially identified the wooden statue as Helen herself, since the local goddess of Sparta (''Helen'' means ''moon'') would naturally have become absorbed into Artemis, the moon-goddess of the Olympian canon, as the prestige of the Zeus-centered religion grew.

Suppiliulimas II (circa 1190 B.C.) and his father, Arnuwandas IV, who ruled from about 1220–1190 B.C., are historical kings of the Hittites. The great empire of the Hittites was destroyed, and its capital city sacked, during the reign of Arnuwandas; this is foreshadowed in the novel. King Akhenaten is also a historical figure, a pharaoh of the XVIIIth dynasty. By the time of the novel, he and his religious revolt will already have acquired a quasi-mythic status. I have made his cult of the sun-disk Aten an aspect of the all-embracing Skyfather cult.

A number of authentic but lesser known mythological characters play prominent roles in *The Shattered Horse*. Pergamos and Pielos were indeed the sons that Astyanax's mother Andromache bore to Neoptolemos; Hermione was indeed the daughter of Helen. A rather garbled version of the sacrifice of Idomeneus is presented in Mozart's opera *Idomeneo;* the accounts differ as to whether he sacrificed a son or a daughter. Pylades, the friend of Orestes, was of course not Astyanax under another name, but this seemed to be a seren-dipitously effective way to link the two tragic scions of the noble houses of Troy and Mycenae, and to bring them to-gether. My version of the deaths of Clytaemnestra and Aigisthos, while differing startlingly from those of Euripides, Sophocles, and Aeschylus (which in any case differ radically from each other as well), is consistent with much that has been theorized about kingship and succession in the Bronze Age. Memnon was not a mage in the myth, but an ''Ethiop'' who fought on the side of Troy; my linking him to Akhenaten is an invention. Such details as the necrophily performed by Akhilleus on Penthesileia, queen of the Amazons, however, are an authentic part of the myth.

As my astute and perspicacious editor Beth Meacham has

pointed out, most of the truly bizarre things that occur in this book are actually realistic depictions of Bronze Age life; it is the mundane details, not the spectacular ones, that I have had to fill in with speculation. This is not to say that *The Shattered Horse* should be read as a compendium of facts about the Bronze Age, or as an exegesis of some anthropologist's pet theories. It is first and foremost a novel; and since choice and freedom are two of its most important underlying themes, I felt it was only right to exercise both attributes to the utmost. Although I have spent years researching the subject (I wrote my first version of this book when I was ten years old!) it would be hubristic to claim that I had studied all the data available. Mistakes and inconsistencies may be blamed either on ignorance or on auctorial privilege, depending on the reader's compassion.

One instance of this is in the spelling of the names. I toyed at first with the idea of transliterating in every case the earliest discoverable or hypothesizable form of the characters' names. But certain names, like Priam and Helen, have acquired great mythic resonance to English-speaking people, and I felt that it was pedantic and alienating to use earlier forms. Other cases did not strike me the same way. So the result is a mix of forms, some ancient, some modern. I make no defense of this practice; it's just how it turned out.

I could never have undertaken this novel alone. As mentioned in the dedication of the book, there was a wonderful English teacher, M. R. Smansnid, at the Bangkok British School in Thailand, when I was a child, who first turned my mind toward Greece. I had lived in six countries by then, and my sensibilities were a hodgepodge of cultural ambiguities. The Greek myths brought continuity into my existence for the first time. Then there was my father, who made it possible for me to visit the Bronze Age sites themselves, and to breathe the air of the time of myth. Between those times a wealth of influences must be acknowledged: Mary Renault and Robert Graves, and Evangeline Walton, who has been very kind. I must also give thanks for the unstinting help of Jan Murphy of Berkeley, who located the most arcane texts

for me with ease, and whose interest in and enthusiasm for
this lengthy project have been a constant encouragement.
And I must not forget my editor, Beth Meacham, who suffered long delays in the novel's delivery, who believed in the
book long before she came to be at TOR, and that company's
Vice-President Harriet McDougal, whose affection and respect for writers is a rare quality among those in her position,
and who has helped make this publisher so pleasurable to
work for. I thank you all.

About the Author

Somtow Papinian Sucharitkul (S. P. Somtow) was born in Bangkok in 1952, a grandnephew of the late Queen Indrasakdisachi of Siam and son of celebrated international jurist Sompong Sucharitkul, currently Vice-President of the International Academy of Human Rights. He grew up in Europe and was educated at Eton and Cambridge. His first career was as a composer, and his work has been performed, broadcast and televised on four continents. He was Artistic Director of the Asian Composers EXPO78 in Bangkok and is the Thai representative to the International Music Council of UNESCO. In the late '70s he took up writing speculative fiction, and won the 1981 John W. Campbell Award for best new writer as well as the Locus Award for his first novel, *Starship & Haiku*. His short fiction has twice been nominated for the Hugo Award, SF's equivalent of the Oscar. He has written the galaxy-spanning *Inquestor Tetralogy* as well as the satirical *Mallworld* and *The Aquiliad*. 1984 saw the publication of his first mainstream novel, *Vampire Junction*, under the name S. P. Somtow. He now resides permanently in the U.S. and works alternately on music, books by one alter ego or another, and as a book critic for *The Washington Post*.